Reading the Short Story

Reading the Short Story

A Student's Guide to Selected British, Irish and American Works

ANNA WING-BO TSO
and SCARLETT LEE

Foreword by Andrew Parkin

McFarland & Company, Inc., Publishers
Jefferson, North Carolina

This book has undergone peer review.

LIBRARY OF CONGRESS CATALOGUING-IN-PUBLICATION DATA

Names: Tso, Wing Bo Anna, author. | Lee, Scarlett, 1972– author. | Parkin, Andrew, 1937– writer of foreword.
Title: Reading the short story : a student's guide to selected British, Irish and American works / Anna Wing-Bo Tso and Scarlett Lee ; foreword by Andrew Parkin.
Description: Jefferson, North Carolina : McFarland & Company, Inc., Publishers, 2019 | Includes bibliographical references and index.
Identifiers: LCCN 2019038486 | ISBN 9781476673981 (paperback : acid free paper) ♾
  ISBN 9781476637242 (ebook)
Subjects: LCSH: Short stories, English—History and criticism. | Short stories, Irish—History and criticism. | Short stories, American—History and criticism.
Classification: LCC PR829 .T77 2019 | DDC 823/.0109—dc23
LC record available at https://lccn.loc.gov/2019038486

BRITISH LIBRARY CATALOGUING DATA ARE AVAILABLE

ISBN (print) 978-1-4766-7398-1
ISBN (ebook) 978-1-4766-3724-2

© 2019 Anna Wing-bo Tso and Scarlett Lee. All rights reserved

No part of this book may be reproduced or transmitted in any form or by any means, electronic or mechanical, including photocopying or recording, or by any information storage and retrieval system, without permission in writing from the publisher.

Front cover image © 2019 luchunyu/Shutterstock

Printed in the United States of America

McFarland & Company, Inc., Publishers
  Box 611, Jefferson, North Carolina 28640
    www.mcfarlandpub.com

To my husband Raymond, my daughter Sophia,
and my son Edwin, who make my life complete.
—*Anna Wing-bo Tso*

To my father, who taught me
the value of education.
—*Scarlett Pui-wah Lee*

Acknowledgments
Anna Wing-bo Tso

This book would never have taken shape without Scarlett Lee, its second author. Her passion for literature and her commitment to work never fail to amaze me. Also, it was lucky of us to have received a sponsorship from the Sunrise Charitable and Education Fund (SCEF), Hong Kong (reference no.: S/V/EL in U1[5/2019]). I thank SCEF for placing their trust in us.

I am eternally thankful to Professor Emeritus Andrew Parkin of The Chinese University of Hong Kong, the author of our foreword, who kindly edited and proofread our manuscript, too. I would also like to express my sincere gratitude to Professor Emeritus Julie Holledge of Flinders University, who gave helpful advice and clear suggestions for revising and improving our manuscript. Most importantly, I wish to thank all the students who have taken my language and literature courses throughout the years. They have given me inspiration and encouragement in writing this book.

Table of Contents

Acknowledgments (Anna Wing-bo Tso) — vi
Foreword (Andrew Parkin) — 1
Preface — 3

PART I
SHORT STORIES: GENRE AND LITERARY CRITICISM

1. A Brief History of the Short Story as a Literary Genre — 7
2. Practical Literary Criticism — 40

PART II
CLOSE READING FOR SHORT STORIES

3. Religion and Redemption in O'Connor's "A Good Man Is Hard to Find" — 59
4. Consumerism, Alienation and Digital Dystopia in Bradbury's "The Veldt" — 72
5. Masculinity and Sexuality in Proulx's "Brokeback Mountain" — 85
6. Fantasy and Fan Fiction in Gaiman's "The Problem of Susan" — 98

PART III
LITERARY AND COMPARATIVE ANALYSES OF SHORT STORIES

7. Psychoanalysis and the Gothic in Poe's "The Fall of the House of Usher" and Stevenson's "The Strange Case of Dr. Jekyll and Mr. Hyde" — 113

8. Irony and Paralysis in Joyce's "Grace" and Trevor's
"Of the Cloth" 136
9. Civil Rights and Prejudice in Walker's "Everyday Use"
and Smith's "The Embassy of Cambodia" 154
10. Femininity and Social Pressures in Lessing's "To Room
Nineteen" and Gilman's "The Yellow Wall-Paper" 174

Afterword 190

Index 193

Foreword
Andrew Parkin

  This book on short fiction by Anna Wing-bo Tso and Scarlett Lee deals with the short story and is aimed at students of modern literature in all English-speaking places around the world. It will, in my view, serve them well, for the book details the history of short fiction from Egypt to modern times, defines the genre as such, and offers a chapter on practical literary criticism and others devoted to general information about chosen authors and close readings of a variety of their texts, all fascinating examples of the work of masters of short fiction, such as Edgar Allan Poe, Robert Louis Stevenson, and James Joyce, followed by William Trevor. The book also examines other highly accomplished writers such as Alice Walker and Zadie Smith, who are concerned with civil rights and racial issues in their fiction, and considers how femininity and the social pressures that surround women even today find telling fictional accounts in works by the late, and highly original, Doris Lessing and Charlotte Perkins Gilman.

  For Asian students and others whose native languages may not be English, the book is extremely useful, because short stories offer good reading that can be taken in smaller doses than those offered by novels. Moreover, the timeline of the stories naturally introduces students to a variety of styles, so that they can become familiar with the elegance of nineteenth-century English and the more direct, even pungent manner of some twentieth-century texts.

  The book is arranged in such a way that the reader is led to appreciate through truly riveting fiction the language, social issues and manners of the 1800s in London and America. But the twentieth-century stories can be studied for their ethos, revealing some of the pressing issues in society that still plague us with problems.

  This is not to say that the book is merely a kind of social propaganda. Far from it, because Dr. Tso and Ms. Lee offer us short fiction that is *intriguing in itself* on the level of human situations with believable characters. Even if a story like the celebrated "Dr. Jekyll and Mr. Hyde" still speaks to problems in modern society, such as drug addiction with unexpected effects on the body and mind, the story in itself holds our attention as fiction, rather than as studies in sociology or criminology. The authors are concerned primarily with literary study, not just social propaganda. For this they must be congratulated. Students have plenty of opportunities to study sociology, politics, and economics in modern universities, so it is refreshing for me, as a literary and dramatic critic, to find a book which offers literary experiences to be relished first as literature.

The book, however, is also useful for the insights the stories offer into American and British society at different stages. And as a book that introduces a genre of fiction in a systematic way, it could be used for a course on the short story that serves as a prerequisite for courses in contemporary short fiction in English by younger up-and-coming writers. I can see it being used in such a way, for example, in India, or the United States or the United Kingdom, but also in Germany, where students have an extremely high level of English proficiency, even if they are not English specialists.

Because new media opportunities for students have appeared within the last fifteen years, I can see that a good grasp of short print fiction would go hand-in-glove with the use of examples taken from online sources and linked, for instance, to some examples of flash fiction.

Since Dr. Tso and Ms. Lee have chosen stories with a wide range of styles, valuable work could arise from a consideration of the language and the rhetoric found in the stories. Studies of imagery, symbolism, and tone, especially irony, as the authors demonstrate in their commentaries, can easily arise from readings of the selected stories.

The book makes a real contribution to our understanding of the way in which writers cannot help but to delineate the tensions and the manners of those who lived in the societies that led to the present age.

Andrew Parkin is a professor emeritus at the Chinese University of Hong Kong. He lives in Vancouver and continues to read his academic work, poetry, and fiction in cities around the world.

Preface

What is a short story? As Harmon and Holman define, it is "a relatively brief fictional narrative in prose" (480) which may range from 500 words up to 15,000 words in length. There is no one way to write a short story, and there are different methods of studying short stories in English. To obtain a chronological overview, some may want to study short stories along the timeline for deeper understanding of the historical development, while others may like to study short stories through the genre, the author, the theme, stylistic analysis, and/or the critical literary theory. This book aims to do both. As the book title indicates, our intention is to offer guidance for reading and analyzing British, Irish, and American short stories written by canonical authors in recent decades. While focusing on short stories written in Britain, Ireland, and America, our book suggests mixed methods for studying short stories.

As for the selection of short stories, our book consists of a diverse collection of twelve popular and internationally-acclaimed short stories, half of which are by British and Irish writers, namely James Joyce, William Trevor, Robert Louis Stevenson, Doris Lessing, Zadie Smith, and Neil Gaiman, and half of which are by American writers such as Edgar Allan Poe, Charlotte Perkins Gilman, Ray Bradbury, Flannery O'Connor, Alice Walker, and Annie Proulx. With reference to the course syllabi of literature courses offered by most universities worldwide, the selection of short stories in our book strikes a perfect balance between six male and six female authors of different ethnic backgrounds. In addition, our book illustrates a spectrum of various themes conveyed in an assorted variety of genres, including fantasy, gothic, horror, romance, Southern gothic, science fiction, realist fiction, and historical fiction. All of our focal texts are works that were distributed sporadically between the nineteenth century and the twenty-first century.

For readers' convenience, the book is proportionally divided into three parts. In part one, readers are introduced to influential short story authors in British, Irish, and American literature. The key author overview in chapter one includes brief discussions of various types of short stories, different writers' styles and literary techniques, as well as the evolution of the short story genre. To help readers develop critical views on literature, chapter two provides a summary of the most common critical literary approaches in reading and analyzing literary works, which range from historical criticism, biographical criticism, reader response criticism, Marxist criticism, feminist criticism, psychoanalytic criticism, to formalist criticism. In respect of the introduction to the short story genre and critical theoretical approaches illustrated in part one, part two studies four short stories in context and provides a close reading of O'Connor's "A Good Man Is Hard to Find," Bradbury's "The Veldt," Proulx's "Brokeback Mountain," and Gaiman's "The Problem of Susan." In part three, readers are invited to walk through key topics and main themes in eight more selected masterpieces from British, Irish, and American literature, which are all paired up for contrast and comparison in the context of recent debates regarding language, politics, justice, religion, gender, psychology, fantasy, national identity, and more.

The main intended readers of this beginners' guidebook are undergraduate students who study English and Comparative Literature, but we will also be glad if literature teachers and scholars find this book useful for their teaching and research.

BIBLIOGRAPHY

Harmon, William, and C. Hugh Holman. *A Handbook to Literature*. New Jersey: Prentice Hall, 1996. Print.

Part I

Short Stories: Genre and Literary Criticism

1
A Brief History of the Short Story as a Literary Genre

The Origin of the Short Story

To many modern readers, the short story seems to be a sub-genre with an ephemeral history of no more than 100 years. Though its development may have been surpassed by that of the long narrative at times, its influence on narrative literature as a whole is by no means inferior, nor is it more short-lived. Historical reviews even date the development of the short story long before humans could write. Considered one of the earliest forms of oral recording, the short story was widely practiced by various tribes from different countries, such as Israel, India, Egypt, and Greece, as a means of memorizing and passing down the tales preached by the ancestors. Confined to this function, it was often recited with instrumental music, while the recorded form was mainly in verse and rhyme. Later, the oral tales were inscribed in cuneiform or written in prose, as different tribes developed their own writing systems. This marked the beginning of a long battle for the short narrative to gain its full recognition as a distinct genre in written literature and laid the groundwork for its development in English literature in Britain, Ireland, and America.

Early Development

Britain

(I) **The Early Middle Ages to Chaucer.**
The early development of the short narrative was circumscribed by reli-

gion and Greco-Roman culture. The Catholic Church first exploited the genre in the priest's sermon. *Exemplum*, as it is called, became the earliest source for the development of the short story in English literature, though in reality, the forerunners of the short story genre were rudimentary, didactic, and unoriginal. Saint Gregory the Great (540–604 AD), for example, amassed secular short descriptions from the excerpts of sermons, Bede's history, and direct translations of Bishop Wærferth in his four books that comprise *Dialogues* from 306 to 337 AD. *Dialogues* not only helped the expansion of Roman Christianity and the spread of pagan English, but it also had a subsequent influence on the narrative mode. Hardly any native writers benefited from it, though, as they struggled to rid the stories of foreign influence while nurturing homegrown tales. Not until the end of the fourteenth century did they see the debut of indigenous short stories.

Geoffrey Chaucer (c. 1343–1400) was the first English writer who used his own language, that is, London-based English, not Latin or French but new English, to tell stories about English life. *The Canterbury Tales*, written between 1386 and 1389, collected twenty-four stories narrated by a group of pilgrims on their way from Southwark, London to Canterbury Cathedral. Every character displays individual personalities and lyrical emotions, thus reflecting upon human errors. Digressing from moralizing, Chaucer put the spotlight on human nature in flesh and bona fides, successfully breaking ties with the sacred narrative method and the influence of foreign fabliaux and fables. These homely tales instilled "strong English thought" (Canby 77) and finally set the genre itself upon English soil.

(II) Post-Chaucerian Age to the Eighteenth Century.

After Chaucer, for a long period of time there were hardly any writers who could bring the art of story-telling to another level, let alone carry on the Chaucerian fashion. A lack of vigor and novelty made the development of the short story form stagnant for almost five centuries. At times, it even went backwards. Unimaginative and conservative, writers of the time could only reproduce the medieval works of low literary value, such as exempla and fabliaux. Not until the Renaissance in the sixteenth century did this literary movement in Britain gain momentum. Under the spell of foreign influence—the Italian Renaissance, the British gradually embraced the spirit of the Enlightenment towards the end of the movement. The imported Italian novella widened the scope of the genre to a broader humanistic approach. The rekindling of fervent interest in human life in short fiction bore some resemblance to Chaucerian style, which brought forth the wave of the Elizabethan novella. This new brand of short fiction absorbed every element of the Italian novella, and turned it into the romance and discourses wrought with rhetorical style. However, it was a lavish style, for the story per se was completely overshadowed by the finest thoughts on manners, morals, and life. Such was the hallmark of the seventeenth-century novella. Not surprisingly, its subsequent effect on the later development was evident in short stories replete with English manners and morals. A collage of anecdotes, character sketches, and criticisms became almost a didactic tool to cleanse the ills of the society with the least truthful representation of life. The subservience to morality and didacticism is unique to the development of the British short story of the time.

America

Similar to the development of the British short story, the first prose form of the American short narrative was largely anecdotes and episodic sketches. Fairy tales and folktales aside, notable stories, such as the tale about the young George Washington confessing to chopping down the cherry tree, were considered the primitive form of the genre. They had strong yet loosely described characters, as well as underdeveloped plots void of necessary elements like theme, technique, and narrative point-of-view, which are ascribed to the genre today. Some were written solely for sermons, while others were no more than a few episodes to illustrate morals and virtues. It was not until 1819 that the short story genre became recognizable and was taken seriously. This started with Washington Irving, the pioneer of the short story in America.

Washington Irving

Washington Irving (1783–1859) was born after the Puritan age when most writers were still introspective and deterred from attempting to write or else produced "pale and often unearthly" works (Pattee 2). Irving was an exception, thanks to his British descent, which left him immune to New England puritanism. Growing up in New York, which did not provide an intellectual atmosphere for the young Irving, he could only devour books of the eighteenth century at home and naturally display the writerly temperament of that time—being circumspect, he embraced the idea of classicism. His Celtic ancestry further drew him to Europe, a continent which allowed him to find his origins, indulge himself in the picturesque and romance, and above all, give vent to his emotional temperament. All this gave him the disposition of a short story writer. *The Sketch Book* (1819–1820) was the first American short story collection, and it revolutionized the literary genre. It had some of the most successful stories such as "Rip Van Winkle" (1819) and "The Legend of Sleepy Hollow" (1819). In his review "Essay Writing" in 1822, Prescott compared it to the British short story:

> Although of the same generic character with the British essayists, it has many important specific peculiarities. The former were written ... with a direct moral tendency, to expose and to reform the ignorance and follies of the age. *The Sketch Book*, on the other hand, has no direct moral purpose, but is founded on sentiment and deep feeling [333].

Irving made an exquisite start on the short story solely for America. For the first time, the reader found the distinguishable elements in the genre: amoral, imaginative, entertaining, humorous, realistic, and a rich atmosphere coupled with defiant characters. But it was the unity of tone (finished in one sitting) which decisively marked the short narrative from its counterpart. Because of Irving, sketches and tales became the first fashion in the development of the American short story. Thereafter, the publication of the short story blossomed, thanks also to the fashionable idea, "the annual" from London, where the Industrial Revolution made mass printing accessible to a greater reading public. Readership spiked; demand surged. Many short story writers made use of the platform to achieve their success. Among those include the next prominent figure—Nathanial Hawthorne (1804–1864).

Nathaniel Hawthorne

Anyone reading "Young Goodman Brown" (1835) may feel unsettled by the dark and hushed tone permeating the story. In fact, most of Hawthorne's short stories are shaped by an overtly religious atmosphere, which contrasts starkly with Irving's romantic and picturesque tales. Irving's distant ethnic origin caused him to be unaffected by Puritan attitudes; in contrast, Hawthorne's indigenous ancestral background engrossed him in New England puritanism. In their treatments of the same subjects, the latter's approach was more focused and in-depth with recurring motifs such as morals and spirits. Yet, what placed him in an arguably more influential position in the genre's development than any other contemporary writer was the form. He was the first to exploit a single situation, spin it with successive actions, and then reach a climax with a moral ending. The form may seem sermonic given his Puritan past. Nonetheless, it has a touch of modernity that defined what the short story is today.

Edgar Allan Poe

To round out this golden era of the first stage of short story development in America, we cannot fail to mention a notable figure, Edgar Allan Poe (1809–1849), the founding father of the American short story.

On par with the prominent duo Irving and Hawthorne, Poe had an enormous influence on consolidating the movement with a clear, accurate, and systematic description of the genre. In his brilliant book *The Philosophy of Composition* (1846), he defined the short story and emphasized a few crucial elements—effect, impression, totality, and the ability to read the story in one sitting: "[i]f any literary work is too long to be read at one sitting, we must be content to dispense with the immensely important effect derivable from unity of impression—for, if two sittings be required, the affairs of the world interfere, and everything like totality is at once destroyed" (22).

To embody all these components successfully in a short story, the writer must take readers into account by being precise and meticulous in every step. Poe's approach is scientific and extrospective, Irving's is sentimental and retrospective, whereas Hawthorne's is moral and introspective. Indeed, in his review of Hawthorne's short story collection, *Twice-Told Tales* (1837, 1842), Poe already hinted at a clear distinction between the duo and himself with regard to originality and reposeful manner. His style was artificial, relentless, and purely imaginative, based on reading rather than observing real life, which can be easily traced in his detective stories and psycho-thrillers such as "The Fall of the House of Usher" (1839). Further in the review, he laid out the blueprint for the short story, highlighting the importance of unity: "[w]e need only here say, upon this topic, that, in almost all classes of composition, the unity of effect or impression is a point of the greatest importance" ("Review of Twice-Told Tales" 521).

Poe's contributions to the genre's development may be pure opportunism, if we consider the expanding market of the annuals and the magazines altering the demand of the reader on the short story. It required concision with the most single effect, which Hawthorne's and Irving's stories would hardly satisfy. Yet, it is commonly agreed that Poe's short stories do not fully embody the American spirit. They are not meant to be told from the American's point-of-view pertaining to the legends or indigenous cultures. That said, the early genre development on American soil should be shared equally among the trio—focusing on romance and picturesque, Irving popularized sketches and character study; intrigued by morality and sin, Hawthorne modernized the form; marketing his horror tales, Poe hammered out the first guideline on the technique unique to American short stories.

Mid-Development

Britain

Poe's influence traversed the Atlantic in the early nineteenth century, saving the experimental British writers from a long, disconcerting struggle with short story development. In the almost four centuries since the Chaucerian tales had debuted, hardly any writer could steer away from the influence abroad, be it Romanticism from France, Gothicism from Germany, or Italianate rhetoric from Italy. Some great novelists and poets of different periods such as Lord Byron and George Eliot attempted to write short stories but too often failed to see it as a single genre, not to mention their failure to recognize the form and develop a genuine local taste. A lack of craftsmanship and vision saw Britain lag far behind her counterparts who had already produced some canonical short story writers.

Irving was the first to land ashore with his lighthearted short tales. The humor and poise of his stories awoke the nation with a fresh breeze. Armed with the most useful technique, Poe's later arrival altered writers' perceptions of short story writing to various extents. His manifesto "The Philosophy of Composition" was critically acclaimed and frequently cited among literati. British writers came to realize that the short story possessed distinctive literary value and the essential elements—impressionism and unity (rather than didacticism). Meanwhile, the market opened to a share of short narratives amid the exponential growth of periodical publications. Demands for short stories of all kinds to fill up the literary magazines such as *Granta* (established in 1889) surged. Once favoring the volume to the page, the national taste had finally drifted away from the novel to anecdotes, sketches, and tales that could allow readers to while away the daily commute (James, "Guy de Maupassant" 264).

The current fashion inspired some Victorian writers who drew on their novel writing experience to create short stories with unconventional art forms such as omission and implication, while foregoing the traditional techniques like plotting and characterization. The results were not all impressive. Charles Dickens, for example, imitated Poe's art form while still maintaining the traditional oral narrative mode, the tale-within-a-tale, in one of his short stories, "The Haunted House" (1859). Some other experimental writers were Elizabeth Gaskell, William Makepeace Thackeray, and Anthony Trollope. Robert Louis Stevenson was among a few on the list who successfully mastered the short story technique and turned the genre into an artful form. "A Lodging for the Night" (1878) and "The Strange Case of Dr. Jekyll and Mr. Hyde" (1886) are two prime examples that showcase Stevenson's talent. Under his pen, the stories are crafted with finesse. There are novel ideas and verisimilitude. Readers can trace the influence of Poe on the structure and psychic reality, and that of Hawthorne on moral analysis.

Regardless of whether they failed or succeeded, these attempts proved that the short story could finally and gradually stand on its own feet on British soil and embark upon the road to the modern short story as a respectable genre.

America

While the idea of the short story as a meaningful art was still fermenting in Britain, America had already taken a big leap at the forefront of Anglo-American short story development, thanks to the booming market of literary magazines that provided American writers the opportunity to practice their skills. *The Harper's Magazine* and *The Atlantic Monthly* were founded in 1850 and 1857 respectively, followed by other short-lived magazines such as *Lippincott's Magazine* (1868–1915) and *Scribner's Monthly* (1870–1881). Readership grew. Experimental writers started to find an outlet for their voices. American short stories now set sail into a colorful and diversified era. Not only did some outstanding writers emerge—for example, Bret Harte, Henry James, and O. Henry—but for the first time, women writers, notably Sarah Orne Jewett and Charlotte Perkins Gilman, actively joined the movement, reshaping the themes of the short story and empowering other women through the genre.

Bret Harte

Bret Harte (1836–1902) was a short story writer well-remembered for his critical essay "The Rise of the Short Story" (1899), in which he declares the waning influence of English tradition on American short stories and the rise of a crucial element—humor. He took it as the quintessential American feature from which civilization developed, highlighting the novelty and the individuality that evolved around it. As a result, humor should be highly regarded by writers. He considered Poe's and Hawthorne's short stories not Americanized enough because of their lack of humor. The dialect and the habits of thought of a people or locality were fully voiced through humor rather than by polishing the style and the technique, or underpinning with some moral theme (Pattee 233). Otherwise, the short story would not be recognized nor appreciated by readers. Harte concluded that humor was "the parent of the American 'short story.'"[1] Indeed, his stories such as "The Luck of Roaring Camp" (1868) are dominated by humor and peppered with old west slang, which were inspired by the California Gold Rush. From the peculiar atmosphere to rural landscapes, unique characters, and rustic dialogues, every ingredient is localized to produce romantic, impressionistic, and nostalgic effects.

Harte's advocacy on behalf of the local color story with close-up studies of special people and places sidelined Poe's unsympathetic and meticulous psychoanalytic approach. Some even argue that the latter failed in every single criterion of the modern short story. Especially after the Civil War, readers turned to the distinctive regional flavor, which they rarely found in their hometowns. Humor was desperately needed to offset the tragic mood brought by the war. Writers embraced the trend and infused their stories with humor and local features, notably Mark Twain's "The Celebrated Jumping Frog of Calaveras County" (1865), and decades later William Faulkner's "A Rose for Emily" (1930).

If Poe was the inventor of the technique of the American short story, it would be fair to say that Harte was the re-inventor of the genre. For the first time, verisimilitude had been taken seriously. To be original to locality, the story had to be real (though selective), be it the culture, the custom, or the folks. The story had to be brushed with details to reflect the truth. "Realism," as the critics called it, started to go hand in hand with the American short story, whose development had thus been further strengthened.

Henry James

After Harte popularized the modern short story, someone had to perfect the form. No one could render such service better than Henry James (1843–1916). James's literary contribution to the short story was twofold. First, he was an advocate for the influence of the avant-garde movement on the short story. Keen on exploring a modern definition pertaining to the genre, James was particularly critical of the traditional form. In 1898, James contributed an essay to *Fortnightly Review*, in which he emphasized the need for selective representations of characters, motives, and psychology rather than the plot itself. The qualities of the actions should lead. The complexity or the continuity could then be captured by glimpses of or exposures to such actions, which come finally to fix the effect. Interiority took over from exteriority. The latter, which Poe defended as the indispensable ingredient of creating a dramatic effect, lost its foothold, and was regarded as outmoded and artificial in the literary movement. James's remarks had a great influence on Henry Harland, the editor of the short-lived, high-brow British literary magazine *The Yellow Book* (1894–1897). Seven years later, Harland laid out the desired aesthetic form of the short story, which, he asserted, has to be crafted and refined "by omission, by implication and suggestion" (XVI). The development of the short story had diverged drastically from its origins, ready to be shaped by the force of the avant-garde on both shores.

James's short stories largely reflect the masterful exploitation of situation and realism, namely plotless psychological realism. The intricacy interwoven in a serious situation is fully displayed in his most famous short story, "Daisy Miller" (1878). It is the psychological interplay between internal reality and external reality that helps shape the fictitious life and characters, making his story intriguingly and subtly connected to reality. His legacy is the creation of a new art form for the short story—blending realism and impressionism.

In that sense, James succeeded Hawthorne as one of the masters of the situation in the short story and superseded Harte as a great realistic writer of the period.

Sarah Orne Jewett

Popularizing the local color story did not rest solely on male writers' shoulders. For the first time, we see female writers mark their debut in the genre by exploring the same theme. Sarah Orne Jewett (1849–1909) was the female trailblazer of local color stories. Born in South Berwick and brought up in New England, Jewett naturally took Maine as the background for most of her short stories. The short story collection *Deephaven* (1877) and "The Country of the Pointed Firs" (1896) are some of the stories that offer a glimpse of the isolated coastal towns through intense yet humorous drama. The tranquility and loneliness set against the emotions and the struggle of the locals gives nuance to the stories. *Deephaven* was praised for its sharp local quality. Willa Cather, whom Jewett influenced greatly, remarked that no writer could invent such native language as those spoken by Jewett's personae, for its distinctiveness was drawn from the nature and the experiences of the local people (XVI–XVII). However, it is "The Country of the Pointed Firs" that has become Jewett's masterpiece for its impressionistic portrayal of provincial lives in the declining trading port. Her acute sensitivity brings life to characters that have long been forgotten, or else dismissed as flat and uninspiring.

It is the "everyday aspects" (Cary 51–52) that Jewett called upon as a necessary ingredient for a good story. The ordinary people who go unnoticed in real life are hailed as heroes and heroines and given a voice in her sketches. As a female writer, Jewett especially tailored the voice of her stories to women. Apart from *Deephaven*, which depicts the uphill battles faced by capable and independent women, another short story collection, *A White Heron and Other Stories* (1886), resonates with modern women's fates, in which the frustrations amid achievements and desires of the women in New England strike an accord with the modern reader. Jewett was the first short story writer to successfully blend the local quality and feminist issues in the regionalism genre, and thus earned her double title—the first feminist writer and one of the most influential local color writers.

Charlotte Perkins Gilman

As early as the 1830s, the launch of *The Godey's Lady's Book*, the first female reader-oriented monthly magazine edited by Sarah Josepha Hale, had already foreseen the increasing role of women writers in the short story genre.

It elicited response from outstanding female writers and engaged them in contributing to benefit women education in the literary field. The tone was inviting and encouraging. In less than a decade, the publication had already attracted a cadre of female writers. They were the pioneers of female sketch writing or the forerunners of short stories, such as Caroline M. Kirkland (1801–1864) and Katherine O'Flaherty (1850–1904). Yet, in a male-dominated literary world, their impact was still minimal. Their works were either overshadowed by big names such as Poe[2] and Hawthorne, or remained circulating in their own group. Charlotte Perkins Gilman (1860–1935) was the first to break through and be taken seriously as a feminist writer.

Gilman was a prolific short story writer. Her feminist writing is often interwoven with her adamant belief in gender equality. Born at a time when women's rights were suppressed, she actively participated in social reform movements and advocated for females as an indispensable part of the society rather than just as homemakers in the family. The misdiagnosis of postpartum depression, which resulted in housebound mistreatment, eventually inspired her to write the semi-autobiographical short story "The Yellow Wall-Paper" (1892). Supported with graphic details, the unconventional writing style, which features brief paragraphs and disruption of coherence through its depiction of thought disorder, contrasted with the ineffectual style of most feminist short stories. The story's theme of women and madness defied a traditional framework, extending to social, economic, and linguistic oppression. Its bold and confrontational approach set an example for later female short story writers such as Doris Lessing.

Today, "The Yellow Wall-Paper" is widely acclaimed as a trailblazing feminist work and is studied extensively for its three-dimensional and resounding themes that still echo in different social strata. Such enormous impact undoubtedly placed Gilman as one of the most influential feminist writers in the history of the American short story.

Modern Development

Britain

Near the end of the nineteenth century, British short story writers finally caught up with the progress of the development of the short story genre. The British short story, once a marginalized and devalued genre, boldly strode toward the twentieth century as an independent literary form. It was a period of discovery and experiment as well as a stage of liberation. Attempts were made to break away from the European model and set up their own brand.

Sir Arthur Conan Doyle, the author of the Sherlock Holmes stories (1887–1927) and *The Hound of the Baskervilles* (1902), gained huge international success in publishing short detective stories. Meanwhile, notable modernist writers such as James Joyce and Virginia Woolf exploited the short story for aesthetic trials. Less radical writers like D.H. Lawrence challenged controversial issues including sex and sexuality. No genre could be better than the short narrative for an avant-gardist attempting a new theory. Its intensiveness and inclusiveness were synonymous with modernity, and it provided an excellent platform to showcase high-brow and experimental art, while periodical publication as a venue made the short story accessible to a wider readership.

The most significant change during the period, however, was not just brought by literati but also journalists. Initially trained as journalists, some prominent writers later brought the zeitgeist-journalism into the short story to tap into the age of curiosity and introspection. The principles of journalism infiltrated the art form. It was the law of journalism coupled with the avant-garde movement and high-culture periodical publication that determined the direction of the next development.

Joseph Conrad

Polish ancestry positioned Joseph Conrad (1857–1924) as an outsider in the avant-garde movement from the very beginning. This anti-elitist and anti-populism attitude put him in a period of uncertainty as an established writer. The long struggle to explore an art form of his own, nonetheless, did not stop him from contributing short stories to various literary magazines and newspapers such as *Fortnightly Review*, *Saturday Evening Post*, *Harper's Magazine*, and *Daily Mail*. The boom of periodical publication and his foreign identity gave Conrad a fair chance to experiment with new themes relating to non-English settings and set a wider perspective than any other writers of his time. Many of his short narratives are set in nature, especially at sea. His first published short story "The Lagoon" (1898), for instance, uses an Indonesian rainforest as the backdrop, while one of his finest short narratives, "The Secret Sharer" (1909), takes place on a sailing ship in the Gulf of Thailand. Likewise, his global vision and anti-hero attitude, which none of his contemporaries possessed, gave rise to the Conradian style of characterization. Most of the protagonists he portrayed are unsung sailors or seafarers who struggle with nature, battling for good and against evil. Exploration of the human psyche is the recurring motif. Though evolved around the traditional frame-narrative structure, Conrad's short narratives are complex and powerful in the modern period for their anti-climax, distinct insight, and above all, his highly crafted prose style. The understated mastery of his writing skills had a great influence on many writers, such as Ernest Hemingway and William Faulkner.

Rudyard Kipling

Rudyard Kipling (1865–1936) was born at the height of British imperialism. Influenced by his colonial upbringing in Bombay and journalistic career in several British Indian newspapers, his writing style tapped into the growing curiosity of the native reader who had never traveled to India yet was intrigued by her culture, customs, and religions. It was the exotic link that brought Kipling his first success in the short story. His first short story collection *Plain Tales from the Hills* (1888) became a sensational hit, followed by *Soldiers Three* in the same year. The stories are set in India, and the plots are enveloped by oriental mystery and idiosyncrasy. True portraiture is there but intensified by imperialistic romance. This marked an essential development of the British short story in the late nineteenth century, which saw the shift of localization from the indigenous culture to the colonial one, accompanied by a sharp contrast between races. Kipling certainly took the element of locality from Harte and further colored it with an oriental paintbrush, a unique product of British imperialism. This resulted in vivid, enigmatic, and fascinating, yet disturbing, tales of adventure and exotic lives in almost all his short narratives, from *The Jungle Book* series (1894, 1895) to *Just So Stories* (1902), to name a few. As a prolific short story writer, Kipling witnessed the progressive change of the genre in the literary circle in the turn of the century, while he was celebrated as a charterer boldly experimenting with narrative techniques, like cinematic effects and strategic omission, which later shaped modernist writing. His quintessential British humor and knack for amusing the reader with short narratives made him a phenomenal success in the populist market of not only his own country, but also far across the Atlantic in America.

Hector Hugh Munro

Famously known by the pseudonym Saki, Hector Hugh Munro (1870–1916) was greatly influenced by Kipling. He, too, embarked upon a writing career as a journalist and later became a master of the short story, on par with O. Henry from America. Being a foreign correspondent gave Saki an edge over others because of his ability to write profusely based on rich material gathered during reporting. As a satirist, he ridiculed almost every aspect of life, from religion, females, and the military to Jewish people, and above all, Edwardian pretentious manners. Some of his protagonists are young aristocrats who disdain the bourgeoisie, or miserable women with insufferable attitudes toward money. His humor is witty, sharp, and at times, inhumane. His icy irony, in particular, turns him into a harsh and aloof writer sparing no thought for the plight of his characters. His most famous story "Sredni Vashtar" (1911) ends with the young protagonist Conradin's secret pet—a ferret—killing his overbearing guardian Mrs. de Ropp and concludes, "'[w]hoever will break it to the poor child? I couldn't for the life of me!' exclaimed a shrill voice. And while they debated the matter among themselves, Conradin made himself another piece of toast" (178). This is callous with no mercy.

Saki might not be the most popular short story writer of the early 1900s. Yet, Langguth, Saki's biographer, admitted that Saki "turns out to be one of us" (qtd. in Gale 921) precisely for his aloofness and malice. Readers who favor him relish that ruthless sarcasm. With his exuberant mental energy, Saki could fully expose human vices and follies from which other Edwardian writers refrained. Such appeal remains timeless, even more so today, when we see how greed and selfishness eat our soul and divide a country. Saki's dose of hell may horrify some readers and writers, but eventually offer them a profound analysis of humanity. Roald Dahl, as one of Saki's admirers, acknowledged that "he was the first to employ successfully a wildly outrageous premise to make a serious point" (qtd. in Rundell 33).

E. M. Forster

Though best remembered for his novels, E. M. Forster (1879–1970) also contributed significantly to the short story. In fact, Forster's novels and short stories are superb examples of the dichotomy between the two genres. To Forster, short stories are less restrained, thus setting his imagination free. They are fantasies for pure enjoyment and escapism, without logic and morals. Characters and plots are not necessarily well developed because the reader's attention rests upon the story itself. The Aristotelian unities, namely unity of action, unity of time, and unity of place, should, nevertheless, be well observed. While some of these principles precisely echo Poe's, some new elements are found in Forster's short stories. Magic realism is one such feature that recurs in his stories. For instance, in "The Celestial Omnibus" (1911), a young boy yearning for imagination and life stumbles upon a signpost reading "To Heaven," thus starting a self-discovery journey full of magic and adventures. Another feature is the mythological figure. In "The Story of a Panic" (1904), Forster introduces Pan, the god of nature, as the spirit who scares a group of English tourists away, except for a fourteen-year-old boy who is then transformed and possesses a power akin to that of Pan.

The best theme to demonstrate his wild imagination is travel. Though Forster's novels share the same themes, it is travel through time that distinguishes his short fiction from his long fiction. Forster's personae in the former are particularly endowed with abilities to move physically, geographically, psychologically, and mentally so that the experience ultimately alters their life perspective. "The Machine Stops" published in 1909 is a short science fiction piece which takes the theme of time travel and predicts the invention of instant messaging and the Internet. It was named one of the best novellas of the mid-century.

While Forster's reputation rests upon his novels, it is his short story collections which convince us that the short story cannot be replaced by full-length fiction nor taken as a sub-genre, for the impossible can only be achieved in the realm of the short story.

James Joyce

Born in Dublin,[3] James Joyce (1882–1941) set the background of *Dubliners* (1914), his only short story collection, precisely in Dublin. It is a realistic study of the city and a depiction of the Irish experience, traced chronologically from youth to adulthood, and eventually to death. Echoing James's and Harte's thematic notions on short narratives, the protagonists are mostly from the lower middle class leading common lives. For example, there is Little Chandler in "A Little Cloud," a poetaster who dreams about going to London for a successful career, but eventually finds himself trapped in his familial role. Likewise, there is Mrs. Kearney in "A Mother," an overbearing mother who believes that money and fame will come by signing her daughter up for a series of concerts, but to no avail. The petit bourgeois mentality that permeated the declining city in the early 1900s is exploited in Joyce's "defiant realism." Thus, no matter how dismal and mundane the Dubliners' lives are, there is always a moment of revelation. The ruptures of emotion through gestures, words, or flashbacks manifest themselves through epiphany, a technique famously deployed by Joyce. It is the sudden spiritual transformation from trivial events rather than significant life actions into a decisive moment that finally brings the protagonists back to reality.

Dubliners is no doubt one of the hallmarks in the history of the short story genre. Not only did it unequivocally mark the birth of the modern short story in history, but it also defined what the modern genre today should be. Joyce proved that psychological sketches combined with "prose impression" (Brown xli) could only be achieved through the short narrative form. By the same token, "epiphany" entered into the literary dictionary and has become a byword for the modern short story. This technique further pushed the plotless form into extremity—fragmentary and fleeting. The central idea is "now and here." The revolution Joyce brought to the genre was not transient. For successive generations of writers, *Dubliners* is synonymous with the short narrative bible in which they seek inspiration and guidelines on writing modern short stories.

America

By the end of the nineteenth century, American short story development peaked, basking in its most flourishing and promising era. First, a fervent and serious study of the short story as an independent field of literature commenced. Some prominent scholars such as Brander Mathews, who published *The Philosophy of the Short-Story* in 1907, attempted to pin down the genre. The short narrative was seen on par with science for its law-governed and theorem-bound attributes, hence, teachable in colleges and universities. Ten commandments were prescribed as necessary though arbitrary elements for a contemporary short story. While some elements such as shortness and unity were set as general rules by Poe long before the period, new ones such as culmination, characterization, and verisimilitude were added or emphasized. Culmination, which was further developed as the Iceberg Theory, was widely adopted as a writing technique by Ernest Hemingway in his short stories. The Iceberg Theory suggests less is more. When less is revealed, the story becomes more powerful, such that the reader's imagination will be stimulated. On the other hand, characters and dialogues should be in similitude, which ultimately gives soul to the tale.

Kipling played a key role in this revolutionary change. Kiplingism reached America, the land shaping the genre with a powerful force. The new fashion directed the short narrative to its next development, which is called the "Kiplingized short story" (Pattee 340). To write a short story, it had to be plain. The conventional fictitious elements such as platitudes and fastidiousness were swept aside. Instead, readers demanded truth from the writer, who must have concrete and vicarious experience that could relate to them. The power of vividness and crispness did not rest upon imagination but positive knowledge and firsthand adventures. It was the material that impressed the reader. That was how journalistic writing started to dominate the new era. Especially after the war with Spain, a growing number of war correspondents resorted to writing to uncover the truth that would have never been exposed without the help of the short story. Unsentimental and ugly as it was, the truth, through the short narrative, had nonetheless become a lively and humorous account of the displaced, the suppressed, and the abandoned in an unsettling age.

O. Henry

Also known as William Sydney Porter, O. Henry (1862–1910) had every quality a short story writer in the turn of the century should possess. He wittily sprinkled his works with local color (most of the stories are set in New

York City); surprised readers with twists; amused them with humor; and above all, showed a touch of journalistic sense. His early life was decisively unglamorous—being jailed for embezzlement and mingling with criminals—which, nonetheless, gave him abundant material. Many of his short stories were written while he was in prison. One notable example is "The Gift of the Magi" (1905). It is a classic O. Henry story, with humor and a twist ending in addition to a moral theme. Equally well received was "The Ransom of Red Chief" (1907), which takes the reader aback when the story ends with the kidnappers going berserk because of the hyperactive kidnapped boy, desperately wanting to pay the father to get rid of him. It was a lighthearted read tapping into the taste of readers and the market of literary magazines at that time. Indeed, some of his short stories were famously adapted into the popular culture. The techniques O. Henry deployed in his stories, by and large, fall into the category prescribed in the handbooks of short story formulas, which made him a hugely popular short narrative writer in the early twentieth century.

Jack London

From O. Henry to Jack London (1876–1916), it was a transition from comedy to an unrelenting focus on social change. The former represented an early stage during which the society still remained positive and was unaffected by historical reforms. When the successive waves of enormous changes swept the world, the mood changed drastically, and London projected the impact through his most anthologized short story "To Build a Fire" (1908). It represents the dark power at play between man and nature, aptly capturing prevailing pessimism and preoccupation with social conflicts, familial obligations, and above all, the lost souls throughout the country. Through the specific realistic settings, the reader is reminded of humans' impotence in defying nature. It is an objective and scientific analytical study of the relations between human beings and their surroundings, echoing the idea of the Naturalist Movement in the late nineteenth century. Not surprisingly, London himself was once a war correspondent and acquired the skills of writing in a condensed style with facts and logic while witnessing gruesomeness in life. The short story provided him the best venue to depict the deterministic power in crucial life-and-death moments from an objective angle. With London's powerful vision and masterful skills, "To Build a Fire" is firmly lodged as a classic of naturalism.

Sherwood Anderson

When great names such as Hemingway, Faulkner, and Joyce appear and reappear in the genre, one name may well be eclipsed, and yet, the development of the short story would not have been complete without him—Sherwood Anderson (1876–1941). His major accomplishment comes from a series of short stories collected in the book *Winesburg, Ohio: A Group of Tales of Ohio Small-Town Life* (1919). Centered upon loneliness and isolation, the stories develop in a sprawling community network that sees more than a hundred characters who interact but fail to connect and communicate. It is a grotesque short story cycle threaded with a universal theme—human frustration. Against this conventional theme is the unconventional structure. Built on the character growth of the protagonist George Willard from being a boy to a mature reporter unites the twenty-four sketches in settings, symbols, and mood. In fact, critics often compare *Winesburg, Ohio: A Group of Tales of Ohio Small-Town Life* with *Dubliners*, for they were published in the same decade and share the same schema, namely the modern short story cycle. As Joyce did to the historical movement in the genre, Anderson also influenced a number of prominent American writers such as Ray Bradbury with his short science fiction collection, *The Martian Chronicles* (1950). Offering a glimpse into the distorted psychological view of disconnected characters, his near plotless style pioneered the twentieth-century American style of short story writing, which was later imitated copiously by Hemingway, Faulkner, and the like.

Katherine Anne Porter

Previously a journalist, Katherine Anne Porter (1890–1980) later became a short story writer and reviewer for a few literary magazines such as the *New York Herald Tribune*. Her debut short story "María Concepción" (1922) aside, Porter produced some other remarkable works like "Flowering Judas" (1930). Set in Mexico, the story tells how a young American woman is tormented by her ideology, religious faith, and seduction, and ultimately dreams about suicide to punish herself for her act of betrayal. Porter's experience in the Cultural Revolution in Mexico shaped her unique perspective on politics and religion, which recurs frequently in her stories evolving around the theme of betrayal. Some years later came another acclaimed short story, "Noon Wine" (1937). Set in Porter's native land, Texas, the story alludes to a Greek tragedy, in which the protagonist Earle Thompson takes his own life as punishment for betraying his wife and to end his moral and emotional struggle.

While many of Porter's stories are set in Mexico and the South, Porter never confined herself to one subject. The motifs she explored range from death, race, and gender to sexuality. Witnessing historical changes such as the Civil War and the rise of Nazis inspired her to examine universal issues. Versatility coupled with a dazzling modernist writing style earned Porter numerous prestigious literary prizes such as the Pulitzer Prize, securing her position as a unique writer in American literature.

F. Scott Fitzgerald

F. Scott Fitzgerald (1896–1940) was one of the most influential writers in the Jazz Age, which was characterized by a surge of youth rebellion and a change in morals. Against this backdrop came Fitzgerald's popular short stories that chronicled youth and wealth in the 1920s. For instance, "Bernice Bobs her Hair" (1920) depicts the self-value of and the peer influence among young Americans. During his life, Fitzgerald published one hundred sixty-four short stories, more than any other writer in the same period. For him, writing magazine stories not only gave him a stable income but also an opportunity to experiment across different genres and know the reader's taste. For example, in 1922 he wrote the two fantasies, "The Diamond as Big as the Ritz" and "The Curious Case of Benjamin Button," with the former hailed as one of the best stories in his canon even though it contradicts American values. At his peak, there was "Babylon Revisited" (1931), another story that embodies American values and explores the emotional relationship between a father and his daughter.

Fitzgerald was more avant-garde in theme than in form. Although he used free indirect speech in some of his stories such as "Absolution" (1924), he preferred linear development to the spatial depth explored by other modernist writers. Instead of a fragmentary structure, the plot of his stories is almost always consistent with the beginning-climax-resolution pattern. His poetic writing style is also a far cry from Hemingway's crisp style. For some time, Fitzgerald's popularity as a magazine story writer even surpassed any of his contemporaries. Not only was he paid the most for his stories, but he was also simultaneously sought after by several large quality magazines such as the *Saturday Evening Post* and *Metropolitan*. His top selling stories are now ranked by critics as some of the best American short stories.

William Faulkner

> *Maybe every novelist wants to write poetry first, finds he can't and then tries the short story, which is the most demanding form after poetry. And failing at that, only then does he take up novel writing.*—William Faulkner, 1956

It was such a humble claim made by one of the finest writers in the twentieth century, William Faulkner (1897–1962), who published some of the most anthologized short stories in the century. His first and most acclaimed short story, "A Rose for Emily" (1930), is a notable example. Set in Jefferson, a fictional city in the South, the story examines the changes in the city following the abolishment of slavery, the "peculiar institution" of the Old South, and the protagonist's denial of such change. The plot revolves around a complex structure built upon episodes to show the shift of narrative voices and chronologies. Like other modernist writers, Faulkner used stream-of-consciousness heavily to achieve such effects. In addition to "A Rose for Emily," Faulkner published "Red Leaves" (1930), "That Evening Sun" (1931), and ten more stories, which are all collected in his first volume *These 13* (1931). Not surprisingly, Faulkner's background as a Mississippian has a great impact on the settings and the language of the stories. Of those thirteen stories, six are set in the fictional Yoknapatawpha County, which was modeled on his hometown. The language is typical southern slang. The essential features employed in his stories are a continuation of Harte's tradition that short stories should be brushed with local ingredients to add more color and make it more Americanized. Likewise, Faulkner commented on the demanding form of the genre, which can be seen as a nod to Poe's principle:

> In a short story that's next to the poem, almost every word has got to be almost exactly right. In the novel you can be careless but in the short story you can't.... That's why I rate that second—it's because it demands a nearer absolute exactitude. You have less room to be slovenly and careless. There's less room in it for trash. In poetry, of course, there's no room at all for trash. It's got to be absolutely impeccable, absolutely perfect.[4]

Following the traditions of these two accomplished short story writers, Faulkner not only reinvigorated Southern literature but also achieved his fame through the notoriously demanding genre, which is a remarkable accomplishment for any writer in the history of American short story development.

Ernest Hemingway

Considered one of the greatest writers in American literature in the twentieth century, Ernest Hemingway (1899–1961) bore resemblance to his contemporary Fitzgerald, for both belonged to the lost generation and wrote prolifically for magazines. However, Hemingway's journalistic career that Fitzgerald lacked marks an essential difference in their form, leading to the revolutionary Iceberg Theory. In his critical essay "The Art of the Short Story" (1959), Hemingway argues that simple words, careful selection, and omission of details are indispensable for a good story: "[i]f you leave out important things on events that you know about, the story is strengthened.... The test of any story is how very good the stuff is that you, not your editors, omit" (3). The minimalist style, first acquired when Hemingway was a journalist, was in fact a reaction against the nineteenth-century baroque style. This terse style largely stemmed from the war experience that left him frustrated with western civilization. Like other modernist writers from his country and from Britain, such as Joyce, Hemingway belonged to the lost generation. He lost faith in the institutions. Indeed, some of Hemingway's most remembered short stories such as "Indian Camp" (1924), "Hills Like White Elephants" (1927), "A Clean, Well-Lighted Place" (1933), and "The Snows of Kilimanjaro" (1936) resolutely adopt features that the Iceberg Theory suggests: crisp dialogue, minimal plot development and character development.

Being an adventurer and writer, Hemingway had a gift for relating various life experiences to his short stories, including "The Very Short Story" (1924) and the darkest yet most enduring short stories collected in the series *Men Without Women* (1927) and *Winner Take Nothing* (1933). His themes have no boundaries, from love to bullfighting to war. It was the versatility, the writing style, and the revolutionary short story formula that earned him the Nobel Prize for Literature in 1954 and made him an icon of the modern epoch of the American short story. In 1950, Frank O'Hara acknowledged Hemingway as the second most important literary figure after Shakespeare, while successive writers such as J. D. Salinger and John Updike honored his immense influence on their works. Today, his short stories are still ranked the finest in the English language.

Shirley Jackson

Shirley Jackson (1916–1965) is well remembered for her short story "The Lottery" (1948), one of the most anthologized short stories in the history of American literature. "The Lottery" is set in an unknown small village in modern day that still carries out an ancient ritual. Tessie Hutchinson is selected as the victim through ballots and stones are hurled at her until she dies. It is a twentieth-century version of "Young Goodman Brown" except that Jackson takes the theme of inhumanity with less reserve and more graphic dramatization. Ever since its publication, the story has shocked the world as one of the most brutal in history. Its gruesome effect, nevertheless, coincides with the turbulent time of history of mankind, that is, the end of the Second World War and the beginning of the Cold War. Collective human forces could be vindictive and persecutory. The Nazi concentration camps, the Communist core beliefs about betrayal, and the Stanley Milgram shock experiments on obedience to authority figures are famous examples. "The Lottery" duly reflects the darkest moment of human history in the twentieth century.

Flannery O'Connor

As a devout Catholic and short-lived writer, Flannery O'Connor (1925–1964) blended religion and the fall of humanity in most of her short stories, notably "A Good Man Is Hard to Find" (1955). A grim tale about a family executed by a man while on their way to Florida, it starts with quotidian settings in an exhilarated mood but overwhelms the reader with an ironic and violent ending. In fact, most of O'Connor's works are permeated with such a tone and interwoven with motifs of guilt, alienation, and original sin, which pious readers may find distasteful. Guided by conscientiousness, O'Connor was undaunted by criticism and continued to produce yet more poignant works. Another short story collection, *Everything That Rises Must Converge* (1965), includes some of her most popular stories such as "Revelation" (1965). O'Connor's stories depict the quest for the redeemed soul amid the fall of humanity in which readers may trace the influence of Faulkner and Hawthorne.

Defiantly and adamantly revealing the dark side of humankind and the non-secular world, O'Connor's works also serve as a timely reminder of our overzealous attitudes toward technological advances, which O'Connor believed did more harm than good to the progress of humanity.

POSTMODERN DEVELOPMENT

Britain and Ireland

Near the end of the mid–twentieth century, short story development gradually shifted to Ireland, which saw a growing number of writers committed to short story writing. They were determined to make it a national art and undertook a serious study to revive the tradition of oral culture. Liam O'Flaherty (1896–1984) even took to writing in the Irish language, that is, Gaelic, so as to reignite readers' interest in Celtic culture. It was partially a reaction against modernism that preoccupied the writers with language, partially a desire to reclaim the writer's function as a voice for the community or Gaelic origin in the Celtic Revival. At least two significant critical works were published during that period: *The Short Story* (1948) by Seán Ó Faoláin and *The Lonely Voice: A Study of the Short Story* (1963) by Frank O'Connor. In addition to the booming publication of short stories, British/Irish short story development thrived, which was, to a great extent, sustained by Irish writers. Though some eminent British writers also excelled in the genre, such as Graham Greene (1904–1991), Roald Dahl (1916–1990), and Ian McEwan (1948–), late modern and postmodern art forms of the short narrative were largely redefined and reshaped by Irish writers.

Elizabeth Bowen

As a late modernist writer, Elizabeth Bowen's (1899–1973) reputation may well be eclipsed by that of Virginia Woolf, the central figure of high modernism. Yet, Bowen's contribution to the contemporary study of the short story is no less than hers. Short stories aside, *The Faber Book of Modern Stories* (1937) edited by Bowen occupies an essential position in the genre's development. In the introduction, Bowen likens high modernist literary values to outpourings of mediocre sentiment, which seem to prevail in short stories (40). Instead of advocating the genre as a high-brow art, Bowen believes that it should be a populist art unconfined by class, culture, and form. As much as it serves as a postmodernist manifesto, the introduction gives readers an Anglo-Irish perspective on how the short story could be deployed as the best literary vehicle for an Irish writer living in the time of turbulent Irish history who had to react against human suffering. Creating a character for a short story, she claims, is exempt from any necessity of stating or fathoming motive, which is particularly suitable for capturing the intense emotions in this century (Bowen 45). Indeed, most of the characters in her stories such as "In the Square" (1941) and "The Demon Lover" (1945) are either unknowable or pettifogging. Bowen is concerned with what her characters do rather than who they are, because she believed that focusing on characters' actions brought out the deepest emotions. The short story which allows the writer to create a character with diminishing personae gives one the power to penetrate human plights through psychoanalytic intrigue.

Such was the challenge Bowen took up against the modernist short story form. It was this first masterpiece of criticism of the genre together with her poignant stories that put her in the same ranks as her Irish male peers. In the twentieth century, only two female Irish writers could break the glass ceiling—Bowen and Mary Lavin.

Seán Ó Faoláin

A practitioner, theorist and critic, Seán Ó Faoláin (1900–1991) made his name through writing short stories like "The Trout" (1932). Yet, what made him truly prominent was *The Short Story* (1948), in which he details the historical development of the genre and lays out the theoretical form and techniques that are distinguished from the modernists, such as Joycean extreme metaphorical inventiveness. Seldom has any Irish writer laid out the credo for the genre peculiar to the Irish context as succinctly as his:

> The life now known, or knowable to any modern Irish writer is either the traditional, entirely simple life of the farm (simple intellectually speaking); or the groping, ambiguous, rather artless urban life of these same farmers' sons and daughters who have, this last twenty-five years, been taking over the cities and towns from the Anglo-Irish.... In such an unshaped society there are many subjects for little pieces, that is for the short-story writer; the novelist or the dramatist loses himself in the general amorphism, unthinkingness, brainlessness, egalitarianism and general unsophistication [Ó Faoláin 373, 375, 376].

It was this affiliation and perhaps patriotism that Ó Faoláin strongly attached to that allowed him to draw further remarks upon the stagnant development of the short story in Britain. In an attempt to establish a link between turbulent times and the need for the short narrative, he criticized a lack of admiration for the artistic temperament in the country due to a relatively more stable political, cultural, and social atmosphere, which foresaw long fiction overshadow short fiction. Indeed, Ó Faoláin's early stories such as "Midsummer Night Madness" (1932) and "The Patriot" (1932) decisively use the Irish Revolution as the setting through which the personae's Anglo-Irish identity conflict can be fully displayed. The themes of his works are essentially Irish, from the nationalist struggle to Irish Roman Catholicism, while the characters are from the lower and middle classes in Ireland.

Ó Faoláin's devotion to reigniting the Irish spirit through short stories deserves full credit. Not only is he highly acclaimed as the master of the Irish short story, but he also became the pillar of the genre's development in mid-century.

Frank O'Connor

A prolific short story writer, Frank O'Connor (1903–1966) published more than one hundred fifty works including "Guests of the Nation" (1931), "In the Train" (1935), and "Michael's Wife" (1935). O'Connor frequently drew his experiences in the IRA and the Irish Civil War to create a sense of intense loneliness. "The Uprooted" (1942) is a supreme example of how frustration and pessimism about lives augment that feeling of loneliness. Behind this is the uncertainty caused by political and social upheaval, especially in a turbulent time in Ireland when national identity and conflicts of religions were questioned.

The most remembered work of O'Connor, however, is *The Lonely Voice: A Study of the Short Story* (1963) that details the historical development of the form not of any short story but of silenced population groups. It is a study across nations, from Russia to France, America, and needless to say, his homeland, Ireland. Like Ó Faoláin, he also dismissed England as an ideal place for the short story to thrive because of the national attitude toward society: "[a] young American of our own time ... might look forward with a certain amount of cynicism to a measure of success and influence; nothing but bad luck could prevent a young Englishman's achieving it, even today; while a young Irishman can still expect nothing but incomprehension, ridicule, and injustice. Which is exactly what the author of *Dubliners* got" (O'Connor, "The Lonely Voice" 87). Although O'Connor may have downplayed the merits of young and successful English writers, he persuasively argues that the short story is the best venue to give the marginalized group a voice, which reflects the strong feelings of isolation, dislocation, and loneliness due to rapid modernization. While O'Connor rationalizes the themes of the short story created particularly during the high modernist period, he stresses the need for reviving the tradition of storytelling in which ideology should preside over form, the latter being adamantly adhered to by his contemporaries such as Joyce and the like.

It is this critical study as well as his literary oeuvre that defined O'Conner's legacy and started a new chapter on the development of the Irish short story.

Mary Lavin

Mary Lavin (1912–1996) is another Irish short story writer who used the short narrative to give the reader a glimpse of her homeland, mid-land Ireland. Lavin published her first story "Miss Holland" in *The Dublin Magazine* in 1939. Nineteen collections of short stories ensued, with themes varying from Catholic Ireland to rural lives and feminism. The short story was the only form that allowed her to magnify the complexity and intensity of a single event, especially lives in secluded provincial towns that could normally escape scrutiny due to their triviality. Lavin described the form as "an arrow in flight" or "a flash of lightning," which had "beginning, middle and end, all there at once" (qtd in McKeon). In fact, the stories in her award-winning collection *Tales from Bective Bridge* (1942) are all set in rural mid-land and portray local lives as nuanced and emotional. It is a domestic as well as private world gnawed with troubles, which Lavin proved through short stories as gripping as a national event or a heroic life.

As an Irish feminist inter-modernist, Lavin never shied away from any feminist topics in her writing. Stories such as "Sarah" (1943) and "A Nun's Mother" (1944) give her a voice to criticize the martyr role that Irish women are obliged to play. The heroines should suffer or sacrifice themselves to enshrine femininity. Such an issue was never compatible with the dominant male presence in the genre of the Irish short story in the mid-century. Lavin presented a view otherwise as progressive and unapologetic. Though constantly competing with her male counterparts, especially Joyce, Ó Faoláin, and O'Connor, the first being a giant in crafting the form and the others having successfully established their trademarks on the formula, Lavin proved that her literary oeuvre was as impressive as theirs. She earned several awards including the Katherine Mansfield Prize, and was regarded by Joyce Carol Oates as one of the eminent writers of the twentieth century.

William Trevor

An Irish writer revered by American, British, and his fellow literati, William Trevor (1928–2016) has always been compared with Joyce, for both shared the same techniques and mastered the art so exquisitely that their short story collections are firmly established as the canon of the short story in English. Trevor's masterpiece "The Ballroom of Romance" (1972) speaks of the fate of Bridie, the protagonist from rural Ireland, in "paralysis" and "epiphany," which Joyce also employed in *Dubliners*. Much as Trevor viewed writing as experimental as Joyce did, the former set his stories in and beyond Ireland. Born in Ireland and migrated to Britain after marriage, Trevor showed an aptitude for depicting backward villages of both countries from a distance. His acute observing skill and "unfamiliarity" with both lands gave him an edge in relating the miserable personae to cruel and helpless situations, such as those Bridie faces in a hopeless romance, or the dilemma in which Liam Pat is caught up while being hired to plant a bomb in London in "The Hill Bachelors" (2000).

Having published both short stories and novels prolifically, Trevor had his unique opinion on the two genres. He defined the short story as "the art of the glimpse," and compared the novel and short story as "an impressionist painting" versus "an intricate Renaissance painting." "It should be an explosion of truth. Its strength lies in what it leaves out just as much as what it puts in, if not more.... The novel imitates life, where the short story is bony, and cannot wander. It is essential art" ("William Trevor" 1989).

W. Somerset Maugham

Arguably the best storyteller in the late modernist period, W. Somerset Maugham (1874–1965) published numerous short stories, notably "Rain" (1921), "The Outstation" (1924), "The Vessel of Wrath" (1931), "The Lotus Eater" (1935), and "Virtue" (1943). Maugham saw the short story as the only literary platform to express fully and freely. Short stories aside, Maugham made a significant contribution to literary criticism. In the preface of the first volume of collected short stories *East and West* (1934), Maugham defines the theories of the art of writing short stories based on the models of Guy de Maupassant and Anton Pavlovich Chekhov, which have to be brief, lucid, and "with just the amount of detail that is needed to make the circumstances of the case plain" (qtd. in Nicholas Shakespeare 100). The aim is to allow the reader to exercise discretion and judgment on the story. In another essay, "The Short Story" (1958), Maugham shares Poe's principle and remarks that a short story should be created at night "when the hunter, to beguile the leisure of his fellows when they had eaten and drunk their fill, narrated by the cavern fire some fantastic incident he had heard of" (147). Not surprisingly, most of his short stories such as those collected in *Ashenden: Or the British Agent* (1928) are inspired by incidents that Maugham witnessed or heard.

A crafter rather than an inventor, Maugham nevertheless drew a circle of admirers like Evelyn Waugh and George Orwell. Likewise, the epiphany employed in his stories reminds the reader of Joycean style.

V. S. Pritchett

As a prolific writer, V. S. Pritchett (1900–1997) enjoyed a unique position among other English writers, for he mastered the art of short story so exquisitely that hardly any of his contemporaries could compare. His humble background influenced his writing. Born into a family that frequently moved due to his father's dwindling businesses, Pritchett took up several odd jobs including working in the leather tanning workshops. The early precarious life fraught with low social mobility, nevertheless, gave Pritchett an unusual sense of humor in his stories. His comical yet serious style marked with sharpness and wittiness often turns reality into near surrealism or eccentricity, which successfully proved that a short story writer should not pigeonhole working-class characters as caricature nor address the reader based on hierarchy and class. Pritchett's literary virtuosity is, therefore, not subject to place, time, or class. He was interested in the lives of common people. From shopkeepers and clerks to housewives, he let his dramatis personae tell their own stories[5] and show their quirky character, be it erratic, unscrupulous, or aspiring. They are social stories to connect people regardless of one's qualities, such as a very foolish girl and a man whose family runs a funeral business in "Sense of Humor" (1956), or a defaced woman and a blind man in "Blind Love" (1969).

While Pritchett's art form was influenced by Ó Faoláin and O'Connor, his economical yet poetic language is distinctively colorful and native with old slang like "posh" and "toffs." A superb example to showcase Pritchett's signature style is the dialogue between Mr. Fulmino and Mrs. Fulmino in "When My Girl Comes Home" (1961):

"I wrote to Bombay," said Mr Fulmino.
"He wrote to Singapore," said Mrs Fulmino.
Mr Fulmino drank some tea, wiped his lips and became geography [*Complete Collected Stories* 30].

Swift, arresting, and impulsive like a spark of fire, the language has an immediate effect on the reader. It is the poetic impulses that Pritchett deems important in the short story ("Introduction" xiv).

As a home-grown English short story writer, Pritchett deserves more credit. He wrote stories that show unambiguous Englishness, and he is among a few English writers who made a name for themselves globally through short stories. It was not surprising when H. E. Bates contended that the modern short story should start from Poe to Pritchett.

H. E. Bates

Rarely has any English writer in history been as highly praised for both short stories and critical study as H. E. Bates (1905–1974). His war time stories and *The Modern Short Story* (1941) are considered some of the great contributions in the genre. His literary virtuosity and apprehension of rural English life came at a time when Bates was a provincial journalist. The short story collection *The Beauty of the Dead and Other Stories* (1941), for example, provides deep insights into the human bondage peculiar to the countryside. Commissioned as a wartime writer, Bates even reached greater fame with postwar short stories such as *Colonel Julian and Other Stories*, another short story collection published in 1955, which continues the theme but uses diverse settings. One notable example is "Colonel Julian" (1945), the title story about the two generations' perceptions of war, which is set in India.

The Modern Short Story, on the other hand, is the only literary criticism Bates wrote. It is a critical survey and study of literary history of the short story writers from America and Ireland. Notable writers such as Poe, Harte, O. Henry, London, Hemingway, and Joyce are among those by whom Bates was influenced. Though he avoids mentioning his works or techniques in the book, he discusses his fellow writers like Rudyard Kipling and D. H. Lawrence. Through their works, Bates explores what makes a great short story, and concludes that implication and simplicity instead of description are the essential elements. The writer should refrain from any moral lesson, while the reader should be more responsible. Bates's enthusiasm and imagination give unique insights into the genre's development crisscrossing modernist and postmodernist times.

Bates's success as an English short story writer and critic has no doubt saved the sluggish development of the short story in England during the same period.

Doris Lessing

One of the greatest contemporary British writers, Doris Lessing (1919–2013) contributed prolifically from novels and poems to short stories. While much attention has been given to her novels, her short stories are deemed to be equally important in English literature. As an Iran-born British writer and a communist supporting the Soviet Union until the early 1950s, the themes she dealt with are more progressive in humanity and more diverse in material than any other native writer. Lessing's stories are not just set in England but also Europe and South Africa, the last being where she was brought up and started to write. Her short story collection *African Stories* (1964) was a tribute to the country that she owed a great deal to. Apart from politics, two world wars, and social class, she was also keen on gender issues, which earned her the reputation of the leading feminist writer in the late century. Her main concern was women's rights, which Lessing never shied away from commenting on. Some of her short stories such as "To Room Nineteen" (2000) depict a grim yet profound picture of female suffering in social, mental, and psychological aspects. Provocative and aggressive, her stories can be a challenge to male readers. "One off the Short List" (1963) is a classic example to demonstrate how Lessing employed strong tone and language for a controversial subject—"naked, the fringes of gold at her loins and in her armpits speaking to him in a language quite different from that of her green, bored eyes" (234).

The risks Lessing took as a short story writer were higher than any other writer ever had in literary history. She picked up sensitive and dangerous topics at a time when many others steered clear of controversy. Agonized by her father's painful war experience and deeply disturbed by the violence brought by the wars, Lessing pushed the boundaries to create some powerful stories such as "The Eye of God in Paradise" (1957) based on the Holocaust. In terms of theme, content, and technique, she was ahead of others. It is liberating, insightful, and thought-provoking to read Lessing's stories. For her unparalleled literary contributions, she was awarded the Nobel Prize for Literature in 2007, which signified a triumph over an authority (the British Intelligence Agencies) spying on her for nearly two decades because of her unconventional writing about politics.

Neil Gaiman

A British-born Jewish writer of Polish descent, Neil Gaiman (1960—) is among a few who prove that a writer's interest is not confined by his or her ancestry or religion. From very early on, Gaiman showed a flair for blending contemporary tastes and themes such as enchantment or religion in broad subjects ranging from fantasy, folklore, horror, and short science fiction, resulting in a resurgence of magic and mythology juxtaposed with the pop, futuristic, and technological obsessed culture of this century. *A Calendar of Tales* (2013) and *Trigger Warning: Short Fictions and Disturbances* (2015) are two collections of short stories that showcase the hallmark of Gaiman's versatility. While the former text, which was inspired by tweets, has all of the elements of sci-fi action, the latter emulates the styles of Charles Dickens, Bram Stoker, and Shirley Jackson and takes readers into a dark, unsettling, yet gripping fantasy world. Together with other popular stories such as "The Problem of Susan" (2004), Gaiman not only gained popularity with both children and adults as one of the most widely read contemporary British writers, but also succeeded in bringing Gothic fantasy back to prime time.

Zadie Smith

One of the most popular contemporary British writers, Zadie Smith (1975–), who embraces cross-cultural experiences and is of mixed parentage (English and Jamaican), represents Generation X. Some of her short stories precisely reflect the dynamic and global view of today. Due to her ethnic background, she is particularly interested in interracial exchanges that can bring different nationalities into the same context, as shown in "The Embassy of Cambodia" (2013). Such an approach takes a far broader and more challenging view than that of the writers of the last generation (especially in America) who saw interracial interaction as typically black and white. With the world engulfed in rifts between liberals and nationalists, the short story becomes a bridge to connect people around the globe and brings them hope. Smith, like other contemporary writers, turns herself into a "missionary" to enlighten the world with her poignant stories.

America

From the late twentieth century to the twenty-first century, short story development has advanced simultaneously in two directions. Multi-ethnic writers were first seen hand in hand with American white writers, such as Ray Bradbury, Stephen King, Joyce Carol Oates, Edna Annie Proulx, and John Updike, in shaping and redefining the genre. On the one hand, Bradbury and King popularized short science fiction, while Proulx and Oates write on regionalism and Gothicism. On the other hand, it is the multi-ethnic writers who add to the vibrancy and diversity such that the genre, more than any other kind, readily meets the challenge of a more globalized century.

Though the multi-ethnic short story appeared as early as the late nineteenth century, it was not until the late twentieth century that it started to gain momentum. Themes and subjects have since been expanded from marginalized population groups to multi-ethnic groups including Jewish Americans, Asian Americans, and African Americans. At first glance, the development reflects one of the most significant social changes in American immigration history that started in the 1920s when the immigrant quota was lifted. A huge growth of multi-ethnic populations meant a new demand had to be met. Various media outlets as well as publications sought to reach out to the new audience by incorporating new voices. Magazines, newspapers, and books were no longer restricted to the native readership but open to a new population so that they could still be connected with their homes. One way was to let them access the public discourse, thus indirectly opening the door to non-traditional writers.

Lurking in the background, however, are the grim tales recounted by immigrant writers and those of color. The short story gives them an outlet for voicing their concerns about prejudice, repression, discrimination, segregation, slavery, violence, and brutality that have long shaped their lives as well as their ancestors'. This never-ending struggle of conflicting identity and value between "self" (tribes, communities, countries of origin) and "others" (the United States) taking place on personal, cultural, social, and political levels has become the recurring theme of the multi-ethnic story. Pulitzer Prize winner Alice Walker is one of the most widely read contemporary writers of African origin. Her first short story collection *In Love and Trouble: Stories of Black Women* (1973), which includes the often anthologized story "Everyday Use" (1973), and her second collection *You Can't Keep a Good Woman Down: Short Stories* (1981) chronicle struggles of American Black women through gender stereotypes and traumatic experiences, such as rape and abortion. Both collections reveal the American Black women's inferior role in both black and white communities.

Suffice it to say that African American writers have been a strong pillar of the multi-ethnic short story development for more than a century. First, there has never been a scarcity of talent in this vast community. Less celebrated but equally important writers such as Zora Neale Hurston, Jean Toomer, and Richard Wright dedicated their lives to African American literature. For a period of time, there were periodicals such as *Opportunity* and *The Crisis* that solely published African American short fiction. Second, for their resilient and daunting character, the writers' power to resist, fight, and voice the injustice their communities have experienced has remained one of the strongest aspects of the multi-ethnic groups. This collective voice continues to shape the development of contemporary American short stories.

The second group that dominates the genre is American writers of Jewish descent. The Holocaust in World War II gave rise to the new literary power for the imminent need to reassure Jewish existence after the genocide. Bernard Malamud, Saul Bellow, and Philip Roth are some of the most productive Jewish American writers who have garnered numerous prestigious literary awards like the O. Henry Prize and Nobel Prize for Literature. Stories written by them are frequently selected as the best contemporary American short stories. While most of the stories share similar themes with those of African American ones, the struggle they underpin is quintessentially Jewish—the negotiation between Jewish values and American values, and the impact of the genocide on the survivors and the following generations.

A shaping force that has grown in the last few decades is Asian American writers, mainly of Chinese, Filipino, Indian, and Japanese descent. It is more about globalization and the new immigration policy than wars that pull them together. They form another branch of the multi-ethnic genre which is slightly different from the last two groups partly because they are assimilated into the American mainstream with relatively less blood and tears. Their short stories tend to deal with softer issues on the personal level such as exploring the generation gap in families or probing into their ancestral roots. Yet, the achievement of the writers should not be underrated. In fact, some successful writers such as Gish Jen, Ha Jin, Jhumpa Lahiri, Samrat Upadhyay, Mitsuye Yamada, and Hisaye Yamamoto have established their fame through winning various awards like the Flannery O'Connor Award, the Massachusetts Book Prize, and the Women's Network Alert Literature Award.

The multi-ethnic short story has opened a new chapter of American Literature and further pushed its boundary. Studies of this field have never been so fervent. Experimental writers of diverse backgrounds are eager to try out short narratives because it is a genre that gives them promise and hope. Literature thrives not because of the length of a text but because of the boundless imagination that can only be fulfilled in a short story.

Notes

1. See "Literary Notices: July Magazines [Second Notice]," *The Chester Courant*, 5 July 1899, 7.
2. Poe was a frequent contributor to *The Godey's Lady's Book*, which had its literary quality raised significantly by his presence.
3. Though Joyce's nationality is a controversial issue, different resources, for example, *The Times Literary Supplement*, did suggest that Joyce refused Irish citizenship several times and remained a British citizen until he died.
4. Faulkner, William. Local Public and University Community, 5 June 1957, University of Virginia, 202 Rouss Hall.
5. Pritchett describes writing his first short story, "Sense of Humor," and recalls why he switched from a third-person to a first-person narrator in an interview in 1990: "If only I could jump away, this man could tell his own story. People are much brighter than you think they are. I shan't be interfering with him. I shan't give him my thoughts" (qtd. in Guppa and Weller).

Bibliography

Bendixen, Alfred, and James Nagel, eds. *A Companion to the American Short Story*. West Sussex, UK: Wiley-Blackwell, 2010. Print.
Bowen, Elizabeth. *The Faber Book of Modern Stories*. London: Faber & Faber, 1937. Print/Web.
Bradbury, Malcolm, and James McFarlane, eds. *Modernism: A Guide to European Literature 1890–1930*. 1976. London: Penguin, 1991. Print.
Brown, Terence. "Introduction." *Dubliners*. Edited by Terence Brown. London: Penguin, 2000. vii–xlviii. Print.
Canby, Henry Seidel. *The Short Story in English*. New York: Henry Holt & Co., 1909. Web.
Cary, Richard, ed. *Sarah Orne Jewett Letters*. Waterville, ME: Colby College Press, 1967. Print/Web.
Cather, Willa. "Preface to Sarah Orne Jewett." *The Country of the Pointed Firs and Other Stories*, vol. 1. Boston: Houghton Mifflin Company, 1925. IX–XIX. Web.
Chaucer, Geoffrey. *The Canterbury Tales*. 1386. London: Penguin. 2009. Print.
Conrad, Joseph. "The Lagoon." *Modern Short Stories: For Students of English*. Edited by Peter JW Taylor, 18th ed. Oxford: Oxford University Press, 1992. 10–24. Print.

Davis, Barbara Thompson. "Katherine Anne Porter, The Art of Fiction No. 29." *The Paris Review*, issue 29, 1963. 150–51. Print/Web.

Dickens, Charles. "The Haunted House." *Great English Short Stories*. Edited by Paul Negri. Mineola, NY: Dover, 2005. 1–23. Print.

Faulkner, William. Local Public and University Community, 5 June 1957, University of Virginia, 202 Rouss Hall. Web.

_____. "A Rose for Emily." 1930. *Literature: An Introduction to Fiction, Poetry, and Drama*. Edited by X. J. Kennedy and Dana Gioia, 6th ed. New York: Harper Collins, 1995. Print.

Fischer, Andreas. "Context-Free and Context-Sensitive Literature: Sherwood Anderson's *Winesburg, Ohio* and James Joyce's *Dubliners*." *SPELL Swiss Papers in English Language and Literature 4: Reading Contexts*. Edited by Neil Forsyth and Gunter Narr Verlag, 1988. 13–32. Print/Web.

Fitzgerald, F. Scott. *The Diamond as Big as the Ritz and Other Stories*. 1963. London: Penguin, 1996. Print.

Gale, Steven H. "Saki." *Encyclopedia of British Humorists: Geoffrey Chaucer to John Cleese*. Vol. 2 L-W. New York and London: Garland, 1996. 919–922. Print/Web.

Gilman, Charlotte Perkins. "The Yellow Wall-Paper." *The New England Magazine*, Jan. 1892. 647–656. Web.

Goodyear, Dana. "Kid Goth: Neil Gaiman's Fantasies." *The New Yorker*, 25 Jan. 2010. Web.

Guppy, Shusha, and Anthony Weller. "V. S. Pritchett, The Art of Fiction No. 122." *The Paris Review*, issue 117, 1990. Web.

Harland, Henry. "Yellow Dwarf." Letter. *The Yellow Book*, vol. X. London: Elkin Mathews & John Lane, July 1896. XVI. Web.

Harte, Bret. *The Luck of Roaring Camp and Other Writings*. New York: Penguin, 2001. Print/Web.

Hawthorne, Nathaniel. *Young Goodman Brown and Other Short Stories*. Mineola, NY: Dover Publications, Inc., 1992. Print.

Hemingway, Ernest. "The Art of the Short Story." *New Critical Approaches to the Short Stories of Ernest Hemingway*. Edited by Jackson J. Benson. Durham, NC: Duke University Press, 1990. 1–16. Web.

Hunter, Adrian. *The Cambridge Introduction to the Short Story in English*. Cambridge: Cambridge University Press, 2007. Print.

Jackson, Shirley. "The Lottery." 1948. *50 Great Short Stories*. Edited by Milton Crane. New York: Bantam Books, 1979. 130–137. Print.

James, Henry. "Guy de Maupassant." *Partial Portraits*. 1888. London: Macmillan, 1899. 243–290. Web.

_____. "The StoryTeller at Large: Mr Henry Harland." *Fortnightly Review*, Apr. 1898. 650–654. Web.

Joyce, James. *Dubliners*. 1914. London: Penguin, 1992. Print.

Kenny, John. "Inside Out: A Working Theory of the Irish Short Story." *Frank O'Connor: New Critical Essays*. Edited by H. Lennon. Dublin: Four Courts Press, 2007. 99–113. Print/Web.

Lessing, Doris. *African Stories*. 1965. New York: Simon & Schuster, 2014. Print.

_____. *Doris Lessing Stories*. New York: Vintage, 1980. Print.

"Literary Notices: July Magazines [Second Notice]." *The Chester Courant*, 5 July 1899. 7. Web.

Malcolm, Cheryl Alexander, and David Malcolm, eds. *A Companion to the British and Irish Short Story*. West Sussex, UK: Wiley-Blackwell, 2008. Print.

Matthews, Brander. *The Philosophy of the Short Story*. 1901. Forgotten Books, 2014. www.ForgottenBooks.org. Accessed 30 September 2015.

Maugham, W. Somerset. "The Short Story." *Points of View*. 1958. London: Random House, 2011. 142–188. Print.

_____. *W. Somerset Maugham: Sixty-Five Short Stories*. London: Heinemann/Octopus, 1976. Print/Web.

McKeon, Belinda. "An Arrow in Flight: The Pleasures of Mary Lavin." *The Paris Review*, 12 June 2012. Web.

Murphy, Catherine. Interview with Mary Lavin. *Irish University Review, Mary Lavin Special Issue* 9, no. 2 (1979): 207–224. Web.
O'Connor, Flannery. *A Good Man Is Hard to Find and Other Stories*. Boston and New York: Houghton Mifflin Harcourt, 1955. Print.
O'Connor, Frank. "The Lonely Voice." *Short Story Theories*. Edited by Charles E. May. Athens: Ohio University Press, 1976. 83–93. Print/Web.
Ó Faoláin, Seán. "The Dilemma of Irish Letters." *Month* 2, no. 6 (1949): 366–379. Web.
O'Hehir, Andrew. "Neil Gaiman's 'Trigger Warning.'" *New York Times*, 3 March 2015. BR18. Web.
Pattee, Fred Lewis. *The Development of the American Short Story: An Historical Survey*. New York and London: Harper & Brothers, 1923. Print/Web.
Poe, Edgar Allan. "The Fall of the House of Usher." 1839. *Edgar Allan Poe Selected Poetry, Tales, and Essays*. Edited by Jared Gardner and Elizabeth Hewitt. Boston, New York: Bedford/St. Martin's, 2015. 86–103. Print.
_____. *The Raven and the Philosophy of Composition*. San Francisco, New York: Paul Elder and Company, 1907. Web.
_____. "Review of Twice-Told Tales." 1842. *Great Short Works of Edgar Allan Poe: Poems, Tales, Criticism*. Edited by Gary Richard Thompson. New York: Harper Collins, 1984. 519–527. Print/Web.
Prescott, William. "Essay Writing [Washington Irving]." *The North American Review*. Edited by Jared Sparks, et al., Apr. 1822, vol. XIV, no. XXXV: 319–350. Web.
Pritchett, V. S. "Introduction." *The Oxford Book of Short Stories*. Oxford: Oxford University Press, 1981. XI–XIV. Print.
_____. "When My Girl Comes Home." *Complete Short Stories*. New York: Grove Press, 1965. 30. Print/Web.
Rundell, Katherine. "Ferrets can be Gods." *London Review of Books*, 11 Aug 2016, vol. 38, no. 16. 33. Web.
Saki. "Sredni Vashtar." *The Oxford Book of Short Stories*. Oxford: Oxford University Press, 1981. 174–178. Print.
Sarker, Sunil Kumar. *A Companion to E.M. Forster. Vol. 1*. New Delhi: Atlantic, 2007. Print.
Scofield, Martin. *The Cambridge Introduction to the American Short Story*. Cambridge: Cambridge University Press, 2006. Print.
Shakespeare, Nicholas. "Somerset Maugham." *The Best Australian Essays 2004*. Edited by Robert Dessaix. Melbourne, Australia: Black Inc., 2004. 97–113. Print/Web.
Stein, Jean. "William Faulkner, The Art of Fiction No. 12." *The Paris Review*, issue 12, 1956. Web.
Stevenson, Robert Louis. "A Lodging for the Night." *Great English Short Stories*. Edited by Paul Negri. Mineola, NY: Dover, 2005. 133–148. Print.
_____. *The Strange Case of Dr. Jekyll and Mr. Hyde and Other Tales of Terror*. 2002. Edited by Robert Mighall. London: Penguin, 2003. Print.
Stout, Mira. "The Art of Fiction CVIII: William Trevor." *The Paris Review*, issue 110, 1989. Web.
Trevor, William. *The Ballroom of Romance and Other Stories*. London: Bodley Head, 1972. Print.
_____. *The Hill Bachelors*. London: Penguin, 2001. Print.
Twain, Mark. "The Celebrated Jumping Frog of Calaveras County." *The Oxford Book of Short Stories*. Oxford: Oxford University Press, 1981. 61–66. Print.
Wood, James. "V. S. Pritchett and English Comedy." *On Modern British Fiction*. Edited by Zachary Leader. Oxford: Oxford University Press, 2002. 6–17. Print/Web.

2
Practical Literary Criticism

WHAT IS LITERARY CRITICISM?

Literary criticism is an organized and systematic application of critical theories for the purpose of literary appreciation, evaluation, and interpretation. Drawing on concepts and theories from disciplines such as philosophy, sociology, psychology, and linguistics, literary critics use different critical perspectives to help us understand "what literature is, what it does, and what it is worth" (*Merriam-Webster's Encyclopedia of Literature* 685). In *The Mirror and the Lamp*, M. H. Abrams suggests that each piece of literary criticism examines at least one of the four elements: the literary text itself; the author who wrote the text; the world or nature; and the audience of the work (Abrams 6). More specifically, literary critical approaches are classified as text-oriented, language-oriented, author-oriented, context-oriented, and reader-oriented (Jagadale 180):

1. Author-oriented approaches that include Classicism and Humanism of various kinds.
2. Reader-oriented approaches including the Reception theory/Reader response theory (French/German/American).
3. Context-oriented approaches
    (a) Psychological contexts: Psychoanalytic criticism of various schools;
    (b) Context of gender: Feminist/LGBTQ criticism;
    (c) Historical contexts: New Historicism/Cultural Materialism;
    (d) Colonial contexts: Post/Neo-colonial criticism;
    (e) Socio-economic contexts: Marxism of various kinds;
    (f) Socio-cultural contexts: Myth criticism/Dialogism, etc.

(g) Text-oriented approaches including Formalism, practical/new criticism, structuralism and stylistics, post-structuralism and deconstruction (French/American/Indian).

In the following sections, the seven most commonly used criticisms for analyzing short stories, namely historical criticism, biographical criticism, reader response criticism, Marxist criticism, feminist criticism, psychoanalytic criticism, and formalist criticism, will be introduced and explained one after another with examples. These critical approaches will also be used to evaluate the selected British, Irish, and American short stories in chapters three through ten.

Historical Criticism

Developed between the end of the eighteenth century and the early twentieth century, historical criticism sees a literary work as a creation of its time and place. Historicists believe that to understand a literary work, a thorough investigation of the historical, biographical and socio-cultural contexts of the text must be carried out. Take studying Arthur Miller's *The Crucible* (1953) as an example. First of all, one needs to know the historical setting of the story. It is crucial to have knowledge of the witch hunts that took place in Salem, Massachusetts, in the seventeenth century. Secondly, to apply historical criticism to *The Crucible*, one also must become familiar with the historical and cultural context of the author's time. In other words, the communist "witch hunt" that happened in the U.S. during the Cold War in the 1950s is central to the study.

As the most widely used criticism, historical criticism can be further branched into two approaches: old historicism and new historicism. Old historicism, namely the traditional historical perspective, asserts that history is objective. It is believed that there "are 'facts' that we can know, with some degree of certainty, and as readers we ... need to gather them ... and fit them together ... and cautiously relate them to literary works" (Lynn 145). By contrast, new historicism (1980s–present) does not hold the view that history can be objective. It is more interested in how the literary work is interpreted differently across different time periods:

> [Q]uestions asked by traditional historians and by new historicists are quite different ... traditional historians ask, "What happened?" and "What does the event tell us about history?" In contrast, new historicists ask, "How has the event been interpreted?" and "What do the interpretations tell us about the interpreters?" [Tyson 278].

Simply put, new historicism can go as far as to believe that there are no facts in history. History itself is a series of interpretations represented as facts.

There is not even a single history. Likewise, the literary text does not reflect facts but interpretations shaped by cultural discourses. The literary work is a "textual construct" (Habib 266) based on fragments of interpretations of truth. Nevertheless, whether it is old historicism or new historicism, the following questions are useful for the literary analysis:

1. When and where was the work written and published?
2. According to recorded history, what happened at the time that the work was written?
3. How does the work reveal the ideologies and social values of the time period when it was published?
4. Do the language, characters and events presented in the work mirror those of the author's time? How so?
5. How was the work received by critics and the public during the author's life? Why?
6. How does the reception of the work change over time? Why?
7. Are there any historical documents, cultural artifacts, or social institutions which can be analyzed in conjunction with particular literary works? [Di Yanni 1567]
8. To what extent can we understand history as represented in the literary work?

The historical perspective is particularly effective for studying realist fiction such as James Joyce's short stories. For example, historical criticism of Joyce's "Grace" (1914) involves the close examination of the social, cultural, and intellectual context within which the short story was written. It tells readers a great deal about the Irish nationalists' resistance against the 800-year British rule in Ireland, the religious divides in Dublin, as well as Joyce and his contemporary Dubliners. In the same light, one who studies Alice Walker's "Everyday Use" (1973) with the historical approach will need to look into the Black Power Movement during the 1960s. With a comprehensive understanding of the long suffering of African Americans, one gains a better grasp of complicated issues such as Black-on-Black oppression. For a more detailed historical analysis of Joyce's "Grace" and Walker's "Everyday Use," please refer to chapters eight and nine.

Biographical Criticism

The biographical approach is like historical criticism on a micro, personal level. It sees a literary work as a mirror that reflects the personal life experience, thought and feelings of the author. It is believed that through examining the author's family background, upbringing, education, and life events, one will be able to understand the world view of the author, the values and ideologies that influence the author's writing, as well as the key concerns and main themes conveyed in the literary work. One famous example of the biographical inquiry is Samuel Johnson's *Lives of the Most Eminent English Poets* (1779–1781), which provides a critical analysis of poetry with reference to the biographical accounts of fifty-two poets, revealing the relationship between the life experiences of poets and their writings (Rollyson 363).

To use the biographical approach, one may probe into the author's world by reading his/her personal letters, diaries, essays, blogs, and in the digital era, the author's Twitter, Instagram and other social media accounts. In addition, when studying the short story, special attention should be paid to the following questions:

1. What was the world view like when the author wrote the literary work?
2. To what extent did the author accept or reject the prevailing world view of his/her time?
3. How did the author's personal life encounters affect his/her view?
4. What was the author's major concern(s) in life?
5. How are the author's view and major concern(s) reflected in his/her short story?
6. How are the author's view and major concern(s) reflected in his/her writing other than the short story?
7. Is there any correspondence between the author's life experiences and the events that happen in the short story?
8. Is there any correspondence between the real people in the author's life and the characters in the short story?

For example, scholars who study Edgar Allan Poe and his works are often fascinated by his obsession with the death of a young, beautiful woman. As revealed in his essay "The Philosophy of Composition" (1846), Poe writes: "the death of a beautiful woman is, unquestionably, the most poetical topic in the world" (Cited in Bronfen 59). Indeed, it is found that in many of Poe's short stories and poems such as "Ligeia" (1838), "The Fall of the House of Usher" (1839), "The Raven" (1845) and "Annabel Lee" (1849), there is a recurring motif of the young and beautiful female corpse. To understand Poe's obsession with the beautiful woman's death, Marie Bonaparte, Sigmund Freud's close friend and colleague, takes the biographical approach to study the women who influenced Edgar Allan Poe's view of death and femininity. It is discovered that both Poe's mother and wife died at a young age—Elizabeth

Poe, who had "an unusually close relationship with Poe" (Walden 161), died of tuberculosis after Poe's father abandoned the family. Likewise, Virginia Eliza Clemm Poe, Poe's cousin and later his wife, also suffered from tuberculosis, grew worse, became catatonic and passed away ten years after she married Poe. Throughout the years, Poe witnessed the illness, struggles and suffering of his young dying wife while taking care of her. Her pain and death inspired Poe's writings.

Based upon the biographical inquiry, Bonaparte puts forward the notion that Poe may have been a necrophile, and he was fixated on his dead mother. To remain eternally physically faithful to his mother, he chose to marry Virginia, his ailing thirteen-year-old cousin. Since Virginia was more like a sister than a wife to him, Poe spared "himself the need to consummate the marriage" (Wright 1803), though at the same time, his young wife's illness, suffering and death doubly traumatized Poe, causing him much pain and anxiety. Through the biographical approach, it becomes obvious to readers that Poe's "repressed feeling is transferred ... onto fictional figures and objects" (Wright 1803). In all those tales with the dying young female figure, "Poe is reliving Elizabeth Poe's last agony and death" (Wright 1803). It is not difficult to see that the characterization of the incestuous siblings, Madeline and Roderick Usher, in "The Fall of the House of Usher" (1839) corresponds to Poe's wife and himself. Poe's fragile and beautiful wife, on the other hand, bears points of resemblance with Poe's mother, who died young and beautiful.

Likewise, in Doris Lessing's "To Room Nineteen" (1978), the characterization of Susan Rawlings also corresponds to Doris Lessing herself, who had experienced the pain of being torn between her writing career and motherhood. Lessing, who chose to divorce her husband and leave her two young children to pursue her career in England, once said: "[f]or a long time I felt I had done a very brave thing. There is nothing more boring for an intelligent woman than to spend endless amounts of time with small children. I felt I wasn't the best person to bring them up. I would have ended up an alcoholic or a frustrated intellectual like my mother" (cited in Wood). Although "To Room Nineteen" cannot be viewed as an autobiographical account of Lessing's firsthand experience as a mother and an ambitious writer, the biographical approach illuminates the problems of how traditional female roles in the family may affect the well-being of women.

READER RESPONSE CRITICISM

The biographical approach remained convincing and appealing for most scholars until 1968, when Roland Barthes announced the "death of the author," denouncing authorship together with the relevance of the author's biographical background. It is argued that the meaning of the text is up to the reader but not the author at all. The same text can be interpreted in numerous ways by different readers. Meanwhile, the same reader can also interpret the same text differently at different times and ages. In contrast, once the text is published, the author has no control over how his/her text is read and interpreted by readers across time and different cultures. In brief, the reader is the one who has the power to determine the meaning of the text during the reading process:

> The reader is the space on which all the quotations that make up a writing are inscribed without any of them being lost; a text's unity lies not in its origin but in its destination. Yet this destination cannot any longer be personal: the reader is without history, biography, psychology; he is simply that someone who holds together in a single field all the traces by which the written text is constituted.... Classic criticism has never paid any attention to the reader; for it, the writer is the only person in literature ... we know that to give writing its future, it is necessary to overthrow the myth: the birth of the reader must be at the cost of the death of the Author [Barthes 148].

Ever since then, the relationship between the reader and the text has been brought to center stage. In the late 1960s, Hans-Robert Jauss introduced reception theory, which later became highly influential in Germany and the U.S. in the 1970s and the early 1980s respectively (Fortier 132). Reception theory, a version of reader response theory, puts great emphasis on readers' reactions towards the literary text. Readers are encouraged to participate actively in interpreting the meaning of the text. Every reading experience is unique because each reader's age, gender, race, class, education, etc. is different. No one has the power to tell others how the text should be read:

> A response paper expresses what you experienced in reading and think about the assigned text ... [and] should reflect your background, values, and attitudes in response to the work, not what the instructor thinks about it [Kennedy 1397].

More importantly, readers are not supposed to accept and absorb the literary text passively. Rather, they should use their own values and experiences to create the meaning of a text. Should there be gaps and blanks in the text, readers should complete the text by filling them in. To employ the reader response approach, one can consider the following guiding questions:

1. Who are the intended readers of the literary work?
2. How do readers feel about the text?
3. Does the reader like or dislike the text? Why?
4. What does the text mean to the reader?
5. Is the text connected to the reader's life experience?
6. Can the text have multiple meanings?

7. If so, are there interpretations that are more valid than others?
8. Do meanings and interpretations of texts change over time? If so, how?

Besides giving personal responses, readers may also work as an interpretive community that shares a common ground (Lynn 69). Together they can also contribute to the construction of meaning. Rather than being told how the text should be read, readers who represent different communities express how the author's work influences them and makes them feel. For example, Annie Proulx's "Brokeback Mountain" has received greatly diverse reader responses across time since its publication. To the lesbian, gay, bisexual and transgender (LGBT) community, Proulx's gay-themed short story, which became an Oscar-winning film, is a milestone that celebrates relationships between gay people, bringing LGBT into the mainstream Hollywood cinema. The mass media also see "Brokeback Mountain" and Ang Lee's film version as "a sign of America's readiness to humanize and civilize its attitude towards homosexuality" (cited in Piontek 123). On the other hand, conservative church-based and homophobic audiences feel uncomfortable about the gay content, shaming the gay cowboy film as gay propaganda (Kupelian). As Daems puts it: "[s]uch a reading perceives *Brokeback Mountain* as a straight-up attack on 'American values,' a perverse film neatly summed up in the title of one widely-read virulent response subtitled 'Rape of the Marlboro Man'" (94). Scholars who study "Brokeback Mountain" with the reader response approach should take such widely different reader responses into consideration. Note that the reader response approach is particularly useful and powerful for studies that deal with controversial texts. For instance, diverse perspectives can be drawn from the reader response analysis of Nikos Kazantzakis's *The Last Temptation of Christ* (1955), which draws a stark contrast between Christianity and Secularism.

Marxist Criticism

Another literary criticism commonly used among researchers is the Marxist approach (1930s–present). Interestingly, while the Marxist approach was named after Karl Marx, the father of modern Communism, neither Karl Marx nor Friedrich Engels suggested any comprehensive literary theory for studying literature. Marxism only became a new way of thinking, reading, and understanding literature when critics, theorists, and intellectuals such as Louis Althusser (1918–1990), Frederic Jameson (1934–), and Terry Eagleton (1943–) applied Marxism to literature as an approach for literary analysis. In general, the Marxist approach sees literature either as a tool for a political agenda, or a social construct that reflects the ideology of the social class to which the author belongs. As Barry explains:

> So instead of seeing authors as primarily autonomous "inspired" individuals whose "genius" and creative imagination enables them to bring forth original and timeless works of art, the Marxist sees them as constantly formed by their social contexts in ways which they themselves would usually not admit [167].

In other words, art and literature are propaganda tools for what Althusser calls interpellation, a process in which "the working class is manipulated to accept the ideology of the dominant [class]" (Dobie 81). The individuals who are manipulated are often politically unconscious of "the exploitation and oppression buried in a work" (Dobie 81). The social and political elements of a text are all that matter; the aesthetic elements are of little value. To study a literary work, Marxist critics investigate the author's social class, the history and culture of the author's time, focusing on how class distinctions, struggles and conflicts are represented in literature. It aims to reveal the ideology that blinds readers. To apply Marxist theory in a close reading, one can begin by considering the following guiding questions (Dobie 88–89):

1. What is the power relation, distribution of wealth and social status depicted in the story?
2. Who are the powerful people and who are the powerless ones?
3. How do the powerful ones gain their power? Why is power denied to others?
4. Is there evidence of class conflict and struggle?
5. Is there evidence of repression, manipulation and exploitation?
6. What tools do people of the bourgeois class use to consciously or unconsciously repress and manipulate the powerless ones? Media? Education? Religion? Literature?
7. How does the ideology revealed in the story support the values of capitalism or any other "ism," such as sexism, racism, imperialism, that perpetuates the domination of one group over another?
8. Does the author condemn the unfair system?

The above questions are useful for analyzing short stories such as Doris Lessing's "To Room Nineteen" (1978). In the story, Susan Rawlings is a typical housewife and a victim of financial abuse (Baston 24). She is repressed, exploited and powerless under the patriarchal system. As the mother of four children, Susan takes up the conventional role of the unpaid housewife and gives up her financial freedom and independence. Unfortunately, she has neither a bank account nor any personal savings. This puts her in an embarrassing situation. Every time she needs money, she needs to ask for it from

Matthew Rawlings, the one and only breadwinner of the family, reporting to him on how she will spend the money. For the monthly rent she needs to pay for room nineteen, a private room that can give her moments of relief and peace of mind, Susan has to make up stories and ask her husband for money every month, which causes misunderstandings. It is revealed that one night at bedtime, Susan again asks Matthew for money. Unluckily, Matthew, who has total control over the household spending, suspects that Susan needs money for some secretive, indecent affairs. He then says coldly: "[h]ere's your five pounds," (Lessing 545) and insolently pushes the five-pound bank note to Susan. Feeling humiliated and financially abused, Susan rejects the offer and argues with Matthew. Sadly, because of her pride, Susan tells Matthew nothing about her worrying mental condition. Instead, she covers up her anxiety and depression by inventing an imaginative lover called Michael Plant, "confessing" that she is having an extramarital affair with him. Not having enough money to pay for room nineteen, Susan has to turn to her ex-employer, Mrs. Parkes and asks her for the loan of just one pound. She lies to Mrs. Parkes that her busy husband has forgotten to leave her the housekeeping money. The two women even commiserate about the fact that all husbands are equally "forgetful." When Susan dies, evidence of her husband's financial abuse also dies with her. No one ever knows the intolerable abuse that Susan has to endure since she forfeits her financial independence for her marriage and children. By and large, the Marxist reading of Lessing's realist fiction highlights how a housewife like Susan Rawlings is trapped and oppressed by a dominant force. Though no solution is given, the Marxist reading makes the unfairness against women heard loud and clear.

Interestingly, apart from studying the short story and its author, the Marxist approach can also be used to criticize other existing forms of criticism. Most famously, in *Marxism and Literature* (1977), Raymond Williams addresses his criticism towards other literary criticisms, or what he calls "the established bourgeois practice" (Williams 53). He points out that before Marxist criticism was introduced, the so-called critical reading "never radically questioned or opposed" (Williams 53) "literature" as a received category. Indeed, Marxist criticism has brought new insights to literary studies, historicizing other critical approaches:

> Lukács contributed a profound revaluation of "the aesthetic." The Frankfurt School, with its special emphasis on art, undertook a sustained re-examination of "artistic production," centered on the concept of "mediation." Goldmann undertook a radical revaluation of the "creative subject." Marxist variants of formalism undertook radical redefinition of the processes of writing, with new uses of the concepts of "signs" and "texts," and with a significantly related refusal of "literature" as a category [Williams 53].

Critical approaches such as historicism and formalism, which used to be oblivious to class struggle and the oppression and exploitation of people, have undergone substantial changes in the face of Marxist criticism.

FEMINIST CRITICISM

Just as similar to Marxist criticism, the core belief of feminist criticism (1960s–present) also shares the core belief is that literature is a social construct that reflects social values and ideologies of the society. Following the two world wars which empowered women to take on roles in both the public sphere and the private spheres as well, post–World War II intellectuals started to revisit and renew first wave feminist classics such as Mary Wollstonecraft's *A Vindication of the Rights of Women* (1792), Virginia Woolf's *A Room of One's Own* (1929), and Simone de Beauvoir's *The Second Sex* (1949). Gender issues including gender roles, ideological stereotypes, and the oppression of women within the social structure gained public attention again in the second wave of feminism. In the 1960s–70s, two rudimentary feminist approaches were developed. The first form is the literary critical analysis which studies literature, challenging patriarchy and other power relations that privilege men and subordinate women, in particular in Western culture:

> Western culture is fundamentally patriarchal ... [t]hat social structure, they agree, is reflected in religion, philosophy, economics, education—all aspects of the culture, including literature. The feminist critic works to expose such ideology [Dobie 97].

Alongside feminist literary criticism, gynocriticism, the second form of feminist approach, aims to redefine the literary canon dominated by men. Coined by Elaine Showalter in *A Literature of Their Own* (1977), gynocriticism supports new women writers and unearths neglected literature written by female authors but unknown to readers:

> gynocriticism ... worked to increase the number of female authors available to readers. It did this partly by encouraging the emergence of new writers, and partly by recovering forgotten or unvalued texts and making them available for reassessment [Tolan 328].

By creating a canon of women's writing, gyno-feminists believe that they can bring women back to center stage, and ultimately women's creativity can be truly realized. When using feminist criticism, it is important to observe the depiction of women in literary works, especially how female characters have been silenced and marginalized. The following questions can help one analyze the interactions between gender and power in literature:

1. How are women represented in the text?
2. What gender roles are men and women playing in the text?

3. How do characters embody masculine and feminine traits?
4. How is the patriarchal social structure revealed in the text?
5. Do the female characters show signs of resistance against patriarchy? If so, how?
6. Does the literary work reinforce or undermine patriarchal ideology? How so?
7. How do cultural factors such as race and class intersect with gender in the text?
8. What role does the work play in terms of woman's literary history and literary tradition? [Tyson 101].

It is noteworthy that feminist criticism can take many shapes. It does not necessarily have to be in the form of an essay. It can also be in the form of a speech. For example, Virginia Woolf's *A Room of One's Own* (1928) is the extended book version of the iconic feminist speech that she delivered at Newnham College and Girton College at the University of Cambridge in 1929. Likewise, Neil Gaiman's short story "The Problem of Susan" (2004) is itself a feminist reinterpretation of C. S. Lewis's *The Chronicles of Narnia* (1950–1956). In the Narnia books, female sexuality is portrayed as the evil power that tempts men to leave God. To readers' great disappointment, not only Jadis the White Witch, but also Susan Pevensie are punished and banished from Aslan's heaven because of their beauty and female sexual awakening. Taking the feminist critical approach, Gaiman avenges Susan by rewriting the Narnia ending. After five decades of being silenced, Susan returns as an old professor of children's literature, revealing the agony of being orphaned and the hardship she had experienced after being left behind in England in the post-war period. Meanwhile, Gaiman also shares with readers Susan's sexual fantasy and her first love-making experience through the third-person narrative. Susan becomes a down-to-earth character who lives her life as a real person. Contrary to the gynophobic attitude reflected in C. S. Lewis's Narnia series, in Gaiman's feminist rewriting, Susan is not ashamed of sex. She has nothing to repent for in her life.

Psychoanalytic Approach

Built on the psychological theory known as psychoanalysis founded by Sigmund Freud (1856–1939), psychoanalytic literary criticism (1930–present) employs Freud and his followers' theories to interpret the text as well as the author's psychological state. Unlike Marxist criticism and the feminist approaches, psychoanalytic criticism does not focus on the intention of the author. Rather, it attempts to examine hidden instincts, psychological conflicts, repressed desires and forbidden fantasies of the author's unconscious mind. To a large extent, interpreting a literary work is like interpreting a dream. Attention will have to be paid to symbols and images, which carry subtle implications and meanings. Sometimes, presence-absence such as slips of the tongue and slips of the pen may also open the door to the unconscious.

Among the many psychoanalytic theories, four Freudian concepts are found to be most influential and useful for psychoanalytic readings. The first one is the importance of the unconscious mind, the mysterious driving force behind our behavior. As Tyson elaborates: "human beings are motivated, even driven, by desires, fears, needs, and conflicts of which they are unaware" (15). Making the unconscious conscious is thus of utmost importance. However, it is not easy to unlock the unconscious through the conscious mind. Traces of the unconscious can only emerge in dreams, art, silences, compulsive repetitions in behavior, etc.

The second key concept is repression, which includes the denial and suppression of fears, guilt, aggression, secret conflicts, forbidden desires, and the like. Defense mechanisms such as displacement, selective memory, avoidance and regression are developed so as to bury the repressed feelings in the unconscious. Nevertheless, Freud explains that "[u]nexpressed emotions will never die. They are buried alive and will come forth later in uglier ways" (cited in Rani 162). Hence, understanding repression is one of the ultimate goals of psychoanalysis.

The third key Freudian notion is the tripartite structure of personality, which consists of (1) the id (the pleasure principle), (2) the ego (the reality principle), and (3) the superego (the morality principle). The id is where the libido or primitive drives are located. The superego, on the other hand, is the individual's conscience "which begins to form during childhood" (Richter 1015). Between the opposing forces of the id and the superego, the ego keeps the balance and sustains the individual's mental health. It is noted that our behavior is affected every time there are splits and conflicts among the three principles.

Another cornerstone of psychoanalytic criticism is the Oedipus Complex for boys and the Electra Complex for girls. It is believed that around the age of four, boys will develop an unconscious sexual desire for their mother, whereas girls will desire for their father. The anxious wish to possess the parent of the opposite sex and exclude the parent of the same sex remains strong until the individual learns to shift the sexual desire to another person later in life. Interestingly, it is noted that when choosing a life partner, people do have a tendency to choose a person who resembles his/her parent of the opposite sex.

To apply psychoanalytic criticism when reading literature, one may begin by asking the guiding questions below:

1. What unconscious drives can be observed in the characters?
2. Can Oedipal/family dynamics be found in the literary work?
3. How do early childhood experiences influence the characters?
4. Can the narrative, the plot, and/or the characters' behavior be explained in terms of any psychoanalytic concepts?
5. Are there any images or symbols relevant to death, sexuality, and the unconscious in the text?
6. What hidden meaning can be found in the language used by the author?
7. What does the literary work suggest about the psychological state of mind of the author?
8. What might a given interpretation of a literary work suggest about the psychological motives of the reader?

Most critics agree that psychoanalysis "has always had an affinity with horror" (Dodds), so for short horror stories like Poe's "The Fall of the House of Usher" (1839) and "The Tell-Tale Heart" (1843), a psychoanalytic reading can be fruitful and revealing. Likewise, psychoanalytic reading works particularly well when it is done together with feminist criticism and the biographical approach. For example, scholars discovered that "The Yellow Wall-Paper" (1892) was a short story based on the first-person experience of the author. Jane, the mentally ill housewife in "The Yellow Wall-Paper," is a character whom Charlotte Perkins Gilman intentionally created to resemble herself. As disclosed in her autobiographical writing, Gilman developed severe psychological symptoms because of the oppressive gender role forced onto her. She was given a mental treatment called the "rest cure" (Gilman 265), which worsened her condition. According to Gilman, the specialist confined her to the domestic sphere, constraining her to "two hours' intellectual life a day" (Gilman 265) and advised her "never to touch pen, brush or pencil again" (Gilman 265) as long as she lived. The brutal silencing and the oppressive domestic life forced upon her drove her to the verge of a nervous breakdown. During moments of great anxiety and depression, Gilman could hardly express her thoughts and feelings in writing. The repression was so strong that Gilman was burdened with feelings of guilt and shame:

> You did it yourself! You did it yourself! You had health and strength and hope and glorious work before you—and you threw it all away. You were called to serve humanity, and you cannot save yourself. No good as a wife, no good as a mother, no good at anything. And you did it to yourself! [Gilman 91].

Years after her recovery, she wrote "The Yellow Wall-Paper" to warn people of the traumatic effects of the rest cure. Jane, the hysterical fictional narrator, is a realistic record of what Gilman had been through. As revealed by Gilman, the story is so real that even physicians found it threatening: "[w]hen the story first came out, in the *New England Magazine* about 1891, a Boston physician made protest in *The Transcript*. Such a story ought not to be written, he said; it was enough to drive anyone mad to read it" (Gilman 265). The only difference is that unlike Gilman, Jane also suffers serious hallucinations and regression in addition to the repression and hysteria. Without the insightful information gathered from the biographical and feminist approaches, there is no way that a deep and meaningful psychoanalytic reading could be done.

Formalist Criticism

Arising from the Moscow Linguistic Circle of Russian literary criticism in the late nineteenth century and the early twentieth century, Formalism (1930–present) is interested in the intrinsic literary features, or what Roman Jacobson (1896–1982) called the "poetic language" (Busse and McIntyre 6), of the work. To a formalist, a literary work is a discrete and unique aesthetic object for its own sake. It is not a historical, biographical or social document, and thus it should be treated separately from the author, the era, and the socio-cultural environment: "[t]he natural and sensible starting point for work in literary scholarship is the interpretation and analysis of the works of literature themselves" (Wellek and Warren 256). To understand a literary work, formalists examine and explicate the aesthetics in the text, which interdependently work together to convey thematic messages for readers. The following are some of the guiding questions for the stylistic analysis of the formalist literary approach:

1. What is the plot structure of the short story?
2. What does the setting reveal about the central themes of the short story?
3. What do the protagonists and antagonists represent?
4. How do characters relate to one another?
5. Who is narrating the story?
6. How does the style of the work, such as irony and humor, convey its theme?
7. How do literary devices such as imagery and symbols support the overall meaning of the work?

8. What does the form (e.g., tone, genre and structure) reveal about the story's content?

The close readings of the selected short stories in chapters three through six of this book include a section for stylistic analysis as well. For example, in the next chapter, there is a detailed discussion that examines the way Flannery O'Connor uses literary devices in "A Good Man Is Hard to Find" (1953). Formalist criticism is employed to explore the symbolic meanings of the family car, the car crash, the grandmother's broken hat, and other implicit symbols that appear in O'Connor's story. In the same way, the use of irony and paralysis in Joyce's "Grace" and Trevor's "Of the Cloth" is discussed in chapter eight. Different from the thematic analysis which goes hand in hand with other critical approaches, the formalist stylistic study of the text's style, with an emphasis on literary devices and/or figurative language, can be conducted separately from the part in which historical, biographical and socio-cultural backgrounds of the literary works are investigated.

BIBLIOGRAPHY

Abrams, Meyer Howard. *The Mirror and the Lamp: Romantic Theory and the Critical Tradition*. Oxford: Oxford University Press, 1971. Print.

Barry, Peter. *Beginning Theory: An Introduction to Literary and Cultural Theory*. Manchester, UK: Manchester University Press, 2017. Print.

Barthes, Roland. "The Death of the Author." *Image-Music-Text*, trans. Stephen Heath. London: Fontana, 1977. Print.

Baston, Ajda. "Financial Abuse in Doris Lessing's 'To Room Nineteen.'" *Epitome: International Journal of Multidisciplinary Research* 30.4 (2017): 22–31. Print/Web.

Bennett, Andrew, and Nicholas Royle. *An Introduction to Literature, Criticism and Theory*. Edinburgh: Pearson Education Limited, 2004. Print.

Bronfen, Elisabeth. *Over Her Dead Body: Death, Femininity and the Aesthetic*. Manchester, UK: Manchester University Press, 1996. Print.

Busse, Beatrix, and Dan McIntyre. "Language, literature and stylistics." *Language and Style*, edited by Dan McIntyre and Beatrix Busse. Basingstoke: Palgrave, 2010. 3–14. Print.

Daems, Jim. "'Mister, This Is Cattle Country': Livestock and Gender in Western Films." *A Fistful of Icons: Essays on Frontier Fixtures of the American Western*, edited by Sue Matheson. Jefferson, NC: McFarland, 2017. Print.

Di Yanni, Robert. *Literature Approaches to Fiction, Poetry, and Drama*. Boston: McGraw-Hill, 2008. Print.

Dobie, Anna B. *Theory into Practice: An Introduction to Literary Criticism*. Boston: Wadsworth Cengage Learning, 2002. Print/ Web.

Dodds, Joseph, "The Monstrous Brain: A Neuropsychoanalytic Aesthetics of Horror." *PsyArt*, 15 Dec 2009. http://psyartjournal.com/article/show/dodds-the_monstrous_brain_a_neuropsychoanalyti. Accessed on 12 Jan 2019.

Fortier, Mark. *Theory/theatre: An Introduction*. London and New York: Routledge, 2002. Print.

Gilman, Charlotte Perkins. "Why I Wrote 'The Yellow Wallpaper.'" *The Captive Imagination: A Casebook on "The Yellow Wallpaper,"* edited by Catherine Golden. New York: The Feminist Press, 1992. Print.

Habib, M. A. Rafey. *Literary Criticism from Plato to the Present: An Introduction*. Chichester, UK: Wiley-Blackwell, 2011. Print.

Jagadale, Umesh S. "The Interplay of Text and Context in Sarojini Naidu's Poetry: A Pragmatic Approach." *Indian Poetry in English: Critical Essays*, edited by Zinia Mitra. New Delhi: PHI Learning Private Limited, 2012. Print.

Kennedy, X. J., and Dana Gioia. *Literature: An Introduction to Fiction, Poetry, Drama, and Writing*. New York: Pearson, 2011. Print.

Kupelian, David. "'Brokeback Mountain': Rape of the Marlboro Man." WorldNetDaily, 27 Dec 2005. http://www.wnd.com/2005/12/34076/. Accessed on 20 May 2018.

"Literary Criticism." *Merriam-Webster's Encyclopedia of Literature*, compiled by Merriam-Webster, Inc., Springfield, MA, 1995, 685. Print.

Lynn, Steven. *Texts and Contexts: Writing About Literature with Critical Theory*. 5th ed. New York: Pearson, 2008. Print.

Piontek, Thomas. "Tears for Queers: Ang Lee's *Brokeback Mountain*, Hollywood, and American Attitudes towards Homosexuality." *American Culture* 35.2 (2012): 123–134. Print/Web.

Rani, Rabbia. "Psychoanalytic Study of Abigail's Mind in Arthur Miller's Play 'The Crucible.'" *International Journal of Social Science and Humanities Research*. 5.1 (2017): 160–163. Print/Web.

Richter, David H. *The Critical Tradition: Classic Texts and Contemporary Trends*. Boston: Bedford Books, 1998. Print.

Rollyson, Carl. "Biography Theory and Method: The Case of Samuel Johnson." *Biography* 25.2 (2002): 363–368. Print.

Storey, John. *Cultural Theory and Popular Culture: An Introduction*. London and New York: Routledge, 2015. Print.

Tolan, Fiona. "Feminism." *Literary Theory and Criticism: An Oxford Guide*, edited by Patricia Waugh. New York: Oxford University Press, 2006. 319–339. Print.

Tyson, Lois. *Critical Theory Today*. New York: Garland Publishing, 1999. Print.

Walden, Sarah. *Whistler and His Mother: An Unexpected Relationship*. London: Gibson Square & University of Nebraska Press, 2003. Print.

Wellek, René, and Austin Warren. *Theory of Literature*. New York: Harcourt, Brace & World, 1949. Print.

Williams, Raymond. *Marxism and Literature*. Oxford: Oxford University Press, 1977. Print.

Wood, Gaby. "Doris Lessing: A Woman Ahead of Her Time." *The Telegraph*, 17 Nov 2013. https://www.telegraph.co.uk/culture/books/10455882/Doris-Lessing-a-woman-ahead-of-her-time.html. Accessed 12 Jan 2019.

Wright, Elizabeth. *Psychoanalytic Criticism: A Reappraisal*. Cambridge, UK and Malden, U.S.: Polity Press, 2006. Print.

Part II

Close Reading for Short Stories

3
Religion and Redemption in O'Connor's "A Good Man Is Hard to Find"

BIOGRAPHY OF FLANNERY O'CONNOR

Born into a traditional Catholic family as the only child in Savanna, Georgia, in the southern U.S., Flannery O'Connor (1925–1964) was deeply influenced by her Southern and Catholic upbringing. When she turned 15, her father fell gravely ill with lupus, an autoimmune disease. Her family had to move to a dairy farm called Andalusia in their hometown of Milledgeville, Georgia, in 1940. One year later, her father passed away, and O'Connor continued to live with her mother in Milledgeville. At the age of 17, she received tertiary education at the Georgia State College for Women and obtained her first degree in social sciences in three years (Spivey 4). In 1946, she studied journalism at the University of Iowa, where she met important writers and critics, developed her writing skills, earned her master's degree, and published her first short story, "The Geranium" (1946). For several years, she pursued her writing career and worked at Yaddo, an artists' community in Saratoga Springs, New York. Unfortunately, shortly after she published her first novel, *Wise Blood*, in 1952, she was diagnosed with lupus, the same incurable disease that claimed her father's life. O'Connor then moved back to the farm in Milledgeville and lived with her mother. For twelve years, she battled her illness and wrote the majority of her works, in which religion was a recurring theme. Her most well-known short story collections, *A Good Man Is Hard to Find and Other Stories* (1955) and *Everything That Rises Must Converge* (1965), where unique chemistry was created as she blended Southern culture with her Catholic values, were also published during that period, gaining her numerous honors and awards such as the O. Henry Award in 1957. At 39,

O'Connor died of lupus at the Baldwin County Hospital. She was buried next to her father in Milledgeville in 1964.

SOUTHERN GOTHIC LITERATURE

Flannery O'Connor was one of the pioneer American Southern writers who created the Southern Gothic literary genre. Primarily, the term "Gothic" came from the late eighteenth century in Europe. It refers to a literary genre that combines horror, mystery, suspense, violence, the supernatural, and at times romance. Masterpieces such as Edgar Allan Poe's macabre stories, Mary Shelley's *Frankenstein* (1818), Robert Louis Stevenson's *The Strange Case of Dr. Jekyll and Mr. Hyde* (1886), and Bram Stoker's *Dracula* (1897) are all considered classics of the Gothic canon. In the early to mid–twentieth century, American writers including William Faulkner, Flannery O'Connor and Tennessee Williams experimented with the form and style of the Gothic by building it within a socially realistic framework. As defined by Stamenkovic:

> *Southern Gothic* is a macabre writing style native to the South of the USA. Since the middle of the 20th century, Southern writers have interpreted and illuminated the history and culture of the region through the conventions of the Gothic narrative (or Gothic novel), which at its best provides insight into the horrors institutionalized in societies and social conventions [15].

Yet, rather than relying on the supernatural to build suspense and guide the plot, Southern Gothic writers tell disturbing stories of poverty, violence and sinister events based on the creepy and unusual regional settings in the American South. Grotesque and disturbing characters "who are not accepted or oppressed by traditional Southern culture—African Americans, Native Americans, women, homosexuals, disabled, etc." (Stamenkovic 15) are used to explore unpleasant social and cultural issues in the southern U.S. states. Flannery O'Connor's "A Good Man Is Hard to Find" (1953), for example, is a "totally unexpected, yet totally believable" (O'Connor 113) short story written in the typical Southern Gothic literary style.

PLOT OVERVIEW

Set in the 1950s in the southern U.S., "A Good Man Is Hard to Find" is a scary, brutal yet humorous short story with a most shocking and violent ending. At the beginning of the story, a family man named Bailey plans a car trip from Georgia to Florida with his family. Just like any other typical road trip, Bailey's children play games, read comic books, fight, and have snacks in the car. While driving past Georgia, however, the grandmother insists that they visit east Tennessee instead. She keeps nagging her son Bailey, arguing that they should not head towards Florida because the children have been to Florida before, and because she read in the newspaper that a famous killer known as the Misfit is on the loose in Florida. No one listens to the old lady, and they stop for lunch at Red Sammy's, a filling station and barbecue joint near a town called Timothy. Red Sammy Butts, the owner of Red Sammy's, complains to the grandmother that it is hard to find a good man these days, and that people have become untrustworthy. The grandmother calls Red Sammy "a good man" (O'Connor 15) and agrees with him that everything is going wrong in the world, unlike the golden days in the past. After lunch, Bailey and his family carry on with the journey. The grandmother again requests that they stop at a plantation in Georgia. She directs Bailey to drive up a dirty, deserted path to get to the plantation, when she suddenly realizes that her memories have fooled her. The plantation is in Tennessee, not Georgia. Then, Bailey's car loses control and flips over on the hilly road. The car accident is a shock to the family, but it is not half as shocking as their deadly encounter with the Misfit and his gang. The grandmother recognizes the Misfit right away, and she tries her best to beg for her own life. The three gangsters ignore her plea and systematically kill all her family members one by one. As the old lady gets desperate and turns religious, the Misfit reveals his anger and disappointment towards life, saying that it has "no pleasure but meanness" (O'Connor 28). At the end of the story, the grandmother has a spiritual awakening. A few moments before she is killed, she forgives the Misfit, reaches out and calls him "one of her babies" (O'Connor 29). He then shoots her, and she dies with a smile on her face.

CHARACTERS

Grandmother

The grandmother is a Catholic woman who lives in Georgia with her son Bailey and his family. Though she considers herself a lady and dresses in fine clothes, she is a proud, selfish middle-class white woman who cares only about herself. She freely and frequently passes judgment on others, but her faith in God is fragile and her moral codes are questionable. She is oblivious to social issues such as inequality and racial discrimination. Due to her conceitedness, complacency and bourgeois background, she doesn't reflect upon her own flaws until she faces her own death.

Bailey and His Wife

Bailey and his wife have three children, namely a daughter called June Star, an eight-year-old son named John Wesley, and a baby. They live with Bailey's mother. They are a typical middle-class couple from the South. As parents, they are not very successful, for their children are rude, selfish, rascal-like, and as self-centered as their grandmother.

John Wesley and June Star

They are the son and the daughter of Bailey. John Wesley is a mean, spoiled and unthankful eight-year-old. He calls Tennessee "a hilly dumping ground" (O'Connor 11) and Georgia "a lousy state" (O'Connor 11). During the car trip, he slaps his sister over the grandmother, yells loudly inside the car, and kicks hard on his father's seat, making the baby scream. His grandmother also has to stop him and his sister from throwing snack boxes and paper napkins out of the car window. June Star is also an annoying, sharp-tongued child with poor manners. When she does not get what she wants, she rolls her eyes, screws up her mouth, and screams as noisily as her brother. She also knows little about danger, pain and death. She feels excited about the car accident but is disappointed because "nobody's killed" (O'Connor 19). She also daringly asks the Misfit why he is telling them what to do (O'Connor 21), and she says Hiram reminds her of a pig (O'Connor 27) before the gangster kills her in the woods.

Red Sammy Butts

The owner of Red Sammy's, a barbecue joint with a gas station and a dance hall located near a town called Timothy in Georgia. Because of blind faith and poor judgment, he is fooled by two young swindlers who steal his gasoline from the filling station. Just like the grandmother, he is nostalgic about the old days. Everything in the past seems better, and he thinks he is a good man from an older, better world.

The Misfit

The Misfit is a famous criminal wanted by the police. After being wrongly accused of killing his own father, he becomes a lost, angry, atheist killer who commits crimes and murders anywhere he goes. He thinks there is "no real pleasure in life" (O'Connor 29) but meanness. Yet, ironically, he is also the chosen vessel in O'Connor's story, the most unlikely recipient of

God's divine grace. As Drake notes: "it is often those whom the 'upright' and 'wholesome' regard as grotesque [who] become chosen vessels indeed…. The real grotesques are the self-justified, the apparent grotesques may be the blessed" (22).

Bobby Lee and Hiram

They are two young criminals who are on the loose with the Misfit. Both of them are callous murderers who are indifferent to the pain of others. They kill Bailey, his wife and their children after being told to do so. According to June Star, Hiram is a fat man who reminds her of a pig. Bobby Lee is yet another disturbing criminal who calls the grandmother "a talker" after she dies. He enjoys using violence without thinking about the consequences, saying that the killing is "some fun" (O'Connor 29).

Main Themes

What Is a Good Man?

The title of the short story, "A Good Man Is Hard to Find," can be considered a parody of the grandmother's elusive definition of a "good man." As the story unfolds, the reader sees that the "good man" label has nothing at all to do with morals or goodness. It is in fact close to meaningless because the label is applied every time the grandmother finds that someone does things in her favor, or says things to her benefit. Calling someone "a good man" is also her strategy when she tries to impose her own values upon others, hoping that she can take control or gain the upper hand in circumstances. The first man whom the grandmother thinks highly of is Mr. Edgar Atkins Teagarden, a good-looking man from Jasper, Georgia, who courted the grandmother when she was young. Nostalgically, she shows off to her grandchildren by describing in great detail how Mr. Teagarden romantically wooed her by bringing her a watermelon each Saturday afternoon in her girlhood. She calls him a "gentleman" (O'Connor 13) twice, and she highlights that he became very rich because he was wise enough to buy the Coca-Cola stock when it came out. Whether Mr. Teagarden is really a good man or not, the reader will never know, but the reader realizes that this is indeed an act of narcissism. The underlying message the grandmother conveys is: I am superior, for I was once courted by a decent and wealthy man of good taste. The more she praises Mr. Teagarden, the better she feels about herself.

Then, when Red Sammy Butts, the owner of a filling station and a food-serving dance hall, romanticizes the past and makes clichéd and negative overgeneralized statements about the present, such as "[a] good man is hard to find" (O'Connor 16) and "[e]verything is getting terrible" (O'Connor 16), the grandmother agrees totally with the "good country guy," who "thinks and speaks in clichés" (Somerville 82). Likewise, when Red Sammy Butts tells the grandmother how he stupidly let two young strangers driving a Chrysler take his gasoline, the grandmother immediately pacifies him by saying, "Because you're a good man!" (O'Connor 15). While this is in fact a case of silly blind faith and sheer poor judgment, the grandmother applies the "good man" label indiscriminately. One possible reason why the grandmother reacts in such a way is that Red Sammy Butts has said something which she longs to hear—that old people like her were brought up in the best era; people her age are better, nicer, more trustworthy and respectful, who are true ladies and gentlemen superior to all. The harsher Red Sammy Butts complains about the current situation and people, the rosier the past sounds, and the more pleasing it becomes to the grandmother's ears.

Intriguingly, proud as she is, the grandmother calls the murderer "a good man" three times when facing death. In great panic, she also praises the murderer as "not a bit common" (O'Connor 24), assuring him that he must be a man of "good blood" (O'Connor 22, 28) who comes "from nice people" (O'Connor 22, 28). She desperately uses every flattering expression trying to draw the Misfit to her world and change his mind, in particular reminding him that a good man like him "wouldn't shoot a lady" (O'Connor 22, 28). At the end, her definition of a "good man" loses its meaning entirely. None of her flattering words work. The callous serial killer spares no one. His gangsters, Bobby Lee and Hiram, kill all her family members. The Misfit shoots her through the chest three times without blinking an eye.

Who Is the Real Misfit?

Apparently, the criminal who is on the run is "The Misfit" (O'Connor 15). Everybody calls him this nickname, and when he is recognized by the grandmother, he honestly admits that he is "The Misfit" (O'Connor 22). True to his name, he is a sick, cruel, and anti-social serial killer who randomly kills people he meets on the road, including the luckless grandmother and her family. He is indeed the real misfit in the story. Yet, besides the criminal and his gang, the grandmother may also be read as a misfit in the story. While she has not committed crimes like the criminal has, as a Catholic, her complacency, hypocrisy, dishonesty and selfishness may indicate that she is sinful enough to be called a rascal, if not a misfit.

Right at the beginning of the journey, the grandmother starts manipulating Bailey and his family to convince them of where they should go for vacation. It is her personal wish to go to east Tennessee so she can pay a visit to "her connections" (O'Connor 9), but she presents it as if east Tennessee is the best place for the children, and that it is the one and only sensible place to go on a holiday. First, she dissuades Bailey from going to Florida, claiming that Florida is not safe for the children anymore because, according to the newspaper, the Misfit is also heading towards Florida. Afterwards, she again employs an authoritative tone and lectures Bailey and his wife that they should think of taking their children to places where they have never been to, such as east Tennessee, so that the children will be able to "see different parts of the world and be broad" (O'Connor 9).

She also goes as far as to make up stories about an old house that she wants to visit in Georgia, claiming that there is family silver hidden in a secret panel in the house. When she has successfully convinced everyone to take a hilly dirt road to go on a "treasure hunt," she suddenly remembers that the old house is in fact in Tennessee, not Georgia. Yet, instead of honestly telling her family members that her memories have played a trick on her, she selfishly hides the truth from everyone. Later, when they have a car accident as Bailey drives up the dirt road, the first thing that comes to the grandmother's mind is not the safety of the baby, the children, Bailey and his wife. Rather, she is afraid that Bailey may blame her for her idle wish and insistence on visiting the old house, which caused the car accident. To avoid being blamed, she plays the victim and pretends she has an injured organ.

What most readers find annoying is that when the Misfit and his gang get hold of the family after the car accident, the grandmother cares only for herself. She never once begs the gang to spare the lives of her son, her daughter-in-law, the baby, or the other children as the criminals randomly but systematically murder her loved ones. She pleads only for her own life instead. Shamelessly, she emphasizes that she is a "lady," and that no one should shoot a lady like her. Her only concern is her own death.

Moral Codes

As a devoted Catholic, O'Connor aims to bring moral reflections to center stage in her short fiction. The reflections are not necessarily confined to religious topics, though. As Paulson puts it, O'Connor's short stories often present "class conflicts, racial differences, and the mindless conformity of groups marching in processions or parades and basing their sense of identity on such status symbols as uniforms, possessions, skin color, and the Christian faith" (xii). All this begins as O'Connor invites the reader to use a critical eye to look at the grandmother's superficial moral codes. Just as the shifting definitions of a "good man," the moral codes of the grandmother are wanton and unreliable, especially in the first half of the story. As the story begins, the grandmother is well-assured of her so-called moral codes, which are mostly related to class and social status. For example, she takes the moral high ground by instructing her son and daughter-in-law how to widen their children's horizon by taking them to "different parts of the world" (O'Connor 9). This is a bourgeois suggestion because not everyone can afford to travel around. Her understanding of decency is also shallow. Obsessed with one's attire and physical appearance, she thinks that dressing up decently is important because that is how people will recognize her as a lady, even if she dies in an accident: "[i]n case of an accident, anyone seeing her dead on the highway would know at once that she was a lady" (O'Connor 11). She has double standards, too. On the one hand, she teaches her grandchildren not to pass judgment about the place they are from, but to love and pay respect to people, one's parents and native state (O'Connor 12). On the other hand, she fails to show respect to others. When she sees a poor African American child, she points her finger at him and calls him "a cute little pickaninny" (O'Connor 12). She casually makes mean, racist comments about African Americans, saying that poor "[l]ittle niggers" (O'Connor 12) don't have things like white people do, and that a poor Black child with no britches on is a worthy subject for a painted picture. In the second half of the story, however, the moral codes that the grandmother holds boil down to nothing. When the Misfit challenges her about spiritual beliefs and the meaning of life, she is mentally crushed and forced to deny her hypocritical and meaningless moral codes in her bourgeois state of mind. She has to step down from the high moral ground, and her faith in God becomes shaky, too. When she knows the Misfit may kill her, she mutters in panic, "[m]aybe He [Jesus Christ] didn't raise the dead" (O'Connor 28).

The Unlikely Recipient of Grace

Nevertheless, the power of Catholic faith still shines through despite the disappointment in humans and violence in the text. As O'Connor explains, "in my own stories I have found that violence is strangely capable of returning my characters to reality and preparing them to accept their moment of grace" (O'Connor, "On Her Own Work" 111). By violence, O'Connor refers to how grace can be suddenly forced upon "an individual who has shown no signs of cooperation" (Strong 103), who least expects the arrival of God's grace and his or her own death. Facing death and being put through the most agonizing pain, a person as despicable as the grandmother can still be rescued and become a recipient of God's grace. Towards the end of the story, the grandmother realizes that her life is coming to an end. What is truly left of her is just her faith in God. Though briefly, she starts to show the signs of experiencing a spiritual awakening. She listens to the Misfit's life story patiently and does not pass judgment, except for asking him to pray: "[i]f you would pray, ... Jesus would help you," "why don't you pray?" (O'Connor 26). She holds tight to her religion and calls for Jesus (O'Connor 27). Before the Misfit kills her, she shows a moment of grace—like Jesus to a sinner, she reaches out to touch the Misfit on the shoulder, forgiving his sins and recognizing him as "one of my babies," "one of my children" (O'Connor 29). With God's grace and forgiveness, the grandmother dies with a smile in her face.

Incredible as it may seem, besides the grandmother, the devilish Misfit can also be read as another undeserving recipient of God's grace. In "Novelist and Believer," O'Connor has made it clear to her readers, "I prefer to think that, however unlikely this may seem, the old lady's gesture, like the mustard seed, will grow to be a great crow-filled tree in the Misfit's heart, and will be enough of a pain to him there to turn him into the prophet he was meant to be" (112–113). In other words, the Gothic story is supposed to be an epiphanic self-discovery for the Misfit. The Misfit, though not a Catholic, is true to himself and serious about the meaning of life. He reveals that when he was young, he was never "a bad boy" (O'Connor 25). He remembers clearly that his father died of epidemic flu, but people wrongfully accused him of killing his own father. Having been punished for what he has not done, he feels that there is "[n]o pleasure but meanness" (O'Connor 28) in life. Feeling angry at society, he indulges in delinquent acts as evil as killing people and burning down people's houses (O'Connor 28). He becomes an outcast who commits crimes wherever he goes, consistently living out his personal moral code of "no pleasure but meanness." Unlike Bobby Lee who thinks killing is fun, the lack of purpose and meaning in life pains the Misfit. O'Connor manages to drop hints of spiritual repentance to the reader that the Misfit may change for the better, too; he admits to the grandmother that he wishes he were with Jesus when He raised the dead, so that he would not be what he is. Also, upon seeing God's grace manifested through the old lady, his voice seems to crack and his face twists as if he is going to cry. All these signs of awakening conscience imply that there is still hope for the Misfit. He can be the next person to receive God's divine grace.

STYLE

Symbol

Multiple symbols can be found in the short story, and the most straightforward one is probably the journey in the family car and how it ends with the unexpected accident, which symbolizes the sudden and tragic death of the entire family. In the 1950s, most middle-class families in the U.S. living in the suburbs had two cars, and it was common for families to go on a road trip during weekends. To a large extent, the family car symbolizes the typical American nuclear family, where the mother, father and children live under the same roof. In the short story, Bailey's car turns over in the road accident and the flipped car can no longer function. This connotes that the family's ordinary life is turned upside down, and that the unexpected predicament shall end their lives.

Another symbol that most readers would probably notice is the old lady's hat, which symbolizes the grandmother's misguided moral code. At the beginning of the journey, the grandmother wears a carefully selected "navy blue straw sailor hat with a bunch of white violets on the brim" (O'Connor 11). The classy hat is not just a decoration. It represents her social standing too, for she has the ridiculous belief that dressing up as a lady is the most important virtue of all. Yet, after the car accident, the hat is no longer in good shape. The front brim comes off, and the violet spray hangs off the side. This foreshadows that the flimsy moral conviction to which she holds on tightly shall eventually fall apart when the Misfit and his gang arrive. While the broken hat is still pinned to her hair, the grandmother still tries her very best to remind the criminals that a lady like her should not be shot. However, shortly thereafter, as the grandmother reaches up to adjust the hat brim, the entire brim comes off in her hand. After thinking for a second, she gives it up and just lets the hat brim fall on the ground. Again, this subtle description in the story carries significant symbolic meaning. First, it implies that the old lady's superficial moral code has finally totally collapsed. More importantly, it indicates she has finally come to the realization that it is time to let go of her meaningless social image as a well-attired lady. Her moral code is just not solid enough to withstand the blow when it is put to test.

Besides the obvious symbolic meanings of the family car, the car crash, and the grandmother's broken hat, implicit symbols can also be discovered in O'Connor's story. As Bryant suggests, "the name of the town where the family stops for lunch is carefully chosen, so is the name of Red Sammy's café" (305). The town in which Bailey and his family choose to stop and have lunch is called "Timothy" (O'Connor 13), which is the name of one of the books in the New Testament. Also, Red Sammy's café is called "The Tower" (O'Connor 13). From the Christian point of view, both names were chosen with solid religious reasons: Timothy is a biblical text that teaches Christians how to avoid being conceited and self-centered, which echoes the painful lesson the grandmother experiences upon encountering the Misfit. On the other hand, the Tower may just as well be read as the Tower of Babel, which symbolizes vanity and arrogance, the nasty character traits we see in the grandmother.

Irony

Irony is yet another powerful literary device O'Connor uses to introduce her Christian beliefs. As previously mentioned, the town name Timothy is by no means a coincidence. It is closely associated with the messages conveyed in the book of Timothy in the Bible, though in an ironic sense. Interestingly, most of the characters we meet in O'Connor's short story show exactly the opposite qualities that the Bible suggests good Christians should have. For example, in the First Epistle of Paul to Timothy, the Bible says, "[h]e [the husband] must manage his own family well and see that his children obey him with proper respect" (I Tim. 3:4–5). However, Bailey, as the father of the family, has not been doing a good job, because both his daughter and son, June Star and John Wesley, are impolite and inconsiderate. When Red Sammy's wife asks if June Star would like to be her little girl, June Star replies to her with the rudest comment: "I wouldn't live in a broken-down place like this for a million bucks!" (O'Connor 14). John Wesley is as nasty as his sister. He keeps yelling in the car until the baby cries and kicks Bailey's car seat so hard that Bailey feels the blows in his kidney (O'Connor 17) just because he wants his father to drive them to the old house with a secret panel filled with family silver. Ironically, Bailey, June Star and John Wesley are the negative examples of how good Christians should behave.

Likewise, the talkative, conceited and manipulative grandmother who always uses an authoritative tone to tell others what to do is a total negative example of what the book of Timothy requires of women: "[a] woman should learn in quietness and full submission. I do not permit a woman to teach or to assume authority over a man; she must be quiet" (I Tim. 2:11–12). The ironic effect is doubled as O'Connor reveals the old lady's obstinate obsession with ladylike attire, for the book of Timothy also advises women to "adorn themselves in modest apparel, with decency and propriety; not with braided hair, or gold, or pearls, or costly array" (I Tim. 2:9). The ultimate irony in the story, however, is that conceited Christians like the grandmother and her kind actually feel good about themselves. In order to get rid of her obstinately misguided moral conviction, it takes extreme violence and suffering, like someone will have to "shoot her every minute of her life" to make sure she stays spiritually awake. Intriguingly enough, God's lesson in faith is also a mean and ironic joke, for the Christian epiphany cannot happen without the Misfit, the lost soul who is angry at society. As Fitzgerald points out, "[o]n the tragic scene, each time, the presence of her humor is like the presence of grace" (xxxiii). The irony at the end of the story is so violently cruel and extreme that some critics even believe O'Connor "does not care about her characters" (Park 257). Nevertheless, it is now widely recognized that presenting cruelty as dark humor is a famous characteristic of Flannery O'Connor's writing.

Humor

It may be difficult to imagine that there is room for jokes and humor in Southern Gothic, but under the pen of O'Connor, chemistry does happen when she puts various elements together at the same time. In "A Good Man Is Hard to Find," the story is told through a third person point of view which constantly ridicules the grandmother. For instance, at the beginning of the road trip, the narrative "explains" to readers why the grandmother has to secretly bring the cat with her on the family car trip: "he would miss her too much and she was afraid he might brush against one of the gas burners and accidentally asphyxiate himself" (O'Connor 10). The "explanation" is so narcissistic and preposterous that it becomes a joke instantly, distancing the readers from the hilarious character. Furthermore, just as every family member in the car feels fed up with the grandmother because she cannot stop talking, the third person narrative says the grandmother's talk is interesting: "[s]he pointed out interesting details of the scenery" (O'Connor 11). Comically, immediately after this comment is made, the narrative continues to inform readers that Bailey's wife has gone to sleep and the children have paid zero attention to what their grandmother is saying—they are reading comic books. The stark contrast between reality and the narrative's comments about the grandmother creates a most humorous effect. Later on, when Bailey refuses to dance to the jukebox music at Red Sammy's, the narrator remarks that Bailey "didn't have a natural sunny disposition as she did and trips made him nervous" (O'Connor 14). Clever readers would realize the narrative is again making fun of the grandmother, because she is no Miss Sunshine, and it is she who gets on the nerves of Bailey, making him feel anxious and uncomfortable. Regarding why O'Connor's story offers humor, some perceive it as a method for sugarcoating the serious religious preaching in her writing.

BIBLIOGRAPHY

Bryant, Hallman B. "Reading the Map in 'A Good Man Is Hard to Find.'" *Studies in Short Fiction* 18 (1981): 301–307. Print.
Drake, Robert. *Flannery O'Connor: A Critical Essay*. Grand Rapids, MI: William B. Eerdmans Publishing Co., 1966. Print.
Fitzgerald, Robert. "Introduction." *Everything that Rises Must Converge*, by Flannery O'Connor. New York: Farrar, 1965. vii–xxxiv. Print.
O'Connor, Flannery. "A Good Man Is Hard to Find." *A Good Man Is Hard to Find*. London: The Women's Press Ltd., 1980. 9–29. Print.
_____. "Novelist and Believer." *Mystery and Manners: Occasional Prose*. Edited by Sally Fitzgerald and Robert Fitzgerald. New York: Farrar, Straus & Giroux, 1969, 154–168. Print.
_____. "On Her Own Work." *Mystery and Manners: Occasional Prose*. Edited by Sally Fitzgerald and Robert Fitzgerald. New York: Farrar, Straus & Giroux, 1969, 107–118. Print.
Park, Clara C. "Crippled Laughter: Towards Understanding Flannery O'Connor." *American Scholar* 51.2 (1982): 249–257. Print.

Paulson, Suzanne M. *Flannery O'Connor: A Study of the Short Fiction.* Boston: Twayne Publishers, 1988. Print.

Somerville, John N., Jr. "A Reflection of Grace: The Place of Humor in the Theology of Flannery O'Connor." *Ilha do Desterro* 30 (1993): 79–90. Print.

Spivey, Ted. R. *Flannery O'Connor: The Woman, the Thinker, the Visionary.* Macon, GA: Mercer University Press, 1997. Print.

Stamenkovic, Dusan. "Conceptualization of 'the South' in Southern Gothic Literature: Changing Perception through Metaphor and Image Schemas." *Arctic & Antarctic: International Journal of Circumpolar Sociocultural Issues* 6.6 (2012): 7–25. Print.

Strong, Emily. "Flannery O'Connor's Protestant Grace." *Criterion: A Journal of Literary Criticism* 9.1 (2016): 101–109. Print.

4

Consumerism, Alienation and Digital Dystopia in Bradbury's "The Veldt"

BIOGRAPHY OF RAY BRADBURY

Raymond Douglas Bradbury (1920–2012) was born in Waukegan, Illinois, a place upon which Bradbury based the setting of his stories and novels in the years to come (Beley 20). In his formative years, young Ray Bradbury was exposed to thriller films like *The Phantom of the Opera* (1925) (Reid 105) and *The Hunchback of Notre Dame* (1923) (Reid 1). He was also inspired by his artistic Aunt Neva, who read him Edgar Allan Poe's horror stories and introduced him to the world of literature (Aggelis xii). He then read heavily the influential works of "Charles Dickens, George Bernard Shaw, Edgar Allan Poe, H.G. Wells, Arthur Conan Doyle, L. Frank Baum, and Edgar Rice Burroughs" (Weiner 80), developing a lifelong passion for books and writing, especially horror and science fiction stories. After spending about twelve years in Waukegan in his childhood, at age 14, Ray Bradbury moved to Los Angeles with his family in 1934. In the same year, he became a paid writer of science fiction for the first time.

Although his family did not have the money to send him to college, Ray Bradbury's writing career continued to take shape. Upon completion of his secondary education at the Los Angeles High School in 1938, he was first invited to join the Los Angeles Science Fiction Society, where he met numerous writers. In the following year, he joined the Wilshire Players Guild, where he had the chance to try playwriting and act in a number of plays. He also published four issues of his own fanzine, *Futuria Fantasia*. Starting from age 24, he became a prolific full-time writer of various genres that range from novels, short stories, poems, essays, and drama to screenplays.

Among the eleven novels, thirty books and about 600 short stories that he wrote over his 70-year career, *The Martian Chronicles* (1950) was the science fiction that first aroused awareness from critics and readers. Shortly thereafter, the publication of *The Illustrated Man* (1951), an anthologized collection of his best short stories, established his reputation as a dystopian science fiction author. Up through the present, numerous schools and colleges still include Bradbury's short stories as recommended readings in the curriculum. Most importantly, in 1953, he published his dystopian masterpiece, *Fahrenheit 451* (1953), which is widely acclaimed as one of the most influential books of the 20th century (Bankston 141). Hailed as America's best science fiction writer who has deeply impacted generations of readers, including fiction writers like Stephen King and film directors such as Steven Spielberg, Ray Bradbury was granted multifarious literary awards, including the O. Henry Prize for short fiction in 1947 and 1948 (Eller 141), the National Institute of Arts and Letters award in 1954 (Otten 3), the World Fantasy Award in 1977 (Reid 4), and the National Book Foundation's medal for "Distinguished Contribution to American Letters" in 2000 (Piddock 92).

Dystopian Science Fiction

According to Luckhurst (2005), the literary genre of science fiction (SF) had gone through multiple transformations prior to its consolidation in the late 1920s. While H. G. Wells and Jules Verne paved the way for science fiction traditions (Stockwell 9), the term "science fiction" emerged only as the "radio entrepreneur, journalist and magazine proprietor Hugo Gernsback ... coined 'science fiction' in his magazine *Science Wonder Stories* in 1929" (Luckhurst 15). Since SF originated from cheap magazines and "lowly and kinetic pulp fiction" (Luckhurst 16), at first many perceived it merely as a tasteless and embarrassing modern genre category. Ray Bradbury, alongside British authors such as Aldous Huxley and George Orwell, was one of the fiction writers who brought sophistication to the genre. As the *New York Times* remarks, Bradbury "helped transport science fiction out of the pulp fiction ghetto and into the mainstream" (Kakutani).

Besides the uncanonical origin, it is also noted that compared to other literary genres, the SF genre has relatively loose boundaries and a fluid genre identity. As Kincaid describes:

> [S]cience fiction is not one thing. Rather, it is any number of things—a future setting, a marvelous device, an ideal society, an alien creature, a twist in time, an interstellar journey, a satirical perspective, a particular approach to the matter of story, whatever

we are looking for when we look for science fiction, here more overt, here more subtle—which are braided together in an endless variety of combinations [cited in Rieder 14].

Nonetheless, essential elements can still be found in classic SF works, especially those written and published in the late 1930s to the late 1950s, namely "the Golden Age of Science Fiction" (Booker and Thomas 24). Following the dystopian SF novel formula employed by Aldous Huxley's *Brave New World* (1932) and George Orwell's *1984* (1949), Ray Bradbury's SF novels and short story masterpieces published in the 1950s function as warnings and social criticism towards the contemporary society. On the one hand, they draw on the speculative notion of "what if" in SF. On the other hand, they depict a futuristic dystopian society derived from people's fear and anxieties toward reality. For example, in "The Veldt" (1950), Bradbury makes a warning about the danger we may face as our lives become increasingly overwhelmed with technology. He presents to his readers how a futuristic automated home can ruin family relationships, turning everyday life into a walking nightmare. Put simply, unlike pulp science fiction that focuses mostly on actions and fantastic adventures only, dystopian science fiction can act as a prophecy that voices political and cultural concerns, taking the SF genre to another level.

Plot Overview

"The Veldt" is a SF thriller written by Ray Bradbury in 1950. In the story, George and Lydia, the parents of the Hadley family, spent thirty thousand dollars to install a fully automated system called Happylife Home in their home. Happylife Home is supposed to provide comfort and convenience for the family. The intelligent home is designed with "the voice clocks, the stoves, the heaters, the shoe shiners, the shoe lacers, the body scrubbers and swabbers and massagers" (Bradbury 45) so as to take care of the housework for all family members. It even brushes the teeth, gives baths to the family members and rocks everyone to sleep. Of all its functions, the nursery is the most powerful. It can read the children's minds and project their thoughts as virtual reality (VR) in the nursery room. Numerous make-believe places and characters, such as "Wonderland, Alice, the Mock Turtle, or Aladdin and his Magical Lamp, or Jack Pumpkinhead of Oz, or Dr. Doolittle, or the cow jumping over a very real-appearing moon" (Bradbury 34), have been created by the nursery. While George is proud and happy to be the owner of this "miracle of efficiency" (Bradbury 28), Lydia feels uncomfortable about it, especially the three-dimensional VR function of the nursery, which gives her an uncanny feeling. She urges her husband to take a look at the nursery, and she suggests asking a psychologist to check the nursery, too.

Upon Lydia's request, George enters the nursery with Lydia. At first, the nursery is empty and silent. The glass screens on the walls and the ceiling are blank. Then, as it detects the presence of the two people, it gradually transforms itself into an African veldt. Besides creating the authentic visual effect, the nursery simulates the heat of the sun, the sounds in the veldtland, as well as the smells of animals, blood and death. The lions in the African setting even set eyes on the couple and run towards them. The simulation in the nursery is so real and threatening that the couple can't help but flee and shut the nursery door. As George checks the nursery for a second time, it is soon found that the nursery does not respond to George's request for a new VR setting. It just stays showing the same old African veldt, which reveals that the veldt has been on the mind of their children, Peter and Wendy, for a long period of time, though the children utterly deny that they have conjured up Africa and the hungry lions. The nursery gets on the nerves of the parents when George finds his old wallet in the nursery, which is chewed and drenched with blood and saliva and smells of a lion. It becomes increasingly disturbing when they hear lions' roars and people's screams coming from the nursery. Worried about the mental state of their children, the couple consults the psychologist, who happens to find Lydia's scarf smeared in blood upon his visit to the nursery. Lydia and George then lock up the nursery and turn off Happylife Home all together, but their children get hysterical and sob uncontrollably. The couple hears their miserable cry, so they turn on the nursery for a short while once again before leaving the house for a vacation. Soon afterwards, they hear their children calling for them from the nursery. They rush to the nursery, but the children are nowhere to be found. The door slams close, and the lions are awaiting their prey.

CHARACTERS

Characterization in a short story is often constrained by the story length and form. Nevertheless, characters in Ray Bradbury's short stories, be they quiet or outspoken, are all telling in their own ways. In an autobiographical essay published in the January 1945 issue of *Weird Tales*, Bradbury confirms the importance of characterization in his fiction: "[t]he kind of people in [the author's] story, their beliefs, their fears, their reactions, their tastes, are pretty indicative of the author's mind; even if some of the people in the yarn appear to be exact opposites" (cited in Eller 100). In "The Veldt," the parents and the children in the Hadley family also appear to be exact opposites to one another:

George Hadley

George is the father of the Hadley family. With all good intentions, he equips his house with Happylife Home to take care of his family. He thinks he has "given the children everything they ever wanted" (Bradbury 38), only to find that he has brought a nightmare home. Being aware that his "[p]ride, money, foolishness" (Bradbury 47) have turned his son and daughter into insufferable monsters, he tries to resolve the situation by switching off the automated home. His decision is rational and sensible, but his moment of realization has arrived too late.

Lydia Hadley

Married to George Hadley, Lydia is a housewife with two ten-year-old children. Yet, unlike typical housewives, Lydia does not need to do any housework because Happylife Home, the fully automated home, has already done all the work in the house and the nursery for her family. Deprived of her traditional gender role as a mother and housewife, Lydia feels uneasy and anxious at home. She misses the old days of looking after her children herself and taking care of the chores on her own. She also senses that things have gone wrong with her children. Before George notices the real danger of the nursery, she has already suggested calling a psychologist to inspect the nursery. She is also the one who first proposes shutting down the automated house in exchange for "a breath of honest air" (Bradbury 45).

Peter Hadley

Ten-year-old Peter is the son of George and Lydia. He is cool-headed and intelligent, but spoiled by his parents, and he relies thoroughly on Happylife Home both physically and mentally. For him, tying his own shoes, brushing his own teeth, combing his own hair, and giving himself a bath without the help of Happylife Home are unimaginably dreadful to him. He is also deeply attached and totally addicted to the nursery, which to him is more important than his real parents. To protect the nursery from being turned off, he tells lies, rebels against his parents, and goes as far as to formulate a plot to murder his parents.

Wendy Hadley

Both Wendy and Peter are said to be good-looking, who have "cheeks like peppermint candy, eyes like bright blue agate marbles" (Bradbury 36). Despite her good looks, Wendy is crooked-minded and overtly obsessed with the nursery. Just like her brother, she can no longer tell right from wrong.

When Peter lies about not remembering any Africa, she covers for him and lies to her father as well. Like Peter, she hates her parents when they threaten to shut down Happylife Home and lock up the nursery. In collusion with Peter, she hatches the evil plan of having her parents eaten by lions in the veldt.

David McClean

David McClean is the psychologist whom Lydia and George invite to inspect the nursery. The VR setting of the nursery rooms always makes him nervous, and he calls them "damned rooms" (Bradbury 44). He warns the couple of the dangerous situation which the nursery and automated home have put the children into, but he is also worried that shutting down the automated system all in one go may have a detrimental effect on the Hadley family. Nonetheless, on discovering Lydia's bloodstained scarf in the nursery, he follows the couple to the fuse box and together they switch off the nursery.

Main Themes

Consumerism and Mass Culture

At the time when "The Veldt" was written, the U.S. had experienced prosperity and become an unparalleled superpower following World War II. During this Golden Age of Capitalism, the U.S. experienced industrial advancement, economic bloom, and flourishing technological innovation. With the explosion of job opportunities in the 1950s, the annual income of the working population soared more than 200 percent (Carosso 9). This gave rise to a sudden expansion of the middle class, alongside the rise of the idealized nuclear family unit. Meanwhile, such phenomenal social affluence also pushed Americans towards the dark twins, namely mass culture and "insatiable consumerism" (Carosso 9). Under the influence of mass culture, personal uniqueness was suppressed and independent thinking was numbed. More unfortunately, the "reductionist, materialist image of human nature and human culture" (Mogen 107) was reinforced "through mass entertainment media" (Mogen 107) such as TV, radio and advertisements. The "deceived masses" (Adorno and Horkheimer 133) were encouraged to conform to "consumeristic excess" (Lopez 103), where consumers were overwhelmed by homogenous goods packaged as symbols of success and good taste, giving "a false fulfillment of wish-dreams, like wealth, adventure, passionate love, power and sensationalism in general" (Lowenthal 11). For example, for most nuclear families in the fifties, owning a big family car and a suburban house filled with new appliances such as the television was the social norm. Rarely would anyone question whether what they wanted was what they really needed. As long as the consumer goods made them feel good about themselves, the quality and usefulness of the products did not matter at all. As Marcuse contends:

> The products indoctrinate and manipulate; they promote a false consciousness which is immune against its falsehood ... it becomes a way of life. It is a good way of life—much better than before—and as a good way of life, it militates against qualitative change [12].

In "The Veldt," George Hadley represents the majority of middle-class Americans in the 1950s. He thinks money can buy his family physical comfort and happiness. In fact, the intelligent home and the nursery not only frighten his wife, but also dehumanize his children. Yet, blinded by "[p]ride, money, foolishness" (Bradbury 47), he is "filled with admiration for the mechanical genius" (Bradbury 29) who designed the nursery. He is proud of being the owner of what he calls the "miracle of efficiency selling for an absurdly low price" (Bradbury 29), which he believes "[e]very home should have" (Bradbury 29). The first time he hears Lydia's plea to shut down the house for a break, he replies, "[b]ut I thought that's why we bought this house, so we wouldn't have to do anything?" (Bradbury 32). The consumerist ideology is so strong that George is not even aware that he is experiencing anxiety, which turns him into a chain smoker.

Abandonment and Alienation

Apart from the stark warning against the dangers of consumerism and mechanization, Ray Bradbury also wants people to embrace humanity. In a lecture at Stanford University in 1982, he shared his optimism in humanity: "[t]he race doesn't have to die, because we don't deserve it. We're too good for that" (cited in Drassinower and Kemkow 112). Though his SF stories are mostly dystopian thrillers, he keeps reminding his readers that true happiness can only be pursued when we spend time with our family and loved ones. Technology gadgets may be fun, but they should never be allowed to take the place of human interaction, or of expressions of love and emotions. Sadly, the Hadley family in Bradbury's story gets it all wrong from the start. The parents abandon their children once the voice-activated smart home system is installed in their house. As the housewife, Lydia does not prepare meals for Peter and Wendy, nor does she give them baths, play with them, teach them, or read them bedtime stories. Spoiled by the technology, Lydia can no longer compete with the nursery: "[c]an I give a bath and scrub the children as efficiently or quickly as the automatic scrub bath can? I cannot" (Bradbury 32). As a father, George does not play his role well, either. He fails to notice

Peter and Wendy's problem until Lydia shares her worries with him. It is sad and ironic that while the Hadley family lives under the same roof, Lydia and George fail to show their parental love and look after their children. The child abandonment continues until their children abandon them.

Brought up by the machines, Peter and Wendy are dehumanized, detached and alienated from their parents. They do not need their parents anymore, which is why Lydia feels like she does not belong. When talking with his dad, Peter no longer looks at his parents: "Peter looked at his shoes. He never looked at his father anymore, nor at his mother" (Bradbury 40). The children have also developed mental problems—like Peter Pan and Wendy in Neverland, Peter and Wendy in "The Veldt" conjure up a dreamland of their own—a sick, twisted killing field that smells of blood and the predators' breath created by the evil nursery room. The psychologist, David McClean, finds the alienation and the children's abnormal behavior alarming:

> You've let this room and this house replace you and your wife in your children's affections. This room is their mother and father, far more important in their lives than their real parents [Bradbury 43].

When George and Lydia try to shut off the smart home and start anew, the children are not afraid of killing their own parents. The parent-child alienation and resentment are so deep that after the parents are murdered by the lions, Wendy can still serve David with tea, pretending nothing has happened. The tragedy of the Hadleys is a negative example for us all.

Man Versus Machine

It is not hard to tell that Ray Bradbury has a cautious view of science and technology. "The Veldt" is yet another cautionary SF story in which machines come alive, "devouring" people who dare to challenge their existence by turning them off. However, Bradbury once pointed out that the progress of technology itself is not a bad thing. If technology ever poses a threat to humanity and human existence, humans, not technology, should take full responsibility:

> machines themselves are empty gloves. And the hand that fills them can be good or evil. Today we stand on the rim of space, and man, in his immense tidal motion, is about to flow out toward far new worlds ... but he must conquer the seed of his own self-destruction. Man is half-idealist, half-destroyer, and the real and terrible fear is that he can still destroy himself before reaching for the stars [cited in Zipes 11].

In Bradbury's visionary SF tales, the self-destruction of men starts when they create machines to bring them physical comforts, not knowing that they may have a high price to pay. The Hadley family is a negative role model showing human indulgence in technology: the family members lose most of their basic survival skills when the artificial intelligence (AI) of the smart home takes charge of everything in the household. The psychologist's comments on the Hadleys are laughable but true: "[w]hy, you'd starve tomorrow if something went wrong in your kitchen. You wouldn't know how to tap an egg" (Bradbury 43). Extending the phenomenon from the micro to the macro level, men are losing ground to AI and machines in the job market, too. As in the Hadley family, no one would think of employing a cook or a nursery caretaker anymore. Job opportunities have been taken over by technology everywhere, and men can no longer compete with their own creation. After over sixty years of automation and technological advancement, this worrying situation is already happening. As reported by *The Guardian*, "[r]egular reports warn us that an automation apocalypse is nigh. In January [2017], a McKinsey & Company study found that about 30% of tasks in 60% of occupations could be computerized and last year [2016], the Bank of England's chief economist said that 80m US and 15m UK jobs might be taken over by robots" (Mahdawi). Though new jobs may be created in the digital age, to a large extent, statistics have proved that technology is destroying the jobs of people from all walks of life.

Reality Versus Illusion

The ultra-realistic, three-dimensional simulation generated by the nursery is what we called virtual reality (VR) nowadays. It is amazing to see how Bradbury prophesied the invention of the VR technique back in the 1950s, when TV sets had only started to become popular in the U.S. More incredibly, Bradbury had also foreseen the addictive potentiality of virtual reality technology long before VR reached its users and was brought to the mainstream. In "The Veldt," Peter and Wendy are obsessed with the VR illusion created by the nursery. Not only are they detached from reality, "[t]hey live for the nursery" (Bradbury 31). The simulated world is everything to the children. When the nursery is locked up, they break into it; when their parents shut off the VR system, they get it turned on again at all cost.

George and Lydia fail to resolve the situation mainly because they have overestimated their control over the machines. George thinks that they have no problem separating the simulated world from reality: "[w]alls, Lydia, remember; crystal walls, that's all they are. Oh, they look real, … but it's all dimensional superactionary, supersensitive color film and mental tape film behind glass screens. It's all odorophonics and sonics" (Bradbury 30). Lydia also thought it was okay to switch the nursery back on just for a few moments. The couple's overconfidence and poor judgment take them down the road to perdition. They end up being eaten alive by the lions in the African veldt simulated by the nursery.

As critics and scholars have noticed (Anderson 33–34; Diskin 47; Smith 44), Bradbury's "The Veldt" is in fact a literary allusion to J. M. Barrie's *Peter Pan* (1911). Named after Peter Pan and Wendy Darling, who have a jolly time together in Neverland, Peter Hadley and Wendy Hadley build their own world of fantasy:

> The characters' names were not chosen by chance, but augment the themes of the story. "Wendy" and "Peter" obviously refer to the characters in *Peter Pan*, a tale about children who refuse to grow up. Wendy and Peter, like their namesakes in the children's story, live in a make-believe fantasy world instead of the "real" world. In *Peter Pan*, the violent fantasies of the children are domesticated; in "The Veldt," however, these fantasies take over and the domestic technology turns violent [Anderson 33–34].

More intriguingly, just like "Neverland," the fantasy world created by the nursery is a place of no return. The Hadley children are the "Lost Boys" in *Peter Pan*. Once they enter the simulated world, they can no longer stay away from it. The illusionary world has become reality for them. Likewise, George and Lydia are devoured by the illusion constructed by VR. For them, the nursery is also a place of no return.

STYLE

Foreshadowing

Ray Bradbury is good at giving advance hints of what is to come later in his story. The death of George and Lydia has been foretold several times in the exposition and the rising action of the story plot. In the opening scene of "The Veldt," readers are, for the first time, given the foreshadowing hint when Lydia shares her concerns with George. First, she says she doesn't know exactly what is wrong with the nursery, but then immediately afterwards, she suggests calling a psychologist to inspect the room. Her sixth sense is not backed up by any solid proof at that time. Nevertheless, this serves as an omen indicating that the nursery is causing mental harm to Peter and Mary, and something abnormal might soon happen to the Hadley family.

The rising action of the plot is also filled with instances of foreshadowing, each getting more obvious and terrifying than the one before. The hungry lions that chase George and Lydia out of the nursery are just the beginning of the nightmare. As the story unfolds, missing accessory items that belong to the couple are found torn and/or blood-filled in the nursery room—George's lost old wallet is found to be chewed and smeared with blood and saliva that smells like a lion. David also happens to pick up a bloody scarf that belongs to Lydia. These eerie items are advance hints indicating that George and

Lydia shall soon fall prey to the lions conjured up by their children. The foreshadowing is most explicit when the couple hears two screams coming from the nursery: "[t]wo screams. Two people screaming from downstairs. And then a roar of lions" (Bradbury 39). Bradbury has not spelled out who the two screaming people really are and why they are there, but according to Lydia, the screams sound awfully familiar. It is highly likely that they are the screams of George and Lydia themselves. Some readers interpret the uncanny screams as a reflection of Peter and Wendy's desire to kill their parents; others see the screams as part of the self-defense mechanism regulated by the intelligent nursery, which scares off whomever wants to switch it off. Whichever interpretation prevails, the foreshadowing is just as powerful.

Personification

The concept of artificial intelligence (AI) was unknown to many in the 1950s, but as a visionary SF writer, Ray Bradbury often transports his readers into the future, sharing his insights on how AI, modeled after the human brain, can mimic and eventually replace humans. In "The Veldt," the stylistic device of personification is used whenever Happylife Home is referred to. Lydia is the first character to personify the intelligent home. Feeling upset at being replaced by the human-like house, she complains to her husband, "[t]he house is wife and mother now and nursemaid" (Bradbury 32). In fact, the house owners are indeed expected to talk with the smart house as if it is a real person, for it is programmed to speak like a human. When George wants ketchup for his food, he asks the house for it in the most natural tone: "[w]e forgot the ketchup" (Bradbury 33). In response to George's request, the house apologizes immediately in a most gentleman-like manner.

Because of the uncanny humanness of the intelligent home, George and David cannot help but personify the nursery room, too. Verbs of emotion such as "likes" and "hates" are used to describe the emotions that the room may be feeling. Moreover, ridiculous as it may seem, turning off the room is compared to killing a conscious, living being. George and David wondered if the nursery room would find it life-threatening should they turn it off:

> "I don't imagine the room will like being turned off," said the father.
> "Nothing ever likes to die—even a room."
> "I wonder if it hates me for wanting to switch it off?" [Bradbury 44].

Later on in the story, George announces the "death" of the room: "the whole damn house dies as of here and now" (Bradbury 45). The reaction of Peter and Wendy towards the "death" of their dearest nursery then further personifies the room. They cannot believe their parents would "murder" their beloved, so they grieve the "death" of their "loved one" by screaming, prancing, yelling, sobbing, swearing and throwing things hysterically. In addition, in the third-person omniscient narration, death similes have been used to refer to the machines and the automated home: the electronic appliances are compared to "dead bodies" (Bradbury 45), whilst the house is called a "mechanical cemetery" (Bradbury 45). The use of such figurative language helps to perpetuate the personification effect as well.

Bibliography

Adorno, Theodor, and Max Horkheimer. *Dialectic of Enlightenment*. London: Verso, 1979. Print.
Aggelis, Steven L. "Introduction." *Conversations with Ray Bradbury*. Edited by Steven L. Aggelis. Jackson: University Press of Mississippi, 2004, xi–xxvi. Print.
Anderson, James Arthur. *The Illustrated Ray Bradbury: A Structuralist Reading of Bradbury's The Illustrated Man*. Rockville, MD: The Borgo Press, 2013. Print.
Bankston, John. *Ray Bradbury (Who Wrote That?)*. New York: Infobase Learning, 2013. Print.
Beley, Gene. *Ray Bradbury: Uncensored! The Unauthorized Biography*. Lincoln, NE: iUniverse, Inc., 2006. Print.
Booker, M. Keith, and Anne-Marie Thomas. *The Science Fiction Handbook*. Singapore: Wiley-Blackwell, 2009. Print.
Bradbury, Ray. "The Veldt." *The Illustrated Man*. Thorndike, Maine, U.S. and Bath, England: G. K. Hall & Chivers Press, 1999, 27–48. Print.
Carosso, Andrea. *Cold War Narratives: American Culture in the 1950s*. Bern, Switzerland: Peter Lang, 2012. Print.
Diskin, Lahna. "Bradbury on Children." *Ray Bradbury*. Edited by Harold Bloom. New York: Bloom's Literary Criticism, 2010, 23–50. Print.
Drassinower, Abraham, and Cheryl Kemkow. "Ray Bradbury: An Interview." *Conversations with Ray Bradbury*. Edited by Steven L. Aggelis. Jackson: University Press of Mississippi, 2004, 122–138. Print.
Eller, Jonathan R. *Becoming Ray Bradbury*. Baltimore: University of Illinois Press, 2011. Print.
_____. "The Body Eclectic: Sources of Ray Bradbury's Martian Chronicles." *Ray Bradbury*. Edited by Harold Bloom. New York: Bloom's Literary Criticism, 2010, 141–172. Print.
Kakutani, Michiko. "Up from the Depths of Pulp and into the Mainstream." *New York Times*. 6 June 2012. Web. 28 Feb 2018.
Lopez, Ilse Marie Bussing. "Architecture, Technology and the Uncanny: Infiltrating Space in 'The Veldt' and in 'The Digital House Project.'" *Revista de Lenguas Modernas* 25 (2016): 101–111. Print.
Lowenthal, Leo. *Literature, Popular Culture and Society*. Palo Alto, CA: Pacific Books, 1961. Print.
Luckhurst, Roger. *Science Fiction*. Cambridge, UK: Polity Press, 2005. Print.
Mahdawi, Arwa. "What Jobs Will Still Be Around in 20 Years? Read This to Prepare Your Future." *The Guardian*, 26 June 2017. https://www.theguardian.com/us-news/2017/jun/26/jobs-future-automation-robots-skills-creative-health. Accessed 6 March 2018.
Marcuse, Herbert. *One Dimensional Man*. Boston: Beacon, 1964. Print.
Mogen, David. *Ray Bradbury*. Boston: Twayne Publishers, 1986. Print.
Otten, Nick. *Fahrenheit 451: The Teacher's Companion*. Saint Louis, MO: Milliken Publishing Company, 1990. Print.
Piddock, Charles. *Ray Bradbury: Legendary Fantasy Writer*. Pleasantville, NY: Gareth Stevens Publishing, 2009. Print.
Reid, Robin Anne. *Ray Bradbury: A Critical Companion*. Westport, CT: Greenwood Press, 2000. Print.
Rieder, John. *Science Fiction and the Mass Cultural Genre System*. Middletown, CT: Wesleyan University Press, 2017. Print.

Smith, Patrick A. *Thematic Guide to Popular Short Stories*. Westport, CT and London: Greenwood Press, 2002. Print.
Stockwell, Peter. *The Poetics of Science Fiction*. London and New York: Routledge, 2014. Print.
Weiner, Lauren. "The Dark and Starry Eyes of Ray Bradbury." *The New Atlantis: A Journal of Technology & Society* 36 (Summer 2012): 79–91. Print/Web.
Zipes, Jack. "Mass Degradation of Humanity and Massive Contradictions in Bradbury's Vision of America in *Fahrenheit 451*." Ray Bradbury's *Fahrenheit 451*. Edited by Harold Bloom. New York: Bloom's Literary Criticism, 2008, 3–18. Print.

5

Masculinity and Sexuality in Proulx's "Brokeback Mountain"

BIOGRAPHY OF ANNIE PROULX

Edna Annie Proulx was born to George Napoleon Proulx and Lois Gill as the eldest of five daughters in Norwich, Connecticut, in 1935 (Asquith 4). Due to her father's work in the textile industry, Annie Proulx and her family moved around and grew up in various towns in Vermont, North Carolina, Maine, and Rhode Island (Rood 2). This filled her childhood with adventures in different geographical areas. Her mother, a naturalist and painter, taught her how to see the world by paying close attention to details. Proulx then channeled those skills in her writing and wrote her first short story at the age of ten. She also developed her love of reading when she attended the high school in Brookfield, Vermont, Black Mountain High School in North Carolina, and Deering High School in Portland, Maine (Rood 2).

After graduating from Deering High School, Proulx continued her education and earned a B.A. degree in History from the University of Vermont, Burlington in 1969, a M.A. degree in History from Sir George Williams University, Montreal in 1973, and passed the oral examinations of her PhD in Renaissance Economic History in 1975 (but did not complete her degree). During her studies, she married three times, divorced two times, and gave birth to one daughter with her first husband, two sons with her second husband, and one son with her third husband. After twenty years, her third marriage also ended in divorce. As a single parent who needed to raise three sons, Proulx had to make ends meet. She had worked as a freelance journalist and founded a local newspaper called *The Vershire Behind the Times*. From 1975 to 1988, she also wrote non-fiction magazine articles in addition to publishing how-to guidebooks such as *Sweet and Hard Cider* (1980) and *The*

Complete Dairy Food Cookbook (1982). Proulx found the non-fiction writing tasks tedious, and she was more passionate about writing short stories. Nevertheless, because of her money shortage, each year she could only afford to write one to two short stories in *Gray's Sporting Journal* (Kort 259).

At the age of 53, Proulx managed to secure a book contract from Scribners for a collection of short stories. She then anthologized nine short stories she had written throughout the years, all of which were set in geographical locations in rural New England, where she has lived for over 30 years. Though considered a late bloomer, Proulx successfully attracted attention through the publication of her first short story collection titled *Heart Songs and Other Stories* (1988). In the 1990s, she started publishing novels, including her debut novel *Postcards* (1992), which won her the PEN/Faulkner Award for Fiction, as well as her second novel *The Shipping News* (1993), which won notable awards such as the U.S. National Book Award for Fiction in 1993 and the Pulitzer Prize for Fiction in 1994. In 1997, she published her internationally acclaimed tragic gay love short story "Brokeback Mountain" in *The New Yorker*. The time she spent living in Wyoming, the life experiences she had in the rural regions, and the difficulties she encountered in her marriages all contributed to shape the setting, plot and characterization in her work. The short story not only brought her an O. Henry Award in 1998, but also the chance to get her work introduced to a wide audience through Ang Lee's *Brokeback Mountain* (2005), an Oscar-winning film. Today, Annie Proulx is recognized as one of America's greatest writers, comparable to Ernest Hemingway and William Faulkner (Varvogli 7).

Queer Politics in the U.S.

Among the many short stories of Annie Proulx, "Brokeback Mountain" is considered the most significant because it puts queer issues center stage, powerfully changing the representation and perception of homosexual people in mainstream American culture. Before "Brokeback Mountain," gay people were often marginalized, mocked and medicalized in the mass media. Hardly any popular writers would use homosexuals as main characters in their fiction. The sissy gay character, if any at all, is either a laughing stock in the plot or a terrifying threat (e.g., a carrier of HIV, a deadly disease with no cure) to the social order. In her most famous short story, Proulx breaks the stereotypical prejudice and "offers a refreshing, counter-stereotypical representation of gay and/or bisexual men in a U.S. media offering" (Hart 213). By revealing the pain and hardship of a closeted gay couple, she fearlessly stood up for gay rights at a time when homosexual sex and same-sex marriage were still illegal.

She also shares frankly with readers how her story "Brokeback Mountain" took shape:

> One night in a bar in upstate I had noticed an older ranch hand ... He leaned against the back wall and his eyes were fastened not on the dozens of handsome and flashing women in the room but on the young cowboys playing pool.... [T]here was something in his expression, a kind of bitter longing, that made me wonder if he was country gay. Then I began to consider what it might have been like for him—not the real person against the wall, but for any ill-informed, confused, not-sure-what-he-was-feeling youth growing up in homophobic Wyoming ... "Brokeback" was constructed on the small but tight idea of a couple of home-grown country kids, opinions and self-knowledge shaped by the world around them, finding themselves in emotional waters of increasing depth [...].
>
> The urban critics dubbed it a tale of two gay cowboys. No. It is a story of destructive rural homophobia [...].
>
> I wanted to explore both long-lasting love and its possible steep price tag, both homophobic antipathy and denial. I knew this was a story loaded with taboos but I was driven to write it [...]. Jack and Ennis soon seemed more vivid than many of the flesh-and-blood people around me ["Getting Moved" 129–131].

The gay protagonists of "Brokeback Mountain" may be modeled on the defendant of the United States Supreme Court case *Bowers v. Hardwick*, 478 U.S. 186 (1986). In the controversial case, Michael Hardwick and another adult male were arrested by a police officer for having consensual oral and anal sex in the bedroom of his private home in Atlanta. They were both charged with a criminal offence for violating a Georgia state law that banned homosexual sodomy (Roughton 84). The unfair decision influenced a long line of similar cases, raising social concerns and bringing heated debates in the U.S. After a long period of 17 years, the Supreme Court decision was overturned by *Lawrence v. Texas*, 539 U.S. 558 (2003). Based on the Fourteenth Amendment's guarantee of equal protection, the landmark case in 2003 invalidated the sodomy laws. Ever since then, consensual same-sex sexual acts became legal in all states and territories in the U.S.

"Brokeback Mountain" is a milestone for the lesbian, gay, bisexual, and transgender (LGBT) community and its supporters. Due to the huge impact it has had on mainstream culture in the U.S. and beyond, it remains a classic decades after it was published in 1997.

Plot Overview

In the summer of 1963, Ennis del Mar and Jack Twist, two nineteen-year-old boys who grew up on Wyoming ranches, first meet as they work as sheep herders for Joe Aguirre, the Forest Service foreman on Brokeback Mountain.

Having spent much time alone with each other day and night surrounded only by sheep, Ennis and Jack become good friends. One cold evening, Ennis gets drunk and stays with Jack in the same tent. When the two of them share the same bedroll, Jack suddenly directs Ennis's hand to his genitals. Ennis is inexperienced, but he instinctively responds to Jack's strong desire. After that first night together, the two boys secretly continue their romantic relationship throughout the summer until the job ends in August. It is only on the last day of work that the lovers realize Joe Aguirre has spied on them and discovered their relationship. Before they depart, Jack hints to Ennis that he would like to continue their intimate relationship, but Ennis avoids the matter by saying that he and Alma will soon get married and settle down. Suppressing their true feelings for each other, the two boys separate and move on with their lives.

Four years after the summer of 1963, Jack finds Ennis, sends him a letter, telling him that he is coming over to Riverton, Wyoming, to see him. When the gay lovers finally see each other again, both of them are already tied down by marriage and children—Ennis is living with his wife Alma and their two daughters, whereas Jack has married a rich woman named Lureen and they have an eight-month-old son in Texas. Nevertheless, they find that their hunger for each other has remained the same, if not increased. When they are alone in the hallway outside the apartment door, they can no longer hold themselves back. They hug erotically and kiss breathlessly, not noticing that Alma, who opens the door to look for her husband, witnesses everything. Alma remains quiet when Ennis says he is going out with Jack to get a drink, though she knows very well what is happening between Jack and her husband. After the drink, the two men sleep in a motel and have a serious conversation about their relationship. Jack says they need to "figure out what to do" ("Brokeback Mountain" 299), and he bravely suggests that they can leave everything behind, start anew, work on a little ranch and have "some sweet life" ("Brokeback Mountain" 300) together somewhere. Yet, Ennis is too scared to come out of the closet. He tells Jack that they can get themselves beaten to a "bloody pulp" ("Brokeback Mountain" 301). He recalls that when he was only nine years old, his father made him look at the mutilated body of a gay man who had been violently murdered by homophobes. Same as four years earlier, Ennis escapes from the matter again. Much to Jack's disappointment, Ennis only wants to pretend that all is well and carry on with his joyless life. However, the two continue to meet up once or twice a year.

After ten years of a loveless marriage, Alma can no longer tolerate the abnormal and unhealthy relationship with her husband. She confronts Ennis, divorces him and remarries a grocer. In the following years, Jack and Ennis still get away from time to time, going "fishing" together and spending romantic time alone in various wild mountainous areas far away from the public, but never again do they revisit Brokeback Mountain. In their last getaway in 1983, Jack urges Ennis to think about going to Mexico and living together. After twenty years, his love and desire for Ennis are still as strong as ever. It is painful for him every time they separate, knowing that they can only meet for a few days once or twice a year. Once again, Ennis refuses sorrowfully and dares not look at how upset Jack is. The couple ends their holiday break with a sad farewell.

After a few months, Ennis tries to send a postcard to Jack but it is returned and stamped "deceased." Shocked and petrified, Ennis called Jack's wife, who confirms that Jack broke his nose and jaw in a weird car accident. He dies drowning in his own blood. She also tells Ennis that Jack once told her that when he died, he wanted his ashes to be scattered on Brokeback Mountain. She has no idea where the mountain is, so she buried half of his ashes in Texas and sent the other half to Jack's parents. Ennis then figures out the truth: Jack was murdered because of his sexual orientation. Shortly thereafter, he pays a visit to Jack's parents' small, rundown ranch in Lightning Flat, Wyoming. Jack's father is an angry old man who seems to know there was something going on between Ennis and his son. Jack's mother, however, welcomes Ennis and shows him Jack's childhood bedroom. Shattered by sadness, Ennis finds inside Jack's closet his own shirt hidden underneath Jack's shirt, "the pair like two skins, one inside the other, two in one" ("Brokeback Mountain" 316).

At the end of the story, Jack's father refuses to let Ennis have Jack's ashes buried on Brokeback Mountain. Having lost the most important person in his life, Ennis is like a prisoner of the past. He always dreams of Jack, and he often wakes up wetting his pillow with tears, and sometimes the sheets (implying nocturnal emissions).

CHARACTERS

Ennis del Mar

Ennis is a fictional closeted gay character whose perspective is constantly used by the third-person narrator to convey the story. Having grown up in a conservative family in rural Wyoming, Ennis is stoic and introverted. After his parents die in a car accident, Ennis is raised by his elder brother and sister. Due to financial constraints, he drops out of high school at a young age and works as a rancher. One summer, he works on Brokeback Mountain and falls in love with his co-worker Jack Twist. His genuine affection towards Jack is long-lasting, and he has no sexual and romantic relationships with men other than Jack. Nonetheless, because of the difficult circumstances, he suppresses his love and desire for Jack. He leads an unhappy double life by marrying Alma Beers and has two daughters.

Jack Twist

Jack is the carefree and passionate gay protagonist who is deeply in love with Ennis after sheep ranching with him on Brokeback Mountain. Though Jack is also a country cowboy brought up in a conservative family, unlike Ennis, he is outspoken about his attraction to men and assertive about his pursuit of happiness. He dreams about going away with Ennis, but he fails to convince Ennis to come out of the closet. He then marries Lureen and has a son. Over a span of twenty years, his longing for Ennis never stops and they keep having secret getaways together. Feeling empty and restless, he indulges himself in rodeo and has sex with gigolos in Mexico. He is found dead with his nose and jaw broken in a roadside accident, but Ennis suspects that Jack was violently murdered by homophobes.

Alma Beers

Alma was Ennis's childhood sweetheart. She is already engaged to Ennis before he meets Jack on Brokeback Mountain. Her loveless marriage with Ennis, which drags on for ten years, brings them two daughters, Alma Junior and Francine. Much to her disappointment, Ennis never takes her and her girls on vacation. Moreover, Ennis often fails to earn enough money to feed the family. She has to work as a clerk in a grocery store to make ends meet. Yet, the main cause of her despair is Ennis's love relationship with Jack. She sees Ennis and Jack kissing each other in the hallway, and she knows very well that when the two men go on holiday together, it is definitely not to fish, as they claim. After some time, the long-suffering Alma bravely confronts her husband, who twists her wrist violently and leaves home resentfully. She then divorces Ennis and marries a grocer in Riverton.

Lureen

Lureen is the wife of Jack Twist. Having inherited a farm machinery business from her father in Childress, Texas, Lureen has "some serious money" ("Brokeback Mountain" 297), which gives her the upper hand in the marriage. She never meets her in-laws, and she is the one who "had the money and called the shots" ("Brokeback Mountain" 307). Her primary contribution is providing financial stability for Jack and her family. She and Jack also have a fifteen-year-old son, who is "dyslexic or something, couldn't get anything right … and could hardly read" ("Brokeback Mountain" 307). She, however, refuses to admit that her son has problems and "pretended the kid was o.k." ("Brokeback Mountain" 307), depriving him access to proper treatment. Whether she knows of Ennis and Jack's affair is not made known to the readers, but it is possible that she has sensed something special between Jack and his "fishing buddy or the hunting buddy" ("Brokeback Mountain" 311), for she is described to be "polite but ... cold as snow" ("Brokeback Mountain" 312) when she talks with Ennis on the phone.

Jack Twist's Parents

Jack's father, John C. Twist, is a typical male patriarch who controls the family. He is harsh, hot-tempered, homophobic, and hardly knows how to express his affection towards his son. When Jack showed signs of failed toilet training at the age of three to four, John was so angry that he knocked his son down on the bathroom floor and whipped him with his belt. Even after the death of his son, John still complains about Jack not helping enough with the ranch work. He also suspects that Jack and Ennis have an erotic homosexual relationship. He stares at Ennis "with an angry, knowing expression" (Proulx 313) when Ennis pays him a visit. Mrs. Twist, on the other hand, is a kind and gentle woman who loves her son for what he is. She still keeps Jack's room intact after his tragic death. Knowing that Ennis is someone important to her son, she invites Ennis to enter Jack's room after treating Ennis with cherry cake and coffee.

Joe Aguirre

Joe is the Forest Service foreman who employs Jack and Ennis to work as sheep herder and camp tender. He is a voyeur who uses his binoculars to spy on Jack and Ennis on the mountain, discovering the secret between the two nineteen-year-old gay lovers.

MAIN THEMES

The Construction of Masculinity

One of the most daring attempts of Proulx's "Brokeback Mountain" is the way it locates homosexual love and desire "within the iconic system of the American Western landscape and the figures of masculine Westerners" (Patterson 46–47). Readers are invited to rethink what masculinity is and how it works. Considering the backgrounds and upbringing of Ennis and

Jack, most readers would agree that they do accurately represent typical Western cowboys: "[t]hey were raised on small, poor ranches in opposite corners of the state ... both high school dropout country boys with no prospects, brought up to hard work and privation, both rough-mannered, rough-spoken, inured to the stoic life" ("Brokeback Mountain" 284). As for their upbringing, both protagonists are trained by a tough and hypermasculine father. It has been revealed to readers that Jack received harsh, military-style training from his father. He was whipped for not performing well in his potty training when he was still a toddler. Ennis's father has a similar teaching style. When Ennis was only six, his father taught him to resolve disputes with violence:

> Dad says ... make him feel some pain ... keep doin it until he takes the message. Nothin like hurtin somebody to make him hear good ["Brokeback Mountain" 300].

Ennis and Jack's masculine physical appearances conform to the patriarchal norms as well. Tall, muscular and born with quick reflexes, Ennis has a body "made for the horse and for fighting" ("Brokeback Mountain" 286). Likewise, Jack carries "some weight in the haunch" ("Brokeback Mountain" 286) and is keen on rodeo. Heavily influenced by the hypermasculine culture in the Western cowboy environment, both Ennis and Jack engage in masculine activities such as fighting, coyote hunting, and truck repairing.

However, despite the coercive hypermasculine training and the seemingly essential masculinity presented by Ennis and Jack, they cannot help but fall in love with each other all of a sudden. Natural and genuine, their passion and sexual desire for each other require "no instruction manual" at all ("Brokeback Mountain" 290). A queer reading of the story opens readers' eyes, making them see that masculinity and femininity are only a social construct, "a regime of representation" (Nixon 4). Just as Beaver describes, "[w]hat is 'natural' is neither heterosexual nor homosexual desire but simply desire. [...] Desire is like the pull of a gravitational field, the magnet that draws body to body" (161). As opposed to desire, "gender is the repeated stylization of the body, a set of repeated acts within a highly rigid regulatory frame that congeal over time to produce the appearance of substance, of a natural sort of being" (Butler 43–44). In other words, masculinity, just as femininity and heteronormative identities, are "constructed, represented, repeated and, in turn, reinforced as if they are ordained by Nature. They are fabricated at the moment when they are performed" (Tso 113).

Nature Versus Culture

According to Hunt, the geographical settings presented in many of Annie Proulx's stories are half-real, half-imagined spaces derived from "literary tradition, scholarly research and personal experience" (Hunt 6), and Brokeback

Mountain is no exception. In Eastern Wyoming, there are a number of Brokebacks, such as Brokeback Road, Brokeback Creek, and Brokeback Ranch, but there is no real Brokeback Mountain ("Where is Brokeback Mountain"). An imaginary place romanticized by Proulx, Brokeback Mountain accentuates "the eternal forces of nature" (Van Belle 6) that transcend "cultural, geographical, gender and sexuality boundaries" (Dhawa 84). The "state of timelessness" (Morrison 91) of Brokeback Mountain allows them to express their homosexual love and desire for each other as "a part of nature, just as the mountains and the rivers are a part of the character of this continent [Wyoming]" (Kitterman 51). Intentionally set as a contrast with rural Wyoming, the mountain is a secret, natural haven where Ennis and Jack can find themselves and be themselves. It is the place they build their love upon; it is the place where they temporarily get away from family duties and commitments, not to mention the suffocating social oppression against homosexuals. The gay couple cannot hide on Brokeback Mountain forever, though. Once they come down from the mountain, reality sets in and they have to conform to the heteronormative culture in society again. When Jack urges Ennis to figure out what the two of them should do, Ennis replies that there is nothing they can do to go against the patriarchal social order:

> Jack, I built a life up in them years. Love my little girls. Alma? It ain't her fault. You got your baby and wife, that place in Texas. You and me can't hardly be decent together if what happened back there ... We do that in the wrong place we'll be dead. There's no reins on this one. It scares the piss out a me ["Brokeback Mountain" 299].

In Proulx's tragic story, nature and culture are set as a pair in a binary opposition that cannot go together. Should the gay protagonist (i.e., Jack) follow his heart and go against the social norms in the mainstream culture, then he risks getting punished and killed by homophobes. Yet, should the gay protagonist suppress his homosexual nature, then like Ennis, he shall live with self-denial and self-deception, which leads to a slow, inward death.

Homophobia and Internalized Surveillance

Set in the 1960s to the 1980s, the sexual discrimination and homophobic threat depicted in "Brokeback Mountain" are real and frightening. As Ennis clearly recounts, when he was nine years old, a homosexual man named Earl was beaten to death with a tire iron just because he ranched with another man. His body was so badly mutilated that it became just "bloody pulp" ("Brokeback Mountain" 301). Ennis still remembers how his father made him look at the corpse in the irrigation ditch and then laughed about the man's death as if it were a funny joke. Having seen the violent death of Earl, Ennis is reluctant to admit his queer desire for Jack: "I'm not no queer" ("Brokeback Mountain" 291). He also denies himself the pursuit of pleasure and happiness when Jack suggests living together: "[t]wo guys living together? No" ("Brokeback Mountain" 301). Out of fear, he internalizes the surveillance and is always on his guard against being spied: "[w]e do that in the wrong place we'll be dead.... It scares the piss out a me" ("Brokeback Mountain" 301). Ennis feels that no matter where they go, they will be spied on, bullied and refused work. The paranoia of being judged and harmed follows Ennis everywhere, and he never feels entirely safe.

Above all, Jack's tragic death is a most traumatic shock to Ennis. On the phone, Lureen tells Ennis that Jack died in an extremely rare accident on the road. As he was trying to pump up the flat tire of his truck, the tire suddenly exploded. The rim hit across his face, breaking his nose and jaw. No one came to his rescue. He passed out and "drowned in his own blood" ("Brokeback Mountain" 311). The real cause of Jack's sudden death is never revealed. Yet, for Ennis, a fear-filled gay male who has been living under the threat of homophobia for decades, Jack's death is not an accident, but rather a homophobic murder in which Jack was callously beaten to death. Just like what happened to Earl, the homophobes got Jack with the tire iron.

STYLE

Motifs

In literature, motifs are defined as "recurrent images, words, objects, phrases, or actions that tend to unify the work" (Harmon and Holman 330). These recurrent items can occur in different forms: they can be (1) multiple appearances of a single object; (2) appearances of multiple related objects; or (3) appearances of a series of seemingly unrelated objects. In "Brokeback Mountain," motifs of all three forms can be found. For example, the first motif that most readers shall notice is the series of letters between the gay lovers. The first letter appears when Jack tracks down Ennis in Riverton, Wyoming. In return, Ennis writes a short letter back to Jack. The letter motif can be classified as motif type (1), where the series of letters refers straightforwardly to the special relationship between Jack and Ennis—despite the fact that the two are thousands of miles apart from each other for four years, the two men remain connected.

Motif type (2), on the other hand, is the "water motif" (Isola 40) or the "wet metaphor" (Isola 39), which comes in the forms of different bodily fluids such as spit, saliva, sweat, semen and blood. The first occurrence of the water motif is the spit that Ennis uses to have anal sex with Jack: "Ennis ... hauled Jack onto all fours and, with the help of the clear slick and a little spit, entered him" ("Brokeback Mountain" 290). The water motif also occurs when the gay lovers meet again after four years of separation. Their erotic kiss is wet and messy: "Jack's big teeth bringing blood, his hat falling to the floor, stubble rasping, wet saliva swelling" ("Brokeback Mountain" 295). Likewise, the motel room in which they have passionate sex smells of bodily fluids: "[t]he room stank of semen and smoke and sweat and whiskey.... Ennis lay spread-eagled, spent and wet, breathing deep" ("Brokeback Mountain" 297). Ennis uses the water-related expression "wrang it out" ("Brokeback Mountain" 298) to describe his feelings towards Jack as well: "I never had no thoughts a doin it with another guy except I sure wrang it out a hundred times thinking about you" ("Brokeback Mountain" 298). More intriguingly, the names of the protagonists are also related to the water motif. On the one hand, "del Mar," the surname of Ennis, means "of the sea." On the other hand, the name Jack subtly refers to "jacking off" (Isola 41). The messy bodily fluids can be read as a motif for the unquenchable sexual desire, uncontrollable emotions and unstoppable love of the gay protagonists.

No less significant than the letter motif and the water motif is the loop motif, which belongs to motif type (3). The notion of the loop appears repeatedly in three seemingly unrelated forms. First and foremost, the narrative structure is a loop. It starts and ends with Ennis daydreaming/dreaming about Jack day and night. As Fitzpatrick points out: "[t]he loop is a closed narrative structure that disrupts the expectation of linear time" (7). Secondly, the lack of progress in Ennis and Jack's love affair can be viewed as a loop as well. For twenty years, the gay lovers have been going in circles and running on empty. Even in the final camp trip together: "[n]othing ended, nothing begun, nothing resolved ... they'd never got much farther than that" ("Brokeback Mountain" 311). The loop motif can be found in Ennis's conversation with Jack, too: "I'm stuck with what I got, caught in my own loop. Can't get out of it" ("Brokeback Mountain" 300). In brief, the loop is not only an iconic figure of the Western cowboys, but also a motif that refers to the fruitless gay romance.

Third Person Limited Point of View

Third person limited narration is used in the short story. Powerfully, the narrative tool tells the story through the perspective of Ennis, showing readers what Ennis sees, hears, smells, senses, thinks, and feels. It limits the narrative scope within the context of rural North America and its Western society in the early 1960s to 1980s. Readers are invited to experience the tough cowboy life on the mountains, which includes horse riding, sheep herding, tent camping, and coyote hunting. To create a regional sensibility, in the narrative, Proulx also includes discrete geographical places that are known to

Ennis and local residents, such as "Big Horns, Medicine Bows" and "Owl Creeks" ("Brokeback Mountain" 304). The attachments and meanings that Ennis associates with the Wyoming landscape often come through the narration.

Another highlight of the third person limited narration is the gay gaze delicately captured in the narrative. For example, after four years of separation on Brokeback Mountain, Ennis misses Jack so much that the scent of Jack is magnified, sexualized and romanticized: "[h]e could smell Jack—the intensively familiar odor of cigarettes, musky sweat and a faint sweetness like grass, and with it the rushing cold of the mountain" ("Brokeback Mountain" 295). Though Ennis never talks about his hidden and forbidden love affair with Jack, readers still get to know from the narrative that after Jack's death, Ennis continues to dream about Jack, which suffuses Ennis with "a sense of pleasure" ("Brokeback Mountain" 283), "grief," and at times an "old sense of joy and release" ("Brokeback Mountain" 318). The up-close and personal narrative serves to elicit readers' sympathy.

BIBLIOGRAPHY

Asquith, Mark. *Annie Proulx's "Brokeback Mountain" and Postcards*. London and New York: Continuum, 2009. Print.
Beaver, Harold. "Homosexual Signs: In Memory of Roland Barthes." *Camp: Queer Aesthetics and the Performing Subject: A Reader*. Edited by Fabio Cleto. Edinburgh: Edinburgh University Press, 1999. 160–178. Print.
Butler, Judith. *Gender Trouble: Feminism and the Subversion of Identity*. New York: Routledge, 1999. Print.
Dhawa, Huai Bao. "Repression, Silence and Cinematic Language: Eastern Sensibility in Visualizing *Brokeback Mountain*." *Journal of East-West Thought* 4.1 (2014): 83–94. Print.
Fitzpatrick, Andrea D. "Love's Letter Lost: Reading 'Brokeback Mountain.'" *Mosaic: A Journal for the Interdisciplinary Study of Literature* 43.1 (2010): 1–21. Print.
Harmon, William, and C. Hugh Holman. *A Handbook to Literature*. New Jersey: Prentice Hall, 1996. Print.
Hart, Kylo-Patrick R. "Annie Proulx's Imaginative Leap: Constructing Gay Masculinity in 'Brokeback Mountain.'" *Text Matters* 2.2 (2012): 209–220. Print.
Hunt, Alex. "Introduction." *The Geographical Imagination of Annie Proulx: Rethinking Regionalism*. Edited by Alex Hunt. Plymouth, UK: Lexington Books, 2009. 1–10. Print.
Isola, Mark John. "Disciplining Desire: The Fluid Textuality of Annie Proulx's 'Brokeback Mountain.'" *Nordic Journal of English Studies* 7.1 (2008): 33–47. Print.
Kitterman, John. "Love and Death in an American Story: A 'Vulgar' Reading of Brokeback Mountain." *Reading Brokeback Mountain: Essays on the Story and the Film*. Edited by Jim Stacey. Jefferson: McFarland, 2007. 45–58. Print.
Kort, Carol. *A to Z of American Women Writers*. New York: Facts on File, 2007. Print.
Morrison, James. "Back to the Ranch Ag'in: *Brokeback Mountain* and Gay Civil Rights." *The Brokeback Book*. Edited by William R. Handley. Lincoln: University of Nebraska Press, 2011. 81–100. Print.
Nixon, Sean. *Hard Looks: Masculinities, Spectatorship and Contemporary Consumption*. London: UCL Press, 1996. Print.
Patterson, Eric. *On Brokeback Mountain: Meditations About Masculinity, Fear and Love in the Story and the Film*. New York: Lexington Books, 2008. Print.

Proulx, Annie. "Brokeback Mountain." *Close Range: Brokeback Mountain and Other Stories*. London: Harper Perennial, 1999. 283–318. Print.

———. "Getting Moved." *Brokeback Mountain: Story to Screenplay*. Edited by Annie Proulx, Larry McMurtry, and Diana Ossana. New York: Scribner's, 2005. 129–138. Print.

Rood, Karen Lane. *Understanding Annie Proulx*. Columbia: University of South Carolina Press, 2001. Print.

Roughton, Ralph. "The Significance of *Brokeback Mountain*." *Journal of Gay & Lesbian Mental Health* 18.1 (2013): 83–94. Print.

Tso, Anna Wing Bo. "Female Cross-dressing in Chinese Literature Classics and Their English Versions." *International Studies: Interdisciplinary Political and Cultural Journal* 16.1 (2014): 111–124. Print/Web.

Van Belle, Jono. "A Cross-cultural Approach to *Brokeback Mountain*." *CLC Web: Comparative Literature and Culture* 17.2 (2015): 1–8. Web. 30 Apr 2018.

Varvogli, Aliki. *Annie Proulx's* The Shipping News: *A Reader's Guide*. New York and London: Continuum, 2002. Print.

"Where Is Brokeback Mountain? Maybe Nowhere." abcnews.go.com, ABC News, 5 March 2006. http://abcnews.go.com/WNT/Oscars2006/story?id=1689983&page=1. Accessed on 23 Apr 2018.

6

Fantasy and Fan Fiction in Gaiman's "The Problem of Susan"

Biography of Neil Gaiman

Born in 1960 in Portchester, Hampshire, in Southern England, Neil Gaiman grew up in Sussex and received education at the Whitgift School in Croydon. Influenced by the masterpieces of C. S. Lewis, J. R. R. Tolkien, Lewis Carroll, Rudyard Kipling, Edgar Allan Poe, Ray Bradbury and other fantasy writers, Gaiman became passionate about composing stories, in particular fairy tale and myth, which are "at the core of his writing" (Campbell 11). After graduation, Gaiman first worked as a freelance journalist and published a biography for Duran Duran in 1984, followed by a biography for Douglas Adams in 1988. However, the works that launched his career and brought him the nickname of "Literary Rock Star" were his wildly creative, sometimes dark and humorous comics, graphic novels, children's fantasy, horror stories, fan fiction, speculative sci-fi and genre blends for TV series and films. Among adult readers, Neil Gaiman's most notable works include *American Gods* (2001), a work of fiction that blends fantasy and ancient and modern mythology, which won numerous best novel awards in 2002, including the Hugo Award, the Nebula Award, the Locus Award, and the Bram Stoker Award. Gaiman's *Sandman* (1989–1996), the best-selling, epic comic book series published by DC Comics, is yet another genre blend that attracts a great deal of fans. His *Stardust* (1999) is also a best-selling, award-winning fantasy novel which earned him the Mythopoetic Fantasy Award for Adult Literature in 1999 and the American Library Association's Alex Award in 2000.

Internationally acclaimed as one of the most prominent post-modern writers in the twenty-first century, Neil Gaiman is also well-loved by child readers. He is the first children's author to win both the Newbery Medal in 2009 and the Newbery Medal in 2010 for his children's fantasy, *The Graveyard Book* (2008). His children's novella *Coraline* (2002), a dark horror version of Lewis Carroll's *Alice's Adventures in Wonderland*, was also awarded the Hugo Award for Best Novella in 2003, the Nebula Award for Best Novella in 2003, and the Bram Stoker Award for Best Work for Young Readers in 2002. It has also been made into a film, a comic book, a musical, an opera and a video game. Up through today, Neil Gaiman has accumulated over 2.72 million followers on Twitter.

Fantasy and Fan Fiction

Fantasy (or the fantastic), an increasingly popular literary genre nowadays, was once considered trivial and insignificant until J. R. R. Tolkien and Tzvetan Todorov popularized it, encouraging critics to include the genre in the literary canon. In his essay "On Fairy Tales" (1938), Tolkien first brings up the binary distinctions between the real and the unreal. He introduces "the primary world of reality" and "the secondary world of fantasy" (cited in Vaden 88), defining fantasy as nonreality, i.e., anything that does not actually exist in the primary world (Tolkien 6). Equally importantly, Todorov gives an even more detailed distinction. According to Todorov, the fantasy genre can be further classified into three sub-genres: the fantastic and its neighboring genre, the uncanny and the marvelous:

> In a world which is indeed our world, the one we know, a world without devils, sylphides, or vampires, there occurs an event which cannot be explained by the laws of this same familiar world. The person who experiences the event must opt for one of two possible solutions: either he is the victim of an illusion of the senses, of a product of the imagination—and the laws of the world then remain what they are; or else the event has indeed taken place, it is an integral part of reality—but then this reality is controlled by laws unknown to us.... The fantastic occupies the duration of this uncertainty. Once we choose one answer or the other, we leave the fantastic for a neighboring genre, the uncanny or the marvelous [Todorov 25].

In other words, under the umbrella of fantasy, the uncanny occurs when the deceiving mind of the protagonist causes weird and bizarre occurrences. Natural explanations such as intoxication, madness, dementia, dreams, hypnosis, etc. can be given. On the contrary, the marvelous refers to supernatural events that "cannot be explained by rational laws" (Reeder 187). The fantastic, on the other hand, refers to the uncertainty and hesitation in between the uncanny and the marvelous. Under such genre definitions, C. S. Lewis's *The Chronicles of Narnia* (1950–1956) belongs to the marvelous because Narnia is a secondary world, whereas Neil Gaiman's "The Problem of Susan" belongs to the uncanny because its Narnia occurs only in dreams. Though the Land of Narnia occurs in both fictional texts, Gaiman's rewriting changes the literary genre.

Classified as the uncanny, "The Problem of Susan" also falls under the fan fiction genre. Based on C. S. Lewis's *The Chronicles of Narnia* (1950–1956), Gaiman's short story is a derivative work that develops a new plot using the existing setting, characters, plotlines and motifs. Upon being asked the reason for writing "The Problem of Susan," Gaiman explains to the his fans and the public that he feels irritated by the ill fate of Susan in the *Narnia* series:

> I read the Narnia books to myself hundreds of times as a boy, and then aloud as an adult, twice, to my children. There is so much in the books that I love, but each time I found the disposal of Susan to be intensely problematic and deeply irritating. I suppose I wanted to write a different story that would be equally problematic, and just as much of an irritant, if from a different direction, and to talk about the remarkable power of children's literature [Gaiman, *Fragile Things* 8].

Gaiman's deep response to the character of Susan Pevensie shows that he too is a fan of the Narnia books. As Van Steenhuyse observes, "fans respond to characters as if they were real people because they have a whole store of memories ... about how they behave in certain situations, about their past, about their likes and dislikes" (6). By reinterpreting the characterization of Susan Pevensie in the fan fiction, Gaiman, as a fan himself, turns his opinions into a story which he wants to share, providing Narnia fans with what C. S. Lewis fails to provide in the original text.

Plot Overview

Neil Gaiman's "The Problem of Susan" is both "a dark and terrifying version of Narnia" (Godfrey 93) and a metafiction of the *Chronicles of Narnia* (1950–1956) with a special focus on what happens to Susan Pevensie in the real world after she is excluded from Aslan's paradise. The story is set in England, where Greta Campion, a young reporter for the *Literary Chronicle*, visits and interviews Professor Hastings, an aged female professor of children's literature, the day before she dies. At the beginning of the interview, the old professor talks about the rise of children's fiction. From Charles Kingsley's *The Water Babies* (1862), *Grimms' Fairy Tales* (1812–1857), Charles Perrault's "Sleeping Beauty in the Woods" (1697), to Roald Dahl's *Matilda* (1988), the discussion remains academic. It is not until Greta asks the professor about her family and mentions C. S. Lewis's *Narnia* books that the discussion becomes personal and emotional. The professor reveals the torturous ordeal that she went through when she lost all her family members in a tragic train crash.

Having experienced the same traumatic loss that Susan Pevensie experiences in the *Narnia* books, Professor Hastings speaks for Susan, providing a graphic and firsthand description of the damage and tough challenges which a young orphaned girl had to face—the hardest part was to identify the mutilated bodies of her siblings alone. Afterwards, she also had a hard time making ends meet because her parents had left her very little money for food and shelter. The professor points out that it is naïve to think that Susan Pevensie will still have the time and leisure to indulge in fashion and beauty. She accuses C. S. Lewis of imposing cruel punishment on Susan, who is not only traumatized by the family's fatal accident, but also denied entrance to heaven due to her awakened female sexuality. The night when Greta returns home after the interview, she dreams of becoming Susan Pevensie, too. In her dream, the world of Narnia is no heaven but a total nightmare. The Pevensie children are betrayed by Aslan, who allows the evil witch to take Peter and Edmund with her as trophies. Even more shockingly, the lion devours the two sisters. Then, in front of Susan's dead head, he enjoys sex with the White Witch before crunching Susan's skull into pieces.

CHARACTERS

Professor Hastings

Professor Hastings is an exported character based on Susan Pevensie of C. S. Lewis's *The Chronicles of Narnia* (1950–1956). In Neil Gaiman's short story, Hastings is an old retired female professor. Specialized in children's literature, she has published a book titled *A Quest for Meanings in Children's Fiction*, which echoes one of the main themes of Gaiman's short story. Just like Susan, she experienced the pain of losing all her family members in a train crash when she was young. As the lone survivor of the deadly train accident, she had to identify her brothers' and younger sister's bodies. She also reveals in the interview that life had not been easy after her family was killed. There was hardly enough money for food and shelter, not to mention spending money on luxuries like nylons and lipsticks. On the night before her death, she still believes she has led a good life, rather than a life of repentance.

Susan Pevensie

Neil Gaiman's short story is named after Susan Pevensie, a key female character in *The Chronicles of Narnia*. Susan is the elder sister and the second eldest among the four siblings of the Pevensie family. Gentle, brave, young and beautiful, she was crowned by Aslan the Lion as the Queen of Narnia at age twelve, sharing the kingdom with her siblings, Peter, Edmund, and Lucy in *The Lion, the Witch and the Wardrobe* (1950). During the nine years that she reigned in the Golden Age of Narnia, she was known to all as Queen Susan the Gentle and Queen Susan of the Horn. Yet, as she becomes interested in make-up, nylons and parties with boys in her puberty, the Narnians leave her and enter Aslan's country without her. She is silenced, exiled and forgotten by all characters at the end of C. S. Lewis's series. In "The Problem of Susan," Gaiman gives Susan back her voice through Professor Hastings, a person who strongly resembles the adult version of Susan Pevensie.

Greta Campion

Greta is the young journalist who interviews Professor Hastings, an old female scholar who studies children's literature. During the interview with Professor Hastings, Greta reveals her anger and dissatisfaction over Susan Pevensie's ultimate exclusion from Aslan's New Narnia simply because Susan has committed "the unforgivable sin of growing up" (Brown 96). She even talked to her English teacher about the problem of Susan in *The Chronicles of Narnia* when she was twelve. The night after her interview with Professor Hastings, Greta becomes Susan Pevensie in her dream. In the nightmare, both she and her sister Lucy are engulfed by the lion.

The Lion

In C. S. Lewis's *Narnia* series, Aslan the Lion is not only the gentle, loving and powerful ruler of Narnia, but also an analogy to Jesus Christ. To rescue Edmund, who betrays his siblings and the Narnians, Aslan sacrifices his life, just as Jesus sacrificed himself and shed His blood for sinners. However, in Gaiman's metafictive short story, the lion is no less evil than the White Witch in Greta's dream. He betrays the Pevensie children, allowing the witch to take Peter and Edmund. Having eaten Susan and Lucy alive, the beast also sleeps with the witch on the grass hill.

The Witch

Jadis the White Witch is the antagonist in both C. S. Lewis's *Narnia* and Neil Gaiman's short story. Like Satan in the Holy Bible, she is evil, powerful, manipulative and mesmerizing. In Gaiman's story, she is the ice queen that has "a body no less white [than her white robes], with high, small breasts, and nipples so dark" (Lewis 180). In Greta's dream, the lion lets the witch have the Pevensie boys. The lion also allows her to have sex with him and ride on him naked.

Main Themes

The Problem of Susan

"The Problem of Susan" is not only the title of Gaiman's short story, but also the main concern and core matter to which Gaiman wants everyone to pay attention. In fact, for generations, numerous fans of C. S. Lewis's *Narnia* series have not been happy about Susan Pevensie being shut out of Aslan's country. What they find most unacceptable is that Susan is considered "no longer a friend of Narnia" (*The Last Battle* 127) merely because she, like most teenage girls, becomes interested in fashion, make-up and boys. In *The Last Battle* (1956), Susan is absent from the gathering for the final victory. King Tirian asks, "Where is Queen Susan?" (*The Last Battle* 127). Peter Pevensie, the High King over all Kings in Narnia and, most of all, the elder brother of Susan, proclaims that his sister is not a friend of Narnia anymore. His view is instantly supported by Eustace, the cousin of the Pevensies. Jill Pole and Lady Polly also criticize Susan for her adolescent pride and vanity:

> "Oh Susan!" said Jill. "She's interested in nothing nowadays except nylons and lipstick and invitations. She always was a jolly sight too keen on being grown-up."
>
> "Grown-up, indeed," said the Lady Polly. "I *wish* she would grow up. She wasted all her school time wanting to be the age she is now, and she'll waste all the rest of her life trying to stay that age. Her whole idea is to race on to the silliest time of one's life as quick as she can and then stop there as long as she can" [*The Last Battle* 128].

After the Last Battle has ended, the exclusion of Susan continues. While others are sent to the post–Narnia paradise in the train wreck, Susan is neither in the train nor at the train station. She becomes the lone survivor in her family excluded from Aslan's heaven, despite the fact that she has entered Narnia twice to fight the enemies of Narnians. All the way through the end of *The Chronicles of Narnia*, not a single character seems to care about Susan at all. This unsatisfactory ending creates distress in readers. Although readers understand that C. S. Lewis was a man of his time, it is disappointing to see how the Narnians could forget about Susan so easily. Some also feel offended by the way C. S. Lewis, Aslan, and maybe God himself give up on Susan. As Nickel points out:

> Perhaps the children do not question Susan's fate because they trust Aslan's judgement completely, but readers are saddened that Susan does not get to take part in this joyous reunion [Nickel 263].

Responding to the cruel ending in *The Chronicles of Narnia*, Gaiman exports the character of Susan Pevensie to his short story, which handles "the questions of aging with an undertone of subversion" (Zarzycka 221). Gaiman also guides Narnian fans to think about multiple issues arising from "the problem of Susan": Why is Susan treated so unkindly? What are the grounds of the damnation of Susan? Is growing up such an unforgivable crime? Why can't a person be "both a participant in matters spiritual and a sexual being" (Mills 17)? Are people like Susan predestined to be damned and excluded from heaven? Does anyone deserve anything dreadful and punishing, like the kind of tragedy experienced by Susan? These queries can be grouped into three big categories, namely (1) the question about the grounds of damnation, (2) the question about predestination, and (3) the question about suffering as a punishment for sins.

Misogyny and the Grounds for the Damnation of Susan

In *The Lion, the Witch and the Wardrobe* (1950), Professor Digory Kirke once says, "[y]es, of course you'll get back to Narnia again some day. Once a King in Narnia, always a King in Narnia" (*The Lion, the Witch and the Wardrobe* 170). Unfortunately, this does not seem to apply to Susan. Once a queen in Narnia, she is no longer a queen when Peter proclaims so in *The Last Battle* (1956). Susan is not getting back to Narnia either after appearing in three of the seven Narnia books. To pacify readers who do not feel comfortable about the mean treatment of Susan at the end of the Narnia series, C. S. Lewis says:

> The books don't tell us what happened to Susan. She is left alive in this world at the end, having by then turned into a rather silly, conceited young woman. But there's plenty of time for her to mend and perhaps she will get to Aslan's country in the end— in her own way [cited in Schakel 159].

However, what remains truly offensive is not whether Susan is given a second chance or not, but the grounds for damnation in Susan's case. Strictly following his Christian beliefs, C. S. Lewis disapproves of Susan's interest in fashion and beauty. Indeed, in the Holy Bible, the Proverbs disapproves of beauty: "[c]harm is deceptive, and beauty is fleeting" (*New International Version*, Prov. 31.30). In alignment with Solomon's remarks recited in Proverbs, Peter the Rock also warns women to guard against worldly possession: "[y]our beauty should not come from outward adornment, such as braided hair and the wearing of gold jewelry and fine clothes" (*New International Version*, 1 Pet. 3.3). A few Christian critics still support C. S. Lewis for shutting Susan out of heaven. It is argued that "Lewis does not condemn anyone's interests in nylons and lipsticks and invitations *per se*. Here he is critical of the fact that ... these have become Susan's *only* interest" (Brown 98). Nevertheless, in an interview with *Time*, J. K. Rowling expressed her concerns about the way Lewis condemns sex:

> There comes a point where Susan, who was the older girl, is lost to Narnia because she becomes interested in lipstick. She's become irreligious basically because she found sex. I have a big problem with that [cited in Grossman].

Philip Pullman, a prize-winning and best-selling British fantasy writer, finds Lewis's negative portrayal of Susan mean and unsympathetic as well. He suspects that Lewis is not only a misogynist, but also gynophobic, for his fear of womanhood and sexual maturity is blown out of proportion:

> Susan, like Cinderella, is undergoing a transition from one phase of her life to another. Lewis didn't approve of that. He didn't like women in general, or sexuality at all, at least at the stage in his life when he wrote the Narnia books. He was frightened and appalled at the notion of wanting to grow up [Pullman].

Gaiman, on the other hand, analyzes the matter from the perspective of Professor Hastings, who, just like Susan, has experienced the same tragic ordeal when she was a teenager. Through the voice of Professor Hastings, Gaiman reminds readers that the punishment for Susan is too devastating. It is hard to imagine that anyone orphaned by a trauma like Susan's would still have the desire to enjoy make-up and nice clothes: "I doubt there was much opportunity for nylons and lipsticks after her family was killed. There certainly wasn't for me" (Gaiman 177). By and large, as shown in Rowling's, Pullman's and Gaiman's responses, C. S. Lewis's antagonistic attitude towards the teenage girl's feminine beauty and female sexuality is largely perceived as unreasonable and unacceptable nowadays.

Predestination, or Restricted Heaven

Besides the issue of sexism towards women, the Calvinist notion of predestination subtly suggested in C. S. Lewis also irritates readers from far and wide. Firstly, in regards to the gravity of crime that the characters commit in *The Chronicles of Narnia*, Susan's feminine pride barely causes harm to others. It cannot be more sinful than Edmund Pevensie's gluttony and Eustace Scrubb's greed. As Kempton states: "Edmund ... quickly sells his siblings and ultimately his freedom to the White Witch for the promise of Turkish Delight. Eustace Scrubb sells his human form ... for a dragon's hoard of gold" (5–6). If God can forgive Edmund the traitor and Eustace the moneyholic, why can't God forgive Susan for her "lighter" sin? In Gaiman's short story, Greta Campion, the young journalist who also wondered why Susan is damned and denied access to heaven, says: "[t]here must have been something else wrong with Susan ... something they didn't tell us. Otherwise she wouldn't have been damned like that" (Gaiman 177).

Such unfairness illustrates the doctrine of Calvinist Christianity that the unchosen ones, regardless of how little they have sinned, remain damned.

Salvation is only granted to those who are preselected. Likewise, Aslan's heaven is restricted, and the Lion does not want everyone to enter heaven. People who were once followers can be kicked out if they are not ultimately the chosen ones. Interestingly, as long as they are chosen, undeserving sinners such as Edmund and Eustace shall nonetheless receive God's grace. Simply put, one's belief in God does not necessarily bring peace of mind, for no one can be certain whether he or she is chosen by God. Thus, rather than relying entirely on God's predestination, one should, despite all hardships, live one's life to the fullest so that there will be no regrets when looking back on one's life. This blissful transcendence is experienced by Professor Hastings in Gaiman's story: "the professor ... dreams that she is reading her own obituary. It has been a good life, she thinks, as she reads it, discovering her history laid out in black and white" (Gaiman 179). As Gaiman's short story suggests, with or without God's grace, the person who has led a meaningful life has already experienced the amazing grace. Entering heaven or not, it no longer matters.

Suffering as a Punishment for Sins

The loneliness and pain that Susan has to go through after the tragic train crash is also hair-raising. In "The Problem of Susan," Gaiman highlights Susan's suffering as he allows Professor Hastings, Susan Pevensie's exported character, to speak for Susan:

> My younger brother was decapitated, you know. A god who would punish me for liking nylons and parties by making me walk through that school dining room, with the flies, to identify Ed, well... he's enjoying himself a bit too much, isn't he? [Gaiman 178].

As Professor Hastings reveals, nothing can be compared to the shock, pain and horror she experienced when she had to identify her siblings' dead and mutilated bodies after the train wreck. In her blog, Nussbaum poses powerful discussion questions regarding C. S. Lewis's disturbingly unkind treatment of Susan:

> Nowadays, when I think of Susan, I think of what it must have been like for her to get the news. Her siblings, her parents, her cousin, her adopted aunt and uncle—everyone she loves in the world—have died a horrible, sudden death. Did Lewis really believe that Susan deserved that pain, or did he truly imagine that "but they're all in heaven" was sufficient to comfort her? Did he even care? [Nussbaum].

Such unreasonable cruelty is nothing new, though, for it is probably modeled after the notion of the rapture and the left behind. According to the Holy Bible, during the rapture, all Christian believers, dead or alive, will rise into the sky to join God. The non-believers who are not chosen by God will be left behind to suffer and die: "[t]wo men will be in the field: one will be taken and the other left. Two women will be grinding at the mill: one will be taken and the other left" (*New International Version*, Mat. 24.40). The triple punishment for the left behind includes the dreadful sudden loss of their loved ones, the unbearable burden to take care of all aftermaths, and the endless, intolerable suffering to come as they burn in hell forever.

Through "The Problem of Susan," Gaiman revisits the preposterous concept of the rapture. He reveals C. S. Lewis's sadistic cruelty towards Susan, as well as the anxiety and anger that Susan may have experienced when her family and friends suddenly left her after the train crash. The recollections of Professor Hastings bring up the most poignant but unanswerable religious questions of all time again: is God not all loving and forgiving? Why does God allow pain and suffering to happen? Does anyone ever deserve anything dreadful and punishing? Is God a sadist? Does God exist?

STYLE

Based upon the fantasy world of Narnia, Gaiman's short story is a metafiction that revisits C. S. Lewis's children's classic and reflects on "the adults' construct of the child, childhood and children's literature" (Skowera 73). According to Waugh, metafiction can be defined as follows:

> Metafiction is a term given to fictional writing which self-consciously and systematically draws attention to its status as an artefact in order to pose questions about the relationship between fiction and reality. In providing a critique of their own methods of construction, such writings not only examine the functional structures of narrative fiction, they also explore the possible fictionality of the world outside the literary fictional text [2].

In "The Problem of Susan," both female protagonists are educated feminists who are conscious of the impact children's fiction can have on young readers. In their conversation during the interview, the misogynistic tendency of C. S. Lewis is blatantly criticized. In addition to the interview, attention is drawn to Narnia's problematic gender stereotypes in different innovative forms. Three common features of metafiction, namely (1) the use of parody, (2) the use of characters' comments on their own or other stories, and (3) the mixing of genres, can be found in Gaiman's writing.

Parody

As a major form of "modern self-reflexivity" (Hutcheon 2), "parody consists in the imitation of external characteristics of any phenomenon in our life (a person's manners, expressions, etc.) that completely overshadows or negates the inner meaning of what is being parodied" (Propp 60). In Gaiman's short story, the creation of the protagonist Professor Hastings can be viewed as the parody which challenges C. S. Lewis's questionable treatment of Susan Pevensie in *The Chronicles of Narnia*. Having suffered the sudden loss of all her siblings in a train crash, Professor Hastings grew up with the pain that Susan Pevensie experiences. However, instead of being merely the mimicry of Susan, this grown-up version of Susan overthrows the superficial vanity girl image created by C. S. Lewis—like many women, Professor Hastings uses scented water, dresses up and wears lipstick not because of vainglory, but because of self-respect and politeness:

> [s]he smells like her grandmother smelled, like old women smell, and for this she cannot forgive herself ... so ... she dabs several drops of Chanel toilet water beneath her arms and on her neck [Gaiman 173].

As the device for parody in Gaiman's metafiction, the main character Professor Hastings also invites readers to get into Susan's shoes—in the real world outside of C. S. Lewis's Narnia books, how was it possible for a poor young woman like Susan to enjoy luxuries such as nylons and lipsticks during World War II? No way. The financial difficulty she had to face would not allow it. C. S. Lewis was not fair to Susan.

Characters Commenting on Their Own or Other Stories

Another fun characteristic of metafiction is that characters often comment on either their own story or other stories known to readers. For example, in "The Problem of Susan," Professor Hastings and Greta Campion make sensible comments on the plots and the characters of a number of children's classics. In the interview, Professor Hastings makes the comment that in Perrault's "Sleeping Beauty in the Wood" (1697), the plot is deeply questionable and therefore not meant for child readers. To support her view, she recites one of the most awkward moments of the fairy tale, where "the Prince's cannibal ogre mother attempts to frame the Sleeping Beauty for having eaten her own children" (Gaiman 175–176). Likewise, Greta brings up her dissatisfaction at Susan being rejected from heaven in the *Narnia* series. She comments: "[y]ou know, that [exile of Susan] used to make me so angry.... All the other kids go off to Paradise, and Susan can't go ... because she's too fond of lipsticks and nylons and invitations to parties" (Gaiman 176–177). As a matter of fact, the comments made by Greta are in alignment with the comments made by Neil Gaiman in a radio interview in 2005:

> each time I'd read them, I would get more and more irritated by the way that C. S. Lewis treated women of, let's say, reproductive age. Girls are cool and he had some terrific girls and there are some nice elderly women in there, but when it gets to sort of beautiful, nice women of reproductive age, they're wicked witches, they're ditsy, they're strange, they're evil, they're not to be relied upon [Conan].

Apparently, it is through the voices of the characters in the metafiction that Gaiman conveys his feelings about C. S. Lewis and the ending he wrote for the *Narnia* books.

Genre Mixing

Gaiman's metafiction also manifests features of genre mixing. On the one hand, the short story is a realistic fiction where the setting is believable; the story resembles real everyday life in contemporary England, and fictional characters such as Professor Hastings and Greta Campion react similarly to real people. On the other hand, the dream sequence in the text echoes the fantasy setting in Narnia, a magical place in which animals and creatures can talk and behave like men. Besides mixing realistic fiction with fantasy, the metafiction serves both as a literary critique and fictional work. While characters can criticize C. S. Lewis for his unkind treatment of Susan, they are still fictional characters created and dictated by the author, Neil Gaiman. Last but not least, the children's fantasy world of Narnia now shows signs of abject horror in the new version—in "The Problem of Susan," Susan's brothers, the Kings of Narnia, are betrayed by the lion and then uncannily transformed into "twisted thing[s]" (Gaiman 180) by the witch. As for Susan and her sister, there is also a detailed and disturbing description of how they are torn into pieces and devoured by the lion. Similarly, C. S. Lewis's children's series is now rewritten with erotic content. Through the omniscient narrative, readers read the mind of Susan/Professor Hastings/Greta, browsing through their wild sexual fantasy:

> The horse half of it [the centaur] is a vivid chestnut. Its human skin is nut-brown from the sun. She finds herself staring at the horse's penis, wondering about centaurs mating, imagines being kissed by that bearded face [Gaiman 172].

More controversially, Gaiman inserts an erotic scene between the White Witch and Aslan the Lion. The oral sex is initiated by the witch:

> The witch lies back upon the grass, spreads her legs. Beneath her body, the grass becomes rimed with frost. "Now," she says.
> The lion licks her white cleft with its pink tongue, until she can take no more of it [Gaiman 180].

Vibrant female sexuality is no longer suppressed in Gaiman's version. His use of hybrid genres totally subverts the fans and readers' perception of C. S. Lewis's Land of Narnia.

BIBLIOGRAPHY

Brown, Devin. "Are the Chronicles of Narnia Sexist?" *Women and C.S. Lewis: What His Life and Literature Reveal for Today's Culture*. Edited by Carolyn Curtis and Mary Pomroy Key. Oxford, England: Lion Books, 2015. 93–106. Print.

Campbell, Hayley. *The Art of Neil Gaiman*. East Sussex, UK: The Ilex Press, Ltd, 2014. Print.
Conan, Neal. "Children's Fantasy Lit in the Modern World." National Public Radio, 5 Dec 2005. https://www.npr.org/templates/transcript/transcript.php?storyId=5039319. Accessed on 11 May 2018.
Gaiman, Neil. "The Problem of Susan." *Fragile Things: Short Fictions and Wonders*. New York: HarperCollins Publishers, 2006. 172–181. Print.
Godfrey, Carole. "The 'Other' Narnia: Manifestations and Mutations of C.S. Lewis's *The Lion, The Witch and the Wardrobe* in Neil Gaiman's *Coraline*." *Mousaion* 33.2 (2015): 92–110. Print/web.
Grossman, Lev. "J.K. Rowling Hogwarts and All." *Time*, 17 July 2005. http://content.time.com/time/printout/0,8816,1083935,00.html. Accessed on 1 May 2018.
The Holy Bible, New International Version. Lutterworth, UK: Gideon, 1992. Print.
Hutcheon, Linda. *A Theory of Parody: The Teachings of Twentieth-Century Art Forms*. Urbana and Chicago: University of Illinois Press, 2000. Print.
Kempton, Emily Rose. *Hope for Susan: Moral Imagination in* The Chronicles of Narnia. Diss. Brigham Young University, 2016. Web. 25 April 2018.
Lewis, Clive Staples. *The Last Battle*. London: Grafton, 2002. Print.
_____. *The Lion, the Witch and the Wardrobe*. London: Grafton, 2002. Print.
Mills, Alice. "Spiritual, Not Sexual: The Plight of the Adolescent Human Wizard in Diane Duane's *Young Wizards* Series." *Supernatural Youth: The Rise of the Teen Hero in Literature and Popular Culture*. Edited by Jes Battis. Plymouth, UK: Lexington Books, 2011. 15–27. Print.
Nickel, Eleanor Hersey. "Whiner or Warrior? Susan Pevensie's Role in the Novel and Film Versions of The Chronicles of Narnia." *C.S. Lewis and the Inklings: Reflections on Faith, Imagination and Modern Technology*. Edited by Salwa Khoddam, Mark R. Hall, and Jason Fisher. New Castle upon Tyne, UK: Cambridge Scholars Publishing, 2015. Print/Web.
Nussbaum, Abigail. "All We Know of Heaven: The Problem of Susan." *Asking the Wrong Question*, 1 Dec 2005. http://wrongquestions.blogspot.hk/2005/12/all-we-know-of-heaven-problem-of-susan.html. Accessed on 14 Jan 2019.
Propp, Vladimir Iakovlevich. *On the Comic and Laughter*. Edited and translated by Jean-Patrick Debbeche and Paul Perron. Toronto, Buffalo and London: University of Toronto Press, 2009. Print.
Pullman, Philip. "The Dark Side of Narnia." *The Guardian*, 1 Oct 1998. http://www.crlamppost.org/darkside.htm. Accessed on 1 May 2018.
Reeder, Roberta. "The Fantastic: A Structural Approach to a Literary Genre by Tzvetan Todorov." *The Slavic and East European Journal* 20.2 (Summer, 1976): 196–189. Web.
Schakel, Peter J. *The Way into Narnia: A Reader's Guide*. Grand Rapids, Michigan and Cambridge, UK: William B. Eerdmans Publishing Company, 2005. Print.
Skowera, Maciej. "Fracturing the Canon: Towards Adulterated Children's Literature." *Fractures and Disruptions in Children's Literature*. Edited by Ana Margarida Ramos, Sandie Mourao, and Maria Teresa Cortez. New Castle upon Tyne, UK: Cambridge Scholars Publishing, 2017. 62–79. Print/Web.
Todorov, Tzvetan. *The Fantastic: A Structural Approach to a Literary Genre*. Translated by Richard Howard. Ithaca, NY: Cornell University Press, 1975. Print.
Tolkien, John Ronald Reuel. "On Fairy Tales." *Tree and Leaf* (1964): 11–70. Web.
Vaden, Matthew Brett. "Literature and Film: Fantasy Across Media." *Caesura* 2.2 (2015): 87–107. Print/Web.
Van Steenhuyse, Veerle. "The Writing and Reading of Fan Fiction and Transformation Theory." *CLCWeb: Comparative Literature and Culture* 13.4 (2011): 1–9. Web.
Waugh, Patricia. *Metafiction: The Theory and Practice of Self-Conscious Fiction*. London: Routledge, 2003. Print.
Zarzycka, Agata. "Liminality and Empowerment: The Aged Woman in Neil Gaiman's 'Queen of Knives' and 'Chivalry.'" *Feminism in the Worlds of Neil Gaiman: Essays on the Comics, Poetry and Prose*. Jefferson, NC: McFarland, 2012. 221–245. Print.

Part III

Literary and Comparative Analyses of Short Stories

7

Psychoanalysis and the Gothic in Poe's "The Fall of the House of Usher" and Stevenson's "The Strange Case of Dr. Jekyll and Mr. Hyde"

Whenever readers pick up a Gothic story, they will anticipate dark, gloomy, ghastly, and fearful elements in it. These are the bywords of Gothic that give rise to the almost formulaic perception of one of the most popular genres in literary history. Within this nearly calculable formula, readers who enjoy Gothic stories find the appeal irresistible and ever-lasting, and devour story after story even though envisaging the same kind of revulsion and horror. Gothic literature is like the dark arts hypnotizing readers without reason and logic. Such timeless and inexplicable success is attested by some classic novels such as *Frankenstein* (1818) by Mary Shelley and *Dracula* (1897) by Bram Stoker. Yet, to succinctly define the genre, delineate its development, and unravel the secret of its appeal, one must examine the Gothic short story. In this chapter, we are going to uncover the "dark psychic" behind the most mesmerizing genre in the world. Though our two references, "The Fall of the House of Usher" (1839) by Edgar Allan Poe and "The Strange Case of Dr. Jekyll and Mr. Hyde" (1886) by Robert Louis Stevenson, belong to the nineteenth century, they still remain massively influential today because they revolutionized the Gothic genre in their unique yet comparable style. Poe, an America writer, and Stevenson, a Scottish writer, were fascinated by Gothic fear and the human psyche; both deployed scientific art and elements of detective stories in their narratives, that are different from each other in settings and structures. Our analysis of the two Gothic stories mainly derives from Freudian, Lacanian, and Kohut's psychoanalytical approaches, of which the major tenets are ego psychology, the mirror stage, and self psychology. These serve our purpose to explore more in the individual than in the social and collective psyche. The Kantian philosophical perception of the sublime is also referred to in order to shed light on the psychological mechanism driven throughout a Gothic story. Within the scope of our study, we not only offer insight into the interplay between the mental process of dramatis personae and Gothic features distinctly found in short fiction, as well as the subtle literary nuances henceforth given rise to, but also question the validity and relevance of the three schools of psychoanalysis in explicating the Gothic elements of the genre, and consider if they are still reliable and applicable concepts.

ANALYTICAL CONCEPTS OF PSYCHOANALYSIS

The consensus to choose the three schools of thoughts is based on their influence on psychoanalysis and their relevance to our study. The psychoanalytic premise of our study does not seek to disregard other theories altogether nor rely on one set of theories. A comprehensive picture that can reflect complexity needs a collective sample of mainstream psychoanalysis, though some of the theories are certainly not free of problems. Freud's theories are subject to the fiercest attacks and continuous reassessment. His groundbreaking tenets rest upon the concept of the unconscious, which Freud posits as central to human consciousness. The structural model or its equivalent (the topographical or iceberg model) proposed consists of three components: id, ego, and superego, which are also known as unconscious, preconscious, and conscious. The developmental model pertaining to psychological development in childhood takes five psychosexual stages: oral, anal, phallic, latency, and genital. These three models simultaneously and interchangeably represent the mental structure, which marks a distinct Freudian view from his contemporaries. Post-Freudian models attempt to avoid such ambiguity and controversy by taking a more specific direction. Heinz Kohut, for example, built his model on the more comprehensible and constructive latent factor of "self" instead of libido, the evasive and, at times, destructive term Freud assigned as the core of unity. Kohut believes that consolidating and maintaining a positive, cohesive self is essential to our mental development. Whether such positivity can be achieved depends on the "self-selfobject" relationship and the three selfobject needs that help to shape the relationship. Among the three needs, namely, mirroring needs, idealizing needs, and twinship,[1] the last comes as the most crucial to our study. For the essential likeness shared between self and selfobject can be found in a wide range of contexts, from family to human race, which are all applicable to our example texts.

A further difference between Freud and Kohut lies in their views on narcissism. Instead of libido,[2] Kohut emphasizes the development of the self and object relations, and their responsibility for the transference of narcissism. Indeed, narcissism is an important concept in psychoanalysis, as it offers explanations to various kinds of psychotic disorders such as paranoia and multiple personality disorder, and is one of the themes of our selected works of Poe and Stevenson. The double they employed for each of their personae reflects the condition that personality disorders exert a mirror effect and arouse unpleasant feelings, namely the "uncanny" as Freud thought. In fact, many literary critics cannot touch on the Gothic subject without associating it with uncanniness. Its elusiveness and inclusiveness make it relevant to almost everything. Freud, who popularized the term in psychoanalytic criticism, was the first to demonstrate how it is visible throughout a horror story. In his paper "The Uncanny" (1919), Freud applies the concept to a number of literary examples to prove how some writers successfully manipulate uncanny factors to reach a horrendous effect. Our concern, however, is more than application. We shall prove the efficacy of Freud's theory of the uncanny with reference to our selected texts.

In a nutshell, the following comparison lends itself to the understanding of ego psychology from the perspective of self. Ego is like a specialized aspect of self; superego is the same as the internalized other as part of the self-structure, where narcissism is self-love, guilt is self-reproach, and censorship in dreams is self-observation in dreams (Rogers 33). Some other post–Freudian models classifying the atomistic elements include container of forces—libido and aggression; container of representations—memories, wishes, fantasies; the structure of representations—id, ego, superego, internalized others. Ego and internalized others in the last structure are some of Lacan's focuses. Seeing the conflicts between the models, Jacques Lacan asserts that the conflicts can be resolved if we first recognize the three basic Others, namely, Imaginary Other, Symbolic Other and Real Other,[3] which operate in transference. Each of these Others represents a different psychic level through which we obtain various kinds of gratification, but the last as a non-meaning entity also relates back to the Freudian concept of uncanniness. All three Others, which originate from the infantile mirror stage, depend on external objects such as friends, an organization, or a system. However, we shall extend the scope of the mirror stage to inanimate objects, which in the Gothic context provide abundant sublime gratification. The three Others, thus, represent a more rigorous set of models to further elaborate on the protagonists' psyche, as their deep structures can be mapped, to various extents, onto those of the protagonists and yield a clearer picture.

The Genre Development of Gothic Literature

Alongside the analytical concepts, the genre development is equally fascinating but no less complicated. Like every genre, Gothic literature has its own history; unlike others, the development embarked upon a peculiar course. It all started with Horace Walpole using his novella *The Castle of Otranto* (1764) for subterfuge.[4] Proclaiming its "truthfulness" from the origin of the script to the setting (Walpole, "Preface to the First Edition" 11–12), the novella successfully deceived readers who had never experienced such nightmarish reading. As absurd as the story seems, it laid the groundwork for the Gothic genre thereafter as no other previous works had. The key ingredients to assail yet entertain readers are set forth in the prefaces of both the first and the second editions: "[m]iracles, visions, necromancy, dreams, and other preternatural events" (ibid. 8–9), blending with the ancient and the modern Romances (Walpole, "Preface to this Second Edition" vi), the sublime (ibid. viii), and the following rules:

> There is no bombast, no similes, flowers, digressions, or unnecessary descriptions. Everything tends directly to the catastrophe.... Terror, the author's principal engine, prevents the story from ever languishing; and it is so often contrasted by pity, that the mind is kept up in a constant vicissitude of interesting passions [Walpole, "Preface to the First Edition" 9].

Barbaric, derogatory, and distasteful, the tone of the novella is determinedly set against the moralistic, aesthetic, modern, and bourgeois values upheld in the Age of Enlightenment. Lacking the knowledge, reason, and logic that define the Enlightenment, the Gothic story was initially seen as a mockery of self-righteousness, excessive norms and arrogance of the advancement of the period, and was rightly trivialized by critics. However, the first wave (around the 1810s) and the second wave (between the 1820s and the 1830s) of Gothic literature proved that the genre deserved much higher regard than it had received. It was during the second wave that Poe took inspiration from Walpole's "recipe" and created the timeless Gothic tale "The Fall of the House of Usher." Yet, Poe was not the first short story writer to create using Walpole's machinery. In 1773, John Aikin published "Sir Bertrand: A Fragment," a sketch considered to be the first Gothic tale, which ticks off many items on the Gothic spreadsheet: a dark and moonlit night; an abandoned, large, antique mansion in disrepair; a vault; an intricate, winding passage; a knight caught up in terror; ghostly figures; and a spell. In short, it is a chivalric Gothic folk tale with a touch of the human psyche. Some critics contend that it was also an experiment using the Gothic principles laid out by his sister,

Anna Laetitia Aikin, in "On the Pleasure Derived from Objects of Terror." The manifesto echoes as well as elaborates on Walpole's prefaces. On the one hand, the key substances are reiterated—"the well-wrought scenes of artificial terror which are formed by a sublime and vigorous imagination" (*Miscellaneous Pieces* 125). On the other, it reveals how our mental faculties are worked up through the painful pleasure of reading:

> A strange and unexpected event awakens the mind, and keeps it on the stretch; and where the agency of invisible beings is introduced, of "forms unseen, and mightier far than we," our imagination, darting forth, explores with rapture the new world which is laid open to its view, and rejoices in the expansion of its powers. Passion and fancy cooperating elevate the soul to its highest pitch; and the pain of terror is lost in amazement [ibid.].

The paradox is laid bare. Our conflicting sensations—fears and pleasures— arouse craving for painful yet sensual desire such that sensible and moral resistance has to but yield. This aptly explains why terror in literature, from the Greco-Roman tragedy to the Eastern Tale, has never lost its appeal and is emphasized in Gothic stories.

Although Aikin's psychoanalytical approach is reader-oriented rather than content- and form-oriented, it was the first to offer a glimpse of how our mind works on Gothic romance. More than a hundred years later, Freud developed his theory in "Beyond the Pleasure Principle" (1920), which takes a similar yet more scientific and comprehensive approach. Once our inquisitiveness is stimulated, it will not be suppressed until it is satisfied. It is an instinctual response to an external stimulus. The more negative (in Aikin's case, the wilder and more fanciful [ibid. 126]) it is, the more excitement it induces: "[t]he repressed instinct never ceases to strive for complete satisfaction, which would consist in the repetition of a primary experience of satisfaction. No substitutive or reactive formations and no sublimations will suffice to remove the repressed instinct's persisting tension" ("Beyond the Pleasure Principle" 42). The common goals and the key to success that Gothic writers strive for are to reach the height of internal excitation, as well as to prolong tensions regardless of morality and sense so as to entertain.

In the Gothic world, it is the negativity of the form and the content that makes the maneuver towards sensual pleasure. From wild landscapes to ruinous buildings, unspeakable secrets and inconspicuous intruders, they all possess the negative power to disrupt our natural law, order, harmony, and ultimately, subjective unity. That unpleasure is itself a kind of sublime peculiar to the Gothic genre.[5] The aesthetic value subsumed under the Gothic sublimity is neither beauty nor norms validated universally but an intellectual feeling that elevates our imagination towards dark and profound truth, which apparent (or positive) beauty disguises.[6] The psychical energies from the quest-driven life instinct attempt to surpass the limit of imagination until they reach the deepest level, which is the unconscious, and heighten the shocking effect. The unpleasure aroused will then be pacified by pleasure, as one eventually apprehends the hidden truth or the fact that the limit cannot be surpassed anymore. As such, the recurring motif in Gothic literature revolves around the sublime in two feelings—unpleasure foreshadowed by pleasure. The human psyche essentially operates as the interface between them. From the Freudian point of view, the unconscious cannot be unlocked without probing into one's early (usually from toddlerhood to childhood) traumatic experiences. Through the process, the memories repressed will be unleashed to reveal the darkest secrets. This might account for Gothic writers' penchant for relating, directly or indirectly, protagonists' inexplicable past (sometimes a reflection of writers' own pasts, such as Poe's) to the present occurrence. The psychological complexity largely depends on how the surroundings arouse yet repress the intricate feelings. Gothic settings are the catalyst for protagonists' psychic journeys. The transference of sublimity from nature and objects to the beholder's mind completes the journey of unpleasure and eventually returns to pleasure.

THE MIRROR MOTIF OF THE GOTHIC

One type of external force exploited in Gothic settings is the moon. Its obscurity and remoteness are always interpreted as an inauspicious sign, so much so that the perceived almighty and supernatural power is on par with catastrophes. Moonlight, for example, plays a significant role in transforming human beings into werewolves or vampires in Bram Stoker's classic stories. Likewise, in "The Strange Case of Dr. Jekyll and Mr. Hyde," Hyde, the doppelgänger of Jekyll, turns violent and murders Sir Danvers Carew on a moonlit night. The moon's power over human beings is as transformative as it is ominous. The moon deployed in "The Fall of the House of Usher," on the other hand, takes on the power to transform an object: "[t]he radiance was that of the full, setting, and blood-red moon, which now shone vividly through that once barely-discernible fissure ... extending from the roof of the building, in a zigzag direction, to the base" (102). The whirlwind adds to the force and aggravates the damage, making the cleavage visible and cracking it open until the wall can no longer hold. Yet, the moon conceived as the external causative force for the collapse cannot complete itself without a yet darker and more elusive force. The force lies within and without. Thus, when it emits the power upon the object, the moon itself also serves as a mirror for the character, which fits Gothic narratives and is compatible with Lacanian theories. The transformation into a complete image of self through an internal force cannot take place without a mirror. It is the catalyst to accelerate the transformative process until its finality. As such, the bright, full moon appearing at the end of the story is synonymous with a mirror that gives an image of wholeness. It constitutes the ego and counteracts the fragmented entity symbolized by the facade of the house. Roderick has regained the complete ego through collating its fragmented pieces. It ends his inexplicable suffering and inner torments.

The lake near the mansion where the narrator ventures to in the hope of altering the aura of misery is another mirror. It absorbs the power of nature and pierces into the unconscious so that the image not only becomes crystal clear but unnerving. It is not at all surprising when in reality many mysterious and supernatural things are found in lakes, as our fantasies and wishes projected onto the water's surface give us a haunted feeling. For example, lake monsters, with the Loch Ness Monster the most famous, are reported all over the world from time to time. In Welsh folklore and American and Scottish literature, lakes play an important part in passing on legends to descendants. Ray Bradbury set his story "The Lake" (1944) precisely in a lake to bring out the traumatic experience the protagonist had with his female childhood playmate and to show how it has haunted him for a decade. Poe himself was so fascinated by the mystic power of lakes that he wrote the poem "The Lake" in 1827 based on a legend of a young couple that drowned in Dismal Swamp in Virginia.

The lake as the "natural" mirror has such an impact on the personae that they are either seduced unaware or determined to avoid it, like Roderick, who confines himself in the barely lit, dilapidated, gloomily decorated mansion, and acts as another person whom the narrator barely knows or has not wished to recognize since boyhood. Roderick lets his self fragment, until destiny calls upon his soul and body to unite. Such a desperate attempt to avoid being caught by the lights (both indoors and outdoors) is fathomable when one does not wish to have a complete self. By the same token, Jekyll takes the laboratory in a building in a backyard as his shelter so that he can gather all the dark power from the gloomy surroundings. The windowless theater in the building in which he once lectured is now deserted, messy, and deadly silent. Its stillness is a chilling reminder of the olden days as if everybody was petrified and everything was frozen. Such an atmosphere is oppressive in an illogical and speechless sense. It is there on the upper floor that he, like Roderick, hides himself when succumbing to fate, while Dr. Jekyll's doppelgänger, Mr. Hyde, acts at night most of the time like any vampire or werewolf.

Away from nature posed as a mirror, we do have loved ones at home or elsewhere that suit the purpose of reflection, and through them, Lacan believes our image can be identified (*Écrits* 76). The fundamental premise of the mirror stage and the symbolic order posits that when an infant encounters a mirror, he or she is struck by an image of himself or herself as a whole. This contrasts with the previous experience of a fragmented entity with libidinal needs. Lacan describes the mirror image as the "Ideal-I," in other words, the ideal ego that provides an image of wholeness against the chaotic reality of the body. Unlike Freud, who proposes the cause for such image as the exertion of an external force, Lacan sees it as a sudden self-realization acted upon by a latent force already possessed by the person. Jekyll acquires a mirror to indulge himself in the transformation into his double Hyde because his intuition tells him that there is nothing to be ashamed of in seeing another side of him even though it is "tenfold more wicked" ("The Strange Case of Dr. Jekyll and Mr. Hyde" 57), as it is just every man's "dual nature" (ibid. 55). The mirror, therefore, functions as the liberation of his repressed ego and regaining of his ideal ego. It can be our human instinctual desire to release ourselves from the ego bondage, as Jekyll feels instantly relieved looking at himself in the mirror and admiring his double. It spares him all kinds of effort to pursue perfection and to please others, an act that cannot and does not speak his real self. Returning to his ideal ego gratifies himself enormously, as he regains total control of his body and mind. He is not subject to anyone but himself. Playing between the virtual complex and reality, he thinks he has become the master of himself or humanity at large, for fate is finally in his hand. Egocentric, he is ultimately granted freedom as well as choice of his own to manipulate the two selves. Such "delight terror" is no more than a narcissistic act and symbolic stage of infancy. The mirror is here to fulfill his egoistic dream.

Looming as a shadow, the mirror image nevertheless dominates our lives. It is the nucleus of all matters, such as life and death. Henceforth, Madeline, the image and twin sister of Roderick, is revived after being coffined for days to take her brother's life. Even though she is in a cataleptic state, the scene mythically and romantically links to strigoica[7]—the entombed body transforming into a full-fledged vampire, leaving her casket in a stormy night, reinvigorating through blood-sucking. Her brother is the only surviving close family member who becomes a victim. Although on the surface, it looks like a revengeful act of one's oppressed ego, it is, in fact, an urge to complete the ego as a whole. On the way to completion, the superstitious belief torments his soul and the psychic power of the witch-like sister depletes his body. Similarly, the laboratory is a casket for Jekyll, where he gathers all the psychic power to rejuvenate himself—a "mature vampire" launching onslaughts at night. It is part of the ego that possesses and exhausts him through "assaults of temptation" (ibid. 65) until the power of Hyde takes hold of sickly Jekyll, eats up his body and soul, then makes him perish.

While mirrors serve a microscopic function in a Gothic text, dwellings take the macroscopic role. Kohut's self psychology offers a lucid account for the operation of the latter in a Gothic text. The four key elements that compose the model are nuclear, virtual, cohesive, and grandiose selves. Although Kohut applied the theory in the human mental apparatus, we believe that it can extend to objects for similar results. Conceptually speaking, the facade of the house reveals the "outside" you. The inside of the house reflects one's true nature, that is, the "inside" you. In "The Strange Case of Dr. Jekyll and Mr. Hyde," the front and the back entrances of the same house exemplify such difference. The front door through which Jekyll enters is located in an upscale part of the city, while the back door Hyde uses is on a shabby, downmarket side street. A significant part is devoted to the description of the glamorous decoration of the entrance hall at the front door compared to the less than impressive description of the back entrance. As such, the house manifests itself as the cohesive self or, more precisely, as an integral part of body and soul, which is divided between the nuclear self grimly portrayed as a hideout for hideous Hyde and the virtual self fancifully depicted as a dream room for respectable Jekyll.

THE GOTHIC HOMES AND HAUNTS

The opposite is demonstrated in the setting of "The Fall of the House of Usher." The inside and the outside of the house are both permeated with an air of stiffness and staleness. The uninviting atmosphere is consistent in and out. To the narrator, the outside of the house is an unbearable scene: "the bleak walls ... the vacant eye-like windows ... a few rank sedges ... a few white trunks of decayed trees" ("The Fall of the House of Usher" 87). Yet, the inside is equally insufferable: "the somber tapestries of the walls, the ebon blackness of the floors" (ibid. 89). The strange fancy that grows in the narrator's mind upon seeing Usher's home is further enhanced by "the phantasmagoric armorial trophies" (ibid.). The nuclear self and the virtual self both merge into the cohesive self seamlessly as if it were needless to forge a difference. Undisguised, the outside of the house reveals the naked self. Roderick apparently wishes guests and neighbors (if any) to judge him as they do to the house: "[t]he now ghastly pallor of the skin, and the now miraculous lustre of the eye" (ibid. 90). The "wild inconsistency between its still perfect adaptation of parts and the crumbling condition of the individual stones" (ibid. 89) observed by the narrator also speaks mostly of Roderick's inconsistent manner—vivacious and sullen, indecision and concision (ibid. 90–91).

Freud sees a dwelling synonymous with a powerhouse that charges libido so that the inexplicable horror is generated throughout. His most anthologized essay "The 'Uncanny'" sets Poe's story right at the heart of the genre. The word "house" appears now and then in the list of definitions of "uncanny" and its antonym "canny." It is there we find the antithesis of comfort and discomfort, familiarity and unfamiliarity, friendliness and unfriendliness, peace and "unpeace," pleasure and "unpleasure," security and insecurity. A "house" is thus a hothouse of intense struggles yet a place to hide our deepest secrets, which psychoanalysts and Gothic writers like to imagine as the mother's womb. When the narrator happens to find in Usher's house "a small picture [that] presented the interior of an immensely long and rectangular vault or tunnel, with low walls, smooth, white, and without interruption or device" (ibid. 93), it is not at all surprising if we coincidentally conjure up an image of female genitalia. In fact, Freud sees the womb as the source of infantile libidinal energy. Right from birth we are brought into a world of unfamiliarity and taught to understand the world as it is, but all the time our childhood phantasies forewarn us otherwise: the world is not as familiar as we like to believe. Our mental struggle is between familiarity and unfamiliarity, and that, as Freud argues, gives rise to the uncanny effect in horror stories. No one does a better job than the narrator in "The Fall of the House of Usher" to elucidate the uncanny feeling: "[w]hile the objects around me ... were ... which, I had been accustomed from my infancy—while I hesitated not to acknowledge how familiar was all this—I still wondered to find how unfamiliar were the fancies which ordinary images were stirring up" (89).

Gothic buildings and surroundings are props writers heavily deploy in stories to bring out the uncanny effect. The negative energy feeds on the seclusion and darkness so as to preserve and empower the libido in the unconscious. Backdrops such as (semi-)deserted castles and mansions in wild landscapes take the enormous and labyrinthine structure with vaults and passages to portend evil so that the persona is enveloped in isolation and rendered helpless rather than rationally seeking positivity outside. The sheer size creates such an opposite effect that instead of comforting and liberating oneself at home, the persona is imprisoned as long as the unspeakable truth holds. Thus, we found the vaults in Usher's ruinous mansion reappear in Jekyll's stately house, albeit a laboratory, and the labyrinths in both, all of which function as a form of physical and mental confinement rather than a cozy dwelling. The oppressive force is neither diminished nor changed but combats the conscious. The psychic power manifests in ominous forms like paintings, vaults, or more ghastly, a combination of both in Usher's mansion sucks the soul and, at times, distorts the shape of the body, while simultaneously supplying the victim with abundant energy to act impetuously. That energy repressed in the unconscious and masked by consciousness finds the outlet when daylight vanishes. The inertia that freezes one's mental state and self-perpetuates one's own superstitious belief accumulates more libidinal energies. Self-fulfillment of prophecy spins violently like a merry-go-round except that "merry" is replaced by scaremongering. It is that repetition-compulsion in the unconscious mind Freud ascribes to the uncanny. The involuntary repetition is as fateful as inescapable, and creepy enough to disturb people so that they can only resort to superstitious and other irrational causes to explain away the situation. When Roderick and Jekyll display similar repetitive patterns, they look as if they are spell-bound. Choosing to withdraw from the social circle, the former ardently believes that it is an unbreakable curse put on the bloodline, and unknowingly yields to superstition, which in reality can be dispelled through positivity, as the narrator tries to do during the first few days of his visit. The latter, on the other hand, puts himself into a test in an attempt to break the curse of mankind at the risk of death as well as a condemnable and unrepentant human failing.

Reclusive setting as the quintessential element forms the backbone of Gothic stories. Castles, wild and rural landscapes among others provide writers with plentiful resources and ignite their imagination, apart from inciting the spooky and unspeakable sensations, which remain deeply locked in the unconscious. A fascinating, thrilling, and mysterious atmosphere does arouse our bodily, mental, or sexual desire. It is an instinctual response to an abysmal setting. In a city, it is the by-street that does the magic. Stevenson is particularly famous for reinventing Gothic settings in urban cities like London. In the late nineteenth century, London had already garnered its literary fame through Dickensian Gothic portrayal. Yet, compared to Stevenson's portrayal, Dickens's is akin to a geographical description and alludes to the political atmosphere, while the former establishes a link between the cityscape and the persona's complex psychology (Mighall, "Introduction" xxxi). It is in this sense that Stevenson's depiction of London draws greater similarity to Poe's rural settings than Dickens's. When readers visualize the city wrapped up in fog and dimness, they are chilled by the same kind of nightmarish aspects of the wild landscape. Such a technique of defamiliarization making the recognizable city strikingly remote and unreal enhances the uncanny effect. Right at the heart of this "familiarity" breeds an evil which eventually takes every reader and every persona by shock.

Worth noting, though, is that the direct formula developed for Gothic stories may lose its effect when applied in other genres. The fairy tale is a clear example. "Cinderella" deploys the necessary elements yet hardly scares readers. The mirror that speaks in "Snow White" fails to evoke the uncanny feeling. It is because we are well aware that fairy tales have their settings and personae completely detached from reality. So long as the writer faithfully presents the animistic system of beliefs, the reader and, to a large extent, the persona will not be painfully stirred by the sudden transformation of an inanimate object into an animate one or thunder into a monster. Only when the norm prescribed to such a genre is deviated from can the stories achieve the effect of horror. Aikin's "Sir Bertrand, a Fragment" is an early attempt to blur the antithesis between fantasy and reality to procure the uncanny quality. The personae are crafted to fit the framework of the traditional fairy tale and yet the atmosphere impregnated with pure terror[8] is decisively against the norm. The typical medieval setting associated with vastness and emptiness contributes to sublime horror capable of making readers and the protagonist shiver (Burke, *Philosophical Enquiry* Part II Sect. VI, VII), the latter being overwhelmed by scenes of a powerful nature and the immense building of terror and passion. That the irresistible temptation urges him to repeat the painful and distressful experience even when he perceives the danger of venturing is itself evidence of repetition-compulsion.

Poe and Stevenson stepped up their game with their psychological fantasies by pushing the boundary so that readers and the personae can no longer distinguish reality from fantasy. The skills required to take the personae to their psychological complexity rest mainly upon characterization, settings, situations, and events governed by the pleasure principle. Theoretically speaking, we all have a mental reservoir of unconscious repression that seeks to surface to consciousness, which is reflected by our senseless compulsive repetition of contemporary experiences with little conviction. While the conservative instincts impel toward repetition, the unconscious containing all the instincts that drive towards the restoration of an earlier state of things becomes a driving force and the true reality of the psyche as well as the prior stage to the conscious. To turn repression into remembrance, in other words, from the unconscious to the conscious, such that an earlier state of things will be restored, requires significant work mainly through transference. Gothic settings are synonymous with this transference and correspond to the aforementioned catalyst. The protagonist under siege in such surroundings is constantly seduced by external excitement, which adds to the tension between unpleasure and pleasure. Between unknowing and knowing, liberating and limiting, the protagonist has to survive the test of physical and mental strength such that a subjective judgment upon the sublime nature and objects is reached, which procures sublimity and resides in the mind of the beholder. Put in a psychological perspective, the psychic journey can be readily called to completion when order and time are restored, repressed material surfaces to the conscious so that the experience will stop repeating itself. While many Gothic writers emphasize the latter process in their works, time and order might be seen as less important elements. The manner in which the knight proceeds to his finality in "Sir Bertrand, a Fragment" is calculating and chronological—a defiance of the unconscious regardless of the intimidating atmosphere the setting creates. The turbulent journey as such can only partially reflect the mental process of the unconscious.

POE'S TWIN ENIGMA AND STEVENSON'S SPLIT SELF

Interestingly, the abrupt transition from the vault to the feast in the final scene of the story gives the reader a sense of dreaminess. Although transitioning from negative pleasure to positive pleasure and from pain to delight, the knight seems to complete his psychic journey, yet the abruptness suggests otherwise, as if two discrete timeless episodes were jumbled together. Deconstruction of the time delineation indicates that such a pairing of consistency and inconsistency raises the question of the validity of actions taken by the personae. The boundary between real and unreal is obscured. In such cases, some readers fancy the adventure as reality and the feast as the dream, and others vice versa. The fluidity open to multi-faceted interpretations makes the Gothic tale more than a psycho thriller. It is about human defiance of nature and resetting the boundary. In "The Strange Case of Dr. Jekyll and Mr. Hyde," the devil always finds a chance to sneak into Jekyll's dream and transform into Hyde: "if I slept, or even dozed for a moment in my chair, it was always as Hyde that I awakened" (68). Hyde is a product Jekyll creates to test the inborn biological system, which in reality is aided by drugs. Yet, a fanciful version is that the dream-like process kicks in with the help of the potion and empowers itself day by day through dreams such that in the later transformation, Hyde manages to conquer the body of Jekyll, presumably his master, with no medical help, and reverses the relations. It is the former who now becomes the master and the latter the corpse-like servant "eaten up and emptied by fever ... and solely occupied by one thought: the horror of my other self" (ibid.). In the dream, it is the unconscious that takes over the reins and introduces the impossible. What is so unsettling about Gothic tales is that we are warned that reality could possibly be subverted and the norms taken for granted might not necessarily hold water. Our fantasy is the realm of troubled water, yet it could dominate reality one day. With the medical advancement Stevenson projected that muddles fantasy and reality, we might be tempted to reevaluate Freud's remark: "a wishful phantasy that emerges in a dream" ("Beyond the Pleasure Principle" 36). Some day when a dream will not be a dream anymore, when the borderline between imagination and reality can be effaced, will an uncanny effect still be able to successfully create what will terrify us?

For all the possibilities, therein lies yet a bigger and indestructible charm to allure readers to the nightmarish reading. Fear is the most powerful engine that propels the Gothic gospel—the grim phantasm that lurks in Roderick's and other personae's mind. The fear upon discovering the daemonic power of the unconscious is a theme that recurs throughout the genre. The devilish victor licks the blood of the vanquished. The savage leaves one petrified. Yet, the unconscious always overpowers the conscious. The shadowy yet invincible object pulls the strings and puppeteers its master. It is not as much of a tug of war as the subject-object relation that pedals the fear and keeps up the tension. In "Beyond the Pleasure Principle," Freud defines fear with reference to danger that it "requires a definite object of which to be afraid" (12). The relation between subject and object in Gothic stories is, thus, a manifestation of fear. Put simply, the excitement cannot do without a fearful object, be it animate or inanimate. Settings, for example, are overt objects to manipulate for an immediate effect. Human beings or half humans are covert subjects and normally require more subtleties than settings to depict and incite horror, though the pronounced features of vampires and werewolves alone are frightful enough to induce the effect. Personae without noticeable differences of physique from any of us are the most complex to deploy to arouse the uncanny feelings. Such arousal must, therefore, be incited by the mental apparatus, for instance, the antithesis between the conscious and the unconscious.

In Poe's Gothic tale, the narrator cannot tell the difference between twin brother and sister, Roderick and Madeline. Only through the psychological lens that magnifies the nuances can they be torn apart. They mirror each other and each constitutes half of the split personality, which, according to Freud, is ego split—I and You. Madeline, who never speaks to the narrator, takes the covert form of a fearful object analogous to the unconscious. The mentally fragile Roderick exhibits the symptoms of the weakened conscious. Stevenson in his Victorian Gothic story took it further by toying with the idea of both physical and psychological factors. On the one hand, it is young Hyde's distorted countenance, short stature, and light body that distinguish him from old Jekyll's smooth face, large figure, and aging body. On the other hand, their temperaments mark them as father-like and son-like figures respectively: "Jekyll had more than a father's interest; Hyde had more than a son's indifference" ("The Strange Case of Dr. Jekyll and Mr. Hyde" 63).

A more dynamic approach to explore I and You is through Kohut's self psychology that steers away from the classical Freudian terms. As mentioned at the beginning of the chapter, Kohut's tenets differ from the traditional principles of psychoanalysis in that he ascribes self rather than the conflict between the drives to human essential nature. The four components previously applied to objects are proposed vis-à-vis the human—the nuclear self ("inside" you), the virtual self ("outside" you), the cohesive self ("inside" and "outside" you), and the grandiose self ("big" you)—throughout the development of the self and object relations. When we are born, a nuclear self has already assumed its place, and then comes the virtual self—an image of the newborn's self that resides in the minds of the parents. The interaction between the nuclear self and the virtual self subsequently forms the child's cohesive self with which a living self organizes the ego activities (Brinich 46). Appearing at a later stage out of the normal infantile experience is the omnipotent grandiose self—the center of all experience and reflection of perfectionism every child is macde to pursue by the doting par ents who revive and reproduce their own narcissism. It echoes Freud's quip "His Majesty the Baby" (91) in his paper "On Narcissism: An Introduction" (1914).

The insight Kohut offers is critical to our study. Self cannot exist by itself but requires an object to interact with in order to complete the development. The self-object relations feed on the needs of mirroring and idealizing, and are commonly found between children and parents, the latter being available, satisfying the needs of the former. The theory brings light to the development of the relationship between Jekyll and Hyde. As the "father," Jekyll presumes at the beginning that what he needs to do is just indulge his "son" Hyde with all the needs that "[center] on self" ("The Strange Case of Dr. Jekyll and Mr. Hyde" 60). To Jekyll's dismay, it does the opposite. The more he gives, the more Hyde wants, to such an extent that the give-and-take can no longer be justified as purely good pleasure but "an inherently malign and villainous" (ibid.) act. He who laughs last, laughs longest. Not only has Jekyll grossly miscalculated the result, but he has turned himself into a slave. Such a grave mishap could have been avoided had the doting father set limits in order to cultivate a healthy and balanced relationship. The problem is, how do we delimit that relationship? When should parents decide to take things in hand and stop their child's behavior? Jekyll probably has not thought of that, let alone the dire consequences of such a relationship. At the back of his mind, it is just an experiment to free the dark side from being caged. With hindsight, he should have a hunch that the relationship would be destined to doom because the patriarchal system always prefers an inflexible, unified self to the divided, disintegrating selves, which disturb the Symbolic Order (Tso 223). The conflict between Jekyll and Hyde was a replica of our daily yet perennial struggle of the conscious and the unconscious. It shall never be resolved, nor the unconscious be appeased.

Regarding the twinship model fulfilling another self-object need, Kohut argues that the likeness twins share with each other in a family, a community, or the human race is important to develop in order to maintain a positive, cohesive sense of self (Fosshage 240). Although the childhood of the Usher twins is not disclosed in detail in Poe's tale, we can see that the intimate bond shared between them is so tight that when one physically collapses, the other is affected immediately to an alarming extent (mentally and physically), synonymous with a domino effect. The positive sense of self sought through the twinship can barely be sustained because of the loss of the self-object portrayed by his twin sister Madeline. Misfortunes never come singly. The negative impact culminated not only destroys the positive self of Roderick but the entire Usher race, for Madeline has mirrored their parents, especially their mother, and their female ancestral line long since he lost them. Her existence is the key to feeding Roderick's mirroring needs and idealizing needs. Being deprived of this is as detrimental as parental criticism and denigration. It is a small wonder that Roderick suffers from manic depression. In Kohut's opinion, Roderick is no more than a "Tragic Man" ("Introspection, Empathy, and the Semi-circle of Mental Health" 402), who fails to exercise his own life plan, and should, therefore, be spared from all kinds of guilt that Freud alleges. The charges pressed on him by Freud naturally go back to our perennial instinctual struggles. Cruel as the verdict seems, Freudian narcissistic theory may otherwise explain the fate that befalls Roderick and Jekyll—they reap what they sow.

It is clear from the onset that Roderick and Jekyll have been preoccupied with the issue of self-preservation. They do it for their own dignity, thereby, benefiting their families. As Freud attributes this instinctual measure to part of our ego, it is assumed that we are all born with certain primary narcissistic traits and gradually learn to direct the libidinal energy thereof to objects in the external world. The success rate varies but the threshold we painfully avoid to trespass is the same, that is, not to turn it into perversion. Yet, it does not guarantee a lifelong success, and this is the case of Roderick and Jekyll. Regardless of the justifiable causes each brings to his own audience, Freud would pin them down to the same category—megalomania, "an over-estimation of the power of their wishes and mental acts, the 'omnipotence of thoughts,' a belief in the thaumaturgic force of words" ("On Narcissism: An Introduction" 75). In other words, it is their delusion about their own power or importance (Jekyll in his medical knowledge and Roderick about the Usher family) that costs them their lives, rather than a lack of love or attention from the "selfobject," as Kohut argues. The phantasy they each build manifests simultaneously the opposition between ego-libido and object-libido, and self-destructive power in extremity, doubly so in Roderick when all his libidinal cathexes are poured into Madeline as the object fantasy on the one end, but flow altogether back to his ego on the other when frustration overwhelms him. His self-perception of the end of the world looms large, which nothing can stop, not even when the narrator, with good intentions, directs his attention toward the external object—his favorite romance "The Mad Trist." Aside from the doubt raised by the choice of the object to displace the morbid anxiety, his mental resistance is almost impossible to temper in any case.

As in Poe's tale, there is no clear clue about Jekyll's upbringing in "The Strange Case of Dr. Jekyll and Mr. Hyde," but his narcissistic attitude is not hard to trace from the beginning. His strong but naive self-belief is deeply rooted in his upbringing.

The creation of his object fantasy, Hyde, is but to gratify Jekyll himself or to fulfill an impossible childhood dream. Blindfolded by his greed, he daringly challenges the law of nature and dreams to separate the self into two entities so that the unjust will walk free without the just bearing any guilt. For some time, he also pours all his libidinal cathexes into Hyde to maintain the erotic relations. Little does he know that the love he professes to the latter is no more than a reflection of his own narcissism. He does what all narcissistic parents would do to revive and reproduce self-love so much that hush money has to be paid out to conceal the harm Hyde has done to a girl. It is a disgrace Jekyll soon discovers, but as he languishes with narcissistic perfection and obsession with the medical achievement to the brink of dissociative identity disorder, moral conscience in accordance with reality wears thin. All comes too late when he decides to withdraw from the game. Lying in the laboratory contorted and twitching, he seals his fate with Freud's damning verdict.

The Gothic Doppelgänger and Psychoanalysis

Like psychoanalysts, Gothic writers throw light on personality but through a different set of schemes. They create personae and pull the strings behind the scene, hence making the stories sound more credible than the research done by psychoanalysts. Stevenson's portrayal of Jekyll and Hyde in 1886 set a clear example of split personality and, to date, is widely adopted as the definition of the psychotic disease in dictionaries or alluded to in texts concerning the issue. The legacy Stevenson left ascertains the possible mission other Gothic writers undertake to rewrite the rules of human psychology. Twins and the doppelgänger are particularly their favorite choice to use for such a challenge, since human personalities are ungraspable without the signified role of the double. The connection the double establishes is far more than just a physical form. Besides the mirror reflection we have discussed, they are the guardian spirits with the belief in the soul and the fear of death (Freud, "The Uncanny" 9). The doppelgänger traditionally carries eerie and paranormal allegorical meaning, as Otto Rank equals it to morbid self-love, which prevents the formation of a happily balanced personality (Tucker xv). Der doppelgänger, in this sense, holds the key to the unconscious of another assuring the latter immortality while threatening to destabilize his or her ego, hence destroying life thereof at any moment (Rank 73–76). That the embodiment of both—immortality and mortality—in the double sends ripples of fear to the one the double shadows generates another issue of defamiliarization. The once familiar figure somehow becomes unfamiliar in an inexplicable way and the uncanny effect has become more imminent than ever. To Roderick, Madeline is the guardian spirit and potential Satan. Her existence can expel yet propel his morbid fear. By the same token, Hyde injects in Jekyll the belief that the human soul should not be encaged, a yearning sign of immortality itself. The adrenaline rush—"a current of disordered sensual images running like a mill race in my fancy" ("The Strange Case of Dr. Jekyll and Mr. Hyde" 57)—at the birth of Hyde is a telltale sign of the power against death. When the demise comes, "a soul boiling with causeless hatreds, and ... the raging energies of life" (ibid. 68) emitted by Hyde and the revenge to destroy everything treasured by Jekyll speak volumes for Hyde's fear of death and Jekyll's will against the destruction of his own ego. It is in Hyde that we also recognize the fear unique to Victorian times—the struggle between public self and private self. The fin-de-siècle saw the decadence of social values in that pleasure was obtained through exposing one's public image as a familiar self to deceive others (Braun 1). The rebellion of the doppelgänger Hyde is a reaction against the threat to him as the true yet suppressed identity.

At first glance, the uncanny effect Freud associates with the double seems solely grounded on mental status. He argues that the double must be created in the mind from very early on and present itself with a friendly quality so as to give a vision of terror when it is in contrast to its later form. While we are inclined to believe so in Madeline's case, it is hard to trace a shade of friendliness in Hyde from the beginning. A more plausible explanation for the effect should, therefore, be twofold—mental and physical. Through the latter, namely epileptic seizure, can both personae simultaneously provoke the uncanny feeling? In "The Fall of the House of Usher," when the narrator looks at Madeline's "suspiciously lingering smile upon the lip which is so terrible in death" (97), the uncertainty he has regarding her as a human being or an automation is temporarily suspended since there is no urgency to clarify. He has been spared from any emotional affect until he is caught off guard by the reemergence of Madeline in the end. The moment of Hyde dying exhibits the same symptoms of epilepsy, which leaves the witnesses (Poole and Utterson) with a series of questions. Not until Jekyll's full statement of the case came to light could they and readers find out the truth.

The uncanny effect the double evokes obscures sense and logic while triggering horror and intrigue beyond grasp. Manipulating the double can, on the one hand, enhance the chilling visual effect as in the case of Roderick and Madeline, and on the other, make one's mind penetrable through another, which results in an utterly odd and usually revolting match of two drastically different people in all aspects. When Lanyon eventually finds out the secret of his friend Jekyll, he is shocked to real death, as if to prove that the scene is so deeply disturbing that nausea alone fails completely to counteract the effect. Neither he nor readers have been able to read Jekyll's mind until this precise moment. The dual shock comes not just from the bodily transformation but also the dark psychological revelation. The credibility of Jekyll as a reputable gentleman of noble background has instantly gone to dust and ashes, and betrays itself as a downright disillusion to his friend. In another classic example "The Secret Sharer" (1909), Joseph Conrad also employed the concept of the double in that Leggatt is conceived as a doppelgänger.

As the development of the Gothic genre continues in the twenty-first century, the doppelgänger has gradually grown to a mature form and the uncanniness it associates with has never been so strong. Its use has since extended from literature to various media productions such as films. A touch of modernity synchronizing with contemporary times also adds to Gothic settings. Yet, the indispensable elements shaping them still remain—seclusion, enormity, grimness. Likewise, the human psyche is always the pivot of themes and motifs to interweave and recur in the genre, only that the scale of complexity is expanding to spice up the story. To tap into technological advancements, anything can happen in a Gothic tale so long as it delivers the necessary effect. One day, we will probably read a story about an army of half-human, half-ghost machines rampaging in a castle in early medieval times, for example. The imagination is unbound; the principle is unaltered. The guidelines set by Walpole, Aikin, Poe, and Stevenson are fundamental to creating a successful Gothic story, notably when chronicling in this chapter the development of the genre from the first sketch ("Sir Bertrand: A Fragment") in the late eighteenth century, to the golden era of the short story ("The Fall of the House of Usher") in the early nineteenth century, then the Victorian novella ("The Strange Case of Dr. Jekyll and Mr. Hyde"), the extended form in the late century. Aikin, Poe, and Stevenson, albeit of different periods and origins (England, America, Scotland respectively), happened to take short fiction as a platform to experiment with the Gothic.

Poe as the founding father of the American short story and leading reviver of Gothic tales implanted delight in horror in psychologically reflexive personae by making use of his blueprints set for the short story in "The Philosophy of Composition" to exemplify how Gothic elements interact with each other to bring out the most chilling effect. When one compares Poe's manifesto with Walpole's prefaces, it is not hard to find that both writers adopt a similar stance on the principles of the Gothic. The exactitude and meticulousness to craft a story for the single strongest effect strike in similar ways. Poe declares so by stating his clear preference for commencing with the consideration of an effect and keeping originality always in view (*The Raven and the Philosophy of Composition* 20). A daunting task as it is, yet only by carefully choosing the best out of "innumerable effects, or impressions, of which the heart, the intellect, or (more generally) the soul is susceptible" (ibid.) can the effectual quality shine through. A short story is like liqueur, distilled with great pungency to guarantee absolute intoxication. To reach the effect, it has to be condensed. Conciseness and complexity must be accomplished simultaneously without digression, which long fiction is privileged to and has the luxury to do. For Poe's strict adherence to the principle, some literary critics today may brand his stories too artificial. Notwithstanding the contrivance, the passion and studious effort Poe devoted to establish his trademark in the genre is indisputable. It is in this artful work "The Fall of the House of Usher" we found the ingenuity of merging Gothic, scientific, detective, and morbid psychological elements in a compact form, thenceforth a classic exemplar no succeeding Gothic writers shall miss.

Poe had a soul of romance. Though an ocean apart, he ardently admired the British romantic tradition and shared the same traits with Walpole, Stevenson, and the like. For Walpole and Stevenson, romance was deeply ingrained in their mind, which is evident with Walpole's preface to the second edition and Stevenson's essay "A Gossip on Romance" (1882), and the latter particularly contributed to the Romantic revival in fin de siècle literature. It is also in another essay "A Chapter on Dreams" published ten years later that we witness how his Gothic story "The Strange Case of Dr. Jekyll and Mr. Hyde" was born. His writerly self was liberated through dreams and led him to the Gothic romance experiment of creating the double. It is a conscious yet unconscious, romantic yet realistic accomplishment to which hardly any previous work is comparable.

Gothic machinery does not solely depend on writers. Readers also play a part. The relations between the text and the reader are as crucial as the atmospheric machinery churned by the writer. Aside from Aikin, who depicts readers' mental faculties necessitating terror in a story, Holland also proposed the model of the Introjecting Reader in 1968 to reflect the essential relations. The reader-oriented explication has it that the internalized object relations discussed above tend to take the figures in a text as temporary introjects by readers (Rogers 32). The interaction between the reader and the persona is indispensable as the reading process taking place presumes an elaborate match between different personae such that a perceived or imagined part of one protagonist becomes internalized by another and further projected onto the former. The reader, therefore, plays a role in materializing the projection through interjecting and matching with his or her own internalizations, and subsequently responds cognitively and affectively at both conscious and unconscious levels (ibid. 32–33).

The Gothic genre exists in diverse forms of short fiction (sketch, short story, novella, etc.), which its counterpart (long fiction) cannot rival for diversity. The irreplaceable status of short Gothic fiction has proved itself time and time again. The appeal, rather than constrained by the compaction, heightens along with the liberation of the unconscious mind. We may well be conscious of our unconscious at times, transform and divert it to high arts. The short story as a pure art form provides a channel for our repressed emotions to surface in a permissible manner, especially with the help of the power it garners and concentrates in one shot. As such, the Gothic story will always have a place in writers' and readers' hearts, for its best service rendered to psychoanalytical exploration and human psychological emancipation.

Notes

1. A child can satisfy his mirroring needs through acknowledgment and affirmation by his or her closest adult(s) who also fulfill(s) the child's idealizing needs at a later stage when the child admires and wants to be like him/her/them. (See Fosshage, "Self Psychology and its Contribution to Psychoanalysis.")

2. Freud claims that in order to stop primary narcissism from growing, the libido has to be directed from the ego system to objects.

3. For ease of understanding, Lacan led us to imagine the relations between the three Others as a Borromean knot. The intricate link shared between them means none of them is dismissible. The Imaginary Other is the formation of the ego through the mirror image. The Symbolic Other is the key to our mental growth, similar to the unconscious. The Real Other is the least conceptualized element for its undefinable nature.

4. Note that before Walpole, Tobias Smollett, a Scottish writer, had already incorporated some of the scenes with Gothic elements in *The Adventures of Ferdinand Count Fathom* (1753), an anticipation of the forthcoming Gothic work. Yet, Walpole was the first writer who gave a clear definition of the Gothic genre and created a story entirely on the theme.

5. While Immanuel Kant grounds his view on nature, the judgment itself invariably applies to external objects. (Kant, *The Critique of Aesthetic Judgement*, 129). Elsewhere, Edmund Burke equals terror to "the ruling principle of the sublime." (Burke, *Philosophical Enquiry*, Part II Sect. II.)

6. Note that on the subject of beauty and the sublime, Burke shares the same view with Kant, though the former's is positive pleasure and the latter's painful (or negative) pleasure. (Kant, *The Critique of Aesthetic Judgement*, 32 and 121; Burke, *Philosophical Enquiry*, Part I Sect. IV.)

7. A Romanian term for a dead or living female vampire.

8. Frederick S. Frank comments on the tale, "[t]he greatness of [this] Gothic fragment lies in its attempt to generate pure terror without an overreliance upon Walpole's machinery" (quoted from Aguirre and Ardoy, "Narrative Morphology," 2).

Bibliography

Abrams, M. H. "Sublime." *A Glossary of Literary Terms*. Orlando, FL: Earl McPeek, 1985. 308–310. Print.

Aguirre, Manuel, and Eva Ardoy. "Narrative Morphology in Barbauld's 'Sir Bertrand: A Fragment.'" N.p.: The NLP/ The Gateway Press, 2009. https://www.northangerlibrary.com/Documentos/Sir%20Bertrand.pdf. Web.

Aikin, John, and Anna Letitia Aikin. "On the Pleasure Derived from Objects of Terror; with Sir Bertrand, a Fragment." *Miscellaneous Pieces, in Prose: by J. and A. L. Aikin.* London: J. Johnson, 1773. 119–137. Web.

Baldick, Chris, and Robert Mighall. "Gothic Criticism." *A New Companion to the Gothic.* Edited by David Punter. Oxford: Wiley-Blackwell, 2012. 267–287. Print.

Blair, David. "Introduction." *Gothic Short Stories.* Hertfordshire, UK: Wordsworth Editions Limited, 2002. VIII–XXVI. Print.

Bonaparte, Marie. *The Life and Works of Edgar Allan Poe: A Psycho-Analytic Interpretation.* London: Imago, 1949. Web.

Bornstein, Robert F. "Reconnecting Psychoanalysis to Mainstream Psychology: Challenges and Opportunities." *Psychoanalytic Psychology* 22.3 (2005): 323–340. Web.

Botting, Fred. *Gothic.* London, New York: Routledge, 2014. Print.

Bradbury, Ray. "The Lake." 1944. *The Stories of Ray Bradbury.* New York: Alfred A. Knopf, 1980. 36–40. Print.

Braun, Heather. "Research Report for *Victorian Doppelgängers.*" https://library.columbia.edu/content/dam/libraryweb/about/awards/Braun_2014_CUL_Libawards.pdf. Accessed 20 Nov 2017.

Brewster, Scott. "Seeing Things: Gothic and the Madness of Interpretation." *A New Companion to the Gothic.* Edited by David Punter. Oxford: Wiley-Blackwell, 2012. 481–495. Print.

Brinich, Paul, and Christopher Shelley. *The Self and Personality Structure.* Buckingham, PA: Open University Press, 2002. Print/Web.

Burke, Edmund. *A Philosophical Inquiry into the Origin of Our Ideas.* New York: P.F. Collier & Son Co., 1909–14. Web.

Conrad, Joseph. "The Secret Sharer." *The Oxford Book of Short Stories.* Edited by V. S. Pritchett. Oxford: Oxford University Press, 1981. 109–146. Print.

Fosshage, James L. "Self Psychology and its Contributions to Psychoanalysis." *Contemporary Perspectives in Psychotherapy and Psychoanalysis,* 1 Sept 1995, The Prague Symposium, Prague. Web.

Freud, Sigmund. "Beyond the Pleasure Principle." 1920. *Beyond the Pleasure Principle, Group Psychology and Other Works: The Standard Edition of the Complete Psychological Works of Sigmund Freud Vol. XVIII 1920–1922.* Translated by James Strachey et al. London: Vintage, 2001. 7–64. Print.

_____. *The Interpretation of Dreams.* 1899. Translated by Joyce Crick. Oxford: Oxford University Press, 1999. Print.

_____. "On Narcissism: An Introduction." 1914. *The Standard Edition of the Complete Psychological Works of Sigmund Freud, Volume XIV (1914–1916): On the History of the Psycho-Analytic Movement, Papers on Metapsychology and Other Works.* Translated by James Strachey. London: Vintage, 2001. 73–102. Print.

_____. "The 'Uncanny.'" 1919. *The Standard Edition of the Complete Psychological Works of Sigmund Freud Vol. XVII 1917–1919: An Infantile Neurosis and Other Works.* Translated by Alix Strachey. London: Vintage, 2001. 219–252. Print.

Guiley, Rosemary Ellen. *The Encyclopedia of Vampires, Werewolves, and Other Monsters.* N.p.: Visionary Living, 2005. Print/Web.

Kant, Immanuel. *Critique of Judgment.* 1790. Translated by Werner S. Pluhar. Cambridge: Hackett Publishing Company, 1987. Print/Web.

Kohut, Heinz. "Introspection, Empathy, and the Semi-Circle of Mental Health." 1959. *The International Journal of Psycho-Analysis* 63 (1982): 395–407. Web.

_____. *The Restoration of the Self.* Chicago, London: University of Chicago Press, 1977. Print/Web.

Kohut, Heinz, and Ernest S. Wolf. "The Disorders of the Self and Their Treatment: An Outline." *The International Journal of Psycho-Analysis* 59 (1978): 413–425. Web.

Lacan, Jacques. *ÉCRITS.* Translated by Bruce Fink. New York, London: W.W. Norton & Company, 1966. Print/Web.

_____. *The Four Fundamental Concepts of Psycho-Analysis*. Translated by Alan Sheridan. London: Penguin, 1979. Print.

_____. *The Sinthome: The Seminar of Jacques Lacan Book XXIII*. (1975–1976). Edited by Jacques-Alain Miller. Cambridge, Maiden, M.A.: Polity Press, 2016. Print.

Malone, Kareen Ror, and Stephen R. Friedlander, eds. *The Subject of Lacan: A Lacanian Reader for Psychologists*. Albany: State University of New York Press, 2000. Print.

Mighall, Robert. "Diagnosing Jekyll: The Scientific Context to Dr. Jekyll's Experiment and Mr. Hyde's Embodiment." *The Strange Case of Dr. Jekyll and Mr. Hyde and Other Tales of Terror*. Edited by Robert Mighall. London: Penguin, 2002. 145–161. Print.

_____. "Introduction." *The Strange Case of Dr. Jekyll and Mr. Hyde and Other Tales of Terror*. Edited by Robert Mighall. London: Penguin, 2002. IX–XXXVIII. Print.

Norton, Rictor, ed. *Gothic Readings: The First Wave 1764–1840*. London, New York: Leicester University Press, 2000. Print/Web.

Poe, Edgar Allan. "The Fall of the House of Usher." 1839. *Edgar Allan Poe Selected Poetry, Tales, and Essays*. Edited by Jared Gardner and Elizabeth Hewitt. Boston, New York: Bedford/St. Martin's, 2015. 86–103. Print.

_____. "The Lake." *The Works of Edgar Allan Poe Vol. III*. Edited by John H. Ingram. London: A. & C. Black, 1899. 88. Web.

Punter, David, ed. *A New Companion to the Gothic*. Oxford: Wiley-Blackwell, 2012. Print.

Rank, Otto. *Double: A Psychoanalytic Study*. Translated and edited by Harry Tucker, Jr. Chapel Hill: University of North Carolina Press, 1971. Web.

Rogers, Robert. *Self and Other: Object Relations in Psychoanalysis and Literature*. New York: New York University Press, 1991. Print.

Skal, David J. *Something in the Blood: The Untold Story of Bram Stoker, the Man Who Wrote Dracula*. New York, London: Liveright Publishing Corporation, 2016. Print.

Stevenson, Robert Louis. "A Chapter on Dreams." *Across the Plains: With Other Memories and Essays*. London: Chatto & Windus, 1892. 229–252. Web.

_____. "A Gossip on Romance." *Longman's Magazine* 1 (1882): 69–79. Web.

_____. "Strange Case of Dr. Jekyll and Mr. Hyde." *The Strange Case of Dr. Jekyll and Mr. Hyde and Other Tales of Terror*. Edited by Robert Mighall. London: Penguin, 2002. 2–70. Print.

Tso, Anna Wing Bo. "Representations of the Monstrous-Feminine in Selected Works of C. S. Lewis, Roald Dahl and Philip Pullman." *Libri & Liberi: Journal of Research on Children's Literature and Culture* 1.2 (2012): 215–234. Print.

Tucker, Harry Jr. "Introduction." *Double: A Psychoanalytic Study*. Chapel Hill: University of North Carolina Press, 1971. XIII–XXII. Web.

Tymms, Ralph. *Doubles in Literary Psychology*. Cambridge: Bowes & Bowes, 1949. Web.

Walpole, Horace. "Preface to the First Edition." 1764. *The Castle of Otranto*. London: Cassell & Co., 1901. 7–12. Web.

_____. "Preface to This Second Edition." *The Castle of Otranto: A Gothic Story*. London: William Bathoe and Thomas Lownds, 1765. V–XVI. Web.

Watson, Alex. "Who Am I? The Self/Subject According to Psychoanalytic Theory." *SAGE Open* 4.3 (2014): 1–6. Web.

8

Irony and Paralysis in Joyce's "Grace" and Trevor's "Of the Cloth"

At the turn of the twentieth century, writers of Irish descent such as Elizabeth Bowen, Frank O'Connor, and Seán Ó Faoláin were increasingly perceived to be as significant as their English counterparts. The short story regarded as a lyrical and hero-less form allows them to channel Irish national spirit, amplify loneliness, and find solace. The "submerged" (86) and the "outlawed" (87), as Frank O'Connor puts it in "The Lonely Voice" (1962), place writers of Irish descent in a unique position. This "otherness" as predisposition and sentiment together with the social antagonistic attitudes and national introversion, be it pre- or post-independence, play a crucial part in defining Irishness in the short story. Irishness lies in the core of settings and personae, which are further magnified by two indispensable elements—irony and paralysis. Subtly and intricately deployed in the short story pertaining to the Irish context, the features have become the hallmark and have made the genre as distinguished as ever. Although critics go to great lengths to pin down the rules, the vast complexity has yet to be explored. In what follows, we shall unbundle such complexity inherent in religion, and put irony and paralysis under the microscope with reference to two texts: "Grace" (1914) by James Joyce and "Of the Cloth" (1998) by William Trevor.

When Joyce completed "Grace" in 1905, Dublin had not only gone through nearly a century of decline but had also been embroiled in religious conflicts between Catholicism and Protestantism. Joyce was born into a bourgeois Catholic family who avowed nationalistic faith. Yet, soon he witnessed the political downfall and demise of Charles Stewart Parnell, an Irish nationalist politician who, in Joyce's eyes, symbolized every new hope of an independent Ireland and a return of Irish Catholicism. His shattered hopes, exacerbated by the indignity due to the prolonged grave family financial situation, sent Joyce into exile both in and out of the country. Being a British citizen all his life, Dublin was, nevertheless, close to his heart. Disillusion and betrayal remained etched in his mind. Unforgiving temperaments seep through his works. Irony and paralysis are the two best tools to seek revenge for all those misfortunes inflicted upon him and appease his unsettling mind.

Trevor, on the other hand, was born into a middle-class Protestant family who, by and large, led a secure life. Drifting from town to town due to his parents' jobs, Trevor was nevertheless more like an estranged Protestant. His imagination spurred between familiarity and unfamiliarity. His method of deploying irony and paralysis was as superb as Joyce's, albeit there were differences between their methods. Trevor lived in provincial towns (in both Ireland and England) most of his life, during which he acquired an acute observation of minute details. Such skill added a subtle undertone to his irony. Like Joyce, Trevor explored religious issues, mainly the tension between Catholics and Protestants, but with a different style.

The two stories, "Grace" and "Of the Cloth," particularly manifest themselves the patent differences between Joyce's and Trevor's styles when approaching the same subject—the religious conflict in Ireland. We shall elucidate it through analyzing the use of irony and paralysis in the texts. As an illumination, we shall first discuss the roles and the development of irony and paralysis in literature, followed by a brief history of religions in Ireland.

Irony in Literature

As early as 350 BCE, irony had already been deployed as a rhetorical style in literature, especially in Greek tragedies. Traditionally speaking, irony was defined as a figurative speech that unraveled the truth opposite to what had been shown at the beginning of a literary text, hence often categorized as classical irony. Later on, various terms and definitions were developed out of the trope: romantic irony, tragic irony, cosmic irony, verbal irony, dramatic irony, and situational irony, etc., depending on their forms and functions. Most of them are closely tied to the development of literature, which speaks clearly to how irony is valued in literature and how it dominates the writer's mind.

In fact, irony has long been valued as an asset among writers, for its satirical and subversive functions empower them to express the inexpressible. Through its use, they are able to examine social, political, cultural, and religious issues with a less restrictive role. Such a role was pinned down as early as the Roman Age: "[t]he stance of the estranged observer who knows he is reluctantly a part of what he is observing is central to the mode, as is an effort on the part of the satirist to create an ethical ... distance from what he is describing" (Freudenburg 247). Its functions, as theorists indisputably claim, are elusive and inconclusive, which explains why irony has never ceased to be favored by writers for centuries. Early practitioners like Socrates and later ones like Saki and Hemingway unanimously inflected their works with the device to convey to the reader the ironic message.

To reflect subtle thoughts, beliefs, and attitudes through irony, words are used as a proposition to subvert, divert, ridicule, and satirize social norms, cultures, religions, and politics rather than an apparent and direct expression of plain truth. Put into perspective, a writer is a craftsman of a sophisticated artwork, and irony is a tool to carve the shaded part of the work. In literary texts, irony is the device to obscure fact and representation, to say otherwise, to empower voices of plurality, and to allude to subversive critiques. Its diverse and elusive nature manifests itself as one of the best and most effective literary techniques other than metaphors and similes to set the tone, so that all the writers who have in themselves zealous emotions and adamant attitudes to write, to express, to affect others as small as a marginalized group or as colossal as the religious world are allowed to convert their sentiments to a subtle and elevated form.

As seen, irony in narrative discourse is concealment as well as revelation of the writer's attitude, emotion, and thought. Its effect is prolonged and profound, doubly so in short fiction. Compared to its counterpart, short fiction takes a more condensed lyrical form, which exploits no more than a couple of settings and a few protagonists. The success of the story lies in words and gestures rather than plots. It is "pure storytelling" (92), as O'Connor suggests. Irony as an art of rhetoric naturally makes a compatible match to high art, and only through such can words accompanied by gestures be effectively employed to give the most desirable effect. The scarce development of characterization even rids the writer of the obligation to mind the humanity, the offences and harm inflicted on the characters, thus taking the reins of caricaturing the personae in whatever role and to whatever extent one relishes. It is, after all, the comical effect and the ironic and/or subversive message that the writer most desires to achieve and convey. When such momentary revelation ruptures, the climax reaches and the truth dawns. The small chamber amplifies the echo, pushing the effect to sheer pitch. Irony in the short story, therefore, has the power to enlighten the reader instantly and spontaneously.

PARALYSIS IN LITERATURE

"Paralysis" originates from the Greek medical term παράλυσις (parálusis), which means "sudden loss of tone and vital power in a certain part of the body" (*Encyclopaedia Britannica* 377). Palsy consists of several subsets based on the severity of the disease. For example, hemiplegia is a severe case in which an entire side of the body is affected. Applied to literary context, parálusis, which is composed of two morphemes—pará and lusis, alludes to immobility and looseness of a persona, an object, or a city physically, mentally, and/or psychologically. Such is revealed in the oft-quoted letter to Grant Richards, the publisher of *Dubliners*, in which Joyce justifies his choice of Dublin for the setting as "that city seemed to me the centre of paralysis" (*Selected Letters* 134), and in another letter to his friend, "I call the series *Dubliners* to betray the soul of that hemiplegia or paralysis which many consider a city" (ibid. 55). Right from the beginning of the series, Joyce has already presented the reader the concept of paralysis: "[e]very night as I gazed up at the window I said softly to myself the word *paralysis*. It had always sounded strangely in my ears, like the word *gnomon* in the Euclid and the word *simony* in the Catechism. But now it sounded to me like the name of some maleficent and sinful being" (*Dubliners* 1).

Joyce broadens the definition of paralysis to two hyponyms: gnomon and simony, each denoting significant religious qualities. Though the literal interpretation of gnomon carries a geometric sense,[1] the word itself can be further derived into "gnosis" meaning secret knowledge, whose noun form "Gnosticism" refers to teaching based on secret knowledge or knowledge of transcendence through internal and intuitive means. It could be associated with one's own religious experience or a sole reference to the Scriptures.

"Simony," on the other hand, becomes more devilish. Originated from Simon Magus in the Acts of the Apostles, simony involves a potential complicit act of selling or buying spiritual objects, which is rightly condemned by Peter.[2] The monetary exchange for spiritual treasures extends to any temporal procurement through material or oral means, or just homage, while spiritual objects refer to all kinds of supernatural things such as sanctifying grace and the sacraments (Weber 2). For example, to obtain the Apostolic Pardon, purchase ecclesiastical favor, or purify and promote through purgatory via complicit acts are all condemned as sins. The Catechism of the Catholic Church categorizes all of these acts as simony and an infringement of the natural law.

From inactiveness, knowledge, to sin, paralysis constitutes a figurative meaning: a regret caused by a lack of knowledge to act, or a transcendence of knowledge, be they vulgar words or gestures, which causes one to be unable to act. In Joyce's and Trevor's worlds, paralysis is a malaise that permeates personal, social, and religious levels. The impediment to one's act and will that perceive the change of life is deemed a moral failure. The socio-economic stagnation of a city or a country is viewed as a shameful dereliction. The lack of religious consensus to help humanity to progress is counted as inadequacy.

The Chemistry Between Irony and Paralysis

What happens when irony and paralysis crisscross in the modern realistic short story? First and foremost, the theory of trope in literature has been developed and modified over centuries, resulting in a more dynamic literary approach than that of paralysis. In the modern context, the use of irony extends such dynamism to a broad spectrum. Be it bitter, sarcastic, or soft, irony functions equivalently as an ultimate tool to heighten and/or contrast the effects: from palpable to impalpable, probable to improbable, speakable to unspeakable, hopeful to hopeless, sour to bitter, emotional to hysterical. This is when the climax presumably arrives followed by the resolution. However, when paralysis interacts with irony, it intercepts and brings the climax to a halt resulting in the suspension or even nullification of the suspense. Anti-climax, as the term suggests, is favored by many a modern writer to bring down their dramatis personae who should deserve or expect a certain outcome after a series of significant built-up actions. The characters' exaltation, joyousness, and hopefulness are squashed, deprived, or trivialized, leaving them at an emotional standstill.

Notwithstanding this frustration, anti-climax can attain a powerful revelation. Epiphany is such a technique Joyce famously adopted in *Dubliners*. The term originates from "epiphaneia," a Greek word meaning apparition or revelation of a deity. The Feast of the Epiphany is the Catholic commemoration of the revelation of Christ's divinity. Joyce, however, further imbued the theological notion of epiphany with the spiritual matter from an artistic point of view:

> By an epiphany he meant a sudden spiritual transformation, whether in the vulgarity of speech or of gesture or in a memorable phrase of the mind itself. He believed that it was for the man of letters to record these epiphanies with extreme care, seeing that they themselves are the most delicate and evanescent of moments [*Stephen Hero* 211].

Such is the aesthetic theory Joyce propounds in his first autobiography *Stephen Hero*. From integrity to wholeness, the qualities of beauty are discovered, analyzed, and synthesized until the third quality—symmetry—is found. As the deepest revelation uncovers itself suddenly, the innermost uniqueness exposes itself and the hidden truth gives the brightest shine. Joyce contends that "[t]his is the moment which I call epiphany.... The soul of the commonest object seems to us radiant. The object achieves its epiphany" (ibid. 213).

The significance of epiphany as a theological and spiritual connotation is multifaceted through the manifestations of symbols, metaphors, and figurative language. In realistic stories such as Joyce's and Trevor's, the apprehension of such significance is even reached through minute details of real and commonplace entities such as places (farms and slums), rooms and buildings (pubs and churches), events (country walks), lives (living beyond one's means), people (clerks and priests), gestures (nods and shrugs), and words (stammering). Trivial, banal, and fleeting as they seem, they often symbolize the most revelatory moment for their least deceptive attributes, thus constituting the epiphany. When the word uttered betrays one's thought and exposes its truth contrary to another's belief, it dawns on the latter's mind and causes inaction, be it verbal or emotional. As epiphanies take various forms, the consequences that ensue from the resultant realization may differ accordingly, from something very slight, such as changing one's mind and shedding tears, to a grave consequence, like an abrupt decision or a drastic action. In a religious context, it brings out a further issue—religious hypocrisy.

Hypocrisy originates from a Greek term associated with impersonation. It is the art of dissimulation conveyed in rhetorical style, which is synonymous with irony, for they both imply ignorance. When the negative connotation is applied to a sacred context, it means the false assumption of an appearance of virtue or religion. It comes as no surprise when a person practicing religion is branded as a hypocrite, as he/she claims or tries to claim to imitate the life of Jesus Christ, which in every sense is bound to fail purely because of human beings' limitations and the circumstances that we are subject to. The irony lies in sheer contradiction and self-ignorance. In such cases, we are either well or partially aware, completely ignore the situation, or overestimate our mental and physical strength. Though it may not be entirely condemnable, he/she will be forgiven only if he/she acts in good faith and makes confession.

Upon the moment of discovering irony interacting with paralysis in a religious context, the effect is as powerful, shocking, speechless, and unresponsive as any aforementioned. In sacred stories, religious hypocrisy is exposed through a fleeting revelation, challenging one's beliefs and raising unsettling questions about the truth read and preached in religious texts. The writer's duty is to lay bare the hypocrisy through different devices. Yet, no devices are better and more effective than irony and paralysis. There is no need to confront the religion head on, for religious matters are always too touchy and too thorny to address, but to shed light on the issues with candor, while giving room to the reader to judge and contemplate.

Religious issues are of immense interest among writers who particularly witness conflicts of religions in their country, which can lead to social unrest and political upheaval for decades. Ireland is one of the prime examples to illustrate how religions take precedence, which influences writers of Irish descent to approach the intriguing theme.

Between Catholicism and Protestantism

Religion in Ireland has long been a complex issue, for it links not solely to politics and society, but also to self-identity and nationalism. Its root can be traced back to the fourth century BCE when the Celtic religion enjoyed its peak through its expansion across Europe. Its influence gradually subsided and eventually converted to Christianity in the following century. Since then, Christianity has been the dominant religion in Ireland and eventually split into two denominations—Irish Catholicism and Anglo-Irish Protestantism— the former being the most popular religious polity in the country.

While the existence of Catholicism dates back to the fifth century BCE, Protestantism became influential much later, that is, from 1537 with the passage of the Irish Act of Supremacy, through which Henry VIII officially declared the separation of the Church of England from the Roman Catholic Church; thereafter, the Church of Ireland, the official church establishment in Ireland, was founded. In a failed attempt to convert Irish Catholics to Protestantism due to the latter's association with Anglicization and Englishness, and the perception as the church of colonialism, the English monarchical wish to impose one institutional religious system in Ireland not only reached a dead end but instigated a further issue—two disjointed churches, two distinct religious identities. The conflict between the two religions marked an eternal struggle between two identities on both national and religious levels. Apparently, the English Reformation was an attempt to break away from the papacy and the Roman Catholic Church. Meanwhile, the Counter-Reformation reacted by building a more effective Catholic Church, training the clergy in Europe instead of England so as to make them distinguish orthodox (Catholic truth) from unorthodox (Protestant heresy) doctrines.

Although for a period of time the Church of Ireland sought a more independent role from the Church of England, it lasted no more than a century when the newly appointed Archbishop, William Laud, determined to cease such a role. By passing laws to purge Presbyterians,[3] the English monarchy not only asserted its absolute authority over its colony but led to a severe division within the Church of Ireland. The rebellion of Irish Catholics against English settlers in Ulster in 1641 further deteriorated the situation and sowed the seed of a long military struggle between Irish Catholics and English Protestants. To restore the Church as the national church, it had to disestablish and regain its foothold; yet, the opposition from Irish Catholics (and Presbyterians) still remained strong. All the time the Catholics were adamant about developing the country as a Catholic state. Revolt after revolt witnessed the sacrifice of some members for the preservation and bequeathal of the ecclesiastical spirit. The consciousness of Irish Catholic identity, albeit oppressed by the English monarchy, never diminished but rather surged, so that even with the sole support of the Catholic Church, the awareness of the inherent culture and Catholic history, it spread voraciously and garnered tremendous force among people. The menace had the Irish Protestants resort to tighter controls by any means, including imposing penalties on Irish Catholics, assigning the loyal archbishops to various government positions, and unifying the two Churches (the Church of Ireland and the Church of England) through the Act of Union in 1800, etc. Notwithstanding these measures, the challenges, backlashes, and attacks from Irish Catholics had not lessened. The Church of Ireland finally and gradually ceded power and authority. First, the Catholic Emancipation Act set the Catholics and dissenters free in 1829. In 1833, the Irish Church Temporalities Act reduced the number of bishoprics significantly. Eventually, in 1869, the Irish Church Disestablishment Act disestablished the Church. Humiliated and betrayed, the Church of Ireland, nevertheless, had a chance to reshape its role in Ireland and reconsider its Irishness. It was highly significant particularly perceiving the home rule movement as developed mostly by Irish Catholics. The Church of Ireland had, thereafter, sought to keep a low profile.

The waning influence of the Church of Ireland had a significant impact on Irish Catholicism. Falling into disarray and disarrangement from the early nineteenth century, the Catholic Church had finally re-emerged as a recognizable establishment. Restructuring and reorganizing led to resumed daily pastoral functions. The modern nationalism that reinforced national as well as religious identity further boosted mass attendance. For instance, the Gaelic League, which was formed in 1893, swept the country with fervency and drew almost 50,000 Irish nationalists as its members. The Revival of the Irish language accompanied Catholic revival and expansion, noticeably in the middle class. Joyce is the first and foremost example of Anglo-Irish writers brought up in a Catholic nationalist bourgeois family in the late nineteenth century, though his attitudes toward the Irish Ireland movement and the religious issue were more skeptical and unimpressive than those of any contemporary literati. His early education was typical Irish Catholic shaped by ecclesiastical views. Putting children in Jesuit-run schools to pave the way for their future was the aspiration of most Catholic nationalist families. Paradoxically, most of the prominent positions in the Irish government and prestigious professions were occupied by Protestants due to their loyalty to the union between Great Britain and Ireland, while the low-paid and undignified jobs were mostly left to Catholics. The Anglo-Irish aristocrats, however, were not particularly supportive of the Irish nationalists. They continued to move out to the U.K, causing the property values to plummet. Such a perverse situation akin to economic punitive measures aggravated the conflict between the two religions. The power, authority, and sovereignty of the country remained in the hands of the English monarchy until 1918.

The landslide victory of Sinn Féin (the Irish Republican Party) in the 1918 parliamentary election and the Irish War of Independence (1919–1921) finally brought an end to colonialism, with Ireland and the British Parliament declaring a free state in 1937. The virtual independence secured the Roman Catholic Church's position as a whole and saw an increase of Catholics up to 95 percent and a further decrease of Protestants down to 5 percent. While the Troubles in Northern Ireland from the 1960s onward further drove Protestants away from the country, the golden era of Catholicism only lasted until the late twentieth century when the post-war economic and social disturbance challenged the traditional notion of nationalism. The change of public attitudes, such as personal conviction towards the orthodox doctrine, severely affected the membership and the congregations. Though the religious ethos was still there, the influence of the Church towards social services was dwindling.

As the society edges along secular and liberal progress today, Catholicism and Protestantism, the two major Irish religions mired in conflict for centuries, ironically face the same problems of repositioning and restructuring in order to socially and culturally integrate into the fast-paced world without being phased out, and to interact with the public and different sectors to provide the best functions for the twenty-first century. It is especially true when religions in Ireland take up such a dynamic and determined role that for centuries they have shaped and reshaped politics and the fate of the country, which is well-known for the south-north division with the north further split into Catholic-nationalist and Protestant-unionist, and within the Catholic heritage, another division between the Augustinian North and the Pelagian South.[4] Intertwined and entangled, religion shows its intrinsic and unique value in the political and social development of the country, a topic that fascinates not just historians and theologians but writers of Irish descent.

Religious Hypocrisy in Joyce's "Grace"

Set in 1901 or 1902, "Grace" registers a tone of defiance, a work that ridicules the two conflicting religions in Ireland, namely, Irish Catholicism and Protestantism. Though Joyce was brought up in a devout Catholic family, he felt deeply betrayed by the faith, partly because of the downfall of Parnell (over his sexual life) and partly due to the collapse of his family's fortune. It was arguably the disgrace and the sheer disappointment that made him and subsequently his story full of contempt for religion. Though Joyce's faith still remains controversial, some of his letters carry such an adamant tone of rejecting "the whole present social order and Christianity" (*Selected Letters* 25–26), or else equaling Protestantism and Catholicism to tyranny (*Critical Writings* 173), that the reader cannot but sense irony in the story.

Brought to the stage of this satirical drama are five personae—Mr. Kernan, Mr. Power, Mr. Cunningham, Mr. Fogarty, and Mr. M'Coy—who conduct a lengthy and "serious" theological conversation at Kernan's bedside. Apart from Kernan, who is Protestant but later converts to Catholicism owing to his marriage with an Irish Catholic woman, the rest are all Irish Catholics. Among them Cunningham is deemed the most knowledgeable and trustworthy man, a philosopher and informant whose face looks like Shakespeare's ("Grace" 156). The simile kicks off the comedy, as Cunningham makes one inaccurate remark after another, while the others unwittingly fall into traps through echoing words, nodding their heads, and remaining silent. From "The General of the Jesuits stands next to the Pope" (ibid. 163), "the Jesuit Order was never once reformed" (ibid.), "Lux upon Lux" (ibid. 166), "Crux upon Crux" (ibid. 167) to "Dolling ... John MacHale" (ibid. 169), the listeners are waltzed into an abyss of ignorance and absurdity. Presumably a religious man, Cunningham fails his memory miserably by mixing up the order (the General of the Jesuit order does not stand next to the Pope), structure (the Jesuit Order was once dissolved by Pope Clement XIV in 1773), mottos (combining Latin and English in "Lux upon Lux" and "Crux upon Crux"), names (Luigi Aloisio Riccio and Edward Mary Fitzgerald instead of Johann Dollinger and John MacHale, who were present at the Vatican Council for the vote against papal infallibility). M'Coy and Fogarty also make some gaffes with the former confusing the motto "Tenebrae" (ibid. 167) with a ceremony of the same name, while the latter misquotes "Great wits are sure to madness near allied/And thin partitions do their bounds divide" (Dryden, "Absalom and Achitophel" Part 1 line 163–164) for "Great minds are very near to madness" ("Grace" 168).

These half-baked truths based on Catholicism by a group of devout Catholics through misrepresentation, misquotation, and misleadingness are the telltale signs that suggest the air of pretentiousness and pomposity permeating the non-secular world. Throughout history, Catholics and Protestants have proclaimed their own doctrine as bona fide, while refuting the other's as heresy, deception, and unorthodox. Publication is not at all an uncommon means of defense and refutation. From 1581 to 1593, Robert Bellarmine published three volumes of *De Controversiis* to disprove Protestant teaching. John MacPhilpin in 1880 published *The Apparitions and Miracles at Knock: Also, the Official Depositions of the Eye-Witnesses* to vindicate the apparition of Mary and St. Joseph in Knock. The war of words is down to different sources of teaching, as Protestants insist on "sola scriptura," meaning the sole reference of the Bible, while Catholics add Roman Catholic tradition, such as venerating the Blessed Virgin Mary, to the scriptural interpretation. Indeed, we are told in "Grace" that the settings of Kernan's home and the Jesuit Church are full of objects that symbolize rituals and sacerdotalism, which are nowhere stated in the Bible but purely observed by sacramental tradition. For example, an image of the sacred heart of Jesus at Kernan's home for Mrs. Kernan to venerate, and candles, the sanctuary lamp, and quincunx in the Church to remind the congregation of the sacred message of Catholicism. Kernan, raised as Protestant before converting, abruptly and firmly rejects the idea of holding a candle, which is regarded as superstition. At one point, he even sheepishly questions if some of the old Popes are up to the standard as if it were a faux pas. While Kernan takes the matter gravely and avoids offense, Joyce, the creator of the persona, decided to make light of it through vulgar allusion. Father Purdon, who gives the retreat in the Church, is named after the red-light district in Dublin. "[T]he distant speck of red light" (ibid. 172) referring to the sanctuary lamp alludes to the brothel area in Purdon Street. Joyce's contempt for the religion reached such an epic scale that no other devices except irony could bring out the grotesque effect as he fervently wished.

Though neither of the religions earned respect nor sympathy from Joyce, it was Roman Catholicism that particularly beset Joyce. He saw the religion as tyrannical as well as disabling, and considered it to be a bigger problem for the country than any others. Presiding over the predominant religion in Ireland, the Catholic Church was, nevertheless, rotten by its crippling system that bred corruption and sexual scandals. It had little regard for ecclesiastical teaching and encouraged a dogmatic and unrepentant approach. Such reality was shunned by the Revival writers but not Joyce, an exile since his early twenties. The preposterous attitudes of the personae and the images of the priesthood are exposed in the story. It directs the confrontation to the Church itself, in which everyone crafts his oratory skill in order to fare well as an orator and professor. When challenged by M'Coy about the proclamation on the Jesuit Order, Cunningham reaffirms it with a double assertion in an authoritative tone, "[t]hat's a fact.... That's history" (ibid. 163). Little do others know that it is empty rhetoric, as it is at once supplemented with evidence (church and congregation) by Mr. Power. Later when he mixes Latin and English in the motto and gets called out by Fogarty, Cunningham is even more assertive about his glaring mistake: "[a]llow me, said Mr. Cunningham positively, it was Lux upon Lux. And Pius IX. his predecessor's motto was Crux upon Crux that is, Cross upon Cross—to show the difference between their two pontificates" (ibid. 167). Kernan also weighs in on the issue of the conduct of some of the Popes, on which Cunningham blithely ignores the graveness of the problem with a hyperbolic claim void of evidence: "[n]ot one of them, not the biggest drunkard, not the most ... out-and-out ruffian, not one of them ever preached ex cathedra a word of false doctrine" (ibid. 168). When Cunningham mentions John MacHale as the Archbishop who opposed papal infallibility, Fogarty again raises doubt about the name and yet again Cunningham reinforces his egregious error: "John of Tuam ... was the man" (ibid. 169). Throughout the conversation, it is Cunningham, with the Shakespearean face, who fares the worst in theological knowledge. His faith is dubious. His understanding of doctrine is ludicrous. Ironically, he is the only man whom Mrs. Kernan fully trusts to turn her husband into a pious Catholic. The deception, frivolousness, and farcicality exposed in the discussion that lacks dialectical exchange make Christian values pale into insignificance, a worrying sign that Joyce had to address. Yet, what he intended to reveal to the reader is the priesthood.

Father Purdon, first introduced by Cunningham and Power to Kernan as a jolly good fellow who is not too hard on the mass attendants, appears in the Jesuit Church as a stout and red-faced preacher. His elaborate style is not only revealed through his gesture but the sermon. Preaching Luke 16:8–9, Father Purdon assures the attendants that Jesuit Christ understands every failing and weakness of businessmen and professional men, who cannot but lead a life of worldliness. For all the temptations in the world, therefore, He understands that they may be the least solicitous in religious matters. Father Purdon pledges himself to speak to the hearers in a business-like manner and vice versa as if he were their spiritual accountant and they the customers. "[T]o be straight and manly with God" (ibid. 174), Father Purdon goes on to end his sermon, "if ... there were some discrepancies, to admit the truth, to be frank and say like a man:—Well, I have looked into my accounts. I find this wrong and this wrong. But, with God's grace, I will rectify this and this. I will set right my accounts" (ibid.).

Father Purdon's interpretation shocks Kernan, not only because he has expected seemly preaching after all the effortful persuasion by his friends and the serious evangelical setting (candles and quincunx), but also some spiritual and inspirational guidance instead of verifying his accounts. It is easy to imagine Kernan's dumb reaction in that instant—not knowing what to do, what to think, and what to say. The transcendence of knowledge has further been reduced to a straight business transaction, which his friends have never uttered a word about before. To receive the grace of God through oral and material means is, in fact, regarded as an act of simony and condemned sinful. The retreat has, thus, become vulgar, superficial, disrespectful, and disgraceful. The four gentlemen—Cunningham, Fogarty, M'Coy, Power— have equally made themselves look ridiculous and ignorant in contrast to the ostentatious and bumptious attitudes they displayed in the conversation.

Yet, who makes them look absurd? They are, after all, humans who are non-omnipotent and fallible in front of God. So whose fault is it? Where does all this come from? The powerful revelation lies in epiphany.

As aforementioned, epiphany, a product of irony and paralysis, is a flash of enlightenment and apprehension. Dramatis personae who expect climaxes yet are deprived of them are left frozen in action and speech, which accounts for Kernan's response at the end of the sermon. As readers, we may also experience an emotional standstill for the unexpected anti-climax. That has, nevertheless, granted us the power to apprehend the truth beyond the spurious claims made by the personae. The way that Father Purdon apparently tailor-makes his sermon for business people and that Cunningham muddles up facts indeed render a profound discovery—religious hypocrisy and the failure of religion. Joyce ultimately took us through this comedy to make a statement about these two pronounced themes. In it, Cunningham and Father Purdon are the two comedians who stage the first and second acts respectively, trying to impersonate Jesus Christ so that they can build up an omnipotent and benevolent image of Him. Their insufficient knowledge, together with Father Purdon's sloppy manner, however, exposes their limitations. Rhetorical skill seems to be the only device to conceal their shortcomings should they wish to inculcate a doctrine they hardly remember. Impression is everything. As a matter of fact, Father Purdon did successfully impress the group, especially Kernan, as he recalls his oratory style and voice with great admiration: "[u]pon my word it was magnificent, the style of the oratory. And his voice! God! hadn't he a voice!" (ibid. 165). Cunningham is less impressed than the others as he recollects the dismissive remarks made by others on Father Purdon's unorthodox preaching. *I perhaps can do better than the priest*, Cunningham may think. Sarcastically, he cannot bring himself to such an orthodox role as well since he makes mistake after mistake without admitting one flaw. Self-ignorance and imperiousness breed religious hypocrisy.

To create imposters, we need a faulty system. For centuries, the Roman Catholic Church has been undergoing different reformations, which seek to eradicate its ills and consolidate its worldwide support. At the height of the reformations came *The Ninety-Five Theses* (1517) by Martin Luther, a German priest who fiercely opposed Catholic views on selling indulgences. Unfortunately, the rottenness is still rampant and the Church is still mired in problems and scandals. The rigid and conservative system is less than desirable to rectify them. Yet, to mask all the flaws, one has to defend the system by blindfolding oneself, which explains the hypocritical attitudes of Cunningham and Father Purdon. Nothing can resort to logic and reason. That is how they see the structure of the Church and how they apply to the sacred life. From preaching to discussing, they all become baseless and hyperbolic. Grace, one of the core beliefs that Catholics have always striven for and sought to preserve, can hardly stand on its own in the system without the support of genuine gracious acts. This can only end in disgrace as expounded in "Grace."

Failure of Religion in Trevor's "Of the Cloth"

A less comical version of "Grace" is "Of the Cloth," in which Trevor portrays two priests, the Rev. Grattan Fitzmaurice of the Protestant Church and Father Leahy of the Catholic Church, in Ennismolach, a half deserted rural town in Ireland. Grattan's father is also a priest in the Church of Ireland. As such, Grattan witnesses the change of time and atmosphere not just through his work but also through his father's account: "the Protestant foundation … had long ago begun to seem too imposing a title, ludicrous almost in its claim. 'We are a remnant,' Grattan's father said" ("Of the Cloth" 23). It does not sound in the least melancholic and depressing seeing the truth laid bare in the dwindling congregation and the disintegrated buildings. The churches which Grattan serves are as dilapidated as ruins, a stark contrast to the adorned and bustling church where Father Leahy preaches. Grattan accepts it as a patent fact and concedes without remonstration that Ennismolach is the tip of the iceberg of such subjugation. "The great Church of Rome inherited all Ireland" (ibid. 24) speaks volumes. The seemingly irremediable disparity between the two Churches for the rivalry and orthodoxy, however, is bridged by the small gestures displayed by the two priests one evening after the Catholic funeral of Con Tonan, a disabled man to whom Grattan has shown benevolence. The ensuing conversation that draws him close to Father Leahy is more peaceful yet no less ironic than the discussion in "Grace."

Father Leahy's sudden visit catches Grattan off guard, and he hastily puts away the paper he is reading. The headline of Father Brendan Smyth being taken into custody for committing pedophilia is perceived as an embarrassment for the visitor. Grattan's kind and thoughtful gesture is ironic in view of the crime committed by Father Smyth. The packed congregations and the impressive funeral service of Con Tonan seen in the church abruptly fall into cliché and superficiality, for they certainly cannot compare to a small but benign and significant gesture. That comparison, nevertheless, does not come to Grattan's mind because of its unworthiness. Has loneliness bothered him? Has the neglect of the churches annoyed him? Not in the least. He has long taken it as destiny. On the contrary, he fathoms that it might be Father Leahy, who patronizes him by making that unplanned visit. The mistrust ironically turns out to be two lonely hearts that perceive the same miserable fate.

As darkness and quietness veil, they stroll in the garden and have a little talk. From restraint to openness, the intimacy has gradually stripped off Father Leahy's holy cloth. Grattan notices his hesitant tone and there is something deeper he inclines to share:

> "Time was, a priest in Ireland wouldn't read the Irish Times.... But we take it in now."
> "I thought maybe that picture—"
> "There's more to it all than what that picture says...."
> "It's where we've ended" [ibid. 35].

A startling revelation of the darkest secret made at the darkest moment betrays the image of Father Leahy, a figure that Grattan has always believed to embolden the congregations. Now it baffles him as much as the purpose of the visit does. The priest with whom he is engaged with in the dark is different from the one he sees and listens to in the church. The confidence he lacks, the secretive man he becomes, the implication he lingers upon are all becoming too perplexing to him. All these, however, strike him as if the dubious remarks made about the priests were reaffirmed: "[w]hy did it seem he was being told that the confidence the priests possessed was a surface that lingered beyond its day? ... Why did it seem he was being told there was illusion, somewhere, in the solemn voices, hands raised in blessing, the holy water, the cross made in the air?" (ibid). As he gathers his thoughts, he cannot help but associate the troubling lives and cultures of the present time with the hypocritical, incredulous, and corrupted image of Father Smyth. His thoughts of rhetorical questions trail off with the last emphatic and ironic question, "[w]ould he say that all he ever did was to reach out and gather in his due, that God had made him so?" (ibid. 36).

As Grattan's mind goes through a dark tunnel desperate for an answer, Father Leahy's successful image still convinces him that Catholicism enjoys a golden era because of priests like Father Leahy, who know how to impress through preaching and mingling with others outside church. The grin, the faith, and the oration are his trademarks, which not only Grattan but Father Leahy himself believes as a necessary compromise to modernity and promise to make "Good Catholic Ireland" (ibid. 37). Not until the last moment when Father Leahy tells him how Father MacPartlan, whom Grattan is not fond of, feels grateful for what he has done for the deceased, do the two priests grasp the quintessence:

> "What he said to me was you'd given Con Tonan his life back. Even though Con Tonan wasn't one of your own."
> "Ah, no, no, I didn't do that."
> "D'you know the way it sometimes is, you want to tell a person a thing?" [ibid. 38].

Contrasting with the startling sermon that leaves Kernan dumbfounded in "Grace," the compliment creates a rippling effect in Grattan's mind. Yet, both

Joyce and Trevor refrain from taking their dramatis personae on a roller coaster of climaxes. Grattan, on taking the compliment, behaves calm and collected; so does Father Leahy, who, on passing the praise, drives away barely saying a word. The anti-climax, nonetheless, takes Grattan out of the tunnel and the light dawns on him, and there, he apprehends the truth—a small gesture can change a life. The gardening work he assigns to Con Tonan, the visit Father Leahy makes, the praise Father MacPartlan gives all become significant. Unfortunately, these unelaborated gestures have been dismissed as too unnoticeable, not showy and flashy enough to get the attention of a huge crowd of followers. That is how religious hypocrisy crops up to compensate for the insufficiency. Image is everything. Even religions today have to consider image instead of substance. It can promote as well as deceive. Yet, the fundamental question is: can it really solve the problems of the Church? Look at Father Smyth—the answer is crystal clear. Father Leahy seems to have the answer too, as he predicts the end of the day will come any time should the approach, practice, and teachings of the Church continue without serious re-examining. The congregations, the Sunday Masses, and the funding, after all, can only deceive the public and conceal the truth. Yet, how long can it last? Father Leahy is aware that changes need to start from small things. A small gesture matters as it keeps genuine faith strong enough to have a profound influence, which is clearly exemplified in Con Tonan's case. Father Leahy himself has sought solace in reciprocal talk, albeit ironically, from a priest whose church he considers archaic and declining. The tokens exchanged between them defy the hierarchical system and constitute real meaning in life guiding each to the right path.

It is time, perhaps, Catholic priests learned from Protestant priests how to perform sincere albeit slight gestures, or else Catholicism may end up in the same plight as Protestantism—dwindling followers and ruined churches due to depopulation and/or progressive secular culture. At the onset, the vestments of the priests of the two Churches denote the past and the future, deception and decorum. Underneath the garment, it is one's perspective that ultimately shapes his path and returns him to his de facto self. Had it not been for the darkness that exposed the naked truth, Grattan, Father Leahy, and Father MacPartlan would not have found themselves converging on the path: "[a]fter all, it was said also, all three of them shared the cloth" (ibid. 33).

From "Grace" to "Of the Cloth," though a leap of around seventy years, Joyce and Trevor both show the power of irony and paralysis as compound tools in a compact fictional form. To them, religion is central to Irish life but also the thorniest issue in Irish history. It is the breeding ground for love, hatred, disputes, and blood. Though the antagonism between Protestantism and Catholicism has been subdued after centuries of battles and wars of words, the gulf between them has not yet been bridged. Joyce and Trevor embraced themselves in an upfront yet evasive position to bring out the issue. Irony and paralysis allow them to comment by foregrounding the personae without authorial affronts. Refraining from being intrusive, they let go of the personae in seamless conversations through which the characters discover the unspeakable truth void of melodrama and emotional outburst.

Joyce's relentless derision in contrast with Trevor's piteous irony have further demonstrated the flexible use of irony and paralysis as a literary compound device particularly in short stories when writers engross readers with one significant yet inexpressible subject. In "Grace" and "Of the Cloth," it is religion that Joyce and Trevor determined to shed light on, and both sought to enlighten the reader on religious hypocrisy and religious ethics. In "Grace," dramatic irony, tragic irony, and situational irony are intertwined. Every historical fact that Kernan is told has already been made known to the reader as untrue. The rig contrived by Cunningham turns into a paradox. From expected to unexpected, Kernan still has his problem unsolved as ever before. "Of the Cloth," on the other hand, uses cosmic irony in an understated manner. When religion is manipulated and corrupted by human beings who naively believe their ideals can override human fallibility and thus make them superior to or different from others, God reminds them who upholds the natural and supernatural order of the universe and who decides their destiny. Divine providence is called upon at the last moment to enlighten them through God's gift, that is, gesture. This is regardless of the doctrine preached and practices advocated by various religious polities, for they are all equal in front of God. The aforementioned forms of irony, howsoever different they may seem, are absorbed by paralysis, which intensifies the single most revelatory moment to enhance the elusive and inconclusive effect. Irony and paralysis, the best partners to maneuver between absurdity and pathos in one sitting, become the quintessence of modern realistic short stories.

Notes

1. Based on *Elements*, Euclid's geometric treatise around 300 BCE, gnomon refers to the remainder of a parallelogram after removing a similar parallelogram from its corner.
2. See *Holy Bible*, NIV, Acts viii 18–24.
3. Most Presbyterians are Protestants descended from Scotland and follow the reformed tradition of Protestantism. Presbyterian churches are mainly governed by elders.
4. An Augustinian follows the doctrines of St. Augustine and firmly believes that the original sin of humankind can only be redeemed through grace. On the contrary, a Pelagian takes a more optimistic ecclesiastical view from Pelagianism (named after an Irish or British monk named Pelagius), whose belief stresses free will and the human capability of distinguishing good from evil without special guidance by the deity.

Bibliography

Aristotle. *The Art of Rhetoric*. 350 BCE London: Harper Press, 2012. Print.
Brown, Terrence. "Introduction." *Dubliners*. 1914. London: Penguin, 1992. vii–xlix. Print.

_____. "Notes." *Dubliners*. 1914. London: Penguin, 1992. 237–317. Print.
Colebrook, Claire. *Irony: The New Critical Idiom*. London, New York: Routledge, 2004. Print.
Donnelly, John Patrick, trans. and ed. *Jesuit Writings of the Early Modern Period 1540–1640*. Indianapolis, IN: Hackett, 2006. Web.
Dryden, John. "Absalom and Achitophel." *The Satires of Dryden: Absalom and Achitophel, The Medal, Mac Flecknoe*. London: Macmillan, 1909. 1–67. Web.
Enright, Anne. "William Trevor: 'An Acute Observer with an Outsider's Eye for Detail.'" *The Guardian*, 25 Nov 2016. https://www.theguardian.com/books/2016/nov/25/anne-enright-william-trevor-acute-observer-eye-for-detail. Accessed 7 July 2017.
Fahey, Tony. "Catholicism and Industrial Society in Ireland." *Proceedings of the British Academy* 79 (1992): 241–263. Web.
Fargnoli, A. Nicholas, and Michael Patrick Gillespie. *Critical Companion to James Joyce: A Literary Reference to His Life and Work*. New York: Facts on File, 2006. Web.
Ford, Alan. "Irish Protestantism to the Present Day." *The Blackwell Companion to Protestantism*. Edited by Alister E. McGrath and Darren C. Marks. Malden, MA: Wiley-Blackwell, 2004. 123–129. Print.
_____. "Religion and National Identity." The Annual Conference of the Irish Association, 14 Nov. 1999, Carrickfergus. Web.
Freudenburg, Kirk. *The Cambridge Companion to Roman Satire*. Cambridge: Cambridge University Press, 2005. Print.
Greeley, Andrew M. "The Religions of Ireland." *Religion in Europe at the End of the Second Millennium: A Sociological Profile*. New Brunswick, NJ: Transaction Publishers, 2009. 133–154. Print/Web.
Harris, Scott L. "Religious Hypocrisy Exposed and Rebuked—Luke 11:37–54." 5 Feb 2017, Grace Bible Church, NY. gracebibleny.org/religious-hypocrisy-exposed-and-rebuked-luke-1137-54. Accessed 23 July 2017.
Hills, L. Rust. "Irony and Point of View." *Writing in General and the Short Story in Particular*. New York: Houghton Mifflin, 2000. 154–157. Print/Web.
Holy Bible. New International Version, 4th ed., Biblica, 2011. Print.
Joyce, James. "*The Critical Writings of James Joyce*. Edited by Ellsworth Mason and Richard Ellmann. London: Faber & Faber, 1959. Print/Web.
_____. Grace." *Dubliners*. 1914. London: Penguin, 1992. 149–174. Print.
_____. *Selected Letters of James Joyce*. Edited by Richard Ellmann. London: Faber & Faber, 1975. Print/Web.
_____. "The Sisters." *Dubliners*. 1914. London: Penguin, 1992. 1–10. Print.
_____. *Stephen Hero*. Edited by Theodore Spencer. New York: New Directions, 1963. Web.
Kenny, John. "Inside Out: A Working Theory of the Irish Short Story." *Frank O'Connor: New Critical Essays*. Edited by H. Lennon. Dublin: Four Courts Press, 2007. 99–113. Print/Web.
O'Connor, Frank. "The Lonely Voice." *Short Story Theories*. Edited by Charles E. May. Ohio: Ohio University Press, 1976. 83–93. Print/Web.
Olson, Roger E. *The Story of Christian Theology: Twenty Centuries of Tradition & Reform*. Downers Grove, IL: IVP Academic, 1999. Print/Web.
"Paralysis." *Encyclopaedia Britannica, Or a Dictionary of Arts, Sciences, and Miscellaneous Literature*, Vol. 13. Edinburgh: Archibald Constable and Company, 1823. Web.
Price, Reynolds. "A Lifetime of Tales from the Land of Broken Hearts." *New York Times*, 28 Feb 1993. www.nytimes.com/books/98/09/06/specials/trevor-stories.html. Accessed 6 July 2017.
Scofield, Martin. *The Cambridge Introduction to the American Short Story*. Cambridge, MA: Cambridge University Press, 2006. Print.
Trevor, William. "Of the Cloth." *The Hill Bachelors*. London: Penguin, 2001. 21–39. Print.
Weber, N.A. "Simony." *The Catholic Encyclopedia, Volume 14: Simony-Tournon*. Edited by Charles George Herbermann, et al. New York: Robert Appleton Company, 1912. 2–4. Web.

9
Civil Rights and Prejudice in Walker's "Everyday Use" and Smith's "The Embassy of Cambodia"

Ever since Christopher Columbus discovered the New World[1] in 1492, and there came, thereafter, an Englishman who brought twenty Africans as indentured servants in a slaving vessel to Virginia in 1619, the longest, most gruesome, and most divisive chapter of black history commenced. This is African American history.

Being the largest ethnic community in America, Afro-Americans have left their sturdy and bloody footprints upon the land more than any other ethnic group fighting prejudice, and procuring and defending civil rights. Account after account of violence and revolts enters into the record, making the plight of the African Americans the most debatable and inconclusive in mankind's history. Politicians, activists, scholars, and students, among others, have participated, witnessed, or changed history in countless protests, movements, wars and battles over more than three centuries. Across the seas, the same race met the same fate. Africans that were brought to Britain long endured treatment no less harsh than those in America. Having dominated the slave trade for nearly two centuries, Britain still feels the impact today. Prejudice against blacks, though downplayed, still remains a thorny issue. The Afro-British have also gone through a long battle for civil rights. The strikingly similar destiny shared between Afro-Americans and Afro-British have inspired their descendants to write stories about the experiences. In the following, we shall unfold the "black" chapter with reference to Alice Walker's "Everyday Use" (1973) and Zadie Smith's "The Embassy of Cambodia" (2013).

Set in the early seventies, "Everyday Use" is a first-person narration of an Afro-American family. The mother being the first-person narrator gives a candid and modest account of the relationships between her and her two daughters, Dee and Maggie. As the story develops into a scene that highlights the most expected meeting between Dee and the family, the conversation between them rips open a wound, exposes a rift, and pushes each of them into an uncompromising position, leading to Dee walking out of the scene in utter contempt and betrayal. The themes essentially evolve around civil rights and prejudice, expanding into multifaceted layers—slavery, racial identity and prejudice, white supremacy, classism, and internalized and externalized racism. The central object, the "quilt" Dee desperately wants, is reminiscent of the past that divides the nation and the Afro-American community itself. It is a shameful, poignant, yet audacious history that dates back to the mid-seventeenth century.

THE DARK HISTORY OF AFRICAN AMERICANS

More than seventy years after the discovery of the Americas, the first batch of Spanish explorers arrived and set up their first colony in the New World in 1565. Other Europeans including the English followed suit, reaching the new land and forming colonies. Within two decades, the number of imported African slaves increased almost fourfold because of the transatlantic slave trade, adding up to a total of twelve million who were forcibly taken to the Americas. The greatest involuntary migration in history turned the Americas into the biggest slave empire since Roman times. The English, who were interested in acquiring and selling the "chattels," set up their own slave trade and exported slaves to other American colonies. It was a "blood-thirsty" business, with nearly two million Africans perishing due to the trade. The harrowing voyages, particularly the ones on the Middle Passage, which have been likened to "the transport of Jews to Nazis concentration camps" (Brendon, *The Decline and Fall* 15), cost many lives as the Africans were treated like nothing but animals and commodities. Slave ships were literally coffins and dungeons for them. They did not know when they would die due to the overcrowded hold that had them stacked in tiers. The stench from the dead and the deadly diseases spread amongst them. The most horrid killing was committed in 1781 when one hundred thirty-three slaves en route to Jamaica were thrown into the sea by a captain who purely wanted to make an insurance claim. It would be called genocide today, but the incident was dismissed as a case of horse slaughter at that time. The inhumane attitudes toward Africans were prevalent and deep-seated in European society, as evidenced by enlightenment French lawyer and philosopher Montesquieu's controversial remark: "[i]t is impossible for us to suppose these creatures to be men, because, allowing them to be men, a suspicion would follow that we ourselves are not Christians" (*The Spirit of Laws* 264).

Ironically, those who survived the slave trafficking would find themselves in charnel houses, which only prolonged and aggravated their tortures. It was in the South that slavery pervaded and racial and sexual prejudice was bred. Although the slave system started as early as 1860 BCE and still exists in parts of the Arab world today, it had been radicalized in the Americas to such an extent that it not only spurred the Southern plantation economy but it was also institutionalized, legalized, and rationalized by all coercive means, such as enacting slave codes and ratifying the Constitution. The rationale behind this was to control and oppress slave societies, which the settlers regarded as a large threatening group of inferior, sinister yet indispensable money-spinners. The inconvenient truth is the Southern economy thrived not because of the elitists (traders, slaveholders, plantation owners) but because of the cheap labor of slaves. Such a paradox naturally triggered the former's inner savageness and devilishness, which could only be appeased by legitimizing the draconian punishments. Besides stripping the slaves of freedom of movement and the right to self-purchase to be freedmen such that the Africans would remain lifetime slaves whose status would be passed on to the next generation, other inhumane measures included castration, severe floggings, cropped ears, slit noses, auto-da-fé, and lynching (Brendon, *The Decline and Fall* 22).

NAME CHANGE AND ITS IMPLICATIONS

As if physical tortures were not enough, psychological ones peddled vice and discrimination. The diaspora tore apart thousand if not millions of African families who were captured or kidnapped and sold to slaveholders, drifted away for life, forced to change their name and abandon their culture. Solomon Northup detailed in his autobiography how he, as a born freedman, was kidnapped and transported to Louisiana, disguised as Platt and enslaved for twelve years. Renaming was the most convenient way to proclaim that slaves were sub-humans bound by their servile condition. A name was a direct link to one's family tree and allowed others to trace the whereabouts of the slaves easily. For the pride of origin and hereditary traits, the enslaved strove to preserve their name that was associated with their tribal language, culture, and customs. That Dee in "Everyday Use" declares her new African name Wangero Leewanika Kemanjo is an example of a direct protest against the disgrace that African descendants have borne throughout history: "I couldn't bear it any longer being named after the people who oppress me" (318). Being named after her great-grandmother renders a painful reminder of how her ancestors were trafficked to a white colony as chattel slaves. By adopting an African name, she apparently believes herself able to regain her African identity, or at least bury part of her history if not its entirety. As well as rejecting whiteness as Groba suggests (223), the reassurance of one's own identity challenges the pre-existing racist assumption that the African is soulless with a heathen culture and of "orangutan" origin. Re-establishing the link between her identity and the indigenous culture supposedly reasserts that Africa, like other western countries, has a long (though unknown) history and an early (though mysterious) civilization, thus deserving the same respect.

That "noble" gesture, nonetheless, baffles others, for the awkward, tactless, and condescending scene staged by Dee whose intention certainly does not sit well with her mother. As Dee pesters her, she admits to herself that the old name can probably be traced back before the American Civil War. Annoyed, the mother only perceives the incessant questions as a belligerent reaction against her, Maggie, and their ancestry, especially the maternal ancestors, while Dee, as usual, puts on presumptuous airs, stands on high moral ground, and lectures everyone with her supreme knowledge of how one should cut loose from the oppressive system. "There I was not ... before 'Dicie' cropped up in our family, so why should I try to trace it that far back?" (Walker, "Everyday Use" 318). It is perhaps a struggle for the mother to understand her daughter's "moralistic" intention, as the former confesses to having little education. Yet, the contrast Dee deliberately sets between herself and her mother as literate vs. illiterate and cultivated vs. uncultivated has also betrayed her inner struggle with her own identity, not to mention her ignorance in rural origin and culture, and above all, her ancestors' continuous battle against inhumanity and indignity.

Dee's mother certainly knows the burden her maternal ancestors bore to keep their families together. To her mind, keeping the "slave name" does little to demean the family. Rather, it is a recognition of generations' concerted efforts as well as the torch of Afro-American spirit to pass on to the next generation. Liberation does not come from rejecting the "slave name," but from acknowledging the past and integrating it into the present. The young radical descendants will not stomach such solidarity and appreciation. Instead of showing reverence for those sacrifices for the common cause, Dee chooses to alienate the recent past and focus on the present and the distinctively remote past, while decrying the passive actions her maternal ancestors took, slamming the "slave name," and refusing to use it. To her, the past is no more than a discrete recollection of memories or flashbacks diverged along a discontinuous continuum. Going back to an African name is a politically correct response to the recent past and a direct link to her true heritage, howsoever remote, odd, and unrelated it seems. The conflicts that typically evolve from two generations mired in a controversial and unsolvable past is one of the issues Walker explores and criticizes in "Everyday Use."

Walker's "Everyday Use" as a Critique of the Black Power Movement

Indeed, the 1970s, the decade during which Walker published the story, was a time of revolts of young Afro-Americans against others—in and out of the black community. They raged at the frustration of integration, which was, by and large, successful in the last few generations. The African Americans who fought and struggled for decades and centuries were more aware than anyone else that integration was not an effortless and seamless process. Insisting yet resisting, negotiating and renegotiating, compromising yet uncompromising had brought generations of Afro-Americans to their current situation, which was hailed less as a milestone in race relations but more as a successful and peaceful attempt for racial coexistence. The younger generation rejected the fruit of their labors and the continuation of non-violent fights for rights and equality, instead demanding drastic improvements and progressive actions, thus instigating the Black Power Movement (1968–1980). Walker challenges the notion of the nationalist ideologies advocated by the Black Panther Party with reference to Dee, who represents the young, educated Afro-Americans who have run out of patience. From her name change (as discussed above) to hairstyle (black straight hair with pigtails locked like lizards ["Everyday Use" 317]), clothing and accessories (loose, loud dress, dangling bracelets, gold hanging earrings [ibid.]), greetings ("Wa-su-zo-Tean-o!" [ibid.]), and dating a black Muslim (Hakim-a-barber), she is determined to revolutionize herself and display all the "glaring heritage" on her body for the extolment of a mystic, remote, and often unknown past, as well as a total rejection of American values. Ironically, it is this rejection that brought the Black Panther Party members close to the ideology of black Muslims. Malcolm X, an activist in the Black Nationalist Movement and leader of the Nation of Islam, lauded Islamic values and preached black dominance while denouncing white supremacy. He changed his surname to Muslim's "X" to acknowledge real but unknown African roots and advocated the separation between blacks and whites. Among other teachings shared between the black Muslims and the members of the movement was forbidding intermarriage, albeit for different motives. Little wonder that the mother suspects Dee and Asalamalakim are not married, as Asalamalakim is Muslim but Dee is not.

While it could be true that Asalamalakim has a major religious concern, Dee's situation might reflect a darker and more complex reality in America.

It was a political and racial issue. Although slavery had been abolished nearly a century ago, the slave past still haunted Americans. Marriage between blacks and whites was taboo in almost every single white social class and a divisive issue in the black community. Dee's disillusionment, therefore, stems from the belief that hierarchy through relationships can increase or secure one's power, which she believes will never be obtained from a white-dominated society through equality. As such, racial hierarchy is internalized into intraracial hierarchy. Failing to climb the hierarchical ladder across races stokes antagonism towards others in their own community whom people like Dee regard as inferior. Classism within black communities is as ugly as that in white communities. Look no further than Dee's use of her relationship with Asalamalakim to reset the hierarchy and elevate her social status. Ironically, it cannot save her from the recent past, but only resurfaces as symptoms of an inferiority complex. Unconsciously, she becomes her own victim.

EXTERNALIZED AND INTERNALIZED RACISM

Does Dee succumb to fate? Not in the least. It is racial hierarchy that she is determined to overcome, but at the expense of the closest people around her. Her resentment of Maggie's and her mother's ungrudging acceptance finally takes its toll, as the mother jumps to Maggie's defense and refuses to give Dee any quilts. The heritage objectified by Dee as a trophy to celebrate victory against her own race and another race has thus been saved from savagery and is re-endowed with distinct value by the mother's dignity. It will be a dowry for Maggie—a token of love and humanity for her descendants. Such is the duel between Dee and her mother—a modern fable of city mouse and country mouse (Walker, *Women Writers: Texts and Contexts* 314). Dee as a city mouse arrives in glamour, then launches a scathing attack in vain and storms off without a snatch of quilts, and finally runs back to the city like a rat. The mother has regained her poise and resumes her country life, as any country mouse would.

When Black Pride[2] was at its peak, many young Afro-Americans were awakened to the beauty of blackness. From art and music to fashion, they were all injected with black rhythm. The slogan "Black is beautiful" captured the essence of the movement and encouraged every Afro-American to embrace black culture and heritage. The cultural movement shifted the standard of beauty from white to black, which should have helped combat inferiority, otherwise known as internalized racism. When Dee dons all kinds of clothing distinctive with African heritage to echo the slogan, her proud demeanor does appeal to some time and her inferiority is repressed, thus boosting her confidence. Yet, it does not take long for the internalized racist attitudes to resurface, and therein lies the problem. The Black Pride Movement took the superficial value of the culture and applied it to certain aspects of life in hopes of making a profound change in the image and perception of the race. No doubt it created a cult with some positive and long-lasting effect, for example, music, but it, too, failed to transcend the material value into a non-material one. When a belief does not reach the soul, it will not transform one's attitude. So Dee is still subject to her own inferiority because her mentality is fixated at the same stage—she fears being victimized and oppressed, and superficially believes rebellious and extreme actions to be the only solution. Her appreciation of black culture may linger as long as the fashion lasts, or fear and despair gnaw at her. Yet, she will always be spiritually detached from her mother and sister, for the different views they hold toward the recent past. The quilt that links generations would have lost its soul had Dee succeeded in snatching it because it should belong to the person who stitches it and uses it indigenously to implant the soul in the object. Maggie embraces the spirit of authentic culture and knows how to enliven it out of true respect, which Dee lacks or belittles, as it contradicts her mythical ideal of black culture. Instead of asking to be taught quilt-making, Dee insists on taking away a finished product. It makes one wonder to what extent "Black is beautiful" is cultivated in one's mind, or if it was sufficient to change one's internalized oppressive attitude. The fundamental goal the movement missed had thus a detrimental effect on the Afro-American community in terms of the progress of black civil rights. The anger and antagonism of young blacks against whites was projected onto the relationships within their own community, as exemplified in Dee's relationship with her mother. The contempt for the backward Southerners was frequently justified by the wrongs they did such as being subservient and lacking cultural awareness. Violence charged against whites was often justified by the insufficient progress of black justice. It is the former Walker particularly condemned amid the resurgence of nationalism among the young. The intolerance toward their own race grew so intensely that the attitude was tantamount to internalized racism—a counter-reaction against externalized racism. Name-calling old Afro-Americans whom the young accused of betraying the race and dissenting from them as "Uncle Tom,"[3] "Auntie Jemima,"[4] "Reverend Pork Chop" was common in internalized racism. It was analogous to "racial policing within black communities," as described by Younge in "Don't blame Uncle Tom," or "keep you and me in check" as Malcolm X warned in his speech "Message to the Grassroots." Though Dee does not call her mother offensive names in the conversation, the accusatory tone no doubt hints the same— "if you are not radical, you must be black with a white heart."

Old Southern Afro-Americans were particularly vulnerable to double racism. The mother in "Everyday Use" bears the brunt of this. Inside and outside her community, she is judged by her looks and intelligence. White superiority against black inferiority was always a thorny issue in both slave states and free states. The complexity lay in the fact that the two races were intertwined so intricately that they were often two sides of the same coin, though black inferiority was subject to tighter authorial scrutiny. Richard Wright, for example, was inspired by Harriet Beecher Stowe's anti-slavery novel *Uncle Tom's Cabin* (1852) and published a collection of short stories *Uncle Tom's Children* (1938) about oppression and white racism in the Deep South. Decades later came Charles Waddell Chesnutt's "The Sheriff's Children" in the short story collection *The Wife of His Youth and Other Stories of the Color-Line* (1899) about racist judgment and lynching. What complicated the whole issue was the addition of prejudice against the same race. The way that Dee's mother is stereotyped as a backward rural Southern woman with rough features and manners—"a large, a big-boned woman with rough, man-working hands ... knocked a bull calf straight in the brain between the eyes with a sledge hammer" ("Everyday Use" 315)—opposite to lily-white skin and white intelligence idealized by Dee, exemplifies double racism. The mother is not just demeaned as powerless in front of white people ("I have talked to them always with one foot raised in flight, with my head turned in whichever way is farthest from them" [ibid]), but also rejected by her daughter for who she is. The value of integrity upheld by the old generation to help preserve the family through hard work and perseverance is diminished in the eye of Dee and other young Afro-Americans. The efforts invested in the Civil Rights Movement in the last two decades are trampled down. The irony is that it was neither changing names nor idolizing the white culture but showing resilience and safeguarding moral principles regardless of situations that cultivated the Afro-American culture. Characteristics such as being home-loving, affectionate,[5] docile, and simple[6] were attributed to the genuine Afro-American culture, yet dismissed by the young generation as an impediment to the legal and social progress of the black community. Internalized racism due to the young's ignorance of the recent and the remote past was as rampant as externalized racism, which might lead one to wonder if the Civil Rights Movement had radicalized or liberated their minds, or if they had ever understood civil rights. Given the movement's elusive and broad definitions, it was not surprising that the young and the old would clash on the common ground via different means toward attaining the same goal.

Civil Rights and Prejudice

Since "civil rights" was defined for the first time in the House of Representatives in 1866 as "those which have no relation to the establishment, support, or management of government" (Cameron 89), the terms pertaining to Afro-Americans such as the rights to vote and own property were spelled out, followed by further guarantee of their rights in courts and equal access to public transportation and accommodations. The Reconstruction era from 1863 to 1877[7] was, in fact, a time for Afro-Americans to realize that securing civil rights and liberties was more than legally abolishing slavery, but fighting in social, economic, and political battles as a consequence of slavery, and that prejudice could extend beyond plantations and manifest itself in various forms apart from physical and verbal abuse. The resistance to change from whites was as fierce as the force to enact by law. Passing and enacting the Black Codes[8] and overruling the Civil Rights Act of 1875[9] turned back the clock. The extension of the codes from slave to black, in other words, the transition of slave economy to labor economy, kept Afro-Americans from benefiting from the economic growth and ensured that the institutionalization of racism continued.

The enforcement of Jim Crow laws after the Reconstruction era was a further blanket ban on black rights and liberties that had previously been guaranteed through the law. The segregated system circumvented such guarantees by separating and impoverishing public and transportation facilities other than schools to degrade the lives of Afro-Americans. The need to teach them to exercise their rights was imminent. W. E. B. Du Bois was among a few Afro-American scholars and activists who increasingly took center stage in debates. In the late 1890s, Du Bois had already published an influential article, "Strivings of the Negro People," in which he coins a term for the peculiar feeling of "double-consciousness":

> [T]his sense of always looking at one's self through the eyes of others, of measuring one's soul by the tape of a world that looks on in amused contempt and pity. One feels his twoness,—an American, a Negro; two souls, two thoughts, two unreconciled strivings; two warring ideals in one dark body, whose dogged strength alone keeps it from being torn asunder [194].

The yardsticks used to judge the blacks themselves and measure their souls were thus both internal and external: inside, the self-awareness of being observed; outside, the relentless social pressure exerted on the psyche. That push-and-pull resulted in binary sensations and brought up the existential questions: Do I exist? Am I an exile? Do I live under someone's shadow? The bipolar division between blacks and whites had never been so sharp and agonizing. The awareness of incompatibility and antagonism between the two races would tear the African American's soul should their mental and physical strength fade. Reconstruction promised them certain rights and liberties, which sadly did not come. They had to learn to grow up from the child of emancipation to the youth with three selves—self-consciousness, self-realization, and self-respect—in order to be themselves (ibid. 196). Someday, as Du Bois dreamed, the world would no longer be black and white but gray. His ultimate vision was to conform to the ideals of the American republic and for white and black people to complement each other. Sadly, it was also what the young Afro-Americans of Walker's generation disdained. Du Bois was Uncle Tom in their eyes. Like him, they realized that prejudice was the root of slavery. However, to compromise was to succumb to fate. If one had to strive to live better with dignity, one must return to his or her indigenous roots. The mother in "Everyday Use" representing the previous generations believes otherwise: when one masters that double consciousness and the three selves, one can merge black and white into an integral part. Thus, it is the mother who maintains her integrity through awareness and self-belief. She knows what is happening in the white world and the yardsticks applied to the black community. Yet, the physique she develops due to manual routines, the unpretentiousness she has in character, the same old house she rebuilds, the handmade quilts she retains, the furniture and utensils passed on through generations, all identify her as a bona fide Afro-American. Dee, instead, shows the binary oppositions, which only exposes her ignorance. For a time in the past, she was against her culture and looked down on her family: "I had offered Dee (Wangero) a quilt when she went away to college. Then she had told me they were old-fashioned, out of style" ("Everyday Use" 320). Now, she embraces her roots and the tradition overzealously, and decides to take the old things away for home decoration. "But they're priceless!" (ibid.) Dee gushes while marveling at the quilts. Her soul is torn between two worlds, oscillating between absolute adoration and downright abhorrence. Her lack of three selves shows that she never goes through the process of self-emancipation and does not live in harmony with double-consciousness. The prejudice she is subject to outside the black community due to her ancestral roots is thus projected onto her family; the strength she is proud to display only reduces her to shallowness and superficiality. Storming and ransacking the house, grabbing the indigenous and exotic items she could never make or produce to adorn her house amount to the barbaric and domineering acts colonizers do to their colonists. While she cannot bear the name that links to the oppressors, she herself acts as one of them: "[s]he used to read to us without pity; forcing words, lies, other folks' habits, whole lives upon us two, sitting trapped and ignorant underneath her voice. She washed us in a river of make-believe, burned us with a lot of knowledge we didn't necessarily need to know" ("Everyday Use" 316). By oppressing her mother and her sister through knowledge, she asserts her own image and believes she can manipulate their minds, thus regaining and boosting her self-esteem. That superiority over one's own race is not a strength but weakness, cowardice, and inferiority. Like other peers of her generation, Dee's inferiority complex comes from being trapped in her own insufficiency amid soul searching and judgments from outside.

"EVERYDAY USE" AND CULTURAL HERITAGE

Du Bois in his most popular work *The Souls of Black Folk* (1903) insists that his black fellows should search their soul to know what they truly need. The soul is always at the heart of the pursuit for integrity, dignity, and humanity. It speaks the impeccable culture one inherits. The quilts as a source of historical and cultural solace in "Everyday Use" forge a close bond between the ancestors, as do the churn and the dasher that bear the wear and tear of all those years. As family heirlooms that preoccupy the female personae, the quilts in particular honor the maternal ancestors. The ubiquity underlying the phenomenal heritage carries a poignant meaning in the story, for the quilts symbolize the crisscross of tradition and history, just like various quilt patterns telling folklore, experiences, and stories of the past. It is the mystic and creative power that pulls Afro-Americans together. Quilting as a distinctive textile tradition has thus united and empowered the maternal community, emboldened the women as well as healed their soul. We see Mama and Maggie, alongside Aunt Dee and Grandma Dee heartened by putting the quilts to everyday use, while Dee distinguishes herself from others by utilizing them as artifacts. They are collective recollections for the race and families, in other words, resources to "reconstruct the experiences of African American women [and] a record of their cultural and political past" (Cash 30). Quilt-making epitomizes such kinship and even helped Afro-American women survive slavery. From bondage to freedom, quilting sustains hope and provides survival strategies. That is why the mother is adamant about keeping the old quilts as she comes to realize they bear the hopes that the maternal ancestors have held onto for decades and desired to pass on to their descendants. To continue the familial spirit, one has to know the core value of quilts and quilt-making attached to the Afro-American community. Maggie possesses every single quality—knowing how to quilt and holding a fond memory of recent family members—that Dee lacks. In the mother's eye, Dee will only degrade and abandon the quilts once the fashion has passed.

History proves fighting for civil rights is a collective rather than individual effort, so much so that success hinges on each individual's potential and the abilities of the group. No one fares better or worse than others. Maggie has a sharp memory and the intelligence for making quilts, while the mother has superior physical strength to do men's jobs. Together, they contribute to the custom and tradition. This is the soft power they display as a reserve, which could turn into a strong force to propel the movement should it be recognized. Instead, it is trampled on by Dee, for it reinforces the stereotype of African slaves—toil hard in abject poverty. Dee's feeling of shame magnifies her indignation and powerlessness, turns herself into an oppressor, and enacts the same systematic and institutionalized mistreatment that was perpetuated throughout the slavery period. The destructive force at times can isolate her from others, as evidenced by Maggie's doubt if she ever had any friends ("Everyday Use" 317), or result in disunity in the movement if her peers gather the same force that turns them against each other. As such, internalized racism and oppression are not only a manifestation of individual suffering but a collective failure of handling distress. The Black Power Movement and its sub-movements unfortunately shared that fatal symptom, which blocked every promising and potentially powerful black liberation effort from success. While the slogan "Black is beautiful" did partially liberate one's mind, it could not effectively deal with the root of the problem. As long as internalized racism existed, the movements to improve blacks' civil rights would likely falter. This is a worrying sign that Walker indicates through the story.

ETHNIC AND RACIAL INEQUALITY IN SMITH'S "THE EMBASSY OF CAMBODIA"

"Everyday Use" is not just a story of the 1970s but an unfinished chapter for the ethnic group today, which is also the case for another story by Zadie Smith, an Afro-British writer. "The Embassy of Cambodia" is a short story of modern times addressing the same issue yet in a broader context. Fatou, an African girl from the Ivory Coast, migrates to London and works as a servant for the Derawals, a wealthy Middle-Eastern family. Her life is a literal reflection of myriad racial issues entrenched in Britain and more so in the multi-ethnic city, which is a magnet for various non-white races from Africa, India and China, for example. The dynamics between ethnic groups are no longer confined to black and white, and neither are the conversations about races. Between Fatou and her Nigerian friend Andrew, the topics can range from the Holocaust, to the Rwandan genocide, to Hiroshima. Globalization does draw them together as pals who can share deeper and wider racial issues than Dee and others in "Everyday Use." However, the same old story still rings true. Fatou and Andrew have to brace themselves for racism, except that it goes beyond simple white superiority. Hence, worse than Dee, Fatou is subject to prejudice from the whites in the swimming pool as well as the Arabic children and adults in the Derawals family. Her self-value sinks further, as now she can only compare herself with people of the same color and seek solace from the wretchedness of an "imprisoned" Sudanese. Little does she know that when the Derawals confiscate her passport and her wages, she has already forfeited her freedom and civil rights like the Sudanese and other African slaves, not to mention drifting involuntarily for work. Yet, she vehemently denies it: "[n]o, on balance she did not think she was a slave" ("The Embassy of Cambodia" 0–7).

For all her denial, Fatou is ultimately leading a life of chattel comparable to a piece of property without value, goods transferred from one owner to another, an item to fill in on the inventory of British plantation records. When Fatou recounts how male and female Africans are both taken as prostitutes by the whites and she is raped at work in Carib Beach in Jamaica, it recalls the unspeakable pain and suffering inflicted upon the slaves in the plantations, who were forced to provide sex for their white masters. If there was one thing that could save her as well as other blacks' lives, it must be the knowledge of civil rights, and that, as Du Bois suggests, is precisely what many of them, including Fatou, lack. At the back of her mind though, Fatou knows that "self-reliance" (ibid. 0–8) holds the key to an individual's and a nation's independence, which can ultimately overcome prejudice, establish and assert one's own identity as not subordinate to other races. Sadly, her thought can never materialize. Her fundamental right to receive a full education is denied mostly due to poverty, hence she loses the opportunity to stand on her own feet.

Fatou's beleaguered situation underscores the intricate link between prejudice and economy. In "Everyday Use," Dee turns herself into a "gold digger" from head to toe—a way to boost her status inside and outside the black community. Fatou bemoans the lack of financial independence that costs her her freedom. She has to steal the Derawals' guest passes in order to swim. She cannot afford a proper swimming costume, but instead wears "a sturdy black bra and a pair of plain black cotton knickers" (ibid. 0–7), which she shamefully and desperately hides in the dark. Money is a curse as well as blessing. Had the Derawals not been rich enough to hire Fatou as a servant, the latter would not have been subject to prejudice by the former. Had Fatou been financially independent, she could have decided her own fate and chosen where and for whom to work under fair conditions.

What Smith points out through the story is that prejudice has become a more alarming, widespread, and complex issue reaching a global and multi-ethnic level. In reality, we do not necessarily see a black person targeted by a white person much as we presume in a typical situation.

The stark contrast between Walker and Smith precisely lies there, as the latter implies that such contentious issues unavoidably go hand in hand with globalization and, more than ever, with capitalism, while in Walker's time, people believed that prejudice in America was largely due to tension between blacks and whites, and purely driven by color. In modern times, there can be tensions between different ethnic groups for manifold factors apart from color such as social status, profession, income, and education. Above all, racial prejudice is no longer an issue unique to America. It will, therefore, be naive for us to solely blame whites for prejudice and superiority, as it exists in different ethnic groups regardless of color and origin, though the former is a clear benchmark for judgment. As educated as Andrew—who acts as Du Bois with his supreme knowledge to enlighten Fatou—is, he equally feels inferior because he is also aware of the stigma carried by his race. His incompetence at swimming reminds him he is no different from other Africans, who can never master the skill.

National stereotypes give rise to prejudice and supremacy. To defy a stereotype and demand equality, one has to make a multitude of efforts to show the world who he or she really is. Apparently, civil rights movements give people hope for a fundamental change in all aspects of their lives and recognition of their ethnic, social as well as cultural identity. It is an opportunity to show their power, intelligence, and quality on par with the whites. What is peculiar and thus setting a different tone from the movements in America is that those in Britain could involve myriad races who have faced the same prejudice. For example, in 1963, Paul Stephenson led a boycott against the Bristol bus company not solely for the blacks but also for the Asians. In the postwar years, one could easily find a sign reading "No blacks, no Irish, no dogs" in a pub.[10] Prejudice was as individual as it was institutional, against blacks as well as other colors. In the case of the pub, it was against their own color. That is why civil rights movements in Britain were not purely a black issue. The British Black Panther movement (1968–1973), for instance, gathered momentum with the help of South Asians. Political coalitions among different ethnic groups such as the Conference of Afro-Asian-Caribbean Organizations in London (1962) blossomed, apart from the organizations initially set up for their own people such as the Pakistani Progressive Party. It was a concerted effort across multi-ethnic minority groups to fight for their own and others' rights in a multi-ethnic society.

Out of all these movements launched by different ethnic groups, black movements are still considered prominent because the unique history of African migration plays a key role in shaping British history. Essentially, it started with the Windrush generation of Afro-Caribbeans in 1948, who opened a new chapter of British multi-ethnic society, and thereafter hundreds of thousands of British colonial subjects of various races followed. It was the consequence of the British Government policy that allowed immigration from British colonies which brought multi-ethnic communities together and particularly to Willesden, where Smith set her story. In fact, it is one of the most diverse areas in the country, as Smith portrays realistically the composition "of the Old and New People of Willesden [who] are not one people" (0–13). Such diversity is what the British government today eagerly promotes to the world—a utopia that champions civil rights issues—and indirectly dismisses systematic racism, as Robin Bunce argues (Brown, "Britain's Black

Power Movement"). Nevertheless, government policy cannot make ordinary people unprejudiced. Racial inequality is still an everyday struggle, and whites against blacks is still a prominent issue. Worse still, the discord between groups with diasporic roots and internalized racism within black communities start to surface (Alexander 1042–1043). All these set against the backdrop—Willesden—become ironic in "The Embassy of Cambodia." Smith brushes aside the narrative as a smoke screen. Racial and ethnic inequality is as entrenched as before and as unsolvable as the situation in America. While it might be true that today the current generation of people of African descent in America and Britain reaps the benefits of social and political movements of centuries, anti-black sentiment is still there thinly disguised as a defense for the safety and self-interest of individuals or white communities. It is especially true in America when police brutality targeted at young Afro-Americans is at a record high.[11] The emergence of Black Lives Matter as a neo–Black Power Movement in America is to strengthen black power against the distressing pattern of violence and the institutionalized mistreatment. Some see it as a proactive way to channel the black spirit such that the sentiment regarding racial prejudice will abate.

It is worth noting that the pattern of oppression is always twofold, as we have discussed throughout the chapter. It is clearly not just a story of "us against them" but "us against us." If externalized racism is hard to obliterate, so is internalized racism. Racial slurs like "Uncle Tom" and "Auntie Jemima" are still used to accuse their own people of having a white heart. Black or white is still an inner struggle for most Afro-Americans. So long as they are denied a proper outlet to heal the distress, internalized racism will still be the solution to vent their negative emotions.

NEOCOLONIALISM IN THE GLOBAL CONTEXT

When two stories separated by forty years relate to similar experiences, we cannot help but wonder: what is the future of the Africans in Britain and America? When Fatou is sacked by the family and calls Andrew for help, all she gets is a promise of another cleaning job. Destiny strips her of her power to change her life, not to mention the rights of education and the right to vote. Civil rights become a luxury to her, which in a fair society should not be, especially in Britain, a country with a proud history of Magna Carta and the abolition of the slave trade. It is not surprising then that Fatou feels dejected and refuses to show gratitude to the receptionist in the pool: "[g]ratitude was just another kind of servitude. Better to make your own arrangements" ("The Embassy of Cambodia" 0–21). As reality bites, disillusion turns into frustration. Like those growing up as the second or the third generation who cannot see a promising future, Fatou gets lost and can only identify herself as a perennial victim under the enduring pattern of prejudice. Watching the shuttlecock flying back and forth in the air inside the Embassy, she knows that it is forever a false hope to live a life free of prejudice, as it is not a fair but violent game.

This endless, unfair game played often on American soil and occasionally on British soil is best seen through multiple lenses. On the macroscopic level, we found different political and social movements aiming at the same targets, mobilizing people and shaping the society constantly. On the microscopic level, there are the interactions between the black, the white and other races, and within the black community that is plagued by its own discrimination problem.

Interestingly, both Walker and Smith chose females as the protagonists in their stories. This could be seen as a nod to the contribution African women have made for their families and communities in an exotic land, as well as an inspiration drawn from their humanistic morals. The latter guides Dee's mother, Fatou, and millions of others to the right path. It is this ardent devotion that has propelled civil rights movements in Britain and America. African women's resilience and robustness further help bridge the recent past and the remote past. That mythical past Dee desperately wants to understand is ironically present in front of her. Nowhere but here can she find such a vivid figure, her mother, who can live up to the ancient Roman personification of Africa—a woman holding a cornucopia of fruit and a scorpion symbolizing hidden treasures and inexhaustible fecundity (Curtis 178). It is a double misfortune when such a "womanist" figure is slighted by her daughter for the house she builds. The pasture it is on is a source of faith, like the gardens of Africa (Adams and McShane 8). It, too, gives her mother and her maternal ancestors the faith of mankind and racial equality.

The garden in Smith's modern version has turned into a swimming pool, in which Fatou attempts to find her African female power, albeit ironically, through "swimming fast and angry" (0–14). It is there she contemplates her identity and recalls bitterly the racial prejudice that happened elsewhere, for example, in Rome. The African spirit of devotion to one's origin regardless of the humiliation of centuries should be magnified in London, a melting pot of mixed races rubbing shoulders every day and thus increasing the chance of multiracial conflicts. Rich and poor gaps due to neocolonialism have widened further instead of narrowed. Africans like Fatou are still exploited as cheap laborers. That Fatou and Andrew are discriminated against in the pool is a familiar scene symptomatic of neocolonialism as a way to perpetuate prejudice in modern times, which reminds us of an instruction issued to the white troops in Nigeria in colonial times: "[t]he British are looked up to, put on a very high level. Don't bring that level down by undue familiarity" (Coleman 152).

Apparently, a resurgence of black nationalism in Britain is evidence of black power against neocolonialism. Protesting against the existence of the statues related to African slavery and demanding that they be torn down (for instance, Cecil Rhodes in Oriel College at the University of Oxford) is the twenty-first century's British civil rights movement. Yet, it is still far less successful than the movement in America. The removal of Confederate statues like Robert E. Lee speaks volumes. In Britain, the actions sometimes meet with either silence or suspicion even though anger is bubbling among the black population. Such diverse attitudes towards handling the same matter are underpinned by the cultural and historical perceptual differences between Africans from the two countries. Of the same ancestral roots, they are shaped by different cultural environments, which might explain the different reactions by Dee and Fatou towards the same situation, with the former being more assertive and the latter more reticent.

History has given the blacks some outstanding female activists such as Sojourner Truth, a slave and abolitionist; Anna Julia Cooper, a black feminist asserting that female Afro-Americans' unique standpoint and contribution render them equally capable to exert influence, fight injustice and better the world as males (*A Voice from the South* 32–33, 134–135); and Toni Morrison, a prominent contemporary Afro-American writer exploring the absence of the black voice—"[I]n matters of race, silence and evasion have historically ruled literary discourse ... to allow the black body a shadowless participation in the dominant cultural body" (9–10). Morrison's view about such absence in the late twentieth century takes subtle form and seeks justification per se. Such absence, as Morrison rightly pointed out in the late twentieth century, takes subtle form and seeks justification per se, for example, altered or disguised in coded language and purposeful restriction in order to conceal racial hostility and moral frailty, which is not all an uncommon practice to fabricate Africanist presence today (6). Censoring and policing to achieve political correctness, giving alternative facts, or marginalizing the race violate freedom and the spirit of Americanism. Likewise, in Britain, voices demanding racial equality are often dismissed as hearsay or discouraged because they threaten the image the British have long built up—that Britain is the first country to emancipate slaves, and today it is the utopia to promote fairness and equality. In such a paradoxical world, distinctive Africanism becomes more indispensable than ever to keep the integrity and define the uniqueness of Africans in America and Britain.

Yet, how can the Africans find the spirit which gives them the strength and dignity to live on? With the quilts, the mother has found the answer. Dee convinces herself by donning all the quintessential African clothes and accessories. Fatou is searching for an answer between the pool and the Embassy of Cambodia. While the power of water like baptizing refreshes her "with a sense of brightness, of being washed clean, that neither the weather nor her new circumstance could dim" ("The Embassy of Cambodia" 0–21), and gives her energy and hope to find her identity, the "pock" and "smash" sound inside the Embassy acts as a slap on her face and sends her back to brutal reality, as if the positivity and hopefulness conveyed in the ending of Walker's story of the 1970s in America have degenerated into negativity and hopelessness in Smith's version of the twenty-first century in Britain. From "Everyday Use" to "The Embassy of Cambodia," we witness a world that has gotten worse and we are, as before, unable to combat different kinds of prejudice. As long as prejudice exists, Fatou's question, "are we born to suffer?" ("The Embassy of Cambodia" 0–10) still rings true and the fight for civil rights shall go on.

Notes

1. A term used to describe the Americas after the discovery, contrasting to the Old World—the world that existed in the pre-Columbian era known to Europe, Asia, and Africa.
2. It was one of the movements related to Black Nationalism, the foremost idea of the political movement.
3. The name originated from the protagonist in the abolitionist novel *Uncle Tom's Cabin* (1852). It initially served as praise for any black who made a sacrifice for freedom. In 1919, the Rev. George Alexander McGuire, who supported the radical black movement, turned it into an epithet for the same reason. See Spingarn, "When 'Uncle Tom' Became an Insult."
4. The female counterpart of Uncle Tom.
5. "In order to appreciate the sufferings of the negroes sold south, it must be remembered that all the instinctive affections of that race are peculiarly strong. Their local attachments are very abiding. They are not naturally daring and enterprising, but home-loving and affectionate" (*Uncle Tom's Cabin* 143).
6. "The negro race is confessedly more simple, docile, childlike, and affectionate, than other races; and hence the divine graces of love and faith, when in-breathed by the Holy Spirit, find in their natural temperament a more congenial atmosphere" (*A Key to Uncle Tom's Cabin* 41).
7. The Reconstruction era refers to two periods: 1865–1877 (covers the whole country) and 1863–1877 (focuses on Southern States).
8. The Black Codes were passed in two consecutive years (1865 and 1866) and had been enacted in some Northern states such as New York and Michigan before the Civil War.
9. The Supreme Court ruled that the 14th amendment about the public accommodation sections was unconstitutional.
10. Though it remains contentious, *Discrimination and the Irish Community in Britain: A Report of Research undertaken for the Commission for Racial Equality* by Hickman and Walter (1997) can still serve as a proof.
11. For an accurate figure, see https://mappingpoliceviolence.org/.

Bibliography

Adams, Jonathan S., and Thomas O. McShane. *The Myth of Wild Africa: Conservation Without Illusion*. Berkeley: University of California Press, 1996. Print.
Alexander, Claire. "Breaking Black: The Death of Ethnic and Racial Studies in Britain." *Ethnic and Racial Studies* 41.6 (2018): 1034–1054. Web.

Beccaro, Thomas Del. *The Divided Era: How We Got Here and the Keys to America's Reconciliation*. Austin, Texas: Greenleaf Book Group Press, 2015. Print.
Bolton, Diane K., Patricia E. C. Croot and M. A. Hicks. "Willesden: Settlement and Growth." *A History of the County of Middlesex: Volume 7, Acton, Chiswick, Ealing and Brentford, West Twyford, Willesden*. Edited by T. F. T. Baker and C. R. Elrington. London: Victoria County History, 1982. 182–204. Print/Web.
Brendon, Piers. "'Renascent Africa': The Gold Coast and Nigeria." *The Decline and Fall of the British Empire 1781–1997*. London: Vintage, 2008. 510–544. Print.
_____. "The World Turned Upside Down: The American Revolution and the Slave Trade." *The Decline and Fall of the British Empire 1781–1997*. London: Vintage, 2008. 1–29. Print.
Brown, Mark. "Britain's Black Power Movement is at Risk of Being Forgotten, Say Historians." *The Guardian*. 27 Dec 2013. https://www.theguardian.com/world/2013/dec/27/britain-black-power-movement-risk-forgotten-historians. Accessed 16 Nov 2018.
Cameron, Jimmy C. *Racism and Hate: An American Reality History, Documents, Essays and Analyses*. Bloomington, IN: AuthorHouse, 2014. Print/Web.
Cash, Floris Barnett. "Kinship and Quilting: An Examination of an African-American Tradition." *The Journal of Negro History* 80.1 (1995): 30–41. Web.
Christian, Barbara T. "Introduction." *Women Writers Texts and Contexts: "Everyday Use" Alice Walker*. New Brunswick, NJ: Rutgers University Press, 1994. 3–18. Print.
Coleman, J. S. *Nigeria: Background to Nationalism*. Berkeley: University of California Press, 1971. Print.
Cooper, Anna J. *The Voice of Anna Julia Cooper: Including a Voice from the South and Other Important Essays, Papers, and Letters*. Edited by Charles Lemert and Esme Bhan. Lanham: Rowman & Littlefield Publishers, Inc., 1998. Print/Web.
Cowart, David. "Heritage and Deracination in Walker's 'Everyday Use.'" *Studies in Short Fiction 33*. Newberry, SC: Newberry College, 1996. 171–184. Print/Web.
Curtin, Philip D. *The Image of Africa: British Ideas and Action, 1780–1850, Volume 1*. London: University of Wisconsin Press, 1964. Print.
Dal Lago, Enrico, and Constantina Katsari, eds. *Slave Systems: Ancient and Modern*. Cambridge: Cambridge University Press, 2008. Print.
Davis, David Brion. *The Problem of Slavery in the Age of Revolution 1770–1823*. Oxford: Oxford University Press, 1999. Print.
Du Bois, W. E. B. "Reconstruction and its Benefits." *The American Historical Review* 15.4 (July 1910): 781–799. Web.
_____. *The Souls of Black Folk*. Chicago: A.C. McClurg & Co., 1903. Web.
_____. "Strivings of the Negro People." *The Atlantic*, Aug. 1897. Web.
Farrar, Max. "Social Movements and the Struggle over 'Race.'" *Democracy and Participation—Popular Protest and New Social Movements*. Edited by Malcolm J. Todd and Gary Taylor. London: Merlin Press, 2004. 78–95. Web.
Germane, Marina. "Minority Coalition-Building and Nation-States." *Journal on Ethnopolitics and Minority Issues in Europe* 14.2 (2015): 51–75. Web.
Groba, Constante González. "Stitching the Self into the Fabric of History and Community: Quilts and Family Tradition in Alice Walker's 'Everyday Use.'" *On Their Own Premises: Southern Women Writers and the Homeplace*. N.p.: Universitat de València, 2008. 213–230. Web.
Johnson, Robin Nicole. *The Psychology of Racism: How Internalized Racism, Academic Self-Concept, and Campus Racial Climate Impact the Academic Experiences and Achievement of African American Undergraduates*. Los Angeles: University of California, 2008. Web.
Kornblith, Gary John. *Slavery and Sectional Strife in the Early American Republic 1776–1821*. Lanham: Rowman & Littlefield, 2010. Print/Web.
Lipsky, Suzanne. *Internalized Racism*. Seattle: Rational Island Publishers, 1978. Print/Web.
Malcolm X. "Message to the Grassroots." Northern Grass Roots Leadership Conference, 10 Nov 1963, Detroit, Michigan. Web.

Montesquieu, Charles de. *The Spirit of Laws*. 1748–1752. Translated by Thomas Nugent. Kitchener, Ontario: Batoche Books, 2001. Print/Web.
Mooney, Chase C., and Barry Grossabach. "Civil Rights and Liberties." *The Encyclopedia Americana Vol. 6: Cathedrals to Civil War*. New York, Chicago: Americana Corporation, 1829. 774–785. Print.
Morrison, Toni. *Playing in the Dark: Whiteness and the Literary Imagination*. New York: Vintage Books, 1992. Print.
Nkrumah, Kwame. *Neo-Colonialism: The Last Stage of Imperialism*. London: Thomas Nelson & Sons, 1965. Print.
Northup, Solomon. *Twelve Years a Slave*. Auburn, New York: Derby & Miller, 1853. Print/Web.
Roberts, Justin. "Race and the Origins of Plantation Slavery." *Oxford Research Encyclopedia of American History*. Edited by John Butler. New York: Oxford University Press, Mar 2016. http://oxfordre.com/americanhistory/view/10.1093/acrefore/9780199329175.001.0001/acrefore-9780199329175-e-268?print=pdf. Accessed 11 Nov 2017.
Robertson, James I. "Civil War: 2. Manpower and Resources." *The Encyclopedia Americana Vol. 6: Cathedrals to Civil War*. New York, Chicago: Americana Corporation, 1829. 793–796. Print.
_____. "Civil War: 3. The Military Campaigns." *The Encyclopedia Americana Vol. 6: Cathedrals to Civil War*. New York, Chicago: Americana Corporation, 1829. 796–811. Print.
Sam, Dicky. *Liverpool and Slavery: An Historical Account of the Liverpool-African Slave Trade by "a Genuine 'Dicky Sam'"* Liverpool: A. Bowker & Son, 1884. Web.
Smith, Zadie. "The Embassy of Cambodia." *The New Yorker*, 11 Feb 2013. https://www.newyorker.com/magazine/2013/02/11/the-embassy-of-cambodia. Accessed 9 Nov 2018.
Spingarn, Adena. "When 'Uncle Tom' Became an Insult." *The Root*, 17 May 2010. www.theroot.com/when-uncle-tom-became-an-insult-1790879561. Accessed 1 March 2017.
Stowe, Harriet Beecher. *A Key to Uncle Tom's Cabin*. Boston: Jewett, 1854. Web.
_____. *Uncle Tom's Cabin*. Boston: John P. Jewett, 1852. Web.
Walker, Alice. "Everyday Use." *Women Writers: Texts and Contexts*. Edited by B.T. Christian. New Brunswick, NJ: Rutgers University Press, 1994. 314–321. Print.
_____. *In Search of Our Mothers' Gardens: Womanist Prose*. Orlando, FL: Harvest Books, 2003. Print.
White, David. "'Everyday Use': Defining African-American Heritage." 2001. *Anniina's Alice Walker Page*. 19 Sept 2002. www.luminarium.org/contemporary/alicew/davidwhite.htm. Accessed 2 Oct 2017.
Younge, Gary. "Don't blame Uncle Tom." *The Guardian*, 30 Mar. 2002. https://www.theguardian.com/books/2002/mar/30/race.society. Accessed 10 March 2017.

10
Femininity and Social Pressures in Lessing's "To Room Nineteen" and Gilman's "The Yellow Wall-Paper"

Gender issues have long been a subject examined in literature. Nathaniel Hawthorne's "The Birthmark" (1843), Charlotte Perkins Gilman's "The Yellow Wall-Paper" (1892), Katherine O'Flaherty's "The Story of an Hour" (1894), Mary Lavin's "Sarah" (1943), Doris Lessing's "To Room Nineteen" (1963) and Alice Walker's short story collection *You Can't Keep a Good Woman Down: Short Stories* (1981), to name a few, are among the classic examples of how a short story is the best genre to explore the complex issues surrounding gender. Such complexity lies in multifaceted layers intertwined in a condensed form which, unlike a novel, does not necessarily give a clear conclusion. Such inconclusiveness best suits the ever-disputed issues on femininity and the problems between the two sexes. Short stories, thus, have the power to crystallize the fleeting moments regardless of a conclusion and draw readers' attention to the irresoluble nature of gender issues. The stories tend to focus on what is happening and how things happened in the episodes that show the protagonists' mental, physical, and psychological pain and suffering. They constitute the telling effect and further probe into the core of the problems: why are all protagonists unanimously women? Why are women always perceived as hysterical and emotional objects? Do biological and psychological factors play a part in determining women's destiny? Why, after all these heated debates over the last century, are women still subject to scrutiny? Why do women still succumb to fate even when women's rights are progressing? How has the society played a role in molding women to fit the stereotypically "desirable" model? These are some of the fundamental questions that many short story writers have in mind when they write stories about feminism. By exploring it through words, writers question and challenge the notion of "femininity" and the problems that surround it. In this chapter, we shall see how Lessing uses "To Room Nineteen" to address these issues. Another prominent feminist work, "The Yellow Wall-Paper" by Gilman, will be examined as well.

LESSING'S "TO ROOM NINETEEN"

"To Room Nineteen" debunks modern fairy tales. The story begins with the narrator's premise of the Rawlings' failed marriage attributed to "intelligence" ("To Room Nineteen" 525). The short yet fundamental beginning foretells the reader in a matter-of-fact tone that the story will not be about a blissful marriage but one at odds with tradition and old wisdom. In a short story confined within a limited sphere, Lessing skillfully and knowingly uses understatement to usher the reader into a crusade against institutional marriage, which has victimized women, including Lessing and her mother, for centuries. In the story, Susan Rawlings is the victim. An English woman with a sound career and a flat of her own, Susan is projected as a member of the middle class who will one day settle down with a man of the same class and probably the same temperament. Matthew Rawlings, who has a well-paid job and property, is seen as an ideal partner for her. Social class and economic status secure their marriage. On the surface, it is a modern marriage in which neither of them marries up. They are also aware of the pitfalls of the old mentality of marriage and try not to submit their personality to the other (ibid. 526). Based on their "intelligent" decision, they, therefore, co-own a flat in South Kensington, one of the most expensive neighborhoods in London, and then move into a house in Richmond in preparation for a big family. To everyone's mind, the couple takes a normal and correct path to have as many children as they can for "their infallible sense for choosing right" (ibid.). As such, every judgment and decision is seen as conformity to social norms and morality without an inch of deviance. The less leeway, the merrier. Has such a maxim brought them genuine happiness? As much as we would like to think so, Lessing clearly does not, as she takes a swift turn to bring this fairy tale to an end in no more than two pages. That "infallible sense" is like a balloon pierced and deflated. Material possessions and children cannot save their marriage, let alone the essential ingredient in every marriage—love. The only savior is intelligence, which they believe can save them from repeating the mistakes other couples make, or at least to minimize the shock and pain of reality. It is the cocoon of privilege and security that they are determined to create for the family.

Ironically, intelligence is also a telltale sign of the Rawlings' failed marriage. The desperate attempt to rationalize every decision they make for their marriage is deemed to be futile, as the bond between a couple should not be merely built upon logic and reasoning. The more they stress intelligence, the further they pull themselves apart from each other. It is intelligence that makes the marriage spiral into oblivion. Lessing's purposeful reiteration of intelligence in a story of fewer than thirty pages amplifies the sarcastic effect not from anywhere but the social perception of how female qualities are measured against a set of parameters, which have never taken women as individuals but as objects. To be intelligent, one has to yield to social pressures with the utmost forbearance. Intelligence forbids women like Susan to use dramatic words such as "unfaithful" and "forgive," not to mention all the emotions like "quarreling, sulking, anger, silences of withdrawal, accusations and tears" (ibid. 529) that one is entitled to vent. What is left here is restraint and reserves that honor the Rawlings' marriage. It is no more than a tightrope the couple is treading; the chance to fail, contrary to their expectation, rises significantly, as do the psychological stakes.

Intelligence has thus done more harm than good to Susan. That her emotions are suppressed further blocks an essential outlet for grievances and insufferableness. Her self-justification and self-reasoning are an attempt to internalize ill feelings, to appear unperturbed and unscathed, to look perfect in everyone's eye, and above all, to conquer the fear that has caused her insanity and eventually led to the demise of the relationship. Such a fate does not solely happen to Susan.

WOMEN AND MADNESS

Over the centuries, historians and psychologists have been studying the relations between mental illnesses and the social demands on women being feminine. It was found that the onset of female maladies forges an intricate link with the social perception of women's behavior and attitudes. Women who deviate from social norms are regarded negatively, hence labeled as insane. Women are especially subject to scrutiny in a patriarchal society, for the social institution has long prescribed a set of rules for women, which are believed to be the best for them. They have to marry when they are young and be faithful to their husband, and then give birth to as many children as possible, take care of them, and serve their husband dutifully without an ounce of complaint. Those not fortunate enough to marry are singled out as outcasts, not to mention women who become pregnant with illegitimate children. The social environment demands strict roles from females from the time they are born. To be desirable, one has to be feminine in every respect, be it appearance or demeanor. Such discipline falls under a big umbrella, which privileges men and enables them to possess the institutional power and authority to legitimize any wrong doing, while perpetuating silence, inferiority, subjection, and passivity from women, limiting their power to the domestic realm. Femininity has been so entrenched as a notion in society that only in the last century did it start being questioned and challenged by scholars and psychologists.

In 1933, the prominent psychologist Sigmund Freud in one of his lectures on psychoanalysis indicated that to define women as feminine, conventionally speaking one would rarely go beyond the attribute of passivity. The culprit was the social custom, which forced women into passive roles (Freud, "Lecture XXXIII: 'Femininity'" 12). Sandra Lee Bartky in her essay "Foucault, Femininity, and the Modernization of Patriarchal Power" (1997) criticizes Michel Foucault for conflating men and women as if they were a single entity, not noticing how differently they are treated in a modern hierarchical disciplined society.[1] She points out that in such a society women are subject to different sets of disciplines, which define femininity as "an artifice, an achievement" (Bartky 95) with regard to body figure, gesture, and movement. None of these achievements is based on intellect, talent, or any inherent qualities. Femininity as a prerequisite and judgment for women has manifested itself in devastating effects over centuries, with regard to bodily harm, disfigurement, and at worst, suicide. Today, femininity is endorsed by activists as a quality possessed by women's righters who have the vision, the power, and the ability to improve women's rights and change their fate.

Lessing was a feminist icon and recognized the impact inflicted upon women whose roles are restricted by society. The desire to conform to the role model of femininity has clung to its societal and familial roots so deeply that even intelligent, educated, independent, and career-minded women such as Susan still succumb to fate. Lessing projects the protagonist as prey trapped in social misjudgment. Susan is an innocent victim, as she still believes that a woman should be the ideal of femininity as someone who accepts instead of fights gender roles. After getting married, a woman should readily give up her job and take up the role of homemaker for the sake of her children and her husband. To sacrifice enshrines femininity:

> Nor did Susan make the mistake of taking a job for the sake of her independence, which she might very well have done.... Children needed their mother to a certain age, that both parents knew and agreed on; and when these four healthy wisely brought up children were of the right age, Susan would work again, because she knew, and so did he, what happened to women of fifty at the height of their energy and ability, with grownup children who no longer needed their full devotion ["To Room Nineteen" 527].

To Susan's mind, it is an intelligent decision justified by the sound reasons put forward for the couple as well as the family. Behind the flawless logic is in fact an old notion of truth held in the hierarchical society that women have to make all the sacrifices, be understanding without holding a grudge, and wait until the young fledge to work again. Susan's intelligence not only fails to save her from being gnawed at but aggravates the situation. She locks herself up in a world of make-believe in which she forfeits her identity. Intelligence has become rhetorical, which only reasserts her sacrificial role. There are moments when Susan reduces the questions of self-value to a list of familial commitments to be ticked off by any married woman:

> Perhaps that was the trouble? It was in the nature of things that the adventures and delights could no longer be hers, because of the four children and the big house that needed so much attention.... Well, was it Susan's fault that after he came home from an adventure he looked harassed rather than fulfilled? ... But none of it by anybody's fault [ibid. 529].

That women have to fully sacrifice without a clear expiration date is an issue that Mary Lavin, the Irish feminist inter-modernist, also probes in some of her stories, such as "A Nun's Mother" (1944), which largely take place in rural areas where women lack the solidarity necessary to subvert the entrenched system. Lessing takes it further by contextualizing the story in a contemporary modish family in London, a global city in the late twentieth century, where advanced women's rights should be expected. What readers witness, however, is episode after episode in which Susan is brought down by the domestic role, becoming fragile and emotionally distraught day by day. Doing the school run turns out to be more than a nuisance but a disarray of thoughts impossible to get rid of:

> On the first morning she was simply restless, worrying about the twins "naturally enough" since this was their first day away at school. She was hardly able to contain herself until they came back.... And the next day ... [she] found herself reluctant to enter her big and beautiful home because it was as if something was waiting for her there that she did not wish to confront.... There she sat on a bench and tried to calm herself looking at trees, at a brown glimpse of the river. But she was filled with tension, like a panic: as if an enemy was in the garden with her [ibid. 530].

That loneliness chronicled in the story first strikes her as "two contrary emotions" (ibid. 531), then slowly takes hold. Freedom is what Susan seeks to calm her nerves. Little had she thought that such freedom could not but further restrain her. The space in which she yearns to be on her own has never gone beyond the house; the lives she is eager to occupy herself with are no more than the household chores; the thoughts about the family she desperately pulls out from her mind always find a way to crawl back. It is the cage Susan has been living in since she married and in which she has been trying to identify herself as a caring motherly figure and dutiful wife after giving birth to the children. Disillusioned as she seems, in reality society has never rewarded any woman like her who adopts such an angelic, feminine role. What we discover is that women are plagued and eventually lose their minds.

Feminine insanity, in fact, is not new in literature. Back in the Elizabethan Age, Shakespeare wrote some plays that depict tragic characters like Lady Macbeth and Ophelia. Women are portrayed as subordinate objects whose self-value is built upon men. Their relations to society are largely shaped by the lives of others. That dichotomy of self/other has never strengthened females but rather weakened them such that they live on the margins of society. Any challenge given rise to can crumble their self-image leaving them vulnerable to any malady. Hence, we see Ophelia turn insane in *Hamlet* (Act 4, Scene 5), Susan develop schizophrenia in "To Room Nineteen," or the protagonist suffer psychosis in "The Yellow Wall-Paper."

Gilman's "The Yellow Wall-Paper"

When Charlotte Perkins Gilman first published "The Yellow Wall-Paper" in 1892, public knowledge about postnatal depression and its diagnosis was next to none. Compounded with this fact was the oppression against women. Gilman herself was a victim in the patriarchal society. When she was first diagnosed with a female malady, she was strongly advised to stay home and rest until she was fully recovered. This misguided treatment was partly due to the fact that psychiatric medication and psychotherapy had not yet been developed, and partly to the social misunderstanding of women's well-being. The best prescription for Gilman at that time was like that for any other female patients—home-bound treatment. Such a counterproductive practice not only failed to cure her but caused her condition to deteriorate, leading to psychosis.

Her account of her experience as a misdiagnosed patient who is prey to social oppression is chronicled in "The Yellow Wall-Paper" through a first-person narrator who first confronts the illness by telling her husband about it, only to receive a dismissive response: "[y]ou see he does not believe I am sick!" (647). Likewise, Susan can imagine how her husband Matthew would respond should she tell him about the strange feelings. "'What enemy, Susan darling?' ... 'Perhaps you should see a doctor?'" ("To Room Nineteen" 531). Matthew's ambivalent if not annoyed attitude is verified when she sheepishly admits to having scolded the children: "'[b]ut Susie, Susie darling ... what is all this about? You shouted at them? What of it? If you shouted at them fifty times a day it wouldn't be more than the little devils deserve'" (ibid. 532). That masculine power to reassure his wife that nothing has happened in fact strengthens the general belief that women are fragile and irrational, the opposite of men. Therefore, women are in need of men's mental and physical protection all the time. That the two sexes are allotted into a strong/weak binary within social institutions further stigmatizes women as dysfunctional objects incapable of reasoning and making a decision on their own, much more so in female maladies. Asking about, revealing, and contemplating the maladies still remain social taboos. Therefore, the protagonist in "The Yellow Wall-Paper" tries to restrain herself in front of others at the expense of self-expression:

> I sometimes fancy that in my condition if I had less opposition and more society and stimulus—but John says the very worst thing I can do is to think about my condition, and I confess it always makes me feel bad. So I will let it alone and talk about the house [648].

The restrictions of freedoms that the patriarchy imposes on women for the sake of femininity have been taken as social norms. Women are stripped of social power and, in the protagonist's case, familial power for the good of well being. The intention of men to take care of their partner may not be malicious, so the protagonist and other women believe: "I have a schedule prescription for each hour in the day; he takes all care from me, and so I feel basely ungrateful not to value it more" (ibid.). Lacking social solidarity, women abase themselves completely, making them powerless to fend for themselves. The abyss of ignorance further perpetuates their feelings of guilt. Hence, we see Susan adopt this self-reproachful tone throughout "To Room Nineteen":

> She tried to tell him, about never being free. And he listened and said: "But Susan, what sort of freedom can you possibly want short of being dead! Am I ever free? I go to the office, and I have to be there at ten.... And I have to do this or that, don't I? Then I've got to come home at a certain time ... but if I'm not going to be back home at six I telephone you. When can I ever say to myself: I have nothing to be responsible for in the next six hours?"
>
> Susan, hearing this, was remorseful. Because it was true. The good marriage, the house, the children, depended just as much on his voluntary bondage as it did on hers ["To Room Nineteen" 534].

Likewise, in "The Yellow Wall-Paper," the protagonist retains her self-reproachful tone until the end: "I meant to be such a help to John, such a real rest and comfort, and here I am a comparative burden already!" (649).

FEMININITY, FEMALE ROLES, AND FEMINIZATION

The social demands for women to conform, yield, and understand regardless of the situation have never been negotiated on any level, nor lowered as the society progresses. Modern women such as Susan also succumb to predestined fate—all the more so because the social pressures on them have mounted twofold, mainly from work and family. Femininity has thus extended beyond familial definitions. Research has yet to show which—work or family—causes more havoc to women or if both can offset each other. Our intuition based on "To Room Nineteen," "The Yellow Wall-Paper," and the like tells us that the latter is tenable. Had Susan in "To Room Nineteen" kept on working, her mental health could have been saved from further deterioration. If the protagonist in "The Yellow Wall-Paper" had been encouraged to work or write, she would have dissuaded John, her husband and physician, from prescribing the physio-therapeutic treatment. In fact, there are moments that her self-belief does make her question the validity of the medical advice:

> So I take phosphates or phosphites—whichever it is, and tonics, and journeys, and air, and exercise, and am absolutely forbidden to "work" until I am well again.
> Personally, I disagree with their ideas.
> Personally, I believe that congenial work, with excitement and change, would do me good ["The Yellow Wall-Paper" 648].

Yet, like other women, she gives in, for females are obliged to accept whatsoever they are told. Against her will, she is forced to withdraw from social contact. The detrimental effect kicks in, turning the malady into severe depression.

The female schizophrenia that Susan suffers from and the psychosis another protagonist develops have been studied by a number of scholars. Elaine Showalter in her book *The Female Malady: Women, Madness and English Culture, 1830–1980* details the recent history of madness, and its relations to culture and society. Statistics have shown that during that period, female patients suffering schizophrenia outnumbered male patients. The main factor that caused such cultural phenomenon was the repression and oppression women faced in the family. Only through madness could women's protesting voice against subjection and abuse be heard (Showalter 222). In "The Yellow Wall-Paper," John as a male physician in the late nineteenth century defines and codifies female maladies purely from the social perception toward women, and comes up with the misdiagnosis. To react to the cure, his wife cannot protest through speaking or writing but gradually lets go of her will; the illness takes full control of her life. Captive internally and externally, the self is torn. That internal conflict pushes her to the borderline. Powerless and socially withdrawn, the protagonist turns to the dull wallpaper and begins hallucinating: "[u]p and down and sideways they crawl, and those absurd, unblinking eyes are everywhere. There is one place where two breaths didn't match, and the eyes go all up and down the line, one a little higher than the other" ("The Yellow Wall-Paper" 650).

The psychosis is driven by double consciousness of conforming and not conforming. On the one hand, the hopeless situation she is in—the prison and the deprivation of self-expression—makes her yearn for writing more than ever, which she deems to be suitable. On the other, she has to yield to the social demands by embracing femininity. The struggle between "what is known but not lived and what is lived but not known" (Kilborne 6) is symptomized by thought disorder:

> I don't know why I should write this.
> I don't want to.
> I don't feel able.
> And I know John would think it absurd. But I must say what I feel and think in some way—it is such a relief! ["The Yellow Wall-Paper" 651].

Double consciousness as a sign of mental illness has been studied by a number of notable psychologists such as Sándor Ferenczi and Sigmund Freud. While the former focused on the cause of traumatic relationships between parents and children, it is the latter whose works on hysteria, absence, and the double conscience we can apply to female maladies. When Freud presented his five lectures about psychoanalysis in 1909, he expounded on the concept of emotion based on one of Breuer's patients' cases as "a quantity which may become increased, derived and displaced" ("About Psychoanalysis"). Any mental illness caused by imprisoned emotions would throw an invalid into a chaos of abnormal changes including constant psychical disturbance, bodily innervations and inhibitions (ibid.). Like the protagonists in the two stories, the patient (a dutiful daughter) went through a similar emotional trauma and could not vent but instead suppressed her strong emotions for the pretense of conventions and her familial role. Femininity is used as a suppressive and oppressive tool in the male-dominated society so as to maintain the status quo. Thus, we see Susan in despair while fully aware of being caged. Nowhere can she release such anger, and she must compromise every time. Her emotions reach the tipping point: "[r]esentment ... was poisoning her.... She was a prisoner.... She was filled with emotions that were utterly ridiculous, that she despised, yet that nevertheless she was feeling so strongly she could not shake them off" ("To Room Nineteen" 533). In "The Yellow Wall-Paper," the protagonist has her mental energy repressed, which should normally be released through words and deeds. She is deprived of "the expression of emotions" ("About Psychoanalysis"), as Freud states, and comes to identify herself with a woman hidden behind the grotesquely patterned wallpaper: "[a]nd it is like a woman stooping down and creeping about behind that pattern.... The faint figure behind seemed to shake the pattern, just as if she wanted to get out" ("The Yellow Wall-Paper" 652).

It is worth noting that when the Freudian analysis on female mental illnesses is applied to the manic roller coaster the two protagonists go through, it contains a dual meaning. First, it highlights the circumstances when a wish of the inflicted has been aroused yet is against other people's desire, and cannot be reconciled with that person's personality on ethical, aesthetic, and personal grounds. After a short inner struggle, the repressed idea resurfaces to consciousness as an unfulfilled wish, which is then repressed again from consciousness and forgotten. It is the woman who exerts the force of the ego on herself against her own and others' repressive force. The intense mental pain the two protagonists in the stories experience, as Freud highlights, is "the protection of the personality" ("About Psychoanalysis"). The bodily and psychical integrity of a female subject to ethnic and social oppression was first called upon as a significant issue when Freud published his paper at the turn of the century.

Second, it reveals a self-discovery process that any female suffering an illness will strive for. Rather than being stigmatized, schizophrenia, hysteria, double consciousness, and other female maladies should be viewed as a positive channel to rebel against social constraints, to seek oneself, and to re-establish self-identity so that the person can regain her mental health. Susan and the protagonist are told to downplay the severity and the remedies of their illnesses for fear of being despised by the family, hence, the society. They pay a high price by falling into a trap that could have been avoided had they confronted the social, institutional, and masculine power. The aforementioned lack of social solidarity makes it almost impossible to resist the immense power. Although history has it that at the start of the last century there was a time when the definitions of masculinity and femininity were being revised, it did not last long. After World War II, the society was pulled back to conservatism and late Victorian institutions built for and owned by middle-class women were demolished, and the focus shifted from female independence back to their relationships with men. After half a century, femininity as a quintessential value was still deeply-rooted in families who raised children on their own. Susan's case is the tip of the iceberg of a society, which still, by and large, upholds Victorian values. Showalter clearly points out in her book that female maladies of Victorian times alluded to the male attitudes:

> In a society that not only perceived women as childlike, irrational, and sexually unstable, but also rendered them legally powerless and economically marginal, it is not surprising that they should have formed the greater part of the residual categories of deviance from which doctors drew a lucrative practice and asylums much of their population [72–73].

These male attitudes, unfortunately, have passed on to successive generations, as displayed by Matthew in "To Room Nineteen":

> She said to Matthew in their bedroom: "I think there must be something wrong with me."

> And he said: "Surely not, Susan? You look marvelous—you're as lovely as ever." ... And she said: "I need to be alone more than I am."
> At which he swung his slow blue gaze at her, and she saw what she had been dreading: Incredulity. Disbelief. And fear. An incredulous blue stare from a stranger who was her husband, as close to her as her own breath ["To Room Nineteen" 534].

Matthew's stare speaks volumes. His role as a husband and breadwinner empowers him more than ever and justifies his scornful attitude toward his wife's request. Any demand outside the familial boundary would be condemned as immoral, rebellious, and a betrayal. Being alone, as a self-discovery process, amounts to an assertion of one's identity, which is readily interpreted by men as a threat to their power and status, not to mention to the integral value of a family. Likewise, in "The Yellow Wall-Paper," even a suggestive tone by the protagonist can evoke a reproving response:

> "It is only three weeks more and then we will take a nice little trip of a few days while Jennie is getting the house ready. Really dear you are better!"
> "Better in body perhaps—" I began, and stopped short, for he sat up straight and looked at me with such a stern, reproachful look that I could not say another word [652].

The plights of the two protagonists are telltale signs of a society that still sees women's requests, be they slight or strong, as aggression. They can never be granted so as to preserve the institutional system intact, while the society in favor of masculinity still develops on course (Freud, "Lecture XXXIII" 12). The circumscription of women's power to think, express, and act according to their own will eventually takes a heavy toll. In the cases of the two protagonists, the endings are uncompromising. In "To Room Nineteen," Susan decides to take her own life. The irreversible relationship with her husband apparently relieves her of the illusion that she could still make him partially if not fully comprehend her situation with empathy. Her body and soul have completely left his: "[a]nd she stretched out her hand to the hollow where her husband's body had lain, but found no comfort there: he was not her husband" ("To Room Nineteen" 547). Nothing but emptiness remains. That hollowness, however, gives her a new perspective of life—not to insist on his understanding nor ask for a divorce. It is time to end the fight between her inner and outer power so that she can take back full control of her soul, which shall never be owned by anyone—not her husband, the children, nor the society. The intense feeling of absence has finally conquered her mind. By imagining returning to the river, her body and her soul are combined into one, which belongs to nobody but Susan herself. In literature, drowning bears a symbolic meaning synonymous with baptism—rebirth "by water and the Spirit"[2]—so that one will be saved from sin. In *Hamlet*, Ophelia is drowned in the river after becoming mad after learning about her father being killed and her lover betraying her. In *The Awakening* (1899) by Kate Chopin, Edna

Pontellier ends her life by drowning. Gassing herself in room nineteen, Susan dreams of drifting into the dark river, with her soul being cleansed and her mind resting forever.

The Mad Women's Escape

From a psychiatric point of view, schizophrenia could be a plausible explanation for Susan's suicide. Statistics have told us that schizophrenia is not a predominant mental illness among females. Rather, it is a reflection of gender inequality, or perhaps more so, the ineffective treatments of schizophrenia peculiar to females, which link to feminization and female roles. Schizophrenia, therefore, among other female maladies epitomizes "the cultural conflation of femininity and insanity" (Showalter 204). From a literary point of view, schizophrenic females have been in the spotlight in literary works since the twentieth century and are regarded as "the symbol of linguistic, religious, and sexual breakdown and rebellion" (ibid.), in which the last is particularly patent in "To Room Nineteen." The couple's asexuality splits Susan's self. To end the mental pain inflicted upon her by the institutional marriage and to rebel against the patriarchal society, nothing could be more overtly expressive than enacting the psychotic suicidal ideation.

The ending of "The Yellow Wall-Paper" does not register the same morbid tone as that of "To Room Nineteen." Yet, the effect is no less alarming. The protagonist locks herself up in the room creeping around the walls as well as in and out of the pattern. When John threatens to barge into the room and manages to open the door, he is horrified by the sight:

> "What is the matter?" he cried. "For God's sake, what are you doing!"
> I kept on creeping just the same, but I looked at him over my shoulder.
> "I've got out at last," said I, "in spite of you and Jane! And I've pulled off most of the paper, so you can't put me back!" ["The Yellow Wall-Paper" 656].

What John witnesses in front of him is a woman who has lost her sanity and acts as if she is an alienated creature. What the protagonist gains, ironically, is her independence and her own space, which have been taken away after pregnancy, by going mad. Postnatal depression is not an uncommon mental disorder among women; however, if not cured with the right treatments, it may lead to severe depression or psychosis, as in the protagonist's case, and even fatality. John certainly does not notice it nor pay much attention to it due to scant knowledge about the condition at that time. Had the physicians had a sound judgment on patients like the protagonist, there could have been a chance to decrease the number of psychotic patients. By the same token, had the society combated the prevailing unfair treatments toward women, they would not have resorted to the ultimate hysterical method as a protest against the patriarchal system. Sadly, until today, the social pressures on women to fulfill their feminine roles have not diminished. Femininity is still perceived as an achievement through body, gesture, and manner instead of quality. The attitude toward stigmatizing female maladies is still rampant.

The two protagonists have their stories told and heard by us. In reality, there are millions of women who are suffering and battling the predestined fate alone without our knowledge. That happens regardless of race, religion, and culture. Yet, little can be done to change the circumstances. Through the short story, a compact but powerful genre, their pleas can be heard. Lessing and Gilman are among other feminist writers who direct our attention to the plight of females. They were not totally immune from the wretched experiences brought about by the male chauvinistic society. Through exploring the protagonists' mental and psychological torment, they could each relate to the respective personae in the most effective manner. Gilman exploited a journalistic writing style to record the protagonist's successive stages of suffering leading to psychosis. It is a first-person account narrated through stream of consciousness, particularly interior monologue, to reveal the mental disorder. It is the absences, incoherent and disconnected speech, as well as the inability to organize thoughts and random associations of topics that betray the power struggle between self and other, inner world and outer world, reality and fantasy images:

> But in the places where it isn't faded and where the sun is just so—I can see a strange, provoking, formless sort of figure, that seems to skulk about behind that silly and conspicuous front design.
> There's sister on the stairs! ["The Yellow Wall-Paper" 650].

The only object that draws the protagonist's attention throughout her stay in the room is a feminine figure conjured up behind the pattern. The more she fantasizes her, the closer she feels to her with regard to emotions and space. The intense emotions and rebellion against the oppression draw her to her fantasy image until they unite body and soul. This is, in fact, the mirror image of her own self, for which she has been desperately searching. Through identifying herself with the woman behind the wallpaper, who creeps around trying to smear it and shakes the bar to escape, the protagonist regains her freedom of space and mind. This is the moment when the image existing as the third person (she) transforms to the first-person narrator (I), shifting the protagonist herself from the vantage point of participating to dominating: "I wonder if they all come out of that wall-paper as I did? ... It is so pleasant to be out in this great room and creep around as I please!" (ibid. 656). By doing so, she also frees thousands of women who are imprisoned in the institutional society, as she fantasizes "so many of those creeping women" (ibid.) outside the room.

In "To Room Nineteen," Lessing deploys third-person narration as the main narrative mode to take us through the background of the Rawlings, up to the first nervous breakdown and through Susan's suicide. Between the episodes, different narrative techniques are intertwined to highlight her psychic pain:

> Except, thought Susan, unaccountably bad-tempered, she was (is?) the first. In ten years. So either the ten years' fidelity was not important, or she isn't. (No, no, there is something wrong with this way of thinking, there must be.) But if she isn't important, presumably it wasn't important either when Matthew and I first went to bed with each other that afternoon whose delight even now (like a very long shadow at sundown) lays a long, wandlike finger over us. (Why did I say sundown?) ... The whole thing is absurd— for him to have come home and told me was absurd. For him not to have told me was absurd. For me to care or, for that matter, not to care, is absurd ... and who is Myra Jenkins? Why, no one at all ["To Room Nineteen" 528].

This short excerpt is Susan's monologue after Matthew tells her about an affair he had with a girl named Myra Jenkins. Lessing uses a few techniques simultaneously and seamlessly. First and foremost, covert free indirect speech ("she was *(is?)* the first") as a prelude to Susan's dubious thoughts. Then we are ushered into her world of uncertainty through the shift of narrative mode from third-person (she) to first-person (I). The inner struggle Susan rages through to attempt to organize her thoughts is further marked by the repetition of "absurd" and prepositional clauses. The self-absorption finally ends with a return of overt free indirect discourse through asking who Myra Jenkins is. Jumbling various techniques in one short paragraph brings out the remarkable psychic effect like an adrenaline rush. Within a split second, Susan rides on a mental roller coaster through loops of thoughts, doubts, images, and flashbacks. The strategy is highly effective in building up a schizophrenic world of phantasy like hers.

It is ironic to see how two women from two different centuries are still caught in the same turmoil. The social injustice decried by Lessing and her predecessor, Gilman, in "To Room Nineteen" and "The Yellow Wall-Paper" has still not been resolved after generations. On the surface, the modern society seems to be more open to novelty and diversity. The concern about gender inequality due to the pay gap and sexual harassment at work, for example, has never been so immense, so has social solidarity. A series of sex scandals involving public figures have sparked fierce debates and various movements on social media platforms—the #MeToo movement being the most dominant—about the unfair treatment of females in various social strata. Punitive measures have been taken to redress wrongs and to reassure people that we are progressing towards creating better, fairer, and more inclusive societies.

The truth is, we still live in a world as backward as that of the eighteenth century when it comes to safeguarding fundamental values such as feminism, and feminist issues are as controversial as ever. While part of the society is chanting the slogan of "breaking the glass ceiling" all the time and willing to take down barriers, we are duly reminded that the factors impeding progress are getting more complicated and are subject to individual, family, social strata as well as the entire community. The issues explored in feminist works have, thus, become multifaceted, such as "To Room Nineteen" dealing with relations between feminism and social, political, familial, and masculine power, as well as identity and female maladies, issues that are still largely off the radar mainly because first, the victim is not a celebrity or a public figure; second, the subject is not newsworthy enough to draw public and/or media attention; third, the problem is too personal to reveal openly.

Rather than propagandizing, "To Room Nineteen" as psychological realism projects a gloomy future for ordinary women's rights. It serves as a wake-up call to those who are too complacent about the achievements they have made, for such achievements only scratch the surface. Not until we recognize that feminist issues should involve all walks of life rather than a selective social sector, and that the efforts should be concerted and campaigns coordinated rather than individual will the day to hail success come. We, therefore, still need writers like Lessing to "whistle blow" to bring issues to the surface and exploit the theme to make it dynamic, manifold, resounding, and contemporary to tap into the concurrent social mood and/or political atmosphere. Doris Lessing, like her prominent predecessor, Charlotte Perkins Gilman, has set a prime example, which will no doubt inspire a new army of writers to fight for women's justice through words.

Notes

1. See Foucault, especially part three of *Discipline and Punish*, for analysis.
2. John 3:5, NIV: Jesus answered, "[v]ery truly, I tell you, no one can enter the kingdom of God without being born of water and Spirit."

Bibliography

Bartky, Sandra Lee. "Foucault, Femininity, and the Modernization of Patriarchal Power." *Femininity and Domination: Studies in the Phenomenology of Oppression*. New York, London: Routledge, 1991. 93–111. Print/Web.
Chopin, Kate. *The Awakening and Selected Short Stories*. N.p.: Simon & Brown, 2013. Print.
Foucault, Michel. *Discipline & Punish: The Birth of the Prison*. Translated by Alan Sheridan, 2nd ed. New York: Vintage Books, 1995. Print.
Freud, Sigmund. "About Psychoanalysis." The 20th Anniversary Celebration of the Founding of Clark University, September 1909, Worcester, MA. Web.
_____. "Lecture XXXIII: 'Femininity' (1933)." *On Freud's "Femininity."* Edited by Graciela Abelin-Sas Rose and Leticia Glocer Fiorini. London: Karnac Books, 2010. 7–34. Print.
Gilman, Charlotte Perkins. "The Yellow Wallpaper." *The New England Magazine*, Jan. 1892. 647–656. Web.

Hawthorne, Nathaniel. "The Birthmark." *The Oxford Book of Short Stories*. Edited by V. S. Pritchett. Oxford: Oxford University Press, 1981. 27–42. Print.
"John 3:5." NETBible. classic.net.bible.org/verse.php?book=joh&chapter=3&verse=5. Accessed 12 Jan 2017.
Junior, Paulo Henrique de Sá. "Schizophrenia or Female Consciousness: Diagnosing a Borderline Personality in Doris Lessing's 'To Room Nineteen.'" *Revista Eletrônica do Instituto de Humanidades* I.IV (2003). Web.
Kilborne, Benjamin. "Trauma and the Unconscious: Double Conscience, the Uncanny and Cruelty." *The American Journal of Psychoanalysis* 74 (2014): 4–20. Web.
Lavin, Mary. *The Stories of Mary Lavin*. Vol. 2. London: Constable, 1970. Print/Web.
Lessing, Doris. "To Room Nineteen." 1963. *The Norton Anthology of Short Fiction*. Edited by R.V. Cassill and R. Bausch. New York: W.W. Norton & Co., 2000. 525–549. Print.
Shakespeare, William. *The Tragedy of Hamlet Prince of Denmark*. 1603. Edited by Sylvan Barnet. New York: New American Library, 1998. Print.
Showalter, Elaine. *The Female Malady: Women, Madness and English Culture, 1830–1980*. London: Virago, 1987. Print/Web.
Walker, Alice. *You Can't Keep a Good Woman Down: Short Stories*. Orlando, FL: Harcourt Inc., 1981. Print.

Afterword

The short story genre can be dated as far back as over 6,000 years ago. As revealed in Egyptian papyri dated from 4,000 BCE, the princes of Cheops in Egypt entertained their father Sneferu with fantastic short stories (Lockett). Through today, the short story remains one of the most popular and important genres in literature. With a view to helping literature students gain a fuller picture, a wider perspective, and a deeper understanding of British, Irish, and American short stories, this book offers a look into how some of the masterpieces from the three countries address various sociocultural topics across different time periods.

While this book suggests "an orderly means of close textual analysis" (Campbell and Jamieson 414) of the short story genre, it is hoped that readers will understand that in the long history of the evolution of the short story, the form, nature and focus of the literary genre are always changing. Although our book has outlined the canonical conventions of the short story genre and overviewed the genre's formal development along the timeline, not by any means will it exhaust ongoing changes that can happen to the genre. After all, as Feuer puts it, "[a] genre is ultimately an abstract conception rather than something that exists empirically in the world" (144). As mentioned in the preface, there is no one way to write a short story, and the ways of storytelling and writing shall increase in time.

Though it can be hard to set a firm and definite list of what constitutes the short story, Milton Crane, the editor of *50 Great Short Stories*, points out what makes a great short story:

> The sudden unforgettable revelation of character; the vision of a world through another's eyes; the glimpse of truth; the capture of a moment in time.
>
> All this the short story, at its best, is uniquely capable of conveying, for in its very shortness lies its greatest strength.
>
> It can discover depths of meaning in the casual word or action; it can suggest in a page what could not be stated in a volume [i].

The future development of the short story genre is itself a story with parallel open endings. With the foundational terms explained, multiple critical approaches introduced, and numerous examples demonstrated, this book shall be an initial guidebook for the reader's exploration of the short story genre with endless possibilities.

BIBLIOGRAPHY

Campbell, Karlyn Kohrs, and Kathleen Hall Jamieson. "Form and Genre in Rhetorical Criticism: An Introduction." *Form and Genre: Shaping Rhetorical Action*. Edited by Karlyn Kohrs Campbell and Kathleen Hall Jamieson. Falls Church, VA: Speech Communication Association, 1978, 18–25. Print.
Crane, Milton. "What Makes a Great Short Story?" *50 Great Short Stories*. Edited by Milton Crane. New York: Bantam Books, 1952. Print.
Feuer, Jane. "Genre Study and Television." *Channels of Discourse, Resembled: Television and Contemporary Criticism*. Edited by Robert C. Allen. London: Routledge, 1992. 138–160. Print.
Lockett, Mike. "The History of Storytelling." http://www.mikelockett.com/downloads/History%20of%Storytelling.pdf. Accessed on 14 Jan 2019.

Index

Abrams, Meyer Howard 40, 54, 133
Adams, Jonathan S. 171
Adorno, Theodor 77, 83
Aggelis, Steven L. 73, 83
Aguirre, Manuel 134
Aikin, Anna Letitia 117, 133
Aikin, John 116–117, 124, 131–133
Alexander, Claire 171
Anderson, James Arthur 81, 83
Anderson, Sherwood 22–23, 38
antagonist 53
Ardoy, Eva 134
Aristotle 152
Asquith, Mark 85, 96
Auntie Jemima 160, 168
avant-garde movement 14, 17

Baldick, Chris 134
Bankston, John 73, 83
Barrie, J.M. 81; *Peter Pan* 81
Barry, Peter 54
Barthes, Roland 54; "Death of the Author" 44
Bartky, Sandra Lee 177, 188
Baston, Ajda 54
Bates, H.E. 32–33
Beaver, Harold 96
Beccaro, Thomas Del. 172
Beley, Gene 83
Bellow, Saul 36
Bendixen, Alfred 37
Bennett, Andrew 54
biographical criticism 41–43
Black Lives Matter 168
black-on-black oppression 42
Black Power Movement 42, 158, 165, 172
Blair, David 134
Bolton, Diane K. 172
Bonaparte, Marie 43–44, 134
Booker, M. Keith 74, 83
Bornstein, Robert F. 134
Botting, Fred 134

Bowen, Elizabeth 27, 28, 37
Bradbury, Malcolm 37
Bradbury, Ray 3, 4, 23, 35, 37, 72–75, 78–84, 98, 119, 134; alienation 79; artificial intelligence 80; *Fahrenheit 451* 83; *Futuria Fantasia* 73; *The Illustrated Man* 73; "The Lake" 119, 134; *The Martian Chronicles* 23, 73; prophecy 73; science fiction 73; simulation 75, 80; technology 74; "The Veldt" 72–84; virtual reality 74, 77, 80; visionary SF tales 79
Braun, Heather 134
Brendon, Piers 172
Brewster, Scott 134
Bronfen, Elisabeth 43, 54
Brown, Devin 104, 109
Brown, Mark 172
Brown, Terrence 152
Bryant, Hallman B. 70
Burke, Edmund 133–134
Busse, Beatrix 54
Butler, Judith 96

Cameron, Jimmy C. 172
Campbell, Hayley 98, 110
Campbell, Karlyn Kohrs 191
Canby, Henry Seidel 37
capitalism 77
Carosso, Andrea 77, 83
Carroll, Lewis 99; *Alice's Adventures in Wonderland* 99; characters 61–63, 75–77, 89–91, 101–102
Cary, Richard 15, 37
Cash, Floris Barnett 172
Cather, Willa 15, 37
Chaucer, Geoffrey 8, 37–38; *The Canterbury Tales* 8, 37
Chesnutt, Charles Waddell 161
Chopin, Kate 184, 188
Christian, Barbara T. 172
civil rights 96, 154–155, 161–162, 165–168, 171–172

Colebrook, Claire 153
Coleman, J.S. 170, 172
Conan, Neal 108, 110
Conan Doyle, Arthur 17
Conrad, Joseph 17, 37, 131, 134
consumerism 77
Cooper, Anna J. 170, 172
Cowart, David 172
Croot, E.C. 172
The Crucible 41
cultural materialism 40
Curtin, Philip D. 172

Daems, Jim 54
Dahl, Roald 19, 27, 100, 135; *Matilda* 100
Dal Lago, Enrico 172
Davis, Barbara Thompson 38
Davis, David Brion 172
deconstruction 41
Dhawa, Huai Bao 93, 96
Dickens, Charles 12, 34, 38
Diskin, Lahna 81, 83
Di Yanni, Robert 42, 54
Dobie, Anna B. 54
Dodds, Joseph 54
Donnelly, John Patrick 153
double consciousness 163, 182–183
Drake, Robert 63, 70
Drassinower, Abraham 78, 83
Dryden, John 153
Du Bois, W.E.B. 162–164, 166–167, 172

Eller, Jonathan R 73, 83
Enright, Anne 153
epiphany 20, 31–32, 69, 140–141, 148

Fahey, Tony 153
fan fiction 98
fantasy 98
Fargnoli, A. Nicholas 153
Farrar, Max 172
Faulkner, William 14, 18, 22–25, 27, 37–39, 60, 86; feminist criticism 41, 49–50; feminist rewriting 50; gender roles 49; patriarchy 49–50
Ferenczi, Sándor 182
Feuer, Jane 191
Fischer, Andreas 38
Fitzgerald, F. Scott 24–25, 38
Fitzgerald, Robert 69–70
Fitzpatrick, Andrea D. 96
Ford, Alan 153
foreshadowing 81–82
formalist criticism 41, 53–54; Moscow Linguistic Circle 53; Russian literary criticism 53
Forster, E.M. 19–20, 39
Fortier, Mark 45, 54
Fosshage, James L. 127, 133–134
Foucault, Michel 177, 188

free indirect speech 24, 187
Freud, Sigmund 50–51, 113–115, 117–118, 120, 122–123, 125–130, 133–134, 188
Freudenburg, Kirk 138, 153
Friedlander, Stephen R. 135

Gaelic 27, 143
Gaiman, Neil 3, 4, 34, 38–39, 50, 98–103, 105–110; *American Gods* 98; Calvinist predestination 104–105; *Coraline* 99; damnation 104; *The Graveyard Book* 99; misogyny 104; "The Problem of Susan" 4, 34, 50, 98–110; punishment for sins 106–107; restricted heaven 105; *Sandman* 98; sex 104; suffering 106–107
Gale, Steven H. 19, 38
genre mixing 10
Gillespie, Michael Patrick 153
Gilman, Charlotte Perkins 1, 3, 13, 15–16, 38, 52–54, 174–175, 179, 186–188; autobiographical writing 52; depression 16, 52, 179, 181, 185; nervous breakdown 52; rest cure 52–53; "The Yellow Wall-Paper" 16, 52–53, 174–175, 179–182, 184–185, 187
Giola, Dana 55
Godfrey, Carole 100, 110
Goodyear, Dana 38
gothic genre: doppelgänger 119, 129, 130–131
Greeley, Andrew M. 153
Greene, Graham 27
Grimms' Fairy Tales 100
Groba, Constante González 157, 172
Grossman, Lev 105, 110
Guiley, Rosemary Ellen 134
Guppy, Shusha 38

Habib, M.A. Rafey 42, 54
Harland, Henry 14, 38
Harmon, William 94, 96
Harris, Scott L. 153
Hart, Kylo-Patrick R. 86, 96
Harte, Bret 13–15, 18, 20, 25, 33, 38
Hawthorne, Nathaniel 10–13, 15–16, 38, 189
Hemingway, Ernest 18, 21–26, 33, 38, 86, 138; The Iceberg Theory 21, 25–26
Henry, O. 13, 18, 21, 22, 33
Hicks, M.A. 172
Hills, L. Rust. 18, 26, 153
historical criticism 41
Holman, C. Hugh 94, 96
The Holy Bible 102, 104, 106, 110, 152–153
Horkheimer, Max 77
humanism 40
humor 53, 70
The Hunchback of Notre Dame (film) 72
Hunt, Alex 92
Hunter, Adrian 38
Hurston, Zora Neale 36
Hutcheon, Linda 107, 110
Huxley, Aldous 73; *Brave New World* 74

imagery 53
Immanuel, Kant 133–134
imperialism 18, 47, 173
irony 53, 69
Irving, Washington 9–12
Isola, Mark John 94–96

Jackson, Shirley 26, 38
Jacobson, Roman 53
Jagadale 40, 55
James, Henry 12, 14, 38
Jamieson, Kathleen Hall 191
Jauss, Hans-Robert: reception theory 45
Jen, Gish 37
Jewett, Sarah Orne 15, 37
Jin, Ha 37
Johnson, Robin Nicole 172
Johnson, Samuel: *Lives of the Most Eminent English Poets* 43
Joyce, James 1, 3, 17, 20, 22–23, 25, 30, 31, 33, 37–38, 42, 54, 136–137, 139, 140, 143–148, 151–153; *Dubliners* 20, 23, 29, 31, 38, 139–140, 152–153; "Grace" 42, 54, 136–137, 144, 146, 149–152
Junior, Paulo Henrique de Sá 189

Kakutani, Michiko 73, 83
Katsari, Constantina 172
Kazantzakis, Nikos: *The Last Temptation of Christ* 46
Kemkow, Cheryl 78
Kempton, Emily Rose 105, 110
Kennedy, X.J. 45–55
Kenny, John 38, 153
Kilborne, Benjamin 182, 189
King, Stephen 35, 73
Kingsley, Charles 100; *The Water Babies* 100
Kipling, Rudyard 18, 21, 33, 98
Kirkland, Caroline M. 16
Kitterman, John 93, 96
Kohut, Heinz 113–115, 134; self psychology 114, 121, 127, 133
Kornblith, Gary John 172
Kort, Carol 96
Kupelian, David 46, 55

Lacan, Jacques 113, 115, 119–120, 134–135
Lahiri, Jhumpa 37
Lavin, Mary 28, 30, 39, 174, 178, 189
Lawrence, D.H. 17
Lessing, Doris 1, 3, 33–34, 39, 44, 47–48, 55, 174–176, 178, 186–189; "To Room Nineteen" 34, 44, 47, 174–175, 179–181, 184–185, 187–188
Lewis, Clive Staples "C.S.": *The Chronicles of Narnia* 99–100, 101, 108; gynophobic 50; *The Last Battle* 103–104 110; *The Lion, the Witch and the Wardrobe* 50, 102, 104, 110 (Aslan 50; Jadis the White Witch 50; Susan Pevensie 50)
LGBT 40, 46

Lipsky, Suzanne 172
Lockett, Mike 191
London, Jack 22, 33
Lopez, Ilse Marie Bussing 77, 83
Lowenthal, Leo 77, 83
Luckhurst, Roger 73, 83
Lynn, Steven 46, 55

Mahdawi, Arwa 80, 83
Malamud, Bernard 36
Malcolm, Chryl Alexander 38
Malcolm, David 38
Malcolm X 173
Malone, Kareen Ror 135
Marcuse, Herbert 78, 83
Marx, Karl 46
Marxism and Literature 48
Marxist approach: class conflict and struggle 47; exploitation 47; ideology of the social class 47; manipulation 47; oppression 47; political agenda 47; repression 47; social construct 47
Marxist criticism 40–41, 46–49; Althusser, Louis 46; Eagleton, Terry 46; Engels, Friedrich 46; The Frankfurt School 48; Jameson, Frederic 46
masculinity 50, 85, 91–92
mass culture 77
Matthews, Brander 21, 38
Maugham, W. Somerset 31–32, 38–39
McEwan, Ian 27
McIntyre, Dan 54
McKeon, Belinda 38
McShane, Thomas O. 171
metafiction 108–109
#MeToo movement 188
Mighall, Robert 123, 134–135
Mills, Alice 104, 110
Milton, Crane 191
The Mirror and the Lamp 40, 54
Mogen, David 77, 83
Montesquieu, Charles de 155, 172
Mooney, Chase C. 172
Morrison, James 93, 96
Morrison, Toni 170, 173
motif 10, 27, 94–95, 100, 118
Murphy, Catherine 39
myth criticism/dialogism 40

Nagel, James 37
New Historicism 40
Nickel, Eleanor Hersey 103, 110
Nixon, Sean 96
Nkrumah, Kwame 156, 173
Northup, Solomon 156, 173
Norton, Rictor 135
Nussbaum, Abigail 106, 110

Oates, Joyce Carol 35
O'Connor, Flannery 3, 4, 26–27, 39, 54, 59–

60, 62, 65–71; Catholic values 59, 66 (grace 66; spritual awakening 66); *Everything That Rises Must Converge* 59; "Geranium" 59; "A Good Man Is Hard to Find" 4, 26, 54, 60, 70; *A Good Man Is Hard to Find and Other Stories* 39, 59; "Novelist and Believer" 70; "On Her Own Work" 70; Southern Gothic (disturbing characters 60; grotesque 60; supernatural 60; violence 60, 66); *Wise Blood* 59
O'Connor, Frank 29, 30, 138, 153
Ó Faoláin, Seán 27–30, 32, 39, 136
O'Flaherty, Katherine 16
O'Flaherty, Liam 27
O'Hehir, Andrew 39
Olson, Roger E. 153
Orwell, George 32, 73, 74; *1984* 74
Otten, Nick 73, 83

Park, Clara, C. 69–70
parody 107–108
Pattee, Fred Lewis 39
Patterson, Eric 91, 96
Paulson, Suzanne M. 65, 71
Perrault, Charles 100; "Sleeping Beauty in the Woods" 100
personification 82–83
The Phantom of the Opera (film) 73
Piddock, Charles 73, 83
Piontek, Thomas 46, 55
plot 53, 60–61, 74–75, 87–89, 100–101
Poe, Edgar Allan 1, 3, 10–14, 16, 19, 21, 25, 31, 33–34, 37, 39, 43–44, 52, 60, 72, 98, 113, 115–116, 118–119, 122–124, 126, 128–129, 131–132, 134–135; "Annabel Lee" 43; "The Fall of the House of Usher" 11, 39, 43–44, 52, 113, 116, 118, 122, 130–132, 135 (female corpse 43; death and femininity 43; Ligeia" 43; "The Philosophy of Composition" 11–12, 39, 43, 131; "The Raven" 39, 43; "The Tell-Tale Heart" 52)
Poe, Elizabeth 43–44
Poe, Virginia Elizabeth Clemm 44
Porter, Katherine Anne 23, 38
post/neo-colonialism 40
post-structuralism 41
practical/new criticism 41
Prescott, William 9, 39
Price, Reynolds 153
Pritchett, V.S. 32, 37–39, 134, 189
Propp, Vladimir Iakovlevich 107, 110
Proulx, Annie 35; "Brokeback Mountain" 85–97 (*Bowers v. Hardwick* 478 U.S. 186 [1986] 87; homophobic 91, 93; homosexual 93; internalized surveillance 93; *Lawrence v. Texas* 539 U.S. 558 [2003] 87; Wyoming 87, 89); *Complete Dairy Food Cookbook* 86; "Getting Moved" 87, 97; *Gray's Sporting Journal* 86; *Heart Songs and Other Stories* 86; nature versus culture 92–93; *Postcards* 86; rodeo 90, 92; *The Shipping News* 86; *Sweet and Hard Cider* 85; *The Vershire Behind the Times* 85; Western cowboys 91–92
psychoanalytic criticism 40–41, 50–53; art 51; compulsive repetitions 51; death 52; defense mechanism 51; dreams 51; Electra Complex 51; forbidden fantasy 51; hidden instinct 51 (libido 51, 114–115, 122, 128, 133); narcissism 115, 127, 129, 133; Oedipus Complex 51; psychological conflicts 51; repressed desires 51; sexuality 51–52; silences 51; tripartite structure of personality 51 (ego 51, 114–115, 119–120, 126, 128, 130, 133, 183; id 51, 114–115; superego 51, 114–115); uncanny 115, 122–126, 129–130; unconscious mind 51–52
Pullman, Philip 110
Punter, David 135

queer politics 86–87

racism 47, 160–162, 165, 167, 172; externalized 155, 160–161, 168; internalized 159–161, 165, 168
Rani, Rabbia 51, 55
Rank, Otto 129, 135
reader response criticism 40–41
Reeder, Roberta 99, 110
Reid, Robin Anne 72–73, 83
Reider, John 84
Reider, Robin Anne 83
religion 4, 18, 23, 26, 34, 47, 49, 59, 67, 136, 141–142, 144–146, 148–149, 151–153, 186; Irish Catholicism 136, 142–144; Protestantism 136, 142, 144–145, 151–152; Roman Catholicism 146
Richter, David H. 55
Roberts, Justin 173
Robertson, James I. 173
Rogers, Robert 135
Rollyson, Carl 43, 55
Rood, Karen Lane 85, 97
Roth, Philip 36
Roughton, Ralph 97
Rowling, J.K. 104
Royle, Nicholas 54
Rundell, Katherine 19, 39

Saki 18, 19, 38–39, 138
Salinger, J.D. 26
Sam, Dicky 173
Sarker, Sunil Kumar 39
Schakel, Peter 104, 110
schizophrenia 179, 181, 183, 185
Scofield, Martin 39, 153
sexuality 50, 85
Shakespeare, Nicholas 31, 39
Shakespeare, William 26, 145, 179, 189; *Hamlet* 179, 184
Shelly, Christopher 134
Shelley, Mary: *Frankenstein* 60, 113

Showalter, Elaine 49, 181, 189
Skal, David J. 135
Skowera, Maciej 107, 110
Smith, Patrick, A. 81, 84
Smith, Zadie 1, 3, 35, 154, 165–169, 171, 173; "The Embassy of Cambodia" 35, 154, 165, 168, 171, 173
Somerville, John N., Jr. 64, 71
Spielberg, Steven 73
Spingarn, Adena 173
Spivey, Ted R. 59, 71
Stamenkovic, D. 60, 71
Stein, Jean 39
Stevenson, Robert Louis 3, 12, 39, 60, 113, 115, 123–126, 129, 131, 132, 135; *The Strange Case of Dr. Jekyll and Mr. Hyde* 12, 39, 60, 113, 118, 121, 125, 129, 131, 132, 135
Stockwell, Peter 73, 84
Stoker, Bram: *Dracula* 60
Storey, J. 55
Stout, Mira 39
Stowe, Harriet Beecher 161, 173
Strong, Emily 71
structuralism 41
style 8, 11, 13, 16–18, 22–26, 32, 53, 54, 60, 67–70, 81–83, 94–96, 107–109, 113, 137, 141, 147, 148, 163, 186
stylistics 41
symbolism 53, 67–68

third person point of view 95–96
Thomas, Anne-Marie 74, 83
Todorov, Tzvetan 99, 110; the fantastic 99; the marvellous 99; the uncanny 99
Tolan, Fiona 55
Tolkien, John Ronald Reuel 99, 110; "On Fairy Tales" 99
tone 2, 10, 16, 27, 34, 54, 65, 69, 82, 116, 138, 144–146, 150, 160, 167, 175, 180, 184–185
Toomer, Jean 36
Trevor, William 1, 3, 30–31, 39, 54, 136–137, 140, 149, 151–153; "Of the Cloth" 54, 136–137, 149, 151–153
Truth, Sojourner 170
Tso, Anna Wing Bo 97, 135
Tucker, Harry, Jr. 129, 135
Twain, Mark 14, 39

Tymms, Ralph 135
Tyson, Lois 41, 55

Uncle Tom 160, 163, 168, 171, 173
Upadhyay, Samrat 37
Updike, John 26, 35

Vaden, Matthew Brett 99, 110
Van Belle, Juno 93, 97
Van Steenhuyse, Veerle 100, 110
Varvogli, Aliki 86, 97
Vern, Jules 73

Walden, Sarah 44, 55
Walker, Alice 1, 3, 36, 42, 154–174, 189; "Everyday Use" 36, 42, 154, 156, 158, 160, 163–166, 171–173
Walpole, Horace 116, 117, 131–133, 135
Warren, Austin 53, 55
Watson, Alex 135
Waugh, Evelyn 32
Waugh, Patricia 110
Weber, N.A. 139, 153
Weiner, Lauren 72, 84
Wellek, René 55, 53
Wells, H.G. 73
"Where Is Brokeback Mountain? Maybe Nowhere" 97
White, David 173
Williams, Raymond 55
Windrush generation 167
Wolf, Ernest S. 134
Wollstonecraft, Mary: *A Vindication of the Rights of Women* 49
Wood, Gaby 44, 55
Wood, James 39
Woolf, Virginia 17, 27, 49–50; *A Room of One's Own* 49–50
Wright, Elizabeth 44, 55
Wright, Richard 36, 161

Yamada, Mitsuye 37
Yamamoto, Hisaye 37
Younge, Gary 173

Zarzycka, Agata 103, 110
Zipes, Jack 79, 84

www.ingramcontent.com/pod-product-compliance
Ingram Content Group UK Ltd.
Pitfield, Milton Keynes, MK11 3LW, UK
UKHW042009140426

5217IPUK00015B/1067